the
SOLACE
of
SHARP
CLAWS

A FAE GUARDIANS NOVEL

the
SOLACE
of
SHARP
CLAWS

A FAE GUARDIANS NOVEL

LANA PECHERCZYK

THE ORDER OF THE WELL

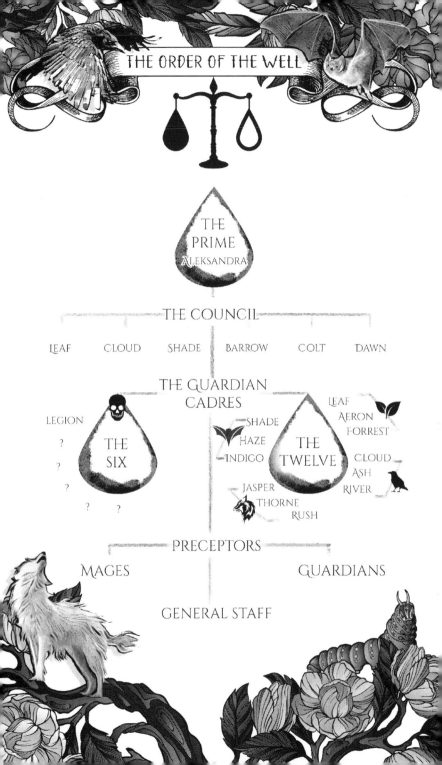

THE PRIME
Aleksandra

THE COUNCIL

LEAF   CLOUD   SHADE   BARROW   COLT   DAWN

THE GUARDIAN CADRES

THE SIX

LEGION
?
?
?
?   ?

THE TWELVE

SHADE
HAZE
INDIGO

JASPER
THORNE
RUSH

LEAF
AERON
FORREST

CLOUD
ASH
RIVER

PRECEPTORS

MAGES   GUARDIANS

GENERAL STAFF

EL

WINTER COUR
ACONITE CITY

ACONITE SEA

ICE WITCH

THE ICE FOREST

HUMAN TERRITORY

CRYSTAL
CITY

RUSH'S
CABIN

MEANDER
WOODS

UNSEELIE KINGDOM

SEELIE KINGDOM

WHISPERING
WOODS

CRESCENT
HOLLOW

NE

OBSIDIAN MINE

OBSCENDIA

CLAW BASIN

ORDER POST

AUTUMN COURT
RUBRUM CITY

CORNUCOPIA
TRADE CITY

FENRYSFIELD

THE CEREMONIAL
LAKE

THE ORDER
OF THE WELL

DELPHINIUM CITY
SPRING COURT

HELIANTHUS CITY
SUMMER COURT

CHAPTER ONE

Thorne stepped through a portal into a field of long grass just outside the burning village of Mornington. Dressed for battle in his Guardian uniform, he unhooked Fury from his holster and held the silver-tipped battle-ax at his side. Decades of use molded the grip to fit his palm perfectly.

He dropped the spent portal stone and took in the scene. The overcast sky hid nothing from his sharp wolf-shifter senses. Screams and desperate cries floated across the field as the nearby village oozed flames and the acrid scent of fear. Caustic ozone from the recent portal mixed with undertones of blood, urine, disturbed dirt... and... Thorne inhaled, tasted notes on the air... A storm is brewing.

Prepare for battle.

Hushed murmurs reached him. He used Fury to cleave a path through the long grass. The voices stopped as his footsteps drew near.

"It's me," he said, voice low.

Aeron and River were huddled together, scratching a game plan in the dirt. The two Guardians were distinguishable not only from the similar leather battle uniform, but the twinkling blue teardrop tattoo under one eye. Aeron's long brown braid trailed down his back and over his baldric. The elf was adept at all forms of magery and was the cadre's most knowledgeable when it came to the monsters they hunted.

River's wings fanned out behind him, a reflection of his unique feathers when in crow form. They shimmered in shades of blue and black, just like his three-inch hair rustling in the wind.

Aeron scowled at Thorne. "I asked for Leaf. Or Forrest."

"Fuck you, too." Thorne kicked dirt on them.

"Harsh, bro," River snapped and then dusted himself off.

"Shh." Aeron waved them back down. "The djinn will hear us."

"A djinn." *Well-damn.* No wonder Aeron wanted another elf. Leaf, in particular, the team leader of their Cadre of Twelve, was adept in airborne elemental magic. Something Thorne could do in small doses but avoided in favor of shifting into a wolf and tearing through things with his fangs.

"What's the plan?" Thorne crouched low, leather breeches creaking.

"I say we trick the damned genie back into its bottle," River suggested. "Then we control it."

"What bottle?" Aeron scoffed. "Have you found it?"

River raised a snarky brow. "So what's your plan then, Preceptor Know-it-all?"

Aeron glared at River and then wiped the dirt until he had a flat surface again. He used his knife to draw a shape. "This is the djinn."

River snorted. "Looks more like a blob."

Aeron pointed at him, and River swallowed his retort.

Aeron then poked a hole in the middle of the shape. "This is the djinn's heart. It's the only solid part of the creature. Actually, the djinn *is* the heart. It just uses copious amounts of energy to create a storm-like smokescreen to hide its true self. We catch that"—he pointed at the heart— "and we live to see another day. The villagers live to see another day."

"How do we destroy it?" Thorne asked.

"We don't. We capture it," Aeron replied sternly and put his knife away.

"Why don't we just get rid of it?" Thorne's tongue swept over his lethal fangs. "It would save a lot of trouble. Djinns have a habit of escaping."

"Isn't a djinn's heart worth a lot of coin?" River asked, blue eyes twinkling.

Well-damned crows, always thinking of coin.

"Forget it. The Prime will want to question it," Aeron confirmed.

The Prime.

Thorne's ears flattened, and he bared his teeth. Her meddling talons had been shredding his fate since before he was born, but as the leader of the Order of the Well, she had

3

a right to do so—as long as it was in the name of protecting the integrity of magic in Elphyne. The last thing any fae wanted was to revert to the barren world of the past where they aged and couldn't access the magic of the Well.

Screw the Prime.

There was one thing Thorne and Fury were good at— decimating. "Let's do this."

He stood and surveyed the field, but the moment his head cleared the long tips of tall grass, a malevolent force struck him in the face, sending him careening backward. He landed with a thud, heavy body crunching over sharp twigs and blades of grass. His breath knocked out of him. Fury skittered to the side. Groaning, Thorne blinked at the stormy sky until his senses became functional. And then he heard River snickering.

Bloody crow.

Thorne's anger, his old friend, swiftly rose to heat his face. He collected his ax and crawled back to the group with a throaty growl. "You could have warned me."

"Where would the fun be in that?" River wiped a tear from his eye.

"Why do you think we're staying hidden?" Aeron shot back. "The djinn is just waiting for your head to clear."

"Tell me how to capture it," he said. And then kill it.

"We need to use a deionizing spell to weaken its tempest and slow it down. But we have to be sure it will be a direct hit. The spell will use the vast majority of my stored mana. Once it's slowed, we cast the silver net over the bulk of its energy." Aeron tossed a fine silver mesh at

River, who caught it and opened it. The elf continued, "River, you hover up high, get ready to cast the trap. Thorne and I will be on the ground to keep it contained. Sound good?"

Thorne's knuckles whitened on Fury. "I'm ready."

River beat his wings until wind gushed around them, and he launched vertically.

Aeron glanced at Thorne. "My hands will be occupied casting spells."

That he had to check made Thorne wonder if trust and camaraderie were ever going to run smooth between them.

"I've got your back," he replied.

Twelve in total, Thorne's unit had once been tight-knit, not only guarding each other's backs, but bonding in friendship. The sad truth was since Jasper, Thorne's wolf-shifter mentor, had disappeared over a decade ago, things had gone downhill. Although, if you asked Aeron, or any of the Guardians around before Thorne's time, they would have said the decline in morale had happened long before, when Rush, Thorne's father, had been exiled.

A curt nod from Aeron, and then they both stood cautiously. Heads above the horizon of grass, they surveyed the field making waves from the gentle, not gushing, wind. Where was it? Eerie silence greeted them. Somewhere above, River hovered, watching with sharp eyes, waiting for the right moment.

"You smell it?" Aeron muttered.

Thorne lifted his chin. Took a sharp breath. Caught it. Then started prowling east, back toward the village. It was stronger there. Perhaps it got tired of waiting for the Guardians to show their heads.

They stalked through the field, listening carefully. The hairs on Thorne's arms lifted, and an almighty crash snapped his head toward another direction—toward the other end of the village—a farm. A female's scream. It had someone.

"Fuck." He ran toward the helpless scream, every protective instinct in his body on high alert.

With his heart pounding, his breath heaving, he pumped his legs and sprinted.

"Wait," Aeron shouted as they cleared the field and came across the outbuilding of a farm.

A gray smokey tornado of destruction tore through the tiny settlement. Wood, debris, crops, it all went flying into the air as the djinn circled through. They were in the midst of a hurricane of roaring chaos.

A female faun crouched under a wagon with a child huddled in her arms. Thorne threw a blast of energy at the tempestuous djinn, but he only angered it more. The storm turned Thorne's way. Two smokey arms peeled from the tornado. Red eyes glowed in the midst.

"That's right, come here." He waved his hands over his head. "Fight someone your own size."

The djinn's elemental body turned back to the female and child.

"We have to lure it away." Aeron pulled up to Thorne's side, chest heaving. "I can't throw my spell at it when they're so close."

Thorne cupped his mouth and shouted. "Here!"

He gritted his teeth. He'd have to expend mana by using a spell—meaning he would have little left to shift into wolf. He hated taking that option off the table. But, Well-damn it, he had no choice.

Drawing on his power, he fashioned another blast of energy and threw it at the elemental. It would do nothing to it, maybe even feed it. But it got the djinn's attention. Red eyes locked on Thorne.

He backed away and pointed his ax at Aeron. "Stay there and attack from behind."

With every backward step into the grass field, Thorne threw more energy at the beast. The djinn followed. Its elemental arms lashed out, slashing at Thorne's face, cutting through his jacket, slicing his skin. Blood dripped from him. Dirt got in his eyes. With every stinging hit, Thorne's rile grew in intensity until he was ready to roar.

"I s-see you, wolf," the djinn hissed. "I s-see into your weak and angry heart."

Thorne faltered. The storm surrounded him, darkening the sky.

"I s-see you have hate. Wantsss revenge. You can use me. Make wisshes."

Flashes of Thorne's past hit him. Orphaned. Living with a cruel uncle. An aunt who tried to save him but failed to protect even herself. Being forced into the ceremonial lake, not knowing if he'd float and bloat, or come out alive. The taunts his childhood peers sent his way for being a child of greedy unsanctioned breeders. Then finding out it was all part of some bigger plan the Prime had cooked up. His pain was nothing but collateral damage. And now he worked for her.

"I'll tell you where my bottle is. S-seek revenge."

No. He wouldn't succumb. This was classic djinn behavior. It fed off the mana of others and used vengeance as a lure. Whoever ruled the djinn now would have little mana left in their body, and because it was leached out by a magical monster, that mana wouldn't be replenished. That fae would no longer be immortal.

Thorne roared his fury, dug deep, and drained his power to hurtle an energy wave at the djinn. Wind gusted from his fingertips, leaving him drained and tired. He stumbled.

"Now!" he yelled.

Nothing.

Crimson, what was Aeron waiting for?

And just as Thorne was out of magical means, Aeron threw his spell at the monster. Air crackled and fizzed. Thorne tasted metal on his tongue. The djinn-storm slowed, the smoke and wind of its tornado disintegrated, and then a sparkling net dropped from the sky.

With a whoosh, the storm was contained under the silver mesh. Thrashing about beneath was a dark, twisted blob of goo with red eyes. It squealed and bucked. And it spat vitriolic and unintelligible words at Thorne.

"Litter box trash," Thorne muttered and then lifted Fury, aimed, and chopped down.

He caught the djinn dead in the middle. It broke in two. A popping sound rent the air, and the remnants of the storm vanished. The clouds cleared, and the sun shone down.

"You idiot," Aeron snapped.

River landed with a windy thud, wings snapping in tight behind him. "Thorne?"

Thorne only grimaced at them, anger still firing in his system. He shrugged.

"Think you can call the shots?" Aeron shoved him. "You can collect the tax from the village, then."

Shock splintered through Thorne. Aeron rarely lost his temper.

"What?" He shook his head. "I'm here on your request. It's not my mission."

"Exactly." Aeron put the net and broken djinn body into Thorne's hands. "It was my mission, and you went against orders. I told you the Prime would want to question it."

Shit. Yes, he did.

"Time to go, River." Aeron threw his hand out and cast the spell to trigger a portal back to the Order.

Bastard. Clearly, Aeron had enough mana left to conjure a portal. He could have cast that deionizing spell earlier.

It seemed like Thorne was the last fae on earth willing to sacrifice his last mana drop for others these days.

River gave Thorne a one-shouldered shrug and then sauntered after Aeron through the portal. The bright shining light flashed and then disappeared as the portal closed, leaving Thorne in a resounding post-battle atmosphere. In one direction was the battle-torn village, in the other, a wild field leading to a forest that called to Thorne's inner wolf.

What he wouldn't give for the mind emptying freedom of running through the woods. The rushing wind. The myriad of scents. The burn of his muscles. All his worries and demons gone.

Simplicity. Bliss.

Sometimes he wondered which part of him came first. The wolf, or the fae. If he let his wolf take over permanently, would anyone miss the fae part of him? Why not just shift, let the beast out, and stay out? Stay animal.

Jasper's voice responded loud and clear from Thorne's memory. *Because the wolf is a part of you, not the other way around. Never forget that.*

CHAPTER TWO

$\mathcal{L}$ooking worse for wear, Thorne returned to the Order through a portal. He ditched the spent stone into some bushes outside the gates and heard a clunk as it hit the others he'd thrown before. He needed to find a new dumping ground, or actually learn to create portals himself. But he didn't have the patience or the reserve mana to waste.

His wolf agreed with him. It liked having reign.

Approaching the gate, he gestured to the guard on the high stone wall and entered the Order grounds. As one of the Twelve, he lived in a house near the back. Having his own room was the only blessing in this place.

The folk at Mornington Village hadn't been pleased to hand over their only red coin, but monster hunting was expensive and resource heavy. They would have felt worse if the Guardians weren't around to stop the djinn. After he'd collected the fee, he'd seen the destruction up close and realized Aeron was right to be furious about the kill. Knowing why the djinn targeted Mornington would have been a good thing.

Damn it.

His pent-up rage and energy had nowhere to go. He felt like a demon pushed beneath his skin, wanting to burst out. It itched. It twitched. All he wanted was to head home, bathe, then go down to the Mess Hall and find a nice soft female to bury himself in. He would take her behind the academy library where the gardens provided plenty of cover, and then head back to his room, alone. Maybe he'd have a few drams of whiskey and—

"D'arn Thorne."

Every muscle in his body locked tight. He turned. "Prime."

In her angel form, the owl-shifter's long white wings brushed the ground. Curly white hair bounced on her bare, brown shoulders, and large knowing eyes took in everything. As usual, she wore the distinctive blue flowing gown that reminded Thorne of a goddess of old. It was probably why the Prime wore it, to attach any association to godliness to herself that she could.

She pursed her lips and held out her hand.

He dug into his pocket and retrieved the coin for her.

"As I understand," she said, "you're the reason there is no djinn to question."

"If you saw the destruction, it left—"

She held up her hand. "We both know excuses aren't what I'm looking for."

Thorne's fists clenched at his side in an attempt to remain stoic, despite the blood boiling in his veins. It would be so easy to let it out. To show her what he'd been thinking and feeling all these years. The rage and the turmoil over her leadership… among other things. Even the wolf inside him howled for a piece of her flesh. He flexed his fingers and exhaled. *I'm not like her.*

He had control of his beast.

Barely.

"What are you looking for then, Prime?"

The loaded question had a double meaning, and rightly so. He was sick and tired of her misdirections and machinations. He was tired of it all. She was the reason his mentor, Jasper, had been missing for over a decade. The only reason he'd learned Jasper was missing, and not on hiatus like the Prime had insisted, was that his father's mate, Clarke, had revealed the truth to Thorne. The psychic human had also said another like her would thaw from a two-thousand-year sleep and would lead him to Jasper. But she had said that two years ago. He started to wonder if it was all another misdirection. Or even an outright lie.

Humans could lie. Fae could not.

The Prime looked him over, long and hard. Then her gaze softened in a rare show of emotion. "It is not I who will be searching soon, D'arn Thorne. You will be going on a journey, and all I ask is that you remember one thing."

"What."

"The Well chose you to protect it. For whatever reason you hate me, believe I had no hand in that. It is real."

A growl slipped out. "You had no hand in shoving me into the ceremonial lake when I was twelve? Because I remember that a little differently. I remember all the tributes differently."

Less than thirty percent of Guardian applicants survived the initiation ceremony. When submerged in the lake, the cosmic Well of Life looked deep into their hearts and judged their worthiness of the extra power it imbued to successful initiates. But to be judged correctly, one was dragged to the bottom of the lake where the connection to the Well was the strongest. One had to truly believe they were dying and to face their moral demons. But if deemed worthy, the new power granted was instantaneous. You could rise a new fae. Stronger, but indentured to preserving the Well.

The six fae who'd entered before him had sunk. Then their bodies had bobbed to the top of the lake, dead, floated, and bloated with the shame of rejection. He knew he'd be the next to do so. He knew that a boy like him, the product of unsanctioned breeding, would never be chosen as a symbol of righteousness. He was the lowest of the low.

The shouts of acolytes and Guardians still rang in his ears when he remembered being pushed down the jetty that led into the sacred lake. He remembered his struggles, the warmth of urine as it ran down his legs on the cold day, and his bare heels burning as they collected splinters from the wood underfoot. He remembered the confusion as some of his captors had fallen into the lake themselves. Then he remembered the wolf inside him taking over, and the all-consuming terror as he looked down into the moving shadows of the deep water.

Something was in there.

Then he was pushed, he went airborne, and into the water's icy embrace.

"What would you have us do, D'arn Thorne?" the Prime asked, snapping him out of his past. "Wait until there are no more novitiates, no more Guardians, and no more protection for the Well? Elphyne will die."

"There has to be another way of getting fae to volunteer."

"There isn't."

He pinched the bridge of his nose. "I've had a long day. Are we done?"

The Prime turned her back, took a deep breath, and then walked away. But not before she tossed some last words over her shoulder. "Your day is only beginning."

He shook his head and continued toward the Twelve's house. The two-story behemoth sat tall and proud at the end of a lawn used as an informal training field. He'd only made it halfway across that field when a small, two-legged, white-haired toddler tottered down the porch steps. She lifted her nose, scented he was kin, and broke into a run toward him, chubby arms flailing in the air. He couldn't help the twitch on his lips at the sheer thrill on his half-sister's face and her high-pitched squeal of delight. It was the look of escape, of pure freedom, probably only linked to her state of undress, but infectious all the same.

He scooped up Willow's wriggling form.

"No no no." She kicked and struggled.

"I think you're a little young to be running across campus with half your clothes off." He cast a wary eye at the house next door where the only other cadre of Guardians lived. The Six were made up of Sluagh, Unseelie fae who'd led the Wild Hunt against the humans who invaded Elphyne centuries ago. They lived in the shadows and rarely came out in daytime, but stranger things had happened.

Some described them as fallen angels; others as demon monsters. Thorne couldn't say. He'd only caught glimpses of them over the decades he'd been at the Order. He'd heard the Sluagh still kidnapped humans. Since Willow was a halfling, he didn't like leaving her unattended on Order grounds. The Sluagh answered only to themselves and on occasion the Prime.

Curtains twitched at the dark windows of the house of the Six.

"Where are your parents?" he asked Willow.

"Mom-mom-mom." Willow pointed back at the house. "Dad-dad-dad."

A panicked woman came tearing out from the house, her long red hair sailing behind her. She saw Willow in Thorne's arms and sagged with relief.

When Thorne arrived, she thanked him—something she kept inexplicably doing, despite knowing that thanking fae would put her in their debt—and then took the wriggling toddler from his arms.

"You're a lifesaver, Thorne," she said, flustered. "Honestly, if Willow would just learn to shift, we'd have no fear with her running around on her own."

He raised a brow. "Still no luck?"

Exasperated, Clarke ushered him in so she could close the door and then released the struggling child into the house. "No, but your father thinks it will happen any day. She's got some long canines coming in. Rush has even tried shifting around her, which apparently is something shifter fathers do with their young to teach them..." Her voice trailed off and she slanted him a guilty look.

He ignored the tweak in his chest at the f-word. It was still odd to hear. He also chose to ignore the fact that Rush hadn't been there to teach Thorne to shift. It had been Rush's sister Kyra. And then later, Jasper.

Thorne cleared his throat. "Where is he?"

"Ah. Yes." Clarke's lips flattened. "That's why we're here."

Her pause gave him a flair of hope. Was this the time?

"Yes," she added, searching his face and reading his expression. "This is the time. Laurel will wake soon and we have to find her before someone else does. Rush is collecting supplies for the journey. It's going to be long and arduous." She flinched. "And unfortunately, Rush and I will have to continue on after you bring Laurel back here for training."

He folded his arms. Laurel. The human. A swarm of old hatred scored his blood. All his life he'd been trained to abhor humans. They stole from Elphyne, from the land and its people. They bled the very life from the soil. Over the past two years, the human raids had petered off and

17

remained small enough to remain negligible to the leaders of Elphyne.

But the Order knew better. One human, a man Clarke had dubbed the Void, was stealing mana from magical creatures, utilizing it for his own means, and planning an invasion that every Seer in the history of Elphyne had warned would mean the end of existence. The problem was, every psychic vision showed a different series of events. The only true common element of victory was that Clarke was leading the way.

This Laurel that Clarke had mentioned was human. She deserved Thorne's suspicion and caution regardless of being a friend of Clarke's.

"This is the human who will lead me to Jasper?"

"Mm-hmm." Clarke scratched her head, seemed to avoid his gaze, and then looked for her daughter who had already vanished somewhere in the big house. "You best be changing, Thorne. We'll head out very soon. And dress warmly. She's in the Elation mountains, but I'm not sure exactly where. We'll have a search on our hands when we arrive."

TRAVELING through the cold Elation mountains hadn't been fun for Thorne. With his mana stores so low from the recent battle with the djinn, he'd been unable to change into wolf and the urgency of their mission prohibited him from stopping off at a natural source of power, like a sacred lake, to rapidly replenish. Instead, the magic slowly seeped back into his body during the journey. He wasn't comfortable knowing his power was so depleted. Especially when his father's was not.

Being Well-blessed meant Rush could borrow mana from Clarke any time he wanted. And Clarke was a rare thing indeed. Human, yet possessing the strongest capacity for holding mana the Order had ever seen. She could go for days at full strength without needing to replenish from the cosmic Well of Life. She could also filter that power to Rush as he did his duty as a Guardian.

Why her? What made this human so important?

A good hour into their journey, snow started to fall as they trekked up the rocky path. Evergreen trees made it difficult to see where they had come from. The snow made it harder. Rush had offered to cast an insulation spell around Thorne, as he had with Clarke, but he'd declined in favor of using his cape. He wasn't in the habit of accepting help from a father who'd never been there for him before.

He now regretted his choice.

They came to a grassed plateau edged by a rocky cliff. Clarke stopped and searched about the cliff before turning to Thorne and Rush.

"There's the cave," she said, pointing to a hidden entrance behind a fallen tree gathering a drift of snow.

They dropped their bags just inside the cave. Thorne also left his cape, as the temperature inside was strangely warmer. Thorne's and Rush's sharp wolf-shifter senses took them a few yards into the tunnel until they came to a three-way fork.

While Clarke and Rush discussed which way to go, Thorne put his hand on the tunnel walls. They were striated, as though the cavity had been drilled by someone... or something. Wyrms were known to inhabit these mountains.

A gasp sent his attention Clarke's way. Residual light shone from the cave entrance, enough to see her irises had turned Seer white. A pinch to her lips and paleness of skin revealed her vision wasn't good. When her blue eyes opened and searched for Rush, she swallowed. "We have to hurry."

"What is it?" Rush asked.

Her hand fluttered to her throat and she shook her head. "Something is wrong. I keep seeing fire."

"So where?" Thorne pointed into the dark recess of the cave system. "Which direction?"

"Unfortunately, my visions haven't shown me where to find Laurel, only that she's hidden somewhere in here."

"So we split up."

"Yes."

Rush frowned at Clarke. "I go with you."

She scowled back. "If the three of us separate, we'll cover more ground."

"You said something is wrong. I can feel you're hiding something from me." Rush folded his arms and stared her down. Like cartography contours, or a fingerprint, their matching bioluminescent Well-blessed markings curved around a hand and arm on each body. It told the world they belonged to each other, and their souls were bound. They could share mana and emotions. Humans could lie, but with that soul-connection, she couldn't lie to him.

Danger sizzled in the air. Urgency. Thorne's heart beat faster and he reached over his shoulder to release Fury.

"Fine," Clarke said. "Rush with me. Thorne, you go on your own. Meet back here in an hour. If the other party isn't back by then..." She looked at Rush. "How do we communicate? Seriously, someone at the academy needs to invent a magical cell phone."

"Because Thorne and I are kin, we can communicate through water with the right link-spell, but that's not always reliable, especially if there is no water around." Rush went to his rucksack and pulled out two glowing glass canisters. He handed one to Thorne who lifted his for inspection. Inside was an air sprite. Made from sparks of light, it shed luminosity wherever it went, leaving a trail. The inside of the canister was already smeared with by-product.

"Sprites," Rush explained. "Already bargained with. They'll also provide light for you to help see."

Thorne raised his brow. Bargained with? That meant the sprite wouldn't just float away on her own agenda, she'd follow Thorne around until she was released from her bargain.

Thorne unscrewed his canister and the tiny winged female zoomed out, circling him with a high-pitched buzz of annoyance.

"Don't listen to her," Rush grumbled. "She got a good deal. A blue coin and all you can eat prickleberries for the rest of the year."

Thorne looked down the three tunnels and sighed. "I'll start with the right."

"We'll take the left."

Thorne was about to head off when he caught Clarke's hesitation. More danger?

"What?" he prompted.

Her eyes widened. "It's just that Laurel has been through a lot. She might not respond well to an unfamiliar face, and you're very… imposing."

"Then hope you find her first."

Crimson, he could handle a female, regardless of the fact she woke from another time. Frustrated, he went down the narrowest tunnel, ducking to avoid the rocky bulk overhead. The tunnel shrank the further he went, until he was half crouched as he walked. Continuing for long minutes, his patience wore thin. Clarke had been frozen for thousands of years and she'd awoken, thawed in a lake. But this human? She had to be hidden in tunnels created by Crimson-knew what. The ridges and striations on the walls solidified his theory that the tunnels were bored by a creature.

Better find the human fast.

Thorne had no clue what kind of human he'd find. Clarke had been difficult to process when she'd first arrived. She spoke strange. She had too much energy. And—

Thorne ducked when the sprite flew across his face, leaving a cold splash on his cheek. No doubt there would be a luminescent track left. He smudged it away, but when he pulled his hand back, an unfamiliar scent halted him. It came from the dark hollow ahead. Sulfur… and—he sneezed—something burned and bitter. The hairs on the back of his neck stood to attention. The sprite flittered about the cavern, knocking into walls erratically. Something was definitely off.

"What is it?" he muttered. Was the borer of the tunnels here?

His grip tightened on Fury's handle.

Smoke oozed from the hollow ahead. The sprite refused to move forward and squeaked with panic.

Shit.

Thorne broke into a jog, pushed through the hollow and into a larger cavern. Fire flickered beyond the smoke. His eyes stung and watered but... there was something in there. He could sense it. It was a tug to his chest. A twist to his heart. A need. An urgency. It went beyond logic. Proceeding could mean imminent death, but he would do it anyway. This incessant need inside urged him forward.

Coughing, he swatted the smoke away and approached with caution. The mana he'd replenished over the journey from the Order might be enough to conjure a spell. He reached deep within to grab the power the Well granted him. He drew on his energy, converted it to water, and sent it toward the epicenter of the inferno. Water shot from his hands and doused the flames. Sizzling smoke hissed. Firelight extinguished, casting the cavern into darkness. He squinted through burning eyes, coughed, and then unbuttoned his jacket. With access to his sweater, he pulled the collar to cover his nose and mouth, filtering the air.

"Get help," he rasped to the sprite then ushered it out of

the cavern. It flew out, taking the light, and a little smoke, with it.

Thorne turned back to the darkness, eyes narrowing toward the corner. His wolf-sight kicked in and picked up a figure laying on the ground. Blood thudded in his ears. It was her. The human. He felt it as surely as if someone had carved her name across her heart. Laurel.

His instinct urged him forward. "All right, wolf. Let's see what this is all about."

He took a step. Then another. The dark shape didn't move. His ears pricked up and strained for a heartbeat. It was there, faint. And fading.

She was unwell.

It was no wonder with this smoke-filled cavern. If he'd been a minute longer, purged the smoke later, she'd have suffocated. Crouching down by her side, he took in her face.

His breath hitched.

His mind stalled.

He blinked, a little befuddled and unsure of what he'd expected. He hadn't really prepared himself. Consumed with the second part of this meeting, the part where this woman would lead him to his lost mentor... he'd failed to think about the woman herself.

She was beautiful. Painstakingly so. Sensual lips like a dream, yet her face held an unyielding harshness even in her repose. Dark short hair cut directly below her sharp jaw. Glorious body swathed in tight black clothes that pronounced every sexy curve. Muscular. Taut. Trim. She looked at peace. Her hands pressed under her face as though she'd fallen asleep.

Somehow Thorne had the sense she wouldn't be caught vulnerable like this often. The arousing thought sparked a kernel of curiosity in his long since dark soul.

And then he saw her ruined and twisted nails. Some of them were thick and stubby.

Laurel has been through a lot, Clarke's voice floated from his memory.

His lip curled in a snarl. He knew why nails grew like that. Someone had done that to her—ripped her nails clean from her fingers.

There was more to her that didn't add up. Scorch marks radiated from her body along the cavern floor. Her clothes were left smoldering, but her skin was blemish free.

Clarke had power. This human—Laurel—probably had it too. Maybe even an inferno's worth. But despite the strange recent fire, her lips held a blue tint. He touched her cheek and hissed. Ice cold. The fire hadn't been enough to thaw her from the ice. The cosmic Well had brought her this far, but she wouldn't survive if he failed to warm her up. He needed to get her blood pumping.

Reaching within himself, he scraped the last remnant of his power and cast a warming spell. But it fizzled and sputtered. His mana was spent. Damn. He glanced at the entrance to the cavern but heard no incoming footsteps. Rush and Clarke could be an hour away or more. Only one thing to do.

He peeled off his jacket, rolled it, and tucked it beneath

her head. Water from his dousing spell sloshed along the rocky floor as he moved. It had already turned cold, like the frozen cavern around him.

Laurel made no move. No sound. The wolf inside him paced and whined in a restless cycle.

"You will survive this," he decreed. *I won't let you die.*

Next was his sweater and undershirt until he was top naked. Shifters were fire-fae. Their body temperature ran high, but since his lack of mana meant he couldn't shift, he'd have to warm her a different way. Lying down next to her, he ripped her shirt open until her chest was bare except for a small dark covering over her breasts. He peeled her wet and torn shirt away and threw it to the side, then gathered her close. He used his sweater to cover her bare back and trapped their body heat.

He cupped the back of her head in one hand, and with the other, he rubbed her back to create friction. He tried not to think of the icy bloom of his breath. She would wake. She had to. She was his key to… everything.

And she was limp, her heart sluggish, her face pale.

Come on. At least shiver.

He placed his palm over the center of her chest. A spark of mana. It was all he had left to give. Heat zinged down his arm, hit his palm and melted into her chest. Warmth spread from his touch. Blue light bloomed on her skin until it pulsed along her veins, striating outward like a star. It should have melted and joined her life-force, but the light didn't leave. It shone brighter. It burned hotter. It spread to her extremities until it wrapped around her arm and his at the same time. He shut his eyes against the shine. When the heat lessened against his face, he opened his eyes and gasped.

Up his arm and hers was the contoured blue bioluminescent markings of a Well-blessed union.

This human was his mate.

CHAPTER THREE

*L*aurel's smart watch buzzed, telling her it was time for her next appointment. She packed up her desk, straightened her papers, locked her computer and gave the picture of her family one last look. It was of her parents and Laurel next to her twin brother, Lionel, in his hospital bed before he died. Taken fifteen years earlier, Laurel and Lionel were freshmen in high school. He never finished.

Her watch buzzed again.

Right. Brunch with the girls.

She strode through the office floor of her business empire. Under the Queen Fitness umbrella, she sold equipment, a fashion line, as well as dominated the franchise gymnasium real estate in Las Vegas. She wanted to be in every hotel by the end of the year. Impossible was not a word in her vocabulary.

A young blond in yoga attire rushed up to Laurel and

held out a smoothie. "Your wheatgrass protein shake is ready, Miss Baker."

"Thank you, Dee." She flicked her gaze down to the woman's feet and frowned. "What's that?"

Dee stopped. Laurel stopped, arched her brows, and then decided it was best they walk and talk, so gestured toward the exit. "Follow."

Laurel had too many things on her agenda to be policing employee fashion. Goddamn, she missed her old assistant, Belinda. That girl had been a walking machine. This one... well... she pursed her lips as Dee scurried to catch up. She was a work in progress.

But Laurel would whip her into shape. Just like she did with everything.

"I'm waiting," Laurel said, walking.

"Um..." Dee scurried. "Sorry, what was the question?"

"What's on your feet?"

"Sneakers?"

"Incorrect. They're the wrong sneakers. The competitor's. Everyone on this floor must wear the Nike-Queen Fitness branded shoes. We didn't spend thousands to secure that partnership for nothing. Do you understand? Good. Grab a pair from the marketing department on your way out today. Next?"

"Sorry, next?"

Good God. "Yes, what's next on my agenda?"

She already knew she had brunch with the girls, then a meeting with the CEO of Luxor, and a quick twenty-minute sojourn down to the shooting range with her father. He'd much rather her take time off to go fishing in the real wilderness, but she'd stopped doing that when she had opened her business. Now she didn't know the meaning of vacation. The shooting range would have to do.

"Okay, first up you have... um... I'm sorry I forgot to bring your planner."

Laurel stopped. She glared. "Well? Chop-chop. Off you go."

Dee scurried away. Laurel tapped her custom Nike covered foot. She took a slow sip of her smoothie and thrummed her glossy blue nails on the cup. Her eyes narrowed with predatory focus on a worker's cell screen— at the brightly colored little gems being locked in a row. Fury tightened her posture. She ground her teeth and strode over. She didn't get to these dizzying heights of success by playing games on her cell, and she expected nothing less from her staff.

She arrived behind the man in question. With a clearing of her throat, the noises in the office died off. There was no other sound except the tapping of her foot. Slowly, the employee rotated in his chair and lifted his gaze to her face. He paled.

She held out her palm. He regretfully placed his cell in it. Then she tossed it into the trash on her way out. What did they think life was? A ride? A game? No. You had to earn your place in it. You, more than any other person, had been given a gift. She certainly didn't squander hers.

A flash of her twin's face hit her hard. Her throat

clogged. But she shook it off before she stepped into the foyer and heard Dee's voice echoing behind her.

"Laurel."

"Laurel."

Dee sounded underwater. Deep. *That's odd*. In fact, everything seemed out of place. The bright lights were blurry. The lobby moved. It smelled like someone had set the trash on fire. Maybe the cell phone had exploded.

She shook her head. *Have to get to brunch with the girls.* No time to dawdle. *Clarke and Ada are waiting.*

Laurel took a step. Felt sluggish.

"Laurel."

Dee's voice had deepened. Suddenly, it wasn't Dee chasing her, but another. A man from her nightmares. His long face warped into something hideously overlong. His expression was a mask of bland depravity—the only emotion she'd ever seen in his dark, soulless eyes.

Pain ripped through her fingertip. She looked down and saw why. He'd pulled her fingernail clean off with a set of pliers.

"No." She thrashed her head. She refused to give this man any satisfaction. "Don't give him the numbers, Clarke!"

"Laurel, wake up."

A spark of heat at her chest punched her out of her dream. Her eyes snapped open to a blue glow in a dim room.

The urge to vomit rose within her like a tidal wave and she puked something disgusting. It dribbled down her chin and landed on her chest. It wasn't smoothie. It was dark,

31

viscous muck. Her heavy eyelids wanted to close again. Every muscle in her body ached. Cold air nipped her face and legs, but inexplicable heat surrounded her torso.

Blue light flashed. Nausea rolled again. She groaned. What the hell was happening? Forcing her gaze open, she tried to take in her surroundings. In the glow, a face. A... man.

Fierce. Handsome. Shockingly blue eyes glowing as much as the surrounding light.

Naked, brawny chest. Powerful arms locked around her.

He caged her in.

She screamed.

He blinked. He let go, and she shuffled back. Rock scrapped against her bare back. Hissing in pain, she looked down at her puke-stained bra and yoga pants. Someone had painted glow-in-the-dark blue lines over her right hand and arm. What was this, a rave? Had she ended up in some nightclub? He had the same on his arm. The markings felt hot... alive... as though something lived beneath her skin. Something powerful.

What the hell?

A quick look around the room showed her it wasn't a room at all, but the inside of a cave. Panic flooded her, threatening to drown out all common sense.

"Laurel." His voice was deep. Calming. He held his hand out like one would to a wounded bear. "You are safe."

Safe? Then why was her heart beating a hundred miles a minute? Where was her t-shirt? Why did the stench of burned things and smoke fill her nose? Where the goddamned hell was she? How did he know her name?

He moved toward her, but she shuffled back and winced when her bare back hit the rocky wall again. "Stay away."

Oh God. What if this was the next step in Bones' torture? What if he hadn't let Clarke and Laurel go? No. She shook her head as more memories came to her.

Bones *had* let them go. He'd pulled out every last one of Laurel's fingernails and was about to move onto her teeth when Clarke caved. She'd given him the numbers. *Bishop, that bastard!* Clarke's ex-boyfriend was the one who'd sold them out to Bones. He'd told the mercenary about Clarke's psychic powers. Laurel's throat choked up. Clarke's eyes had been red and raw from crying. Tears had run in tracks down her face. Until that point, she'd held her tongue. She'd done what Laurel had ordered her to do. Because anyone willing to resort to torture to get some numbers had to be evil. Those numbers had to be bad.

More memories surfaced.

Watching the news reports on TV. Bombs going off around the world. Those numbers had been nuclear codes. Like dominos, civilization collapsed. Then the fallout. The sky. The nuclear winter. The sudden catastrophic ice.

"Did he send you?" she croaked. Maybe Bones wasn't done. Maybe the end of the world wasn't enough for him. "Clarke won't tell you anything now. You can torture me all you like."

Laurel had a stern word to Clarke after Bones had let

them go. She'd told her friend that if they were captured again, to never give anything up. Laurel could take it.

A darkness washed over the strange man's eyes. His jaw set. And then he answered, slowly and calmly. "I'm... ah... friends with Clarke. She sent me to find you."

Laurel pointed her finger at him and accused, "You hesitated."

She caught sight of her damaged fingernail and snatched her hand back.

"I hesitated because she's human," the man muttered. "I'm fae. I'm still getting used to our alliance."

"Fae?"

He gestured at his ears. With a start, Laurel realized they were pointed at the top. Pointed with a light dusting of fur. The sides of his head were buzzed. The pale, silver hair on the top was scraped back from his forehead and pulled into a Viking-like twisted braid that dropped down his brawny back.

His ears twitched. His head cocked, and he slanted a look to the dark hole serving as the cavern exit, and then he tensed. That behavior was decidedly not human, but closer to animal and otherworldly. Laurel sensed danger from him, as though he were a wild, vicious beast calmly watching its prey, getting ready to pounce.

"Something is coming," he muttered.

He scrounged about the floor for something. When his fingers latched onto a dark shape, he tossed it her way. Another scream bubbled in her throat, but when the thing hit her, she realized it was cloth. No. Not cloth. Leather. A jacket. She relaxed.

"Put it on," he grumbled and collected something else, a belt. With a goddamned holster of some sort attached. And in that holster was a big, scary ax glinting with the blue light cast from their matching markings.

When he turned to strap his weapon over his naked torso, Laurel noticed a large tattoo between his shoulder blades. A howling wolf. Back muscles rippled as he lifted the leather straps over his head. The wolf shuddered menacingly. Laurel knew what kind of work it took to carve out a body like that. She'd built her life's business around it.

She also knew how much strength was within his body. His big fists were twice the size of hers. If he wanted to hurt her, she stood no chance. He looked over his shoulder and locked eyes with her, perhaps waiting for something. He didn't find it and frowned.

"You must dress. We have to get out. Danger is coming. Do you understand me?" He spoke as if he expected her to speak another language.

Her cheeks heated. "Of course I understand you. It's the only thing I do understand. What the hell is going on? Where am I?"

"I'm sure Clarke will have plenty to say to you. My name is Thorne."

Clarke.

Her mind got stuck on the familiar name and suddenly there wasn't a place she wanted to be more than near her dear friend. Clarke had been a crafty and sometimes

35

morally ambiguous woman, but she always knew what to say, and she had a knack for knowing what to do. Underneath it all, she had a good heart, and Laurel loved her.

Right. So now Laurel had a plan. Find Clarke. Talk to Clarke. *Work out what the hell is going on.* With this new point to focus on, she slipped her hands within the arms of the fae's oversized and heavy leather jacket. It looked like a badass biker jacket, and it smelled like man. She cast a quick glance at Thorne. He looked like a badass biker. With an ax. And pointed ears.

She shook her head. Again. And couldn't move the feeling of displacement.

Find Clarke. Feel centered. She could do that.

"Where's my top?" she asked.

Thorne bent and picked up something soggy. He squeezed water out of it and offered it to her like some kind of cat with a dead mouse. *Are you fricking kidding me?* Her shirt was torn, in pieces, and half disintegrated. That was a custom Lululemon yoga shirt.

He frowned down at it. Sniffed it. And then remarked, "This has forbidden plastics in it. It will have to be destroyed. But we can do it later."

Forbidden plastics?

Laurel begrudgingly took the top from him but didn't put it on. She wiped her front where her vomit had dribbled, then dumped the top and did up the buttons on the jacket. She gestured to the big guy. "After you."

They'd gone two feet down the exit tunnel when a bright white firefly buzzed and squeaked near Thorne's face. He stopped and inexplicably seemed to listen to the hovering fly. Laurel almost bumped into him. Then he swore. Two-seconds later, his fist clenched around the ax handle.

He craned his neck to look over his shoulder at her. "Can you conjure fire again?"

"What?" she spluttered.

"Fuck."

Panic started to creep up her body. "What's going on?"

But he didn't answer. He started to undress, fingers unbuckling his baldric.

She blinked. What was he doing?

He shoved his baldric at her—battle-ax and all. Then he undid the button at his breeches placket, shoved it all down, and toed off his boots at the same time. "Bring my things. And stay back."

The air around him shimmered. Her blue arm markings burned, and she felt as though something was sucked from her—like the sensation of having blood drawn, but all over —and then he *changed*.

One minute, he was fae, the next a large, white wolf. Two blue eyes locked with hers, looked down at Thorne's clothing in reminder, and then bounded toward the exit.

"Shit." Laurel gaped. "Shit shit shit."

What the hell?

What the goddamned hell?

Was this real? Was she in actual hell? Her mind whirled, spiraling out of control with all the possibilities. She rubbed her eyes. Light from the buzzing white firefly kept her surroundings visible, but it was dark in the direction the wolf had gone.

A growl, an echo, and the sound of something tearing. Snarling.

Laurel's heart stopped beating.

The firefly landed on her finger and bit.

"Ow!" she cried and shook her hand out.

The creature bit her again. This time, Laurel looked closer. It wasn't a bug. It had two arms, two legs, a human face... and wings.

"I'm on drugs," Laurel reasoned. "Must be some kind of psychotropic torture."

Bones was back. There was no other logical explanation.

The little thing jumped off her hand and landed on Thorne's fallen breeches and boots. It squeaked at her with urgency. Laurel jolted with understanding. It wanted her to pick up the things and go.

The tunnel shuddered and groaned. Little rocks and sand fell from above. An almighty roar trembled her bones. That was not... that was not from the wolf. That sounded like a beast. Big. Dinosaur big. In here. In these tunnels.

Danger.

The glowing white firefly tugged on her collar.

"Right. We need to go. Got it."

Urgency skittered up Laurel's spine as she collected Thorne's items and took off after the glowing thing, all the while chanting to herself, "You're not insane. You're *not* insane. Speaking to a firefly is perfectly normal."

She followed until they got to an intersection about ten

feet across and stopped. Which way? There were at least three other passages. Chest heaving, she calmed and focused on where the soft natural light came from. *There.* Glowing streaks were on the same walls, similar in color to the little winged creature. Most of the streaks led down that tunnel. It must be the way out. She took a step, but then jumped back the way she'd come as something big came at her. Snapping piranha teeth and a wet, eyeless face on the body of a giant wyrm. She shrieked, hugged her package and retreated further into the tunnel, hoping to hell the thing would just keep going down another tunnel. And prayed.

The walls rumbled. The giant slug-thing slithered past.

A flash of white followed it, nipping at its tail. The wolf. *Thorne?*

In Laurel's heart she sensed it was him, just like after he'd made the change.

Once again, the feeling of displacement was so big that her mind emptied. She shook her head and thought of Clarke. *Get to Clarke.*

"Can you take me to Clarke?" Laurel asked the lady-fly. She squeaked in return. Then buzzed away, turned back, and hovered. Waiting. "Okay. Let's do this."

CHAPTER FOUR

*L*aurel burst from the dark tunnel system into the light of day. She squinted to protect the ache in her eyes. Fresh air gusted into her face. Snow everywhere. Trees. She blinked as her eyes adjusted and hugged herself.

Goddamn. This wasn't Vegas.

"Laurel?"

She turned. Cried. Her good friend Clarke was sitting on a rocky outcrop beneath a fir tree and next to a fledgling campfire. Laurel dropped her package and ran. The two collided and hugged. God, it was good to feel something familiar in her arms. The same red hair she'd known for years. The same freckle-faced bastion of fun who'd always made it her business to keep Laurel from working too hard.

Sobs wracked her body.

Laurel *never* cried.

Not when her twin had been diagnosed with his auto

immune disease. Not when he died. Not when her finger-nails were ripped from her fingers. And not when the sky had rained ash. Tears weren't useful unless they were the tears of your enemies. Well, that's what her father used to say. The military general had been a driving force in her life.

A new kind of choking took hold of Laurel when she realized she had no clue what had happened to her family. Were they safe? Maybe her father had her mother holed up in some government bunker somewhere. Surely a general had access to something like that.

Swallowing, she drew back and hastily wiped her eyes. She took in Clarke's worried face. The same, but different. Something shrewd existed in her blue-eyed stare that hadn't been there before. Clarke looked... grown up.

And what the hell was she wearing?

Laurel gingerly fingered the fur-lined cape, the carved wooden sundial on a leather cord around her neck, and the scrap of fabric around her hair. Clarke captured Laurel's roving hand.

"There's a lot to tell you," Clarke said. "Come and sit down. The boys will be finished playing soon."

"Boys?"

Clarke bit her lip, eyes assessing. "I'm taking it you've met Thorne?"

Yeah, she'd met that dangerous fae... or wolf. The one who'd been half-naked and hugging her when she'd woken. Intense. That was the only word she had to describe the man. Instead of answering, she looked around at the snow-capped trees. "Where *are* we?"

"I think the better word is when. *When* are we."

"Come again?"

"We're two thousand years into the future—give or take a few years."

Laurel's head swam. "What?"

Clarke sighed. "You really should sit down. And look"— she opened her rucksack to pull out some clothes—"I brought clean clothes for you to change into. Something I wish someone had done for me." She mumbled something about a stubborn wolf and then tossed the clothes to Laurel with a fresh smile. "You'll feel better. Trust me. The praxis wool is warmer too."

"Praxis?"

"A new kind of goat thing. The animals have mutated in this time. Some are the same, but, never-mind. You'll find out one day."

Goat thing? Mutated?

The ground moved beneath Laurel's feet. The horizon shifted. Her head lolled, and she landed hard on her butt. Clarke ran over to her, but she pushed her away. "I'm fine."

Laurel tried to stand. Her eyes rolled. Okay, maybe she wasn't fine. She sat and rested her head between her knees, ignoring the cold snow seeping into her already sodden pants.

"Take it easy, Laurel," Clarke cooed. "Deep breaths."

The cold air was exactly what she needed on her hot and prickly skin. A wave of nausea rolled through her and she retched until more black goo came out. Clarke went to her rucksack and pulled out a waterskin. A *waterskin!*

"Oh, God," Laurel mumbled. "What the hell?"

"Don't worry. I vomited that stuff too. It will pass."

Fight for control. Laurel forced the breath in and out of her lungs. She focused hard on a single twig poking out of the snow. She used the resolve her father taught her. *Tough situations build strong people.* She'd used the same mantra in all her gym centers. Queens don't whine. They work. And then they are *fine.*

Laurel unbuttoned the jacket and peeled it off. She went to add the woolen sweater, but Clarke stopped her. "Bra too. Anything with plastic and metal in it has to go, which, to be honest, is all the clothing you're wearing. Probably why it lasted so many years without completely deteriorating. My clothes practically fell from my body when I woke. Oh. And you'll have to give me your shoes. And your watch."

Laurel gingerly covered her watch. Without it, how would she know what day it was, or when her next appointment was, or how many steps she'd done? She needed it. "Why?"

Clarke's grave expression gave Laurel chills. "Because those bombs that went off destroyed the world. What grew out of the ashes isn't the same. Magic is a part of this world now, but it only flows where no metals or plastics are present. So..." She gestured at Laurel's bra. "The sooner you get it all off, the sooner you can access your full powers."

That took a moment to settle in. Powers. Magic.

Wolf shifter.

Flying fairy thing.

Hungry, giant slug-thing.

Great. Just great. Laurel looked around again as if she could orientate by sight. The sky was blue, not the dusky haze she remembered from… yesterday? Last week? Thousands of years ago? Good lord. *Thousands of years ago!*

She shivered and rubbed her arms. It certainly looked like a new world. What other explanation could there be?

"What happened exactly?" she asked Clarke. "I don't remember how I came to be in that cave."

"We were all at my place. Do you remember that?"

Laurel frowned, squinting to try to recollect, but shook her head.

Clarke continued, "We were in the living room watching the news. Vegas had pretty much shut down at that point. Then it started snowing, and we all went outside to look. Then... I guess the temperature dropped so fast that we froze." She clicked her fingers. "Snap-frozen. Just like that. Rush said the land has shifted since our time. Some ruins remain, but nothing looks the same." Clarke took a breath. "My working theory is that the cosmic Well chose us to survive and somehow worked to keep us frozen and preserved all these years."

"Cosmic Well?"

"Yeah, it's like the life-force that all magic draws from. These fae worship it like a deity. Only, it's not a real person. It's just... life. All powerful. All consuming. All nourishing."

There were so many more questions Laurel wanted to ask but settled on one. "Who's Rush?"

"My husband. I suppose you could call him that." Her lips stretched into a wide-mouthed grin. "He's so awesome.

44

Hot. Sexy. The best. God, I love him. And our daughter, Willow. I can't wait until you meet her."

Daughter? Laurel's brow lifted. Clarke had zero sign of a baby belly. "Goddamn. How—?"

"I thawed about three years ago and had Willow two years ago." Her expression darkened. "There's more I need to tell you, but... Come on. Get dressed and warm first."

Laurel unhooked her bra and quickly slipped the sweater on. Her smartwatch joined the pile. It was dead, anyway. She replaced her yoga pants and sneakers with tight leather pants that fit her like a second skin, and then she tugged on the waterproofed fur-lined boots. The glow from her arm markings glanced off her surroundings every time she moved.

"What is this?" She held her palm out. "You have them too."

"Thorne didn't tell you?" Clarke frowned and then muttered under her breath. "Of course he didn't."

Clarke shook out the cape and wrapped it around Laurel's shoulders. The warmth immediately settled her nerves. Laurel hugged it tightly while Clarke avoided her gaze.

I know that look.

It was the look of secrets.

"Clarke, what are the markings? And why did he ask me if I could conjure fire? And, come to think of it... I saw him turn into a wolf. Right before my eyes. And then there was the glowing little firefly that—"

"It's fine. Don't panic. Remember I said some animals

45

had mutated? Thorne is fae—evolved from both human and animal and with the capacity for using magic—mana—which you now have too. Apparently, fae existed once before, like in the fairytales of old, but as humans industrialized the world, covering it with metal and plastic, magic disappeared." Clarke paused. "And your markings are that of a Well-blessed mating. It means"—she winced—"that... um... your souls are bound. I guess to put it in a way you might understand, you're married to Thorne."

Laurel's heart gave palpitations.

"Uh-uh. No." Nope. Nopety, nope. She shook her head. Married. Never. She was not the marrying type. Let alone to that big, over-muscled warrior that turned into a mother-fricking-wolf? "No fucking way! In no version of life will I ever be married to a feral animal! What the hell, Clarke? You better start bringing out the prank cameras or something, because I'm starting to lose my patience. You know I'm not the marrying type."

Clarke's eyes flashed and caught something over Laurel's shoulder. Laurel stiffened. She turned. Two giant white wolves stood before the cave, holding the tail of the large wyrm between them like a rope, red blood dripping down their maws. One wolf was golden-eyed. The other blue-eyed—Thorne.

horne spat out the wyrm's tail. His side of the catch thumped wetly to the ground. Laurel's words twisted through him.

Feral animal?

This feral animal just protected her from the wyrm. This feral animal just caught her next meal. This feral animal was her Well-blessed *mate*. Anger swirled and churned. Who did she think she was? A human. That's what. A filthy, lying human who hadn't earned her right to hold mana within. She never went through the harrowing initiation he did as a child.

She'd sacrilegiously worn metals and plastics her entire life. No training. Whatsoever. Born in a bed of red coin. That was the kind of female she was. Thorne didn't need to learn any more to see that. Entitled. Sour-faced. Whining woman.

His lip curled, wanting to snarl, but he wouldn't give her the satisfaction. Instead, he drew her mana through their bond and used it to fuel his shift to fae form, reveling when she shivered as the magic left her body to replenish his, smug in the knowledge that she'd have no idea what that feeling meant, or that he'd taken her magic without permission.

It's what she deserved.

Laurel watched him with thinly veiled precaution as he stalked toward her. He stopped inches away. Tension vibrated in the air, but she held her ground while Thorne studied her with open hostility. In the full light of day, she was even more striking. It was a shame she was human and had a soul like murky ink. Good looking. Sharp jaw, small nose, big brown eyes, wide lips, dusky skin. Dark, straight hair cut to her chin. From what he could see of her beneath the cape, and what he remembered from within the cave, she was also fit. Healthy. The kind of body a male drooled over and begged to be under.

Not him.

She did her best to keep her eyes locked on his, but he could tell she wanted to look down. Not to cower to his alpha presence, but to inspect him as much as he had her. Despite her strong outward countenance, her inner turmoil exuded curiosity as much as fear... and a little something beneath it all. Attraction.

Good. Let her pine.

"Jeeze, Thorne." Clarke rolled her eyes. "Put some clothes on."

He stared at Laurel, a silent challenge in his eyes, daring her to turn away, to snarl or squeak at the blood still coating his jaw, to faint or swoon at his nakedness. She stared back, right into his eyes, never losing gumption. It made his heart pound harder, but for which emotion, he was at a loss. Then his rile rose like a flooding river.

Through their bond, he sensed her fear quake. And that made him smile, a baring of teeth. Good. She should fear him. At least then he knew where he stood.

He dipped to the ground, picked up a handful of snow and used it to wash the blood from his mouth, and then ran another handful over his chest to clear the remnants, eyes never leaving hers.

She backed away to the other side of the campfire.

That's right. Move away, human. That's where you belong. Humans on one side, fae on the other. Somewhere behind him, he heard Rush's feet crunching as he came back from wherever he'd transformed, but Thorne kept his gaze stolidly on Laurel.

"Lost my clothes," Rush grumbled. "Somewhere in the cave-system."

"I knew you'd lose them. So I brought extra," she replied.

"What would I do without you?" A kissing sound.

"Probably starve."

A snort.

Finally, Laurel broke eye contact. Her gaze shifted to Rush.

While Rush was Thorne's father, the fae stopped aging

once they achieved maturity at about twenty-one. To a human, he and his father would look like brothers.

Thorne found his clothes and stalked into the dense trees to dress. Not for any sense of propriety, he just didn't want to stare at the human any longer. After he'd slipped his battle uniform on, he worked on his hair. The leather cord binding it had gotten lost in the shift. He fiddled with tying it into some sort of knot to keep it from getting in his face and stared out into the forest, contemplating what to do.

Clarke came up quietly behind him.

"I knew you'd lose it. And I know what it means to you to keep your hair long. Here." She smiled gently at him and held out a new cord.

Damned Seers. A little of his anger released and he touched his fingers to his lips, then pushed his hand out in the fae hand-sign for gratitude. Voicing his explicit gratitude would mean he owed her a boon, and he wasn't ready for that. Even if she treated him like kin and apologized and thanked him all the time. Family would do anything for each other anyway. Debts didn't matter.

"Don't mention it." She returned to where the others sat, leaving him to his peace.

Thorne preferred to shave the sides of his head to keep his ears exposed, and he used to keep the top shorter for ease of care after a shift, but he'd promised himself he wouldn't cut it until he found Jasper. He'd started growing it two years earlier when he'd learned the Prime had sold Jasper to King Mithras in return for keeping the unsanctioned breeding law active. The same law which saw

Thorne's birth mother executed, and Rush exiled. There was nothing good about Mithras, not anymore. Once he was an adventurous king, but now, a cruel coward sitting in his glass palace. No doubt he wanted Jasper because he was a direct descendant. A bastard, but a potential threat to his throne all the same.

Thorne hated Mithras.

He'd ruined Thorne's life. His parents' lives. And now Jasper's. As Mithras's illegitimate son, Jasper had escaped the culling of royal offspring by joining the Order—an organization above the law of the royal courts. For a century or three, Jasper had been safe.

The question was, how much of Jasper, if any, would be left when they found him?

Thorne ran his finger down the long length of his hair. Too long.

Rush approached and cleared his throat.

Thorne should feel some sort of kinship with the fae, but there was a part of him that knew they weren't there yet. He regretted not knowing the kind of fae Rush was, not the way he knew Jasper or the other Guardians. Haze. Shade. Leaf. Even Cloud. They occupied an ever-present space in his mind, like family. But it had been two years since Thorne had learned of Rush's existence, and most of that time Rush had been isolated in his cabin, living his life with his mate and new child, Willow.

But they'd earned the solitude. Even Thorne couldn't fault them for wanting that.

Thorne fitted his ax-baldric over his Guardian jacket,

grateful to have Fury at his back once again.

"Congratulations," Rush said.

"Don't you mean commiserations?" Thorne angled his blue marked arm before his face and sneered.

Silence. Then an awkward sound. "Look, you may not see it now, but she *will* be a blessing to you. And soon, you won't be able to live without her. The Well is never wrong."

Thorne scoffed.

Admittedly, when he'd heard about the rare Well-blessed matings and seen how loved-up Rush and Clarke were, he'd expected more of a visceral reaction when the mating triggered in his own body. But nothing beyond the trickle of her emotions, and the power of her mana pushing at his own, twisting and entwining as though they were one. That part had been good. He actually hadn't meant to take that first amount from her, but when she'd not noticed, he took more. And then the wolf wanted out when he found the wyrm.

The wolf wanted lots of things these days.

When his wolf wanted to mate physically, the fae part of Thorne would have a hard time resisting. Clarke still wore the bite scar on her neck from when Rush had taken her. Thankfully, beyond a general appreciation for her attractiveness, Thorne had felt no such compunction with Laurel.

He supposed the mating response was different with everyone.

"Just because that's your story, doesn't mean it will be mine," he replied to Rush.

Rush folded his arms, brows lowering.

Oh, here we go. The parental talk. The one Rush had no right to give. Being Thorne's sperm donor didn't make him his father. Tension rode Thorne's system as he waited for the lecture.

It didn't come.

"You're right," Rush admitted. "In fact, I hope it's nothing like mine. I want better for you, Thorne. You deserve to be happy."

Thorne ground his teeth. A bird twittered in a nearby tree, hopped from branch to branch, and displaced a clump of snow that landed on Thorne's boot.

"But," Rush continued, "I know as well as anyone how much it hurts to hold that wall up. Just keep an open mind. Take her to the Order. Train her. Put in some effort and she'll lead you to Jasper when the time is right. You never know, you might find you both have more in common than you think. Clarke and I need to head out to find the another frozen human. When we get back, we can hunt for Jasper together. He was a friend."

"Why can't Laurel lead us now?" It grated there was no timeframe, no date, just vague ideas from Clarke about when or how they would find Jasper.

"You know why. A Seer doesn't see all. Just guides. I don't even know if Laurel knows she's meant to go on this quest."

Thorne was sick of waiting.

Rush clapped him on the back. "Come on. Clarke needs to tell you both something before we leave."

When they returned to the camp, Clarke had bolstered

the fire and roasted the wyrm tail on long skewers, much to Laurel's clear distaste. She sat on a stone, hugging her cape, frowning at the fire. Thorne grinned wickedly. He had a feeling he'd enjoy eliciting more discomfort within the woman. He'd make her truly see how animalistic and feral he could be.

There were two kinds of mating. One of the soul and one of the body. His wolf knew that this woman was his soul-match and was curious. It wanted to sniff her. To find out if she was good enough to bite. To feast on. The wolf urged Thorne to go to her, to sit with her, and rub his scent on her... but he didn't. Never. Just because the Well announced them as mates, didn't mean he had to accept it. Did he?

Clarke's head lifted as he neared. She slid out her wooden sundial pendant and left the shadow of the trees to check the time. Concern ghosted her features.

"We have to get going, Rush."

Laurel jumped up. "Great. I'm ready to leave. Where are we going?"

"Oh. Um." Clarke looked at Rush and relaxed, simply by laying eyes on her mate. Thorne wasn't too stubborn to admit a small part of him was jealous. Clarke also had that look when her gaze landed on her daughter. And every time Thorne saw it, an emptiness in his chest hollowed further. It was a look he'd never shared with anyone. Maybe his aunt Kyra in his youth, but that was decades ago.

"You're going to the Order," Clarke continued. "I'll be going somewhere else."

"You're leaving me?" Laurel said in a small voice.

"But not alone. Thorne will be with you."

The look Laurel cut Thorne would hurt if he didn't feel the same way about her.

"Don't worry," he said. "I don't bite." Much.

"But..." Laurel started, then stopped.

"I know it's not ideal," Clarke added. "But we have to search for Ada."

"Ada? Of course I'll come with you. Is she sleeping? Where is she?"

Clarke sighed. "I'm sorry, Laurel. You can't come. You need to train the powers growing inside of you before you have an accident, and Ada will be fine. She's asleep, frozen in ice, just like you were. We'll go to her and bring her to the Order where you can see her. She'll be excited to see a friendly face."

"I'm fine. You know me. I'll work anywhere, anytime. I want to see Ada."

"She's not fine," Thorne added with a sardonic glance at Laurel. "When I found her, she was surrounded in fire, almost dead from smoke inhalation. It was lucky I was able to douse the flames without having time to replenish my stores since my last mission."

Rush's brow rose. "How did you?"

Thorne showed Rush his blue marked arm by way of explanation. "Point is, she needs training."

"*She* is the cat's mother. I have a name and it's none of your business what I can or can't do."

Thorne deadpanned.

55

"Anyway," Clarke said. "You can't come with us, I'm very sorry."

"Where are you going?"

"I can't tell you that either. We learned that the Void is here, and he had Seers working for him. You know, the more I think about it, he may have woken a long time ago. He's worked out how to harvest mana and ingest it to keep himself young. He could be more knowledgeable about this world than we realize. The more people I tell about Ada, the easier it is for him to find out, and the last thing we want is for him to send Bones, or some other henchman to get to Ada before us."

"Bones?" Laurel's face paled.

"Oh shit. I should have warmed up to that part."

Laurel grabbed Clarke by the arm and pulled her to the side where she spoke in a rushed and hushed tone. Thorne fought another grin. Laurel had no idea he could still hear with his keen wolf ears. But his amusement dropped when he caught the word "torture." The woman was so feisty and full of life, he'd forgotten about her past. He supposed it wasn't like people carried a sign around their neck that told the world about their past.

Rush cleared his throat and stood before Thorne, blocking his view of the women. Rush scratched his beard.

"What?" Thorne snapped.

"It's just that I wanted to ask if you could keep an eye on Willow while we're gone."

"As in... babysit?"

"Not babysit. I know that's asking too much. But just to

56

check in on her. You smell like kin. Like it or not, you *are* kin. She'll feel better with you around. I know the house brownies are excellent sitters, but the rest of the cadre won't look out for her as a brother would."

Half-brother. He clenched his jaw but nodded. Even if he wasn't related, young fae were treasures to any fae race. There was a time any birth was celebrated and lauded, as each child was a sign their species would thrive in the harsh post-apocalypse landscape it used to be.

Rush exhaled and hand-signed his thanks.

"If you're worried about the Sluagh, she'll be fine," Thorne said.

"Why do you say that?"

"I have a theory that they only hunt humans because they lack mana. Clarke was never attacked on campus. I don't think Willow will be either."

"I'm not so sure," Rush added. "The Sluagh eat the souls of fae, too."

Thorne shrugged, but then his ears pricked up at the sound of his name, and he listened in on the conversation the two women were having.

"It's much safer for you to be with Thorne," Clarke insisted.

"That means nothing to me. I don't know him."

"He'll protect you with his life."

"I can't trust that. You said we were married! What if he wants... things I don't?"

"You can trust the Well-blessed markings. They connect you both on a metaphysical level. There is no way he'll harm you. It would be like harming himself. And trust me. I've *Seen* things. I know it will all work out fine."

What did that mean?

But Thorne had no chance to ask. Clarke cut the conversation, went back to the campfire, and resumed eating. Fifteen minutes later, everyone had eaten their fill. Laurel chose to wait until they arrived at the Order to eat.

Clarke handed a portal stone to him. "This is imbued with the essence of the Order. It will take you there. We'll leave after you. The less you know about where we're headed, the better."

Thorne activated the stone and a rift in the air opened. Glowing light exploded and buzzed with energy. He stepped through to the other side and waited for Laurel in the field just before the gates of the Order. When she hadn't come after five minutes, he was about to leave without her, but a flash of light and power sparked and then her shape finally appeared.

He closed off the portal. The stone sizzled in his hands.

Alone at last.

He ditched the stone on the floor and bared his teeth. "Let's get this straight. I only want you for one thing—to find my mentor, Jasper. Clarke said you would lead me to him. That's the only reason I'm here."

"What about the... marriage?"

"Marriage. This is what you humans call mating?"

She nodded.

He stared at her long and hard. The Well had matched

them up. Apparently, the Well was never wrong. But he couldn't see it.

"You're the last person I'd choose to be married to."

Turning his back, he strode toward the gates.

CHAPTER SIX

*L*aurel fumed.

She followed the rude wolf-shifter beyond the walls of some medieval type compound—high stone perimeter, oversized gates, and guards questioning anyone who dared approach. Once inside the lush grounds, Laurel could still see the red-leafed forest outside, towering over the perimeter walls. Those trees were huge. She was trapped. A prisoner.

Any hope that she'd find something familiar from her time was dashed, and she both wished for her friend to come back and silently cursed her. Why did Clarke have to leave her so soon?

The sound of trickling water followed Laurel everywhere. There were little gullies of water beside the paths, water fountains, and water dripping from rooftops of buildings as though it had rained recently. But it hadn't.

If she weren't feeling so displaced, she'd appreciate the

verdant landscaping mixed with Byzantine type architecture, simple stone and wooden dwellings.

Fine. Maybe it was like a paradise, or a spa retreat... but she still felt trapped. Lost. Alone.

A wave of irritation washed over her, and strangely, she felt as though it wasn't hers. Like the emotion was a foreign body in her own. Brushing it off, and trying to look inconspicuous, Laurel kept her head down and strode swiftly as she followed Thorne along a path and into the depths of the campus. Large impressive buildings with arched and mosaic windows were to her left, and to the right, behind the barrier of a box hedge, was a grassed training ground for soldiers. Shouts of acknowledgment from the field drew Laurel's attention. Three men, or fae as they were called, were on the outskirts of the field gesturing for Thorne's attention. But he kept walking, staunch and determined, so Laurel followed.

What else could she do?

Clarke had left her. And she got it, she really did. If Laurel had awoken to find herself alone, she might not have survived. Madness or panic would have overwhelmed her if the fire hadn't. That was hard enough to grasp as it was. Fire. From her. Goodness.

If Ada was the next one to wake from their time, she shouldn't have to go through it alone. Ada may be a woman who could look after herself, but even her survivalist training wouldn't cut it at this time.

This training was how Laurel and Ada had met. Laurel had been looking for new ways to bring some spark into her fitness clubs, and survival weekends in the Nevada desert were just the thing. They had trekked a few trails, headed into the canyons, and learned a few empowering skills.

Since arriving through the portal, she'd seen no snow. The air was still nippy, and the vegetation was foreign. Blood-red leafed forests? She shuddered to think what the wildlife was like, and she wasn't keen on exploring. Not until she understood what the hell was going on with her.

Clarke had said Laurel had magic now. It wasn't entirely impossible to believe. She'd seen the evidence in the cave and, on some level, she felt magic living inside of her. It was an energy that reacted to things around her as though it had a life of its own, and it was mainly concentrated on the blue marks on her arm. It almost seemed she could feel someone else's emotions, which was stupid.

Shaking her head, she continued her journey. They made it to a large two-story house toward the back of the campus. Sitting on the porch were two women. One was tiny, about waist high and with small pointy-ears, leathery skin, tufts of hair peeking from random places, and a yellow ribbon in her hair. The other woman had white feathered wings.

She had *wings*.

Laurel's eyes widened as she took in the sight. Glorious white feathers, glossy and catching the sun, swept down from this woman's back to dust the floor. For a moment, Laurel thought perhaps they were a prosthetic, but then the feathers fluffed out, like she'd seen a bird do when cold. Laurel's breath hitched.

Thorne swore under his breath upon seeing the winged-lady. A surge of foreign anger rose within Laurel. Once again, it wasn't her emotion. She had no reason to be angry at the winged woman she hadn't met before.

Could the emotion be coming from the only person scowling in her vicinity? The one with matching twin markings on his arm?

Thorne stomped up the steps and attempted to head straight into the house, but the winged woman cut him off.

"D'arn Thorne." The tone in her voice was hard, sharp, and imperious.

He tensed, knuckles white on the doorknob, then released and met the woman's wide-eyed stare. "What."

"Are you going to introduce us?"

Thorne waved at Laurel. "Laurel, meet the Prime. And the brownie there is Jocinda."

He tried to enter the house again, but the Prime's hand lifted and clenched. Power tingled Laurel's tongue, air whooshed, and the door slammed shut.

"Thin ice, D'arn Thorne."

A low growl rumbled from his throat and he faced her once again. This time, he said nothing and stared.

Laurel rubbed her forearm. The overwhelming urge for anger definitely seemed to come from the markings. She narrowed her eyes at Thorne. It had to be his emotion. There was no other explanation. She concentrated. Something else laced the anger. Hate. Bitterness steeped in regret.

He had a history with this winged-woman. Twisted and painful. The Prime straightened her spine and gave Laurel the once over. Laurel narrowed her eyes suspiciously back.

"It's a pleasure to meet you, Laurel. I'm Prime Aleksandra. You can call me Prime. I am in charge around here. Welcome." She inclined her head regally. "Waking thousands of years after an apocalypse must be harrowing. I'm sure you have many questions and must be tired and hungry. Jocinda has graciously prepared your rooms. There are clothes, bathing water, and refreshments."

Laurel's suspicion eased. Thank God a woman was in charge around here. Laurel held out her hand and said, "Thank you."

Sound stopped. Every hair on Laurel's arms stood on end. Thorne grunted. The Prime glanced down at Laurel's extended hand. Her white brow lifted at the blue glowing marks etched on her skin.

"I will collect on that debt one day in the future. For now, I will leave you to gather your bearings with your new mate. Being Well-blessed so early in your relationship is a boon and a sign that the Well looks favorably on your coupling. I'm sure you will make a formidable team. Tomorrow morning a Guardian will escort you to the temple for testing. Then you will resume your training at the academy."

A team? She and Thorne. Ha! With difficulty, she forced her laughter down, and when Thorne shot her an inquisitive stare, she realized he must sense her emotions too. He was curious about her sardonicism. She felt that echo back at her.

So it was true. The emotions she'd been feeling over the journey were his.

The Prime ignored Thorne's and Laurel's interaction. She hiked her blue floor-length dress to clear her bare feet, nodded to the brownie and then padded down the porch steps and strode away across the lawn, her wings sweeping regally behind her like a glorious white mantle.

The brownie became a bulldozer of action. "Right. Follow me and I will take you to your room." She barged past Thorne and entered the house, stomping right up the grand staircase that led from the foyer to where Laurel presumed were the living quarters.

Without waiting for Thorne, Laurel pushed past him and followed Jocinda. Having her own room was appealing. A bath, some food, and a rest to gather her bearings, even better.

Outside the house had been limestone, arched windows, and terracotta tiles. Inside, the house reminded her of an old medieval castle. Rugs. Glass windows. Tapestries. Leather and wooden furniture. The smell of citrus and cedar. Candles in candlestick holders. Candelabras hanging from the ceiling, but not made from metal. Something else. Glossy pottery perhaps? Opaque glass?

While Laurel ogled at the decor, Thorne took two maroon-carpeted steps at a time to overtake Laurel and catch Jocinda as she scurried to the next floor.

"Where are you going?" he asked the brownie.

"Taking Laurel to her room," Jocinda replied. She took a right on the landing, and stopped at a particular door down the hall.

"But that's my room," he noted.

"You're mated, are you not?"

"Yes, but—"

"Are you arguing with me, D'arn Thorne?"

"No, I'm just… we're not mated like that. Well-blessed mating is different from one of the bodies."

She blinked, flabbergasted at Thorne's tone. "I think not, D'arn Thorne. Would you prefer to arrange these sorts of things yourself?"

Thorne immediately backtracked and showed his palms in surrender. Laurel even sensed a dash of fear down the bond. Fear over a few chores?

"Jocinda, you're completely right," he returned. "We are mated. This is our room." Then he touched his lips and motioned his hand outward and down toward the brownie.

Odd kind of hand signal. Laurel wondered what it meant. She'd seen it a few times already. Another thing to catalog for later.

The brownie opened the door and ushered Laurel inside, brusquely rattling off instructions on how to draw the bath, where more clothes were, and about the food choice selected on the table. Breakfast was served in the kitchen an hour after sunup, lunch at midday, and dinner was an hour after sundown in the main dining room. They'd *foretold* that she was coming, so did their best to find food that Laurel liked, but since the world was vastly changed from Laurel's time, she wasn't so sure.

Again, there were a few things the brownie had said that Laurel didn't understand and hoped she remembered to ask later when she wasn't so brain-fried.

After the whirlwind was gone, it was just Laurel and Thorne together in the chambers.

A window overlooked the large lawn at the front of the house. A decorative temple rose in the distance, tall, regal, and with water running from the roof to cascade over the eaves. Two armchairs faced each other before the window. A table with food was between.

One king-sized bed.

Through an archway, in another chamber, was a steaming bath, and more doors she assumed went to dressing rooms or closets. Hopefully a toilet too.

Good God. What if these people didn't have toilets? It didn't seem like there was electricity. You needed copper wiring for that, right?

Laurel's hands pierced her hair, and she pulled. This was all a bit much. She went to the window and stared while her heart thudded in her chest. She took in air slowly through her nose and exhaled through her mouth, wishing her nerves would calm.

Behind her, Thorne toed off his boots and strode into the bathing room, where he promptly unbuckled his weapons and shed his battle uniform. She had a few seconds to glimpse a taut, shapely rear-end, and then he sank into the bath. The muscles in his back rippled as he supported his weight. The howling wolf tattoo danced.

A long, husky deep sigh escaped him as he immersed, and Laurel felt it vibrate down to her core. For a moment, the anger she sensed from him switched to emptiness and she almost forgot about his caustic attitude. He was just a sexy man in a bath.

With pointed ears.

He rested a muscled arm over the rim of the bath and reclined his head, his long warrior's tail dangling outside the tub.

But he *was* an asshole. Given the chance, most men were. She didn't expect them to be any different in this time than in hers. They'd tried to beat her down when she rose to the top of her fitness game; they'd betrayed her, and one had even tortured her. The only man Laurel had trusted was her father. And he was dead. Gone.

Her throat closed up. Her eyes watered.

They were all gone.

Except for one.

Bones. Apparently he still lived. She shivered, felt the ghost of pain in her fingers, and rubbed them on her thighs. Catching herself in a nervous habit, she tugged her cape around her body until it squeezed tight.

She would *not* cry.

But she missed her father's rigid outlook on life. Her mother's way of softening it. Every creature comfort in her home. Green protein smoothies. Her Nikes. Being CEO of her own company, she owned a penthouse apartment in one of the big chain hotels on the strip. She didn't have to do anything but workout and be a boss. That was her life. She had been a queen. A queen who was living twice as hard because her twin hadn't.

Now what was she?

She shuffled over to the window and sat on an armchair, tucking her feet beneath her bottom. It wasn't so different out there. Blue sky. Green grass. Grumpy people.

Winged people.

Bossy people.

Fae. Not people.

She groaned and grabbed her head. This was going to take some getting used to. She picked through the food on the table, looking for something familiar. Strange fruit. Odd smelling bread. Meat and gravy, which she wasn't a huge fan of. Usually, she stuck to fish or vegetables. Then her gaze landed on one item in particular. Potato croquettes. Her father was part Flemish and would make them at every family gathering. How did they know this about her?

Magic.

Laurel took a bite of the croquette and almost cried. Melt in her mouth. It tasted so good. So like how Papa used to make. She could almost see him standing over a frying pan, testing the sizzling rolls with a spoon. The smell of butter. The friendly ribbing her mother gave her father because he was an overachiever. And then the loving looks her parents shot each other, even though they were well into their third decade of marriage.

What would her father think of this situation?

69

"He who fails to plan is planning to fail," he used to say. She'd hung the quote on the wall of her office in her first gym. It originally came from Winston Churchill who also said, "There is nothing wrong with change if it's in the right direction."

She'd left the world a destroyed husk. A big, empty, gaping hole stretched in her chest. No rock concerts. Famous artwork. All that history. No airplanes to another continent. People, families, children. Gone.

A small sob escaped Laurel, and she covered her mouth, holding it in as she faced the window. It was stupid to try to hide it. Thorne could sense everything. And that made her feel even worse. Not even her thoughts were private.

Outside, she saw the sun setting. The pink and orange hues mixed with turquoise and navy. Beautiful. A group of fae casually strolled across a path at the end of the lawn. They looked to be dressed in long blue robes. And they were laughing.

Laurel's hand touched the glass window pane.

They were happy.

Her world was gone, but now a new one was alive. Alive and seemingly thriving with magic, new life, and hope. If Clarke believed Laurel had a job to do in this world, then she should do it. She was never one to shy away from responsibility, and Laurel would be damned if she let those same evil humans try to take the laughter away from this new world. Not this time.

Tomorrow, Laurel would make her five-step plan. She'd get her body back into shape, work on this magic growing inside her, and then she would find Thorne's missing friend and shove her success in his face.

Because that's the way to deal with naysayers. Prove them wrong.

She knew it was petty, but it was her only defense mechanism at this point. It was something to hold on to.

The sound of water sloshing alerted Laurel to the wolfish fae getting out. With only her instincts thinking, and the need to be somewhere she wouldn't have to interact, she pulled back the covers on the bed, intending to claim it for herself and pretend to be asleep. He got the tub first, fine, but then she would get the bed. He could sleep elsewhere. That was the intention, anyway.

She took off her boots and shed the cape. But the rest she kept on. A bone-deep weariness sank in and she found herself not caring if she dirtied the sheets. She just wanted to sleep and to wake tomorrow clear-headed, like she usually was.

The moment she rested her head on the soft pillow, her body sank into the mattress, and her eyelids grew heavy. An unavoidable sigh fell from her lips. She tucked her hand beside her face and let her lashes slowly drift closed. Tomorrow she would start her plan. Tonight, she would take it easy on herself. Tonight she would mourn the family and friends she'd lost from her time. She would dream about her mother tickling her face when she fell asleep as a child, or even how she brushed Laurel's hair from her face when Laurel was a sad adult. She would pretend she was still only a phone call away.

The padding of feet got closer, and she schooled her emotions to deadpan, and her breath to calm. She feigned sleep. He'd have to physically force her out if he didn't like her taking his spot.

He was quiet so long she thought maybe he'd gone. And she almost fooled herself into sleeping. Oblivion edged in.

Steps drew close, and she didn't have it in her to tense. Maybe it was because there was no hostility coming from him. No. It was an emotion she'd not expected... relief trickled through the markings in her arm. Thorne's calloused fingers traced over hers, lingering around the scars of her nail beds, and then over the fresher scars on her knuckles from when she'd taken up self-defense lessons after Bones' torture. A touch of sadness leaked through the bond. Then... compassion.

The heat of his body—fresh from the bath—blasted her face as he leaned close. Now she tensed, ready to fight, knowing this alerted him to her wakefulness. If he dared touch her... but he took hold of the blanket she'd neglected and drew it over her shoulders. Then he shifted the hair from her face and tucked it behind her ear.

Thorne left the room.

Laurel stayed tense, muscles locked and heart-pounding for long minutes. He'd tucked her hair. He'd covered her with a blanket. The next thing she knew, her eyes flew open and everything was dark.

She'd fallen asleep.

CHAPTER SEVEN

*L*ying in the bed, stretching languidly, Laurel realized it must be close to dawn because she felt rested. She was also an early-to-bed, early-to-rise kind of girl. Perhaps it was something being an army brat gave her. Everywhere they'd moved when she was younger was at some army base. There was always activity in her house during the early hours.

She sat up and rubbed her eyes. The first thing she noticed was an ambient blue glow. Oh. That's right. She had a weird, shimmering tattoo. She poked at the blue lines, testing. On the outside, her skin felt the same. But on the inside, there was a restless energy swimming beneath her skin. Like she'd just taken a pump class, downed a wheat-grass shot, and perhaps even had a coffee.

Coffee. Wheatgrass. Pump class. Her face crumpled at the memory of favorite things she may never see again. But the ache in her heart over losing her family and the rest of the world wasn't so raw after sleep. It was still there, but the deep shock had faded. With that mind numbing emotion gone, she had the clarity to approach her situation with a level head, just like her father had always taught her. *Control your controllables.*

Laurel smiled. She wasn't sure if controllable was even a real word, but her father always made up vocabulary to suit his purpose. His sentiment was right. She couldn't control the fact she was in this time, or that she was in some kind of arranged marriage with this wolf-shifter, but she could control her attitude toward it. The divine source of power they worshipped had chosen Laurel and Thorne as mates, as partners. The Well had imbued her with power. It had faith in her. Laurel should respect that, even if she didn't understand it.

Changing her frame of mind was harder than it sounded. She had to steel herself against her natural objections and ignore her skeptical instincts. It wouldn't happen overnight, but perhaps with time, she'd grow to love this place... maybe even... her mind shifted to Thorne, but she wouldn't finish that train of thought. Not yet.

She had a plan to make. A course of action. But what?

A few things stood out. Clarke believed Laurel was the key to finding this person lost to Thorne. Laurel had to learn to control her powers. And this Prime lady assumed Laurel was going to fall in line, get tested, and go to her academy. There were too many questions, and it was unlikely Laurel would receive answers from Thorne. He also needed an attitude adjustment.

One thing she knew for sure was that she'd solve nothing sitting there thinking about it.

The best thing to do when feeling displaced was to go back to routine, to find something familiar and ground herself. Her favorite old routine was her morning run. It made her feel like she had her shit sorted. She didn't. But it made her *feel* as though she did.

She patted her cheeks. *Wake up beauty, it's time to beast.*

She looked around the moonlit room. No light switch or lamps. But she did find another person in the bed with her. Her jaw dropped. Thorne had slept next to her all night. The steady sound of his breathing ensured her of his slumber. Between the blue glow of their markings and the moonlight, she could see the fae clearly with a blanket draped over his brawny, muscular body. Arms behind his head, his biceps bulged. In rest, he looked attractive. Hot. Mouthwateringly so.

She blinked at the direction of her thoughts, but once started, she couldn't stop. Didn't want to. Her gaze magnetized on his body, starting with a face that almost looked boyish in sleep and in no way as intimidating as in wakefulness. *Puppy* was her first reaction, but then her eyes trailed down, grazed over his scruff covered jaw, thick neck, and sculptured shoulders. Every feminine instinct tingled in appreciation. Down the V of his torso, to the eight-pack stomach where a bolt of desire hit as her gaze snagged on the tantalizing dark hair just below his navel but above the sheet line. She patted her hot cheeks. Must be something wrong with her.

Although... she glanced back at his face... a one-night stand had never bothered her much in the past. Maybe that's what this partnership could be. Physical.

Relationships for her existed only between the sheets, even before Bones ruined her trust in men. Men were intimidated by her drive, they never stuck around, and she ended up finding a use-them-and-lose-them tactic was easier for everyone. Her body reacted. Her skin flushed, her nipples pebbled, and she clenched her thighs together at the thought of how she would use his body to work out her own sensual kinks. She imagined he was the kind of partner who would take all she demanded and then ask for more.

Her hungry eyes shifted to the bulge between his legs. Yes. He could take her demands, and she'd happily give them.

Work to do.

Clearing her throat, she eased softly off the bed, and then quietly explored the anteroom where the bathtub was. More arched windows let in enough light to see. Behind a curtain, she found a closet. Hanging from rails on one side were multiple copies of the blue and black leather battle gear Thorne had worn. On the left side, she found a range of feminine clothes. Thumbing through the collection, she was disappointed to find no yoga pants, no workout clothes, and no sneakers. But Clarke had mentioned plastics being prohibited, and a key proponent of Lycra was synthetic. Still, there were knit fabrics she might be able to source. In the meantime, Laurel would have to be resourceful and come up with alternative active attire.

First, she needed something to bind her breasts. She needed a sports crop top. Tapping her lip, she thought of alternatives. She supposed she could tear a sheet into strips and bind it around her chest. Then her eyes landed on a long, dangling piece of fabric hanging from the rail. Shifting clothing items out of the way, she realized the strip was exactly what she had in mind... as though they'd known about her needs. Clarke had either told them, or they were all truly psychic.

After three attempts, she fashioned the strip around her chest and one shoulder in a way that looked good and felt comfortable. Then she cut off the wool leggings at the thigh with one of Thorne's daggers, and slipped them on, satisfied at how the pants clung to her hips. They wouldn't give her trouble as she ran. Lastly, shoes were a problem. It was either wear solid leather boots or go barefoot. Perhaps they just didn't make the kind of shoes she needed yet. Maybe that was a business opportunity for her.

She decided to keep her feet bare, and tiptoed through the house, intending to be quiet to avoid waking anyone, but soon discovered that was pointless. Three fae were sitting in the open living room near the front, playing cards, carousing loudly. She considered stopping to say hello, but could already see the sky lighten outside. Her favorite time to run was dawn. The rising sun promised a fresh start. Missing it ruined her day.

She slid by and let herself out of the house, closing the door softly behind her. Standing on the porch, she deeply inhaled the fresh air and took a moment to appreciate the smell. She had to force her brain not to take shallow breaths to avoid the air pollution from the nuclear fallout. In her time, the air quality had been abysmal toward the end. But here, early birds were calling, a purple hue ghosted the sky, and the pleasant sound of water trickled. She briefly allowed the memory of helplessness to enter her system, then forced it aside. The time for feeling sorry for herself was over. Another few deep, concerted breaths and she was calm. Strong. Queen.

She was here.

Alive.

She would make the most of it.

Setting off, she jogged down the steps and onto the lawn. Soft grass greeted her feet, and she almost wept at the profound sense of rightness. This was Laurel Baker. Running. In control. Always moving.

On the first lap of the lawn, the pleasant familiar burn in her lungs warmed her and she relaxed. She was able to take in the houses and structures nearby. The house she'd come from dwarfed the house next to it, which was dark and steeped in shadows. It gave her the creeps every time she looked at it, so she passed quickly. After the third lap, all her irrational fears ebbed away. She sank into the fall of her feet, the beat of her heart, and the drag of her breath—at first shallow, and then deep and freeing. Her mind became numb to everything but the next step, the next breath, and her rhythmic heartbeat.

This. Right here.

It felt good. So good she couldn't help smiling.

That was why when the hairs lifted on the back of her neck, she paid no attention. But when hot air, like breath, puffed behind her ear, she stopped suddenly, heart-skipping, and whipped her gaze around. Swallowing nervously, she surveyed the empty lawn. Predawn light glinted through a murky mist and painted the buildings and plants in gold and pink. Like a magnet, her eyes drew toward the smaller house, still somehow creepy and dark, as though even the sun was afraid to touch it. Black curtains were devoid of light. Crow statues sat on the steepled roof, frozen in their regard of her. Cobwebs dusted the porch eaves. And standing in the shadows of the open doorway was a man.

Tall, lithe, hauntingly handsome. He had the kind of beauty that stole her breath. Eyes like gray smoke. Silken medium length black hair. A dark business suit fitted his graceful body like a second skin. A gothic cape hung from his shoulders and kissed the ground beneath him. Long pale delicate fingers tapped his thigh, as though he were deep in thought as he watched her. Laurel's stuttering steps drew her closer until she stopped before his house. It was as though his gaze pulled her there. She couldn't tear her eyes away, nor step in another direction. She was locked in his curious, smoky sights.

Eyes burning with intrigue trailed down her body. Another hot puff of air blew across the back of her neck. A lover's breath. As if he stood behind her, not before her.

She glanced over her shoulder. *Nothing.*

Snapping her gaze back, she almost yelped to see him a

few steps down on his porch. *Closer.* One foot was on a higher step. Those long fingers grasped a rail, but his simmering, intense gaze still locked and devoured. Despite his perfect appearance, every instinct screamed for her to run. But there were other instincts. Baser ones that felt... hot. Heavy. Swollen. Aroused.

What the fuck was going on?

The puff of hot air on her neck shifted. It trailed down behind her ear, tickling her skin, and then it explored her body... wrapping around the blue markings on her arm, and then back up to her torso. It was as though he touched her. Intimately. Brazenly. The whisper of wind entered her clothes, somehow slipped beneath the tight straps she'd wound against her body. Sensation caressed her breasts, nipples, and then navel. She gasped as goosebumps erupted, and the phantom touch went lower.

Terror warred with desire. This was... she couldn't move. Could barely breathe while the beautiful man drank her in, head cocked to the side as though she were a curiosity in a museum. He seemed to look beyond her skin and flesh, to the inside of her very soul. Her body wanted him, would do *anything* if only he came closer and touched her for real.

But while her body engaged in sex, and velvet, and sinful desires, her mind screamed in terror. She opened her mouth... nothing came out.

CHAPTER EIGHT

*T*horne woke with a jolt. Something was wrong.

Terror surged down his bond, hard and sharp. He checked the bed next to him. Empty.

Laurel.

Her scent was fresh. She must have left recently. He shot off the bed, and ran through the house, past the three vampires playing cards in the living room, and out the front door. Two steps later he launched off the porch and had shifted into wolf by the time his paws hit the ground.

Scenting her, he found her standing stiff before the house of the Six. Uncharacteristically, one of the Sluagh was on his porch, staring at Laurel as though she were his next meal. Dumbfounded, Thorne had never seen one of them in the light of dawn before. Only at night. But from the acrid scent of magic in the air, the Sluagh wasn't just staring. He was breaching Laurel's will, the way only a soul-eater could.

Thorne *ran*, prepared to strike. He skidded to a halt

81

between Laurel and the house. Hackles raised, ears down, claws out, he snarled.

Fuck off, Sluagh. She's mine.

The Sluagh's dark eyes slid Thorne's way. He cocked an indignant brow and then darted his gaze to the rising sun as if that were his only concern. For a fleeting moment, the cape draping from his shoulders fluttered with menace. Not a cape. Wings. Big, featherless ones like the vampires... but with draconic talons. Then the Sluagh's gaze snapped down to the blue markings glowing through the fur of Thorne's right paw. The Sluagh's brows lifted in surprise.

A velvety smooth voice entered Thorne's mind. *Truth.*

And then the Sluagh gave a respectful bow and stepped back. Energy blasted from behind Thorne. Wind ruffled his fur. Not energy. The Sluagh's soul. It rejoined its host body and a ghostly outline of the Sluagh's skull crackled and flashed like lightning beneath his skin.

Death. Fallen angels. Soul-stealers.

The Sluagh had many names that fae and humans alike whispered to their children in tales of warning and woe. Never leave a west window open when a loved one was near death because the Sluagh would steal their soul away. But for humans, they cared little if you were near death. They'd steal you alive, kidnap you and keep you in their dark dens, supping on your soul until there was nothing left —if you were lucky. If you weren't, you'd eternally belong to them, a part of the Wild Hunt that flew through the skies during battle, full of locked and moaning souls desperate for release but condemned to live all eternity, serving as the

Sluagh's spectral soldiers, only called out of hibernation to hunt down the enemy or serve as sustenance.

Sluaghs answered to no one, could exist on the spectral plane, and were impossible to control. Unseelie to the core, they were borne of chaos and Queen Maebh's need for protection during the first great war against the humans. It was the Sluagh who'd turned the tide of the battle and pushed the humans back behind their high crystal walls. The humans' war machines could not decimate the spectral offensive of the Wild Hunt.

It baffled Thorne that there were six of them, *here*, ordained by the Well—lauded and accepted by the very nature of life.

These six Sluagh were Guardians who fought magic-warped monsters and upheld the laws of the Well. They were monstrous protectors of fae but were virtually monsters themselves.

But then again, it was the way of the fae. Without darkness, there could be no light. Without the sun, there would be no moon. And... Thorne had been chosen too. One look into his own dark heart confounded most people.

Shifting back to fae form, Thorne rounded on a still shaken Laurel. Her chest rose and fell, fists flexing at her sides, eyes like two big saucers.

"What are you doing out here by yourself?" Thorne ground out before she had a chance to speak. But then frowned when he took in her strange attire, pink cheeks, and sweat-glossed skin. Was she... training? "You should never be out alone, especially at night."

"It was dawn."

"Close enough."

She blinked, and then met his stare. "I was... going for a run. That's all."

"Stupid human. Did you ever stop to think that it wasn't safe?"

All timidness dissolved. Hard fury flashed in her eyes and then she punched him.

In the nose.

Pain and yellow light exploded. A scalding sensation licked his face. His eyes watered and he doubled over, groaning. That hurt more than usual. It also smelled burned. *Fire?* He wiped the blood from the tender flesh of his nose and forced his eyes open. Fire engulfed her fist— the one that punched him. She had no idea.

"No, Thorne," she said. "This *stupid human* did not think that going for a simple run would be dangerous. No one has told me jack about this place. Whatever that *thing* was, it didn't exist in my time except in nightmares or the movies."

He pinned her with murder in his gaze. "So he's a *thing* and I'm a *feral* animal. And yet you're the violent one. You're the one using your mana against me." He gave her fist a scornful look. "And you wonder why no one has volunteered to help you."

She gaped, saw her fist, and the fire guttered out. "I... oh my God. You're right. How the hell did I do that?" She blinked rapidly, eyes shooting all over the place before finally lowering. A pink tinge hit her cheeks. "I'm so sorry."

Thorne stepped back, shocked by her admission

because, to be honest, he *was* being a dick. He'd deserved that punch. There was no need to put herself in debt by apologizing. But then again, she hardly knew about that fae law. Could he fault her for his shortcomings in teaching her?

Her eyes immediately tracked down his naked body. The pink tinge on her cheeks reddened further as she saw what hung between his legs. *Damn.* He should cover up. But then again, that would mean he gave a shit.

She was still looking.

"You want to touch it too?" he drawled. "Maybe paint a picture. It will last longer. Honestly, I don't mind."

Now, where had that come from?

"Um," she stuttered, eyes darting back up to his. "S-sorry. It's hard not to look when it's so—"

Crimson, this was getting messed up. He wasn't... flirting, was he?

No.

Stop it.

He growled, "Don't go anywhere on your own. Understood?"

"Why?" She lifted her chin.

He pointed at the house of the Six. "That's why. The Sluagh steal souls, and they like the taste of humans best. If they don't eat yours, they conscript your soul to fight in their battalion of ghosts for eternity. There are six of them living in that house and their loyalty lies nowhere except to the Well."

For a moment she appeared shocked. But then her eyes

turned thoughtful, and she frowned. "Um... I don't think it was stealing my soul."

"What do you mean?"

"I mean." She lowered her voice in a conspiring way. "It kinda felt me up."

Her words blanked every thought in his head. His inner wolf snarled, wanting to take over, to seek reparations from the Sluagh at this infringement to her person. His next words came out slowly and through a clenched jaw. "It *touched* you. Inappropriately?"

She nodded cautiously, clearly sensing his anger down their bond, perhaps even thinking it was directed at her. And that made him madder. He'd seen her warped fingernails. Knew exactly what had happened. She'd been tortured.

It took Thorne a moment to understand, and then all the frustration he'd been holding exploded. The Sluagh had felt her up. Without permission. Caustic rage surged within him. His wolf snarled, frenzied to get out of the confines of his body. It wanted to tear the Sluagh to pieces.

"Not with his actual hands," she continued, "but with... you know. His energy, soul... or wind, or something. You look pissed. Maybe I shouldn't have told you."

The confident woman dissolved.

Well-damn that Sluagh and its unwelcome and perverted energy. Thorne's fangs sprouted. He stormed back to the Sluagh's house, stomped up the steps and pounded on the door, not caring if he roused all Six and signed the death warrant for his eternal soul. No one touched what belonged to him. His fist kept pounding until eventually, he realized what he was thinking.

She was his.

He'd thought it so adamantly.

But he didn't want it. Did he?

So why was he knocking?

Stupid.

Conflicted, he felt torn apart in many places. On one hand, it offended Thorne on so many levels to see a female taken advantage of like that, on another hand... there was a primal part of him that wanted to be the one she let go there. And that confused him. It was all wrong. This must be the mating marks speaking. Another low growl later and he went back down the steps, glaring at Laurel. "Go back to our house until you're called by the council for your testing."

He strode past her.

"Thorne."

He halted. Turned.

"I think we got off on the wrong foot. I'm... sorry I punched you. I don't like feeling helpless... and... I guess"— her bottom lip quivered—"I'm thousands of years from my world, my family, and my home. Everything here is different. Running makes me feel like I'm in control. I promise I'll ask before I head out again. Please, let's start again." She held her hand out. "My name is Laurel Baker. I know you don't like me, and to be frank, I'm not sure if I like you. But I won't shy away from responsibility. I'll help you find your friend."

His gaze dipped to her outstretched hand. "What do I do with that?"

"Shake it. In greeting."

"Like a bargain."

"I suppose it can also be used as a sign of closing a business deal. Or one of respect."

He straightened. "Then what bargain do you wish of me in return?"

"Nothing."

Shock and hurt flittered down their bond, as though he'd offended her. Thorne narrowed his eyes. She couldn't truly be offering her services for free. "Every fae wants something in return."

It was the way of life in Elphyne.

"In case you missed it, I'm not fae."

He scoffed. Didn't he know it?

She continued, "Well, I suppose if there has to be something, then I would like you to teach me the ways of this new time, including how to use my power." She hugged herself. "You said I made that fire in the cave, yet when that Sluagh had me in his control, I could do nothing to protect myself. I don't even know how I made the fire after I hit you. Again, sorry about that. I don't want to be helpless like that again."

Curious. She not only held her own against his sharp tongue, but it was dipped in honey. In a few sentences, she'd managed to steer the conversation and push further. And potentially put herself in his debt multiple times. He needn't bargain with her to get what he wanted. The laws of

Elphyne said he could just take it from her as part of that debt.

But, again, she had no idea what she'd unwittingly done.

"The academy here will teach you to control your mana. Why not just wait for them to do so?"

"I want you."

Those three words struck a chord inside him. "Why?"

"I suppose," she bit her lip, clearly thinking hard. "I suppose it's a few things I'm slowly coming to terms with. Not only did you come to my rescue, but Clarke trusts you. Your Well chose us to be together, and I should try to honor that. Don't you agree?"

Regretfully, a part of him did. Since the dawn of Elphyne, and Jackson Crimson's discovery of mana and its link to the Well, fae learned that the more they followed the lead the Well set, the longer they stayed alive. That's why metal and plastic were outlawed. It halted the natural flow of mana in nature and in your body. As long as he listened to those laws, he could shift into wolf. He stayed young. He didn't like that a human mate was chosen for him, but he respected the Well.

Laurel mistook his silence for hesitance. She added, "I also want you to teach me because with this bond between us, you can't lie to me."

"Fae can't lie, anyway."

Confusion flittered over her expression, but then shrewd insight shone through. "I'm sure there are ways around that. Remind me to tell you about lawyers one day. But for now, you need something from me. I need something from you. If you don't want to work with this partnership idea, then perhaps consider it a classic business arrangement."

He was probably going to regret this, but he prowled toward her and clasped her hand. "Done. I will help you learn to utilize your mana. You will lead me to Jasper. And then we will go our separate ways."

"Agreed."

He sent mana into his hand. It wrapped around her palm, circling and tattooing the bargain on her soul.

CHAPTER NINE

*H*ours later, Thorne stood in the shadows of the armory, watching a sparring match on the training field while Laurel was being tested for her affinity to different elements at the temple. A winged fae—possibly an eagle shifter—battled a young wolf he'd not met before. Most wolf shifters knew each other, if not by sight, by scent. He must be new.

"You going to show the young pup how it's done?" A deep voice came from over Thorne's shoulder.

He turned and found Caraway, a muskox-shifter who towered at over a foot taller than most others. Two horns curled from the shaggy mop of hair on the top of his head and curved down and out at his scruff covered jaw. His brown doe eyes watched Thorne with amusement. Caraway was big, jolly, and always ready for a laugh, but a surprisingly deadly addition to the Order.

"He seems to have it under control." Thorne nodded at

the sparring match. The wolf had the winged fae's neck in his jaw.

Caraway's eyes darted down to the blue markings on Thorne's arms. "Much has happened since we last saw each other."

Much was an understatement. They hadn't spoken for the past two years, not since Caraway's good friend Anise had been held hostage and Thorne was the one who rescued her, not Caraway. It mattered not to Thorne, but clearly there were some underlying issues between Caraway and Anise. Thorne preferred not to get involved, and the hunt for Jasper had kept him busy.

"How have you been?" Caraway ventured.

"Good. You?"

"Good."

They stood in silence for a few beats, and then Caraway folded his arms. "You haven't seen Anise, have you?"

Thorne frowned. "I thought you were friends. It's been two years."

"At first she wouldn't see me, then she disappeared. I just want to check in with her and make sure she's okay after what happened."

Being in a cage for two weeks, cut from the Well, would have been torture for Anise. Having no access to the lifeblood of nature was akin to a harrowing hangover. The very thought sent a shudder through Thorne. He couldn't grasp how the humans lived without that access permanently.

"You sure you're not keeping her whereabouts from me?"

"Why would I do that?"

Caraway's forlorn flicker made Thorne think the big ox had feelings for the feisty female fae. Thorne's brows knitted together.

"You know Guardians are discouraged from having a relationship for good reason, Caraway."

Caraway laughed, big bellied and loud. "You can talk, wolf. You and your father are lighting the way for all us loners."

"But we didn't have a say in it."

"I don't see Rush complaining. And from the looks of your human, I dare say you won't be either. Stop it. Don't scowl at me. You know I'm right. If I got to wake up next to that every day for eternity, I'd die happy."

A possessive growl rumbled from the base of Thorne's throat and Caraway laughed harder.

"Don't worry, old friend. It's a good thing my type has furry ears. I won't go near your mate."

"You shouldn't go near a female, period. Guardians shouldn't be in long-term relationships. We die sooner than others. It's too complicated."

"Screw the Prime's relationship rule. After what you two have been through, I'd say you deserve a little happiness. It's better to be happy for what little time we have, than none at all. My friendship with Anise has been the best years of my life. Now she won't talk to me... I hate it. I think being cut off from the Well would be worse."

That wasn't true. Rush had been cut from the Well during his fifty-year long exile. He'd almost died from lack of connection. The Prime had cursed Rush as punishment for siring Thorne when the law still stated all new births had to be sanctioned. Rush had suffered because Thorne was born.

Everything inside Thorne clenched tight. Anger surged, and he wondered if he'd ever be free of that weight, of the suffocating self-loathing that encircled him every time he remembered how he'd blamed himself simply for being born unwanted, a thorn in someone's paw.

Irritated, Thorne turned back to the training field. The battle was done. He supposed he had some time to kill before Laurel was done with the testing. He raised his brow at Caraway and then nodded at the field. "You want to go? For old time's sake?"

Caraway shrugged. "All right, but no shifting."

Thorne scoffed.

A change in atmosphere signaled Cloud's arrival. Irrefutable, electrified tension permeated the air. The scent of the night sky and spice hit Thorne's nose as the Prime's assassin landed in a flutter of black feathered wings.

The crow shifter was covered in neck-to-toe power-enhancing tattoos. Like an oil slick, they reflected incandescent, prismatic light and some said the inky depths of the Well—where necromancers and dark mages drew, where anarchy reigned. Thorne preferred not to dabble with the unknown side of their power. It was a dance with disorder that could only end in sorrow. But then again, Cloud was Unseelie, and they were creatures of chaos. Perhaps the enhancing tattoos didn't affect them as it did the Seelie fae.

Blue lightning crackled in Cloud's amused blue gaze.

"Heard about your little mishap this morning," he drawled.

Thorne's eyes narrowed. "Wasn't my mishap."

"But it was your human's, ergo..."

"She's not mine." *Yes, she fucking was.*

Fuck.

As if hearing Thorne's silent turmoil, Cloud grinned knowingly, but the smile didn't reach his eyes. It wasn't genuine humor. It was the cruel, mocking kind. Cloud had been kept captive by the humans in their Crystal City decades ago. It was something he never spoke about, but from the way he spewed vitriol about them, and the way he'd declared to cut every single one of their heads off, the experience hadn't been good.

Thorne gave Cloud and his austere demeanor the once over. Did he need to warn Cloud away from Laurel?

"If the Sluagh wanted a taste of her soul, she must be as desolate as the rest of them," Cloud teased.

Claws sprung from Thorne's fingertips. "Careful."

"Or what?" Cloud stepped closer.

"Or next time I rip into your wings with my teeth, I won't let go."

Blue lightning flashed in Cloud's eyes. Electricity skipped over his skin.

Before he could respond, Thorne continued, "It wasn't Laurel's soul the Sluagh wanted."

Thorne lifted his blue marked hand, meaning, in other words, the Sluagh had wanted Laurel's power. Whether that was true didn't matter. It made Cloud believe Thorne had bested him. Despite Cloud's myriad of enhancing tattoos, the Well-blessed union with Laurel had given Thorne access to more power than Cloud could ever hope for, unless he ended up with his own union. And considering his disdain for humans, or anyone else, that was unlikely. Thorne honestly believed the fae would keel over and vomit if he had to share his sacred mana, let alone his emotions.

If he had any emotions left.

Cloud narrowed his eyes at the markings, then sneered and left.

Caraway scratched his beard. "Well, he's a ray of sunshine."

Thorne raised a brow.

Caraway boomed a laugh and clapped Thorne on the shoulder. "You're not as bad as that. Trust me."

"Fuck you."

This made Caraway double over in a fit. The raucous laughter drew Leaf's attention. The tall blond elf was the team leader of the Twelve, a council member, and an all-out overachiever. He must have come straight from the temple which meant Laurel would be done.

Thorne looked around for an escape route. He didn't particularly feel like being bossed around, but he was too late. Leaf and his Well-damned aristocratic nose arrived.

"D'arn Thorne. D'arn Caraway."

Always with the official titles. Thorne's lip curled. "Leaf."

Leaf glanced at Caraway, who took the hint, mock-saluted Thorne, and strode off.

"As expected, Laurel has tested in abundance with mana. Her capacity for holding it within herself is enough to carry her for days at full power without needing to refill. But I suspect you knew that already."

Thorne gave a tight nod. He didn't need to reveal that he'd already been borrowing from Laurel on occasion.

"Right, well, I'm sure she'll let you know, but her affinity is strongly skewed toward fire. With a little in chaos and spirit, she's basically a ticking time bomb if she can't control it. Her training will resume tomorrow and most likely take weeks. In the meantime, we have a job that requires the nose of a wolf."

Thorne folded his arms. "Give it to someone else. I'll be commencing my hunt for Jasper any day."

A sigh of exasperation left Leaf. This was the same argument they'd had for years. Thorne would want to leave his duties as a Guardian behind and scour Elphyne for signs of Jasper. Leaf would always remind Thorne that his destiny was with the Order, and that Jasper didn't want to be found.

Thorne didn't believe it.

Jasper was not the understated kind. He couldn't hide if he tried. Thorne once remembered Jasper drunkenly declaring to all of Cornucopia that he was the Seelie High King Mithras's bastard son, and that the king wanted him dead, but being a Guardian, Mithras could do nothing to hurt Jasper without aggravating the Order, so who wanted to fuck the king's son.

Jasper had hordes of female fae lining up to bed him. He laughed in the face of danger and taunted destiny. Thorne used to look up to him, but now Jasper was missing, Thorne couldn't help but worry that it was his untouchable, reckless attitude that had put him in danger.

"I'm not asking," Leaf said. "You'll leave first thing tomorrow. Be ready."

Anger surged. "How can you forget one of your own so easily?"

Storm clouds gathered in Leaf's eyes. "While you've been worried about your own little world, Elphyne is on the brink of war. Or have you truly been so blind as to the fresh slate of attacks on Seelie soil?"

"As the Prime always says, if it's not magic, it's not our problem."

"Unseelie unleashing mana-warped monsters *is* magic. It *is* our problem. Two years ago, we learned that humans from Clarke's past have been manipulating fae into doing their bidding. Those humans have been quiet, but we know they want our resources. We have news of a Seelie attack, this time in the Unseelie territory, on Queen Maebh's soil. She's requested an outside opinion of the crime scene before she makes up her own mind as to whether the threat is authentic. It could very well be part of the plot the humans are hatching. Whilst we try to stay out of fae politics, any kind of war will be detrimental to the integrity of the Well, don't you think?"

"This goes against everything the Prime has peddled about getting involved."

"Times are changing. The threat to Elphyne is more complicated. If we war amongst ourselves to the death, the humans will have free reign to come in and take what they want from our soil. They will mine it for metals, and spread their toxins all over the earth, killing it once and for all. Your duty is to the Well, D'arn Thorne. Not to Jasper."

"You're as heartless as the Prime."

"I'm doing my job." Leaf's eyes flashed. "Be ready at sunrise. I'll ensure your mate is kept safe while you're gone."

Like hell, he would.

CHAPTER TEN

*L*aurel eased her aching body into the tub and submerged in hot steaming water.

The so-called testing had taken all day. At the temple, she'd had to stand in various ponds of water and watch a little obelisk light up or not light up. It was the strangest thing. Each pond was apparently keyed to a particular type of element and revealed where her powers were strongest. She was strongest in fire.

She'd always been a practical woman, and the idea of making fire with her mind baffled her, but with each pond she'd stepped in, she'd felt an echo of *something* move deep within her soul and burn down her marked arm.

She sighed and dipped her head back to rest on the lip of the tub, staring at the simple wooden ceiling.

So this was her life now.

No electric lights. No vents from a cooling system. Her gaze trailed around the bathing chamber and tried to make sense of what she saw, how technology was different. No electricity, no computers, no gorgeous rubber-soled shoes. Much of the decor was remarkably familiar. Rugs on the floor. Linen drapes on the window. A closet stacked with clothes—no heeled pumps, dresses or makeup, mind you— but still something so common and mundane that it felt comforting. Pants. Blouses. Jackets.

Soft incense burned with the scent of ocean and forest. Of Thorne, she realized with a start.

The wolf-shifter's grouchy face sprung to mind. Always frowning, that one. Except when she'd seen him sleep and the pressure of his worries had melted away. Had he always been so distant, or had something happened to him to make him so? She held her scarred fingers before her eyes, watched them tremble and then submerged them.

It was none of her business.

But aren't you married to him?

Wasn't that what Clarke had said? Laurel had a sudden stab of longing for her friend. What she wouldn't give for a hug from her mother right now, or a chat. Her mother always knew what to say. She'd tamed her own alpha male, after all. Tears stung Laurel's eyes and she dashed them away. Crying over the matter won't help. *Feeling sorry for herself won't help.*

This time, it was her father's voice drilling her, just like he had when she was younger during one of their "training" sessions. General Baker had always wanted her to join the army. Lionel had been a sickly boy, and preferred the couch and his video games to the outdoors, but Laurel had always liked to run track, and so her father focused his army-trained energy on riding her ass until she made Nationals. At the time, she had hated him. Distance endurance was hard. But when she had won gold, she couldn't argue with his drive. Lionel had also been so proud. Laurel owed much of her success to the discipline her father had taught her.

Laurel cleared her throat and forced herself to rally. She'd been given a second chance at life, none of her family had, so she had to make this worth it. First, she needed to learn how to use these powers building inside her. She hadn't seen Thorne all morning and was already concerned he'd backed out of their bargain. It seemed like none of the fae here at the Order knew he was the one teaching her.

The door burst open and Thorne rushed in, closing it behind.

She craned her neck to see him. Looking fierce, he promptly unbuttoned his leather battle jacket and hung it on a hook behind the door. His white undershirt clung to his form and accentuated every hard muscle as it bunched and rolled with his movements. It took her mind a moment to recover from the impact of the raw male strength he exuded, and then he stormed over, blue fire in his eyes. Spell broken.

Forcing her fingers to remain relaxed on the lip of the tub, she watched him circle the room, pull out a knapsack and fill it with various items—small stones, coin, weapons.

It was on the tip of her tongue to make a retort about privacy, but she knew it would just glance off him. If he had no qualms walking around campus in the nude, then why would he care about her state of undress?

After a few minutes, he still hadn't acknowledged her. She wondered if he'd noticed her. A sense of unrest trickled through their bond and, for once, it wasn't aimed at her. She cleared her throat.

His gaze flicked over to her. He frowned, and then returned to his packing. Finally he collected a small stone bowl, came over and dipped it into the bath water, then went to a vanity with a black shiny mirror. He perched on a stool, lathered a soapy mixture and applied it to the sides of his head. He unclipped a bone knife from his belt and shaved from ear to the strip of silver hair on top.

Two scrapes in, his deep voice rumbled, "We're leaving tonight. Prepare for travel. Dress warm."

Their eyes met in the mirror. Held. Then he resumed shaving. The knife tinkled against the bowl every time he washed it clean of soap.

"They said my training at the academy would commence tomorrow morning and would last for weeks."

He paused. "We agreed I would train you."

Relief washed through her. "Good. I was just checking nothing had changed."

"We made a bargain." He shot her a quizzical look, as if bargains were never broken, and she should know better. "We leave tonight."

Thorne scraped his knife from his neck to his high hair-line. He got to the part at the back of his neck and struggled, trying to find a good angle in the mirror.

Laurel wasn't sure why she did what she did next. Maybe it was because, despite being mated, married, or whatever they were, he was as distant about it as she was. It was the complete opposite to how Rush and Clarke had behaved. They were so loved up, it wasn't funny. Laurel hadn't thought she'd wanted a connection like that, but the emptiness of missing her family was starting to make her feel like maybe she did. Maybe this was a moment of weakness.

She stood up. Water sluiced down her body. Steam curled from the tub.

Thorne froze. He locked eyes with her in the mirror. The air seemed to thicken.

Despite his frozen countenance, and his failure to drop his gaze to her nudity, a bolt of lust seared through the bond and he fumbled with the knife, almost dropping it.

Her body had always been fabulous, shaped from a lifetime in the gym. She never had an issue with showing it off. But this was a bad idea. She lost her nerve, changed her mind, and gathered the towel around her body. What was she thinking?

Hugging the towel, she padded over to him and took the knife from his hand. She smirked. "In case you drop it again, maybe I should finish shaving you."

Without complaint, he acquiesced. She held the blade to his skin and hesitated. If he was her enemy, this would be the perfect opportunity to hurt him. But she met his eyes again, felt the mix of lust and longing he tried to hide, and couldn't move. Couldn't breathe. It was unlike anything she'd experienced before. A tempest whirled in her soul. Outwardly, he looked like he always did, but inside...

He wasn't her enemy. She swallowed and concentrated on the blade scraping roughly along his head.

"Why are we leaving?" she asked, voice huskier than intended.

"Because you won't lead me to Jasper here." His voice sounded dry too.

"Okay," she said. "Fair enough."

He released a breath of relief. Perhaps he'd expected her to argue.

"Tell me about him," she prompted.

"Jasper? He's a wolf-shifter. Of the Mithras line."

"Mithras?"

"The Seelie High King." Thorne grimaced at her confused face. "Elphyne is split into two territories, Seelie— fae of order and light, and Unseelie—fae of chaos and night. Within the Seelie territory, the High King Mithras rules over the Summer and Spring Courts. High Queen Maebh rules over the Unseelie territories, the Winter and Autumn Courts. Mithras is Jasper's biological father."

"Tell me more about Jasper."

"Jasper is the king's illegitimate son, and as such was a target for assassination. Mithras wants no one taking over his throne, and in Elphyne, thrones can be won by blood, whether by war, or by kin. Jasper always knew if the king found out about his existence he would be in danger, and so he volunteered to take the initiation ceremony. He survived and fell under protection of the Order of the Well. Even High Kings have no jurisdiction over the Order. Jasper was safe for years. But now we know Mithras has him, and we don't know where. I've searched everywhere. And still I come up with nothing."

Laurel paused in her shaving. "You don't think Bones or the Void have him?"

"I never thought to look in Crystal City. It's one of the places fae can't enter. It's a city in the wasteland and is full of so much metal that no mana flows there. It's completely cut off. It could be why it's been hard to scry for him." Thorne's gaze turned thoughtful. "But Rush spent time in the human city a few years ago. If Jasper was there, it's likely he'd have heard about it. A fae like Jasper would be big news."

He didn't look too convinced. Neither was she, but she didn't push it. She continued shaving and pretended like that wasn't the most she'd ever heard him speak. "And the Order won't search for him?"

"It was the Prime who sold Jasper to the king for a promise. I highly doubt she has the same motivation to find him as I do."

Jesus. Now she knew why Thorne hated the Prime.

"Then what the fuck are we doing in this place? Why on earth would Clarke align herself with an organization that betrays its own employees?"

Thorne's eyes locked with Laurel's in the mirror. Approval flickered over his expression, and then his brows snapped down. "The Prime isn't the Well. She's one person with a god complex. Ultimately, none of us here have sworn our service to her specifically. We're sworn to the Well. Clarke knows this. She walks to her own tune. The Prime allows it because Clarke is currently working to the same ends—protecting Elphyne."

Thank fuck for Clarke's common sense. And if Clarke didn't trust the Prime, then neither would Laurel. "So where will we start the search?"

"I think we sweep Elphyne before heading into the wasteland. Cornucopia is a neutral trade city between Seelie and Unseelie territory. Jasper used to have an apartment in Cornucopia. May as well start there."

Finished shaving, Laurel took a hand towel and patted the last of the soap from Thorne's head. With a palm pressed on one of his rock-hard shoulders, she took the tail of his hair and let it run through her fingers. It bumped every time she hit a ridge of leather cord. His hair was very long. Down to the middle of his back.

"Does the length mean something?" she asked.

He paused. Then nodded. "I pledged to only cut it when I found Jasper."

"He's been missing that long?"

"Over a decade."

Sadness spread as her fingers trailed back up the hair, slipped over the newly shorn scalp and found the lightly furred tip of his pointed ear. It twitched. Her breath hitched. It *moved*. Like an actual wolf's ear. Unable to help herself, curiosity led her finger down over the fur and stroked.

That lust she'd felt earlier barreled toward her down the bond, kindling her own in response.

A growl came a moment before his strong, vice-like grip took her wrist. Suddenly he was up and facing her. Fire, passion and fury warred over his expression and simultaneously down their bond. He wrenched her offending arm behind her back and pressed her to him. Each time his chest lifted with ragged breath, the towel rubbed her sensitized skin. Confusion danced in his eyes.

"What game are you playing at, human?" he snarled in her face.

"I don't know what you mean, *wolf*," she replied. "I'm still learning. Teach me."

His eyes narrowed, assessing. For all their talk about an alliance, they were still treating each other like enemies. But she didn't shrink back. She held her ground, waiting for whatever sharp words were sitting on the tip of his tongue. They didn't come. Instead, he let go of her hand and said, voice rough, "Don't touch a fae's ears without permission."

She stepped back. "Why?"

"Because they are erogenous."

Oh. Well, that would do it.

A high-pitched squeal at the door came before a little ball of two-legged energy burst through. Pink cheeked and with damp silver hair, the little girl wore simple nightclothes—pale blue linen pants and a t-shirt. Looking severely flustered, the brownie Laurel had met yesterday followed the girl.

"Willow," the brownie admonished. "Leave your brother alone."

Brother?

This must be Clarke's daughter. Laurel's gaze snapped to the girl who had now found her way to Thorne and was attempting to crawl up his legs to tug on his hair. He tried to scoop her up but she deftly evaded him and became a white blur until she climbed on the bed and bounced.

"This is unfortunate, D'arn," Jocinda said. "It's time for her to sleep but she can smell kin in the house."

Laurel expected Thorne to grouse or shout, but he waved Jocinda down and said, "It's fine. I'll get her."

He strode to the bed, but Willow saw him coming. She crouched, fangs sprang from her teeth, her ears elongated until they were severely arched, and claws springing from her fingertips. Transformed before Laurel's eyes, Willow snarled at Thorne.

He paused. "That's new."

"No-no-no sleep." Willow pounced. Thorne caught her midair and tried to take her to Jocinda, but Willow screamed and wiggled and bit Thorne. "No," she whined, tears brimming. "Sleep with you. Here!"

Jocinda gave Thorne a questioning look.

Willow did too.

He sighed heavily. "Fine. I'll put her in her own bed later."

With a nod of approval, Jocinda left.

Laurel followed the two to the bed and was given a possessive warning growl from the little girl. Then she sniffed the air, looked at Laurel's blue marks on her arms, and promptly relaxed.

"She knows you're kin, too," Thorne murmured, seemingly surprised.

A little piece of Laurel's heart melted. Her throat thickened, and she had to force the tears away. She and Lionel used to always jump into their parents' bed, despite her father grumbling. Her mother would always make room.

Clarke was her family. She might not be here, but her daughter was. Soon they would all be together.

"Hi," Laurel whispered, her throat dry. "I'm Laurel, your momma's best friend. Has she spoken about me?"

Willow nodded shyly, then gave a little growl and jumped on Thorne, nipping his face and doing her best to be vicious. Irritation swam over his features. "Willow. It's time for sleep."

But she thought it was fight time. Not sleep time.

Laurel smiled. The girl had moxie, just like her mother. Laurel hugged her body towel and laid down on the bed. She patted the pillow next to her. "Come on. Time to sleep. I'll stay with you."

Reluctantly, Willow peeled off Thorne and came over. She used her claws to pluck the blanket and crawled in circles before finally finding a comfortable position to settle. Her big eyes watched Laurel curiously.

Laurel gently rubbed her finger down the bridge of Willow's nose. With every stroke, the little girl's eyes grew heavier until eventually, they stayed closed. Through it all, Laurel could feel the weight of Thorne's attention and when

Willow finally fell asleep, he whispered, "How did you do that... magic?"

She almost laughed. "No. My mother used to do it to me when I was little. Children just need touch. If she thinks we're family, then she misses hers. I know what that's like."

CHAPTER ELEVEN

*A*fter seeing Willow to her room, Thorne returned to his chambers and was surprised to find Laurel dressed in travel attire as he'd requested. He'd expected a bit of push back, but the woman continued to defy his expectations.

Since he'd seen her with Willow, he'd been in a constant state of unrest. His skin felt tight. His pulse elevated. The wolf in him heartily approved of Laurel's maternal behavior. It also cautiously liked how Willow had treated Laurel like kin.

It was getting harder to keep Laurel at arm's length. And part of him didn't want to. Part of him liked the idea of family. Of her. His father, Clarke, and Willow as a unit. But the other part remembered how cruel the world was. It remembered his mission and that she would lead him to someone who might not smell like kin to Thorne, but *was* family. A fae who had saved Thorne's life in more ways than one.

"Okay," Laurel stated, "I've got warm leggings on, a sweater, and this furred cape on the bed. Was that the kind of warm you're talking about? And what about food? Do we need any?"

The woman rattled off more questions, but harrowing memories forced a burn in his throat. Twelve-year-old Thorne had just arrived at the Order, and Jasper had been chosen to settle him in his room at the barracks.

"Breeches, shirt, sweater, jacket, cape," Jasper said and pointed at the uniform hanging in the closet.

Thorne stood in the doorway to the shared dormitory, hating the single bed in the corner, hating the matching bunk on the other side. It looked like a prison and Jasper was the tattooed prison guard behind him, blocking the exit. Thorne wanted to transform into wolf and run out of there, into the poisonous forest surrounding the Order grounds. Maybe he should. He'd traveled through worse places. Then again, maybe he should eat the toxic red leaves. Never come back.

The idea was so appealing that it consumed his thoughts. Nobody would miss him. They'd just sigh and say, "Oh well, there goes another Guardian."

"You get three sets," D'arn Jasper continued. "You're in charge of laundering them."

Thorne set his simmering gaze on the tall fae, loathing his pretty face. What did Thorne care what he asked him to do? Thorne didn't choose to be shoved into the ceremonial lake. He would have preferred to die—to float—to never worry about where his next beating was going to come from. Never fear the snide looks from people casting him as unwanted. Trash.

"Go away," snapped Thorne.

It only made the d'arn laugh heartily.

"Go float yourself," he snarled again, fury welling to overtake his despair.

"Been there, done that. Didn't stick. Just like you."

"So what, you think we're the same?"

Jasper's dark brow rose. "We're more alike than you think. One day, you'll get that. Until then, launder your uniform, or don't. I don't really care. Here." He removed a small package from his pocket and held it out. "It's a bit of mana-weed. Just don't smoke it before training. Preceptor in charge won't be happy if you turn up wasted."

Thorne took the package and a little thrill skipped up his spine. His aunt Kyra had always said he was too young for this and prohibited any sort of inebriation. At the time, he'd thought she was just being a stick in the mud... but after his Uncle Thaddeus and cohorts had beaten Thorne to a pulp, he knew his aunt was only looking out for him. Better to keep your senses so you could protect yourself, even if that meant lifting your hands to cover your face.

Jasper must have seen the question in Thorne's eyes as he reverently accepted the package. "Yeah, I know you're a bit young, kid, but the training will harden you. Smoke it with some friends. We work hard here, but we play hard too." Jasper's eyes twinkled with humor. Thorne almost missed the angst haunting his expression. Almost. "You're among family now, Nightstalk. Get some rest."

Laurel's hand waved before Thorne's face. "Thorne. Are you listening? I asked about food."

"Food?"

She smirked. "Yeah, I was hoping you'd have smoothie supplies around. But I guess not." She bit her lip at his blank face. "Never heard of the drink?"

"Aren't all drinks smooth?"

Laurel's eyes widened. She blinked. Then she burst out laughing, doubling over and clutching her middle. Her melodious sound pierced his hard shell. Humor shot down their bond and warmth spread throughout his body like whiskey. It was like nothing he'd felt before. No humor, no laugh, no joke had brought this kind of rebellious freedom to his heart. His lip twitched.

He didn't know what to do. She was so... alluring. That smile was transformative. Eyes so bright. Skin flushed.

He took a step closer. And another.

Want to touch her.

Big round eyes watched him approach, and she stopped laughing.

"Do that again," he demanded.

"What... laugh?"

Still mesmerized, he nodded.

"Have you not"—she swallowed—"seen someone laugh before?"

He took her neck gently in his hand and lowered his nose to breathe her in, letting her scent take hold of him further. Something sweet, yet musky. Black raspberries

115

laced with female. No mission, no hate, no Well. Just her. And him.

She stilled, letting him have his moment, and it was bliss. An ache in his fangs. Alpha instincts. *Mark her.*

"Thorne?"

"I have seen it," he murmured against her skin. "I've just not *felt* it."

"Oh."

Such a tiny sound from her. Breathy, soft, feminine. But something in her tone gave him pause, and when he sensed her emotions change down the bond, he stepped back, lip curled. "I don't want your pity, Laurel."

Her eyes turned sad and that made it worse. She'd been tortured, lost her whole world, and yet she felt sorry for him. She didn't even know him.

Fuck this. He finished getting ready, strapping his battle-ax baldric over his jacket and fit weapons to his belt. Then he slung the knapsack over his shoulder and went to the window to peek outside. Darkness swathed the grounds, but it was still early enough that walking to the stables wouldn't appear out of the ordinary. Seelie and Unseelie fae resided in equal amounts on the campus, so the nightlife was as active as the day. Thorne's best bet to avoid Leaf would be to go now, when the elves and other cadre members would often go down to the Mess Hall and take advantage of the Mage Brew and social atmosphere.

"Let's go," he said.

Laurel joined him at the door.

"Are you telling me what the plan is, or am I to follow you around like a lost puppy?"

He frowned. "There is no plan."

"Surely there's something."

"Get to the stables, take a kuturi, and fly to Cornucopia."

"Okay." She thought about it. "Wait... what's a kuturi? Why aren't we using a portal?"

"Because Leaf can trace portals. I don't want anyone knowing where we're going. And you'll find out what a kuturi is when you see one."

"Oh. Sure. That makes sense in no way possible." She searched his face. "Are we going to get in trouble?"

He shrugged, opened the door to his room, and ushered her out. If there was a chance she'd changed her mind, this would be it. But she returned his shrug and followed him.

Just as he'd hoped, the residents of the house were either out, or in their rooms. Thorne led Laurel outside and through the grounds, taking the long winding paths shadowed by trees wherever he could. They bypassed the horse stables and went straight to the kuturi stables without missing a step. Thorne stopped outside the gate and searched around for the only fae who might be here —Forrest.

The auburn-haired elf, also in the Twelve, was almost a permanent fixture at the stables. He had an affinity with animals and art. But like Leaf and Aeron, he should be at the Mess Hall eating and drinking. Scanning the area, Thorne couldn't see him. Good.

He turned his attention to finding a bag of sugared treats. They would keep the kuturi happy and incentivized.

Clawing, squawking, and rustling came from the stalls. The animals knew they were there.

While he scrounged through a supply sack, Laurel shifted uncomfortably.

"What is it?" he asked.

Her gaze darted nervously to a stall. "I'm guessing a kuturi is some kind of giant bird?"

He frowned. "Giant birds were not around in your time?"

She blanched. "I'm right, aren't I? Oh, Jesus. We're going on a bird. Shit."

"How did you fly from one place to another?"

"We made machines that carried us. Planes. Helicopters. We were safe and inside. Not on some bird." She patted her face as though trying to cool it.

So she had no clue. His lip curved slightly as he remembered the warmth of her earlier humor, and in that moment, there was nothing he wanted more than to feel her laughter again. Eagerness twitched through him. With a watchful eye on her reaction, he opened the oversized gate.

"Holy fuck," she gasped.

Inside was a kuturi. With the head of an eagle and the body of a fox, the white-feathered and furred breed was mostly docile, and happy to fly long distances. Useless during a battle, but as long as sugar treats were involved, a perfect alternative for traveling long distances.

The winged beast was big enough to carry two adults on

its back comfortably. It squawked at Thorne and pranced on its paws, long tail swishing in excitement. Black patterns marred the white coat in an artistic way Forrest would probably wax poetic about.

"This is a kuturi," he said.

Laurel gasped and then shoved Thorne. "Get out."

Um. What?

He glanced over his shoulder at her. "Why?"

"No, it's... um. Oh, God, it's a figure of speech. I'm just... wow. It's so beautiful. Can I pat it?"

He nodded. "It won't bite unless it's mistreated, and we spoil them here."

She couldn't stop grinning, and that happiness he'd felt earlier bloomed again. Laurel cooed and fawned over the animal with lively expressions. The kuturi ate up her attention like it was a sugar treat. Rushing warmth flowed down their bond when Laurel hugged the animal and nuzzled its neck. The way her hand stroked rhythmically and tickled under the kuturi's chin made Thorne's chest ache in envy.

He shook his head and cleared his throat.

"Move. I have to put the saddle on."

"Oh, sorry." Laurel jumped back. "I'm in the way."

Her smile didn't leave her face until he'd fitted a double saddle and reins, and when he led the creature out of the stalls to the lawn outside, her skin took on a sickly hue.

He should say something to calm her nerves.

He opened his mouth, but was cut off by a crow cawing in a nearby tree.

Fuck.

Thorne closed his eyes and counted to five. Don't kill it. Don't. He continued counting until he got to ten, then opened his eyes and sought the crow out. Up on a branch, lurking in shadows, was the glossy black crow, watching him with knowing eyes.

"Just let us go, Cloud."

Laurel did a double take as she caught the power struggle but remained silent.

The crow cawed.

"What do you care if we leave?" Thorne asked. "I'm taking the human with me."

The bird's beady eyes flicked to Laurel. Stared. Then left in a flutter of black wings. Whether that meant Cloud was giving Thorne a head start, or simply had flown to tattle on him, Thorne couldn't tell. Best be quick about it or Leaf would be back to haul his ass on that mission.

He gave Laurel a boost onto the kuturi and then climbed on behind her. Laurel fit snuggly between his legs, her body slotting in next to his perfectly. He retrieved a treat from the knapsack at his back, made a clicking sound with his tongue, and reached around Laurel to give the kuturi a treat. It was the promise of more to come at the end of their arduous journey. When he returned to his correct position, Laurel pressed back into him, and a feeling of rightness bloomed further.

Laurel still tickled the kuturi around the head. He couldn't see her smile, but he could feel it.

On a whim, he decided a small detour would be warranted. Holding the reins in his hands on either side of

Laurel, he guided the bird to the lawn runway behind the stables.

"*Hiya.*" He kicked the bird with his heels.

Wings snapped out, taloned paws trotted, and within moments, equilibrium shifted as the animal picked up speed, beat its wings in a frenzy, and lifted. Laurel squeaked in excitement, knuckles white on the grip of the saddle before her. Her short hair billowed and tickled Thorne's face, eliciting a smile from his lips.

Lift off.

CHAPTER TWELVE

*L*aurel was flying. *Can't believe it.* Actually flying atop a bird-animal-thing. Wind buffeted her face. The fresh, clean, and restorative air reminded her of home before the fallout. It was the kind of air that energized her on a hike in the Yosemite National Park with Ada. Tears burned in her eyes, her throat tightened, and she had to force her mind back into the present. She gripped the saddle, kept her knees locked and pressed against the wall of muscle behind her. Not only did she feel safer inside the cage of Thorne's confident arms, but he provided much-needed warmth at this altitude.

It was better to focus on that, on the adventure, than to sink into melancholy over her lost life. Her lost world. She couldn't turn back time, only move forward. Or fly.

Night made the journey extra thrilling. Sometimes she could see lights below on the ground, other times nothing, but the clear air made the stars and moon so bright. It painted the earth below in surprising clarity. She saw blobs of trees and tiny thatch-roofed villages that looked like she'd stepped back in time, not forward. In some places, the stars were beneath them as they flew over water.

Thorne steered the kuturi by the reins and knees, clenching his powerful thighs next to Laurel's. There were so many questions whirling around her mind, but with the wind rushing in her ears, the beat of wings, and her blood quickening, she kept her mouth shut, afraid she would miss the wonder if her attention lapsed.

After an hour or so, Thorne tapped Laurel on the thigh. His lips hit her ear, and he pointed to her right. "Look down."

A shiver ran through her at the sound of his voice, smooth and deep. She tried to angle to the side and peer down, but she wobbled and squeaked. Her arms ached from holding the saddle so tight, for so long, and she didn't trust herself. She shook her head. It was a long way down.

Thorne shifted the reins to one hand and then slid his other tightly around her middle. Steady. "I've got you. Go on. Take a look."

Instinct shifted inside her like a clock ticking or cogs turning. Her eyes landed on the blue glowing marks on her arm, and the twin ones on his forearm circling her stomach. The blue was brighter at night. It painted her front and the kuturi's head. The connection between them pulsed, stronger than before. It felt... it felt... like *trust*. She trusted the fae behind her. It was more than knowing he needed her for a task. It was the kind of person he was, the one he tried to hide. He had stood between her and a Sluagh. He had let his young sister climb into his bed and disrupt his travel plans. He had never felt the joy of laughter, but wanted to. That unguarded moment they'd shared in his chambers had done more to give her insight into her partner than any words. The feel of his fingers curling around her neck. The way his nose dipped to her skin and breathed in deep. The open wonder in his eyes when he'd demanded she laugh again.

I don't want your pity, Laurel.

Somehow that made her trust him more. It meant his small confession had come from an honest place. Inhaling deeply, she nodded, and tilted to the side, confident he would keep her from falling. Lashes lifting from the wind, hair blasting back, she scanned the ground below. She didn't have to look far. Something truly magnificent and full of awe was about one hundred feet below her.

Glowing patterns in all shapes and colors drew a gasp from her lips. What was it? So big and vast. Was it some kind of light show? A circus? She frowned as Thorne guided the kuturi lower. It was nature.

Bioluminescent, ethereal nature.

All of it glowed in shades of blue, pink, purple, yellow, and green. A rainbow of life. Flowers bloomed at night. Leaves, trees, a body of water so large it seemed like a glossy mirror of the night. Lower still brought them perilously close to the lake so vast she couldn't see the end. Their slipstream disturbed the water behind them. When Laurel craned to look behind, she saw they'd rocked the surface of the lake. Swimming stars churned and eddied as though alive and were as excited to meet Laurel as she was for them.

"Where are we?" she asked, trying to meet Thorne's serious stare.

"The ceremonial lake," he replied. "It's the original source of power. Some say it is access to the Well itself."

The Well.

The cradle of life. Of everything the Order dedicated their service to. During her testing, she'd heard plenty about it. Now she truly saw it. It was more than immortality. More than mana. It was the very core of existence. Stardust itself.

Suddenly she felt so small and irrelevant in the grand scheme of things. But she wasn't irrelevant, she was chosen. Maybe not so insignificant after all.

"I need to see it," she declared. "To touch it."

"Now?"

She nodded.

Anguish filtered down their bond and, for a moment, Laurel thought Thorne would shut down, but he didn't. He gripped her middle tight, and the side of his lip curled in a seductive half-smile. "Ready?"

She lost control of her mind. *Dimples.*

"What?" she said.

"Hold tight."

He urged the kuturi faster and Laurel had to turn back to the front. Her cheeks tightened at the speed. She could do nothing but hold on and enjoy the thrill of magic-laden air, of anticipation and awe as they zoomed. Every time the kuturi lifted and dipped, her stomach gave way, and her body filled with sensation. An incomprehensible squeal escaped her lips. She felt like Bastian upon Falkor from the Neverending Story. Thorne must have liked it, too, because he urged the kuturi up higher, despite Laurel's proclamation to go down. His arm became iron around her middle, and then his deep voice whispered near her ear, "Do you trust me?"

"Yes," she replied. No hesitation.

"Then when I say to let go, let go."

She nodded. Okay. Weird. But Okay. Maybe they had to dismount in the lake. She'd sky-dived out of a plane before. She could handle this. Sure.

Then he barked words she didn't understand, clicked his tongue, and the kuturi barrel-rolled. Her stomach lifted into her throat. Her eyes blurred. And the luminescent horizon shifted as they rotated until they were upside down. Her whirling mind only had enough time to grasp they flew upside down and then the gap between them and the water suddenly closed. A scream caught in her throat. Would they crash? On their heads? At this speed, impact on the water would be like hitting concrete.

A second later, the kuturi's wings snapped out, and they glided. The roar of wind whipped past and she could *smell* the salty water as they zoomed.

"Now!" he barked.

She let go of the saddle. Gravity took her hands and flung them toward the lake beneath. Her fingers hit the icy surface. Contact was a hammer to her hand, but the stars in the water, the glowing balls of energy… they were an interstellar galaxy just waiting to zoom up her skin as though iron to a magnet and then the world shifted again and they were upright, flying along as though nothing had changed.

Except everything had.

The contents of her stomach wanted out, an incandescent rainbow patina coated her hands, and… she'd never had more fun in her life. Gasping, heart-pounding so hard it wanted out of her chest, and so full of feeling she would burst, she twisted to see Thorne. But did it too fast, too hard, and they all wobbled.

He steadied them, chuckled, and a puff of hot breath brushed her neck, eliciting shivers that she felt down to her toes. His humor slid into her like a blanket wrapping around her heart.

"Sorry," she gasped. "I just… oh my God, that was fun."

"It's called whiffling," he explained. "It can only be done quickly and for a few beats."

"It was incredible." She shouted another *woohoo* to which he responded with another silent chuckle she felt along her spine. His humor morphed to joy and she almost wept.

I have seen it. I've just not felt it.

He'd lived twice her years, but in all that time he'd not felt true mirth until from her, and now it echoed back at her down their bond.

Her grin stretched until her cheeks hurt.

Thorne directed a descent that took them down to land on a long wooden jetty covered in glowing barnacles. Like the rainbow patina on her arms, it oozed over the under-wood and cast rays of prismatic light through the gaps in the planks. As their ride trotted to a halt, coming off the jetty and onto the sandy shore, Laurel felt a shift in Thorne's demeanor. Joy fled.

Hate. Loathing. Disgust.

It mixed with… duty? An ache?

The trees surrounding the shore provided a tall canopy that seemed to expand into a forest. Not all of it glowed. That glory belonged mainly to vines and creepers growing from the ground, winding into the forest, making it look like a part of the trees.

Crickets chirped. The mating sound of aquatic life called. Something skittered in the foliage. Little balls of lazy lights broke away, as though disturbed. Laurel could have sworn she heard giggling and narrowed her eyes. What had Thorne called the flying firefly thing in the cave, a sprite?

Along the shore, human sized stone huts were scattered among the vegetation. No light came from the windows. Perhaps they were empty.

"Do people live here?" she asked as Thorne helped her from the saddle.

He didn't answer, only fed the kuturi some sugar snacks, and tied its lead to the trunk of a tree. "Wait here," he told it, and then joined Laurel.

Every line of his body was tense.

"What's wrong?" she asked.

Icy fire sparked in his eyes as he glared at the lake. How could he be so irritated in such a wondrous place?

"Thorne?" she prompted.

He scowled, picked up a pebble, and then threw it against the water, making it skip until something in the deep leaped out and sucked it in. "I hate this place."

She gaped at the dark thing in the water, then shook her head and refocused on Thorne. How could he hate this place?

"Why?"

A beat. A breath. An anguished look. "Because they forced me in. No one asked me. I didn't want it... still don't. And do you know what the worst thing was? The Prime herself pushed me in, knowing full well the odds were stacked against my survival."

"That sounds harsh."

"Guardians are a dying breed. No one has volunteered in decades, yet the realm must be protected from the greed of humans and the corruption of fae, so she forces everyone to offer tributes. Even royalty. Even paupers. Farmers. Females. The starting age is twelve."

The greed of humans. Corruption of fae? Wait... "You were twelve?"

His clipped nod was her answer.

"I'm so sorry."

His gaze hardened. "Once again, I don't want your pity."

"Then why tell me?"

"I don't know." He started walking back toward the kuturi. "Let's go."

"Wait." She grasped his hand, tugging him back. At their connection, their bond markings flared brightly. She felt a zing journey down her arm and warmth between their palms. It was as though their souls talked to each other.

As they both considered their blue markings, silence passed. His eyes caught on her gnarled fingernails. To her horror, he shifted them into the light of the moon and inspected them. She snatched her hand away.

"Why do you keep hiding them?" he asked.

A sharp, sad laugh shot out of her. "You know why. They're broken."

His gaze held her captive. It was clear he wanted to say something, but she was a coward. She wouldn't let him. Where he'd just laid out a secret from his past, she ran from it. So she changed the subject. "You said you would teach me, Obi-Wan. I want to be a Jedi like you."

His lip twitched. Something like stifled confusion, awe, and curiosity warred through him. She knew how she must look to him. A strange visitor from another time. Someone who looked like his enemy but acted like something else. Everything inside him wanted to know more about her— she could sense it. He held it all back behind his stiff posture and near implacable expression, but the emotions he tried to corral in his body soared through their bond. She was confounding him. And she liked it. She'd raised the bar her entire life. She was that woman no one expected to succeed, but did.

Your only limit is you.

Yet another quote she rattled off to her clients. They would groan and moan as she put them through their sweaty paces in pump class, but she was living proof. The nails had been ripped out, and when they grew back gnarled, she took up MMA lessons. Then she installed the same training into every Queen Fitness gym. More than self-defense, it was an offense class. Designed to help a woman take the first step in protecting herself. To help her become a powerhouse.

It was something Laurel desperately wanted to believe about herself.

Sometimes she wondered if the motivational quotes she spouted were all a ruse. Just a show. An act. Think yourself strong, and you will be. Maybe. But like a clown who was sad inside but projected jokes, she felt like a fraud sometimes.

"So," she said, "Are there drills? Training exercises? How do I make fire come out of my hand again?"

"We don't have time. It's getting late."

"Give me thirty minutes. You promised you would."

He turned his back on her. She thought maybe he'd declined, but he took two steps, unbuckled the menacing ax from the baldric around his shoulders, and then unbuttoned his leather jacket. He dumped it on the sandy beach and then faced her, now dressed only in a fitted white shirt and breeches.

"Take your cape off," he ordered.

For a single, panic-filled moment, her instinct shouted at her. *Look at his muscles.* That strength. He could rip her in two and not break a sweat. Pulled out nails could be a blessing compared to having a wolf's claws shred her heart.

Cautiously, she studied him and sensed no animosity.

Okay. Let's see where this is going.

A little thrill tripped in her stomach. Good. This was good. She could do this. She unlaced the cape and dropped it to the ground. Her knitted sweater gave her plenty of freedom to move, so she left it on. How would this training go?

What's his plan?

Anticipation thrummed against her skin. She darted a glance at the lake, then to him.

"We're not going for a swim," he noted her direction.

"Then what?"

He lifted his fists, boxer style. "You have a good right hook. Show me more."

A grin split her face. Her MMA training had only lasted a few months before bombs were set loose on the world, but it had been enough to give her the confidence to fight back, or at the very least, the urge to. If Bones came at her again, she wouldn't stop fighting. No matter what.

But he's so much bigger than Bones, a little voice in the back of her head warned. An undercurrent of doubt and fear began to tickle her skin. She shook it off. Surely by now, after everything she'd been through since that terrible day, she could defend herself. Strike first, ask questions later.

He gave her much smaller body a scornful once over and then arched an indignant brow. Was that meant to intimidate?

"You might regret this," she warned, feigning courage.

"Famous last words."

CHAPTER THIRTEEN

*L*aurel's voracity took Thorne by surprise. She didn't stop coming until she'd landed a few hits. Impressive. There was something else driving her actions, and for once, Thorne didn't think it was something he'd done.

He blocked easily, but it didn't stop her from trying. She came at him. He stepped to the side and elbowed her, causing her to stumble. Did she give up? No. She twirled like a dancer and came back, this time learning his patterns.

Clever.

She didn't stumble from the same move again.

Maybe it was the lake's mystic energy filtering into his cracked soul, or the air of anticipation from the sprites watching from both the forest and the water, but he found himself sinking into the sparring match with full-body composure. No anger fired in his veins. No fury. Just... latent fun.

After twenty minutes of rigorous sparring, she paused, chest heaving with effort.

Disappointment flooded him. Was she going to stop?

No. She only removed her sweater, shot him a dazzling grin, and then came at him again—this time making sharp shouts with each strike. *Hya. Hya. Hya*. And he got distracted. Jacket off, there was more of her skin to admire. More fire in her eyes. In her body. She looked alive. Not only did he feel her effervescence whittle his composure, but he saw it on every inch of her face.

Desire speared through him. The woman was a marvel. Sweat cast a pearlescent sheen across her skin, highlighting every feminine curve—the dip of her collar bone, the grace of her neck, the smooth skin on her arms.

Her natural scent invaded his nose, hitting some button in his primitive nature and it took everything he had to stop from jumping her, forcing her down and making her submit. And that would make her run screaming in the other direction. She didn't want a man to dominate her. She wanted an equal.

The bargain they'd made urged him to keep within the boundaries of decency. Onward.

Didn't make it easier.

He slapped her away as she came for his face. "You can't beat me with your fists."

"Watch me." She tried again.

But his patience wore thin. Her musk drove him to distraction. The wolf in him was done with sparring. It wanted between her legs. He shouldn't be here, doing this.

They should be flying toward Cornucopia. For Jasper. He swiftly took her wrist, twisted, and secured her arm behind her back in a punishing maneuver. She cried out in pain, but he held.

"Don't like it?" he taunted. "So get out."

"Not funny." She whimpered. Struggled. "Thorne, I mean it. That hurts. Let me go."

Her scent changed. *Fear.* Every predatory instinct in him perked up. *Laced with sweet feminine musk. Black raspberries.* A growl slipped out. His teeth elongated into fangs. Claws slid from his fingertips, pricking into her. Sensation zipped down his spine and heated at his groin. He was so aroused. Painfully so. Surely she felt the press of his erection against her back. Her hot, sweaty body—trying to be strong—but not enough. When he spoke next, his voice had become gravelly, beastly. "Make me."

He expected her to fight back as she had after the Sluagh. She'd punched fire in his face out of instinct. She should have fought. That's what he would have done. It's what he'd done his entire life. But she didn't. Her terror crashed into him like an ocean storm. He choked on her fear, doubt, and panic. This wasn't her. This wasn't the woman he'd come to know.

"Make me," he said again. He tightened his grip. Hoping the strong woman would resurface, to strike him in the face. The thought sent another wave of arousal over him. He liked his love-making a little rough, passionate. He liked his lovers feisty.

"I can't," she whimpered, squeezing her eyes shut.

"You can. You have the power of a thousand suns at your disposal. Your emotion is your trigger. Use it. The depth of your inner well is deep. And when that's dry, you can access mine. Take it. Your nails might be broken, Laurel, but you aren't."

She gasped, perhaps offended. For long, hard moments, silence compounded. Crickets chirped. And then something must have clicked within her. Fire exploded at his hand, searing his skin. He let go, grinned wolfishly, and bounded back. She whirled on him. Rage transformed her beautiful features, screwing them into a face full of determination. Then she attacked.

The fiery being that came at him was a divine thing. *This is what I want.* Elemental. Goddess. Skin illuminated as though her very blood had incinerated. *Yes.* Flames licked her skin. In her eyes. In her mouth. And still, she advanced.

He stood stock-still, ready to take the hurricane. *Hit me. Make me feel alive.* She kept coming. She wasn't going to stop. He braced.

Volcanic vengeance. A harpy's scream. She dove at him. Catching her, he stumbled back, pain burst along his flesh as it burned. He thought he wanted this. Nope. No, he didn't. He slammed up an insulated wall of protection with his mana, but too late. Searing pain coated him.

Water. Get to water.

It only took seconds, and then they were submerged in the shallows of the lake. Smoke sizzled and hissed. Thorne felt burned in patches over his skin. Laurel spluttered and gasped as he took her under. *Cool off, woman.* But she hit him. Struck him again.

They emerged, gasping.

"Hey." He took her wrists. "Settle."

The survival instinct in her eyes wouldn't fade. *"Don't tell me to settle."*

"Laurel. You got me. You won."

She raged and hit again, but it glanced off his solid chest.

She pushed off and stood back, eyes like wildfire. Water lapped at their waists. The slick rainbow residue from the lake dripped down both their bodies. Her shirt was virtually gone. It hung off her torso in strips of charred mess. His was less ruined, thanks to his last-minute wall of mana, but the skin she'd burned blistered on his arms. Hastily, he splashed water over them. The healing waters soothed the skin. It wasn't bad. He'd survive.

Two steps and he was back in her space, gathering her trembling form gently. She was traumatized.

Guilt flooded him. Shit. Damn. He was a Well-damned cocksucker. A floater. Litter-box trash.

"Are you okay?" he mumbled. *I'm sorry.*

Chest heaving, she wiped the water from her face in irritation. "I'm fine."

"No. You're not." He raised his brows at her shredded top. Perky, perfect nipples glistened in the gaps of her shredded shirt. The arousal he felt earlier bloomed again, hardening between his legs, wanting back into his system.

He swallowed. Couldn't lift his eyes from her chest. He shouldn't be looking.

She glanced down, gasped, and covered herself with an infuriated pout. "How come your shirt is still there?"

"I used my mana as insulation," he rasped, still looking at the same spot, only her arms were covering the pert breasts.

Damn. He scrubbed his face and tore his gaze away.

"You did this on purpose." She pointed at him.

"I didn't. But—" he shrugged. Honestly, if he knew she was going to lose her shirt, maybe he would have.

"I don't mean the top. I mean the goading. You wanted me to hit you."

A growl dragged out of his throat.

It was then he realized their emotions were abnormally heightened. It was the lake. The power.

The wind picked up. Ripples in the water lapped at their skin. But it wasn't cold. It was warm, like between a woman's thighs. Like the dangerous lure of a honey trap, it reacted to Thorne's and Laurel's presence. Energy zinged into him. Into her, too. He could tell by the goosebumps erupting over her flesh. The black of her pupils dilated. Her full lips parted.

Their Well-blessed markings flared, casting blue refractions over the rippling water.

The lake, the source of primordial power around them, urged them together. It *wanted* them together. Wet. Streaked in luminescent color. Sexy. Laurel looked up at him, all lashes, and fizzled fury. Just how he liked it. His warrior's gaze turned heated and she inched closer. She traced a finger down his front and his abs sucked in.

He couldn't breathe. Her lashes lifted to assess his reaction, then she gripped his shirt as though to throw him down.

He tensed. Pushed his jagged lust at her. Let her read it in his eyes. *Do it. Throw me down.*

She raised a dark brow. *You'd like that, wouldn't you?*

I would.

Her grip loosened. His heartbeat raced as her touch turned explorative. Over his pec. Down to his abs. Around. Slippery. Wet. Friction. Everywhere she went, fire ignited like a sharp claw scratching his skin. Fuck, he was so hard. Bursting. Painful. He wanted more. *Scratch me. Make me bleed.*

The wind picked up around them, lifting their hair. He should mind the changing weather. The turbulence. He should warn her about the seductive call of the lake. Its infallible wants. But it was *this* between them. An attraction stronger than any he'd ever known. And it was because it had already been there, simmering beneath his skin from the moment he'd laid eyes on her.

All the more reason to warn her.

To stop this.

"I feel… weird," she admitted.

"It's the power from the lake," he muttered, eyes drinking her moonlit skin in.

Soft lips. Obstinate jaw. And her body… *Crimson.* Glistening. Perfectly toned and begging for touch. His cock twitched. The wolf inside him panted. Want.

Want to kiss her. Taste her. Bite her.

A strangled groan escaped him. He didn't care about

anything else and let his hands roam over the slick surface of her skin. His thumbs brushed her nipples. Her lids fell to half-mast and moan of appreciation shuddered through her.

He couldn't stop this. Whatever was happening.

Stop.

"Laurel." Her name on his tongue. That's all it took. She grabbed at the thick source of his braid and pulled him to her, slamming his lips onto hers. Instant, heady euphoria. He groaned into her mouth and tugged her closer. Her tongue thrust past his fangs, making demands. They licked, sucked, nipped. Incomprehensible pleas chirped out of both of them. More. Deeper. Harder.

This was how he liked it. Fiery. Urgent. Passionate. And she'd instigated the kiss. She was perfect for him.

Mate.

Mark her.

Bite her.

Keep her. His wolf was in a frenzy, but... something was wrong. He could feel it in the water, rippling. Something slick and heavy swirled around his legs. *Alarm. Panic.*

They're here.

He spared no thought for her decency, hefted her over his shoulder and raced out of the water. Three sloshing strides and he was on the shore, settling her back to her feet. Her skin had gone pale. She'd felt it too. Their eyes clashed. She realized she still clutched him, let go and then stepped back.

"What was that?" she asked, hugging herself.

He frowned at the shore, searching for signs. "That was" —everything he hated—"Inkeels."

"What?" she gaped.

"The Well isn't all glowing things and magical powers. There is an inky side. A greedy side." He flinched at the memory of his initiation ceremony. Of the suffocating and horrifying constriction of his body as the *things* slithered around him, dragging him into the deep and further below.

His chest constricted. He flinched, trying to suck in a breath of air. *You're not drowning. Not now.*

He jolted at her touch on his arm. When he looked, he found only concern in her eyes. The fire was gone. And it was this gentler side he had no idea how to handle.

"They're why you hate it here, aren't they?"

She saw right through him. He felt flayed open. Raw. Cowardly. Like a child to be horrified of such things. Was he a warrior, a wolf, or worse? Thorne flexed his fists, as though the action could shift the slimy memory from his skin.

Fuck it. They should never have stopped here. He turned toward the kuturi as it sharpened its beak against a tree trunk.

"Thorne. What about the inky side?" she asked, scurrying to collect her cape and sweater. "Tell me."

He stopped at the kuturi, took a moment to gather his composure, and slid her a dark look. He had to answer her, it was part of her education. He already felt the magical compulsion build from their bargain. Didn't mean he enjoyed it.

143

"It's the stuff of nightmares. Where beings like the Sluagh come from. Where there is no love, no family, no right. Only wrong. Chaos. A dark chasm of despair. Do you understand, or do I have to draw you a diagram?"

"No need to get snippy. Jeeze." A deep line appeared between her brows. "And this is the Well you all worship?"

He snapped around. "We don't worship it. We respect it. And this"—he pointed at the water—"is a place where the connection is strongest. The Well is..." He struggled to come up with the right words. "Life. Cosmic. All-powerful. In our blood. Us."

Slipping her sweater over her shredded shirt, she added, "And the things in the water?"

"Inkeels. They drag you down during the initiation ceremony. They take you to the darkest depths, look into your soul, and strip you of everything you identify with until you feel violated in the most heinous way possible. You would do anything to get out of there. You want to know more? How they invaded me? You want me to take you there? Show you for yourself?" He leaned in close and bared his teeth. "You want those things in you too?"

His harsh words seemed to bounce off her, but then her eyes glistened with tears. Still, she didn't back down. She lifted her chin. "But you didn't, did you? Get out of there, I mean. You took the harrowing experience and... it shaped what you are. A Guardian. Someone the Well chose to keep this world flourishing."

She wouldn't stop staring. Looking into his soul. Awe filled her eyes. "You're—"

"Stop," he snarled.

"You don't know what I was going to say!"

"I'm not a good person."

She scoffed. "Keep telling yourself that. Maybe someday it will stick."

He glared at her, hoping to somehow burn her words away with his sight. "That kiss was a mistake, Laurel. We should leave. The lake has a way of calling you back in. Well-blessed markings don't mean we're exempt. It might decide to test us again."

CHAPTER FOURTEEN

The adrenaline from training and the argument energized Laurel, but after a few hours of flying, not even the buzz of thrill-seeking could sustain her energy levels. Or the awe that she was a frickin' powerful woman.

That fire.

An inferno of power.

It had come from her.

Emotion is your trigger, Thorne had said.

He'd also lost all sense of personality since their kiss, and all she felt down their bond was a coldness that worried her. *That kiss was a mistake.* Try as she might, she couldn't stop thinking about the words he'd hurled at her. Slimy things pulling you down, drowning you… violating you?

No wonder no one wanted to become a Guardian anymore.

And Thorne? He had some issues. That was clear as day. To switch so mercurially in mood when she brought up his morality. He'd done a complete nosedive. It horrified him to think that he might be a good person. But he was. She was sure of it.

Was she? Now, that was another story. Given the power, she had reacted with flames. When he'd taunted her, a switch had flipped inside her. Something dark drove her to attack him, to take no quarter, to burn him alive and make him pay for his words and patronizing grin. It was like he didn't think she could take him.

She'd had to.

A sigh escaped her. Maybe they were a good match. Maybe the Well knew what it was doing when pairing them up. Her body certainly wanted him.

Exhaustion crept in, and she was about to suggest setting down for a rest when something on the horizon piqued her fancy—a yellow stream beaming into the night sky like a spotlight. An ethereal orange glow was near the ground. *More bioluminescence?* No. It was stronger than that. She squinted. More dark shapes, silhouettes of all shapes and sizes before the light. With a start, she realized it was a city of sorts.

Her interest flared.

The closer they flew, the more she saw. No skyscrapers, but a mixture of squat buildings and tall architectural wonders spread out from the orange glow that served as a center beacon. Some buildings were shiny and luxurious, others looked as though they'd been scraped from a forest and brought in. The surrounding citadel wall was almost for show. Its substance, a mixture of solid brick or dilapidated stone next to open and wonky planks of wood. The orange column of light came from a stadium atop a hill, alight with some sort of entertainment currently in progress. Across the currents of the wind she heard roars and shouts. Cheers. Curiosity filled her. Maybe a sports game?

The smell in the air changed. It became a little pungent, a little dirty, and a little like food. Definitely a city.

This must be Cornucopia.

Thorne glided the kuturi down and landed just outside the city limits, alongside a wide river where jetties and docks were punctuated by various warehouses and buildings. It seemed like a common flight path, because they weren't the only ones landing on the dirt airstrip. Other winged creatures, some with passengers on their backs, others with wings sprouting from their own backs, milled about. Many carried cargo in nets. Sometimes the cargo wiggled. It took restraint to stop curiosity and wonder from dominating her expression.

It must be close to midnight, but it was as busy as a midday rush. Not only were there commuters coming in, but soldiers on the ground. It seemed like there were two kinds. Those dressed in coats of red and yellow embroidery, and those in dark tunics. They seemed to stick to their own color groups and looked warily at the others.

With protesting muscles, Laurel dragged herself off the kuturi. Thorne cast a cautious eye at the soldiers milling about and then fished in his pocket for a treat. He retrieved something like sugared jerky and handed it to her.

Upon sniffing the new treat, the kuturi pranced excitedly.

"Give it this," he said. "I'll be back in five."

Laurel's eyes were glued to the griffin-like creature, so she paid little attention to where Thorne disappeared to. Somewhere behind her. Probably to pay for boarding for the kuturi. She didn't care. The kuturi had the only attention her energy allowed. Its lungs heaved as it caught breath, and it nudged her arm with its beak.

"Easy, does it." She fed the animal small pieces of jerky and patted its neck affectionately. She couldn't believe she'd just flown on its back. It was almost like a dinosaur, or a dragon, or... nothing like in her time, that was for sure.

Thorne returned with a tall, mustached, and bald man who had deeply discolored and disfigured features. He had a severe under-bite on his lower jaw. Two fangs protruded up and over his top lip—like a cartoon dog. Arched ears, as was the norm with the fae (so she'd been told), clearly showed his heritage. He narrowed shrewd eyes at her, assessing.

Alarm prickled her skin, and she wanted to check that her hair was covering her ears, but held her fists calmly at her sides. If there was any need to panic, Thorne would let her know. After a moment, Laurel realized the new fae's resentment wasn't aimed solely at her, but at the big warrior at her side. Why?

The attendant's eyes kept darting between the teardrop tattoo beneath Thorne's eye, to his battle-ax strung over his back, and to the jacket—beaten and hardened from countless battles—and the logo of scales over the breast pocket.

Ah. She got it now. He disliked Guardians.

With a final scowl at the attendant, Thorne gathered his knapsack and gave the kuturi a ruffle under the chin. "We'll be back for you in a few days."

Then he gestured for Laurel to head down a long dirt path toward the city. After a few hundred feet, she commented, "He didn't like that you were a Guardian, did he?"

"None of them do."

"Them?"

Thorne glanced at Laurel as though she were crazy. "Everyone."

"Why?" After the sacrifice Guardians had made in the ceremonial lake, after the life of servitude to keep the realm safe and plentiful with magic, it seemed ridiculous. They should be revered. At least lauded.

He shrugged. "Maybe because we can use metals and still access our mana. Maybe it's because we can't fund the Order without taxing them for monster kills. Maybe they resent us prohibiting the use of metals or plastics. Maybe it's jealousy. Who knows? Why don't you ask them?"

More sharp words.

As they entered the city through the unmanned ragtag gates, many passersby looked at Thorne's Guardian uniform and balked. If Laurel wasn't sufficiently overwhelmed with the visual delights of the new mini metropolis, she might have been concerned, or at least angry on his behalf. As it was, her attention was almost completely and irrevocably taken with the atmosphere of Cornucopia.

The streets were a mix of cobblestone and dirt. Shanty type buildings sat next to tall, luxurious and decadent visual delights like the three-spire, mini castle that seemed to be an eating and housing establishment. A hotel! It was that last structure that made her chest swell with nostalgia.

"This is almost like Vegas!" she exclaimed, turning in circles, eyes wide. "My hometown."

Hawkers peddled their wares on street sides, their carts overflowing with an assortment of food, drink, or merchandise. The mouthwatering smell of something salty yet fruity coated the air with a layer of desire. Scantily clad women of all shapes and sizes were next in line as Thorne and Laurel walked past. They stood before a loud raucous establishment with fae leaning out from balconies, laughing and shouting in merriment. Rhythmic drums, lights, and conversation came from inside buildings. The nightlife here was magnificent. Laurel, Clarke, and Ada used to burn up the dance floor on many occasions, in many clubs, and always in sexy dresses. What she wouldn't give to go back to those carefree times.

"Hurry up," Thorne said, already two steps ahead of her. "You can gawk tomorrow."

She caught up with him. "Where are we going—*oof!*"

A body bumped into Laurel at the hip. She almost fell backward.

"Watch where you're going, elf." A grumpy, squat dwarf with a big nose glowered at her.

"Sor—" Thorne slapped his big palm over her mouth, cutting her off.

"Fuck off, dwarf," he barked.

The dwarf took one look at the blue Well-blessed marking on Thorne's hand, widened his eyes, and then stepped back. He seemed to gather himself, he spat at Thorne's feet, and then scurried off.

What was that about?

Suddenly, every sensation in the lane amplified. The shouts and conversation from the balcony above became deafening roars. The sizzle of a food vendor's makeshift stove sparked and spat. A woman with green skin and big, under-bite teeth shouted and waved a fist. She looked like the She-Hulk. A small, furred rat-like creature scampered by Laurel's feet and she jumped to the side.

Thorne let go of her mouth and growled, "Don't get lost. Don't apologize. And don't say thank you."

"Because I'm huma—rfh?"

He did it again! Palm to her mouth. He lowered his face until it was inches from hers. "And *don't* say that."

She glared at him over his hand. After a decidedly dark stare, he released her mouth. Slowly. "Just keep your mouth shut."

Argh! She flattened her mouth and thought of a million nasty things she wanted to say to him, but realized she didn't need to. She could send it all surging into him from their bond. And that was exactly what she did—speared her fury straight to him.

His breath hitched. Nostrils flared, infuriated. He sent

his scolding emotions right back. "Well-damn it, Laurel. Don't push me."

"Or what?" *Go on. Kiss me again.*

"Or I'll—" he bit off his words, glared daggers, and then scanned the lane. "Off you go, then. Take the lead. Clarke said you'll lead me to Jasper, so go."

He folded his arms smugly.

"Yeah. Well. To be honest, I just want to sleep. Is that too much to ask?" They could work out the plan tomorrow.

He smirked, as if he'd won the argument they weren't even having, and then made a flourish with his hand toward the direction he was originally going. "After you, m'lady."

"Cordiality isn't becoming on you." This time, she hurried to stay at his side. "Where are we going?"

He sighed. The tension in his shoulders eased, and he said, "Jasper has a place. We'll start there, rest, and then resume our hunt tomorrow."

Jasper's place turned out to be an apartment in one of the more luxe buildings in the center of the city, not far from the nightlife. Nowhere luxe in comparison to her apartment in Vegas—still no electricity—but not as simple as some places she'd passed. It was a top floor penthouse of a three-story building. Thorne entered via an unlocking spell of some sort that involved a drop of his blood. Inside, the decor was simple bachelor style. Dusty bed in one corner. A couch, table and chairs for entertaining in another. Cool ceramic tiles. No kitchen. But an open fire pit that seemed more appropriate in a backyard if it weren't for its designer decor vibe.

The condo hadn't been visited for a long time, yet the indoor potted plants thrived. When Laurel looked closer, she realized the plants weren't potted, but part of some chain of nature that linked each apartment through gaps in the floor.

"Where is the bathroom?" she asked. The journey had been long, and she was dying to use the toilet.

Lost in thought as he trailed a finger through dust on the tabletop, Thorne indicated toward a door at the back. Laurel's lip curled as she tiptoed through the quiet place. She wasn't sure why she was being quiet. Maybe it was because it felt like walking through a dead person's home. Weird.

Thankfully, the bathroom was in working order. A flushing toilet, small bathtub, and basin under a black glossy mirror. There was a candle on the countertop. She blanched when she realized she'd either have to work out how to light it herself, or call Thorne, and with his mood, she wasn't willing to broach the subject.

So that meant she had to try.

The last time she'd used her fire power, she'd been filled with fury, hatred, and survival instinct. But none of that mattered now. She picked up the candle and stared at it. She tried to remember how it felt to have the shifting power living inside her. Of how it jumped to her call when she was upset. The burn in her cheeks. The roaring of her pulse. She connected all that with the candle and urged it to light, to spark.

The candle spluttered.

It flared brightly, so brightly that she almost dropped it. But she'd had practise at tapering off her power already, so she shut it down.

When she checked the candle, a little flame flickered gently.

She grinned. And look at that, her sweater stayed intact.

Once done in the bathroom, she returned to the main room. Thorne had thrown open the large bifold glass doors and was on the balcony watching over the city. Laurel placed the candle on the table and joined him.

"You seem disappointed," she said.

"No shit."

He was hurting. He probably had hoped Jasper would be there. Laurel bit her lip and looked inside at the decor again. It was simple, but not completely something she'd expect in a Guardian's home.

"I didn't realize the Guardian game was so lucrative. I thought you said you couldn't keep the Order running without taxing monster kills."

"We get a wage. And we live a long time. Most of us have collected holdings and wealth. Jasper liked to frequent Cornucopia during his time off. So he bought this place. I have the family Nightstalk home in Crescent Hollow."

"Crescent Hollow. That sounds cool. I'd like to go there some day."

He frowned at her. "You're here to help me find Jasper. Not go on vacation."

"Ah," she replied, with a twinkle in her eye. "But I'm the

one who will lead you to him. Who's to say it's not while I'm on vacation?"

Nostrils flared.

She laughed. "You hate this, don't you?"

Another glare.

"Relax, Growly." She shuffled back inside. "Tonight, I just want a hot bath, a change of clothes, some food, and sleep."

Thorne followed her, shutting the doors behind him. The sounds of the street muffled. The air inside had lost its staleness. Much better.

"You humans don't want much, do you?" Thorne commented sarcastically.

"What does that mean?"

He watched her rifle through his knapsack. "Rush calls Clarke his princess because she's full of demands."

Laurel snorted. "I'm sure that's a gross exaggeration. And they're not demands. We just know what we want, and we aren't afraid to ask for it. But, for the record, I prefer queen, not princess."

Thorne barked a laugh. "Right. Of course."

"Hey." She pouted at him. "Not for the reasons you think. I used to run a very successful chain of fitness establishments for women. I called my business Queen Fitness. It's a state of mind, not just a title. You think like a queen, you become one. It's very empowering."

"A fitness institution for multiple queens. Sounds horrifying."

"We're not really queens. It's a state of mind. It's just a place women go to work out."

"Like a training yard?"

"Sure. Go with that." She'd pulled out half his knapsack by now, and still, no spare clothes for her. "I can't find another top. Tell me you didn't plan on us being here for a few days and not pack a spare change of clothes."

He gave her a shrug, then headed to the door. "We can go shopping tomorrow. For now, I'll get some food. Don't open the door. Don't open the windows. Just… don't do anything until I get back."

CHAPTER FIFTEEN

*B*y the fourth day in Cornucopia, Thorne had followed Laurel as she'd wandered the entire market square and questioned residents. They'd come up with no intelligible signs that Jasper had been there recently, or even in the past few years. Now they were stuck at a fresh produce vendor Thorne had once saved from the Ring, and who subsequently owed him. He ducked under a brightly covered awning to shield himself from the late afternoon sun and watched Laurel turn a piece of gilly-fruit over in her hands as she haggled with the merchant like a local.

"One clear coin," Laurel said. "That's my final offer."

The merchant laughed. "That's not enough for five gilly-fruit." She raised her brow at Thorne. "Tell her she's joking."

Laurel sighed and put the fruit down. "Very well, then. We'll find another vendor for our needs."

"No, wait!" The merchant said. "I'll take two coin for five gilly-fruit. That's still robbing me blind."

"Deal." Laurel made the gimme-sign to Thorne.

He sighed and fished out two clear glass coins from his pocket and handed them to her. With a wide, triumphant grin, Laurel collected her prize, and they moved to the next stall. The counter was littered with tiny glass animals, baubles and rings. Why on earth Laurel would want to stop there was beyond him.

Thorne leaned against a wooden pole while she sampled the rings. Her attention stayed on a particular blue, clear and gold item. She even held it to the light to catch the rays of sunset.

Frowning, he turned back to the market streets, folded his arms, and kept a wary eye on passers-by. As usual, the population of Cornucopia was as random as its architecture. Seelie and Unseelie together in a mish-mash.

A posh elf in the Seelie gentry walked next to a vampire from the Unseelie gentry. Both dressed disgustingly in wealth. Embroidered jackets, frilled shirts, pompous hair, and a touch of rouge on their cheeks. By rights, the two should have been at each other's throats like the guards loitering in the space they had no jurisdiction in. But in Cornucopia, the companionship between the vampire and the elf was on a level playing field.

Neutral territory.

Neither the Seelie nor the Unseelie could claim it without inciting a war.

It was why Jasper had loved it there. No one cared about

his parentage. No one cared about his pretty face. And if he removed his Guardian uniform, he usually found someone who cared naught about his job. Fae came to Cornucopia for one reason. To have a good time. Whether it was to watch the blood sports at the Ring, to visit the elven-elixir dens, or to dance and fuck a stranger at one of the nightspots. For a few years, even Thorne had fallen prey to the city's allure. That was until Jasper went missing, and he realized the same city that granted anonymity also couldn't care less about each other.

"Hurry up," he declared.

Laurel ignored him and then shifted to the next lot of jewelry.

He wondered how she kept her spirits alive after four days of training, searching, and coming up short. She was still alight, bright with passion and excitement. She was in an element she didn't know she had, or maybe this was Laurel all the time. Confident. Strong. He'd done his best to let her lead the daily expeditions, hoping that if he did, then Clarke's prophecy would come true. But not one fae knew who Jasper was. It had been too long since he'd gone missing. The carousing, charismatic three-hundred-year-old Guardian had disappeared from the collective memory of the city that had cradled him his entire life.

They hadn't hit the nightspots yet.

This will take forever.

Not only did Thorne have to train Laurel in self-defense, but he also had to educate her about their world, and how to use her mana. Some of it came naturally to her, but trying to explain the theory behind the mystical art of accessing one's personal Well was harder than he'd initially thought. She'd blustered her way through lighting a candle, but there were other elements she had an affinity with that he was failing in teaching her about. He could see the benefit of returning to the Order and letting the Mages take over her education.

Laurel wasn't swayed. She woke every morning with a bounce in her step, eager to commence the day. It didn't matter if Thorne wasn't in the mood for a jog around the block, she insisted on going anyway, and he was left scrambling to catch up to avoid a repeat of her incident with the Sluagh. Cornucopia was a strange place. Some said lawless, others said the opposite. One offense declared and you were sent to the Ring—the gladiator pit where differences were settled with blood.

The first morning, he'd had to chase her down the street at dawn, still only in his breeches and casting a glamor on her ears as he went to make them look pointed. While her short hair had covered her ears when they'd disembarked the kuturi, he'd made it a habit to glamor her ears from the first day they'd left Jasper's apartment. There were too many ways this could go wrong and letting Laurel forge her own path was beginning to wear.

Since that first morning, it felt like all Thorne was doing was playing catch up to the woman. Catch up to her as she relentlessly shopped for new clothing in the fabric district. Catch up as she quickly learned the nuances of society and wended and wove through the streets. Catch up as she *made friends* with residents and *redecorated* Jasper's apartment. It was enough to make him snap.

"Time to go," he barked at Laurel.

Her lips pursed, she held her finger up for the merchant to wait and turned to Thorne. "I'm almost done, Growly."

He frowned. Another thing he'd gained over the past few days was that infernal nickname.

"Laurel. I'm done."

She sighed and met Thorne's gaze.

"All right. I'm done too. Let's go home, eat, and then maybe head out and try the only places we've not been to."

She meant the elixir-dens and nightclubs. A surly wash of—something—hit him. He didn't like the idea of Laurel in one of those places, filled with inebriated and horny fae, half-naked Rosebuds, and trigger tempers.

"Not a good idea."

"Unfortunately, it's not your idea. It's mine. And I won't feel like we've exhausted all avenues unless we go there."

He stopped walking and stared at her. "Are you giving me an order?"

She tapped her lip. "Why, yes. Yes, I am. Is that a problem, Growly?"

Everything in him wanted to say yes, it was a fucking problem, but he knew in his gut he had to let her guide the activities. *Crimson*, save him.

"Good," she added, "Chop-chop. Let's go. I want to be bathed, fed, and dressed by the time the Birdcage opens."

He inwardly groaned. The Birdcage was the worst of the elven-elixir dens. He would regret this, but he gestured down the street, tinted in sunset. "After you, my queen."

As THORNE STOOD behind Laurel in the short line for the Birdcage, every instinct inside him screamed to turn the other way. A giant orc in front of him already pawed the behind of a scantily clad elf wearing the mark of a Rosebud courtesan on her upper arm—a rose with no thorns. It was a symbol of beauty, without the pain. The Rosebuds were skilled in their sensuous craft and also physically incapable of getting with child. For the females, their wombs had been removed. For the males, their ability to produce active seed had been cut, ensuring there would be zero repercussions for any regarding the unsanctioned breeding laws.

Clarke had revealed to him the law should have been abolished before Thorne's birth, but King Mithras was not a man of his word. If this same charlatan held Jasper, the sooner they found him, the better. Jasper's move to work at the Order should have pulled him out of the king's crosshairs, but if that was the case, then why had the Prime handed him over to the king?

Like falling dominos, the Prime's machinations all fell into place. The unsanctioned breeding law meant Rush was cursed after Thorne was born. Rush's curse meant he was exiled and invisible to scrying eyes. Because Rush was invisible, when he'd discovered Clarke, and triggered her Well-blessed union, she became irrevocably linked to the Prime's team and would some day turn the tide of the coming war in the favor of the fae.

Infuriatingly, this meant Clarke received many concessions from the Prime the rest of the Order did not. And Jasper had been the victim because of it, nothing but collateral damage. Just like Thorne's mother. Just like Thorne.

Maybe that was why he had left the Order without permission. Part of him resented the woman who'd birthed his half-sister. If it weren't for her arrival in this time, much of Thorne's life would have been different. He'd have two parents alive. Not one. His mentor would be here, and he'd never have been forced into the servitude of the Well. Was that so selfish of him to want?

Rhythmic drumbeats from inside the establishment vibrated the dirt floor and traveled up Thorne's body to itch his ears. They twitched uncontrollably. As did his nose. They weren't even indoors, and yet he could already scent the sex, drugs, and sweat. He hated this place. And he hated that Laurel was pushing him to the edge of red. He'd tried to explain what she would find inside, but all she'd focused on was dancing. It seemed his human companion was a fan.

The dress she wore was no better than a Rosebud courtesan's. Diaphanous silk wrapped her perfectly toned body, giving everyone a clear view of her seductive shape. If it weren't for a strip of opaque linen over her breasts and waist, he'd have an eye of everything. No tattoos, no Well-blessed markings in sight. She'd insisted on extending her glamor from giving the round shell of her ears a pointed look, to hiding their bond. His teardrop marking refused to be glamored, so she painted him with something dark, like a tattoo. He felt ridiculous. She also glamored away his arm markings and insisted he dressed in civilian clothing— buckskin breeches and a form-fitting black shirt rolled up to his elbows.

The worst part was no weapons allowed. He had to leave Fury on the bench at Jasper's apartment. But he never went without a backup. He'd carved a transference rune into Fury's wooden handle. If there came such a time that he needed his old friend, he could summon it. Because he was a Guardian, the metal would come too.

When he questioned Laurel's reasons for hiding their Well-blessed union, she blinked at him innocently and said, "What does it matter to you? You keep insisting we aren't mated in *that* way. That kiss was a mistake. Your words, not mine."

True. Those words had come out of his mouth. Four days ago. He shifted uncomfortably and tugged on his sleeves.

"Besides," she added, "hiding your Guardian status will make you more approachable."

His heart leaped into his throat. Was she trying to make them appear uninvolved? As though they were free to explore others? He narrowed his eyes, studying her intensely. He couldn't flat out ask her. She would think he cared.

A low growl of frustration rumbled in his throat. This was a bad idea.

CHAPTER SIXTEEN

*L*aurel hopped from foot to foot as she stood in the queue for the elixir den Thorne had studiously avoided the entire time they had been in Cornucopia. But she was ready to let loose. She was dressed in a sexy outfit, had kohl makeup around her eyes, and her hair was slicked and clean. She'd also found a shimmering substance to rub over her skin from a really nice female fae who looked more like a sheep than a human, and she was so friendly. The shimmer had always been part of Laurel's routine before she headed out clubbing back in her time. Laurel used to have money, and she enjoyed spending it. She was a self-made queen and didn't deserve the gruff treatment Thorne threw her way. Especially since she *knew* of his undeniable feelings for her. He couldn't lie. Constant lust and attraction simmered down their bond, and yet he stifled it and changed the subject any time she commented.

She might have enjoyed their short moment at the ceremonial lake but wasn't one to wallow or pine. She *was* one to take control of her life and steer it in the right direction. To be honest, spending the past four days doing whatever the hell she'd wanted was invigorating. Finally, she felt like she had control back in her life. Control, strength, and purpose.

What more could she want?

Silently, she glanced over at Thorne's brooding face. He looked uncomfortable in the clothes she'd picked for him. But he looked hot. Sexy. There was no denying it. If he were on her arm at one of the Vegas clubs, they'd have jumped the queue because of all that presence he threw. She could virtually feel his energy in the air. Her dad would have respected him. Her mother would have loved him. The last phone call Laurel had with her parents was about Laurel's need for a big protector in the changing world. That's when they thought the nuclear fallout was the worst thing they had to face.

An image of her family swam into her mind, but she pushed them aside. As much as she missed them, they weren't coming back. So she would live for them. She would flourish for them. And she would do it with the fire she'd been graced with.

Butterflies fluttered in Laurel's stomach. The hard, handsome man on her arm only made tonight better, regardless of his sour expression. The moment he'd seen her dress, he'd paled. As far as she was concerned, when men look like they're going to faint at the sight of your body, it was a compliment. She was ready to party, and perhaps ready for something more from their relationship.

The multilevel Birdcage was the perfect place to explore those feelings. It could have existed in the pages of a magazine. Artisan facades made from a mixture of polished tree limbs and some sort of smooth substance for cage bars. Obviously not metal, but from her vantage point, she couldn't tell the difference. On a balcony above their head, two male fae stood sipping from a glass, eyes languidly drooping from whatever toxin they'd ingested. One had long lustrous brown hair. Very humanlike except the ears. Embroidered jacket, pearlescent buttons, wealth dripping from his pores. His companion was someone of similar social stature, you could tell by the detail in his velvet coat and the stiff spine.

The line moved forward. Thorne guided Laurel closer and she dragged her gaze away from the suave couple.

"Last chance," Thorne murmured. "We can turn around and leave right now."

"Don't be a stick in the mud. You said Jasper frequented here. It's the last place we haven't visited." Well, not *the* last place. The Ring was that. But Thorne didn't think anyone there would know about Jasper. Apparently, his aunt used to work as security and said she'd never seen Jasper there before.

"This isn't a place for someone like you," Thorne mumbled.

"What's that supposed to mean?"

"Nothing."

Nervous tension emanated from him. Looking up at his brooding profile, she appreciated the hard lines, straight nose, and square jaw. She'd urged him to trim his scruff for the night. That dimple in his cheek had been revealed, much to her appreciation. One thing was for certain, she was no longer simply attracted to him, she was in lust for him. Hard. Every cell in her body sang when they touched, and it was starting to hurt when she restrained her desires.

She wanted the touch of his sweet lips on hers again.

"Well, I say we go in. If anything, it will be good to let off some steam. I can have a drink and a dance, maybe get lucky while I'm at it." She paused, waited for a reaction—down their bond, or otherwise.

Icy thunder snapped her way. "What does get lucky mean?"

She arched a brow salaciously. "I think you know what it means."

A low growl rumbled in his throat. "And what exactly will I be doing while you *get lucky*?"

Trying to hide a teasing smirk, she thwacked him on the chest. "Oh, I don't know. I'm sure you'll think of something. Scope out the joint. Find a lady. Ask questions. Up to you."

"Find a lady?" His eyes widened. "You're serious. But we're—"

"What... mated?" She leveled her stare at him. "You said it wasn't like that. You said there was another kind of mating that Rush and Clarke shared, and we don't have it. So... I guess, call this an open marriage."

Angry eyes turned away and glared at some indeterminate spot in the distance. Part of her churned, but she kept her doubts down and out of their bond. If she didn't force him to think about what he wanted, he would continue to keep her at arm's length, and she couldn't live her life like that. Being in Cornucopia had helped Laurel take back control. It was time Thorne learned that his actions had consequences.

"You know," she continued, "the fae really aren't that bad. After talking to them at the markets, I'm starting to feel like I'm fitting in."

"Don't get complacent. Some might look normal, but they could be using a glamor to hide their true form. They could also turn on you the moment they find out who you really are."

"I'm sure I'll be fine. Ooh goodie. Look. Our turn." The queue had brought them right up to the front entrance, where a pink-haired pixie collected a door fee. She was flanked on either side by two male pixies in charge of security. They also had pink hair, but where the female was small and dainty, the males were Laurel's height and packed plenty of muscle.

The female pixie narrowed her eyes at Thorne, but then shifted to Laurel with a broad smile. "Welcome to the Birdcage. We ask all patrons to leave their weapons at the door and to keep their wings latent." She received Laurel's cape and continued rattling off information. "Happy hour is at nine, and we have a special on contraceptive elixirs tonight. Two for one."

"There you go," Thorne grumbled. "Perfect night for

you."

She ignored his snippy remark, despite the hurt simmering beneath her skin. This was the reaction she wanted from him. Jealousy never reared a pretty head, and he had to know that if he was jealous, then there was a reason for it. Namely that he liked her too. Her brow puckered, and she did her best to get on with it.

"What do you mean by keeping wings latent?" Laurel asked the pixie.

"Some of us can't shift, but if we're caught spreading our wings, it's immediate eviction. Despite being called the Birdcage, we respectfully ask that all patrons keep their wings dormant."

Thorne dug into his pants and handed some coin to the pixie.

The pixie handed Laurel a cloakroom token and ushered them inside. Two-seconds later and they were walking through a dark tunnel, following the tribal beat of drums. Nearing the end of the tunnel, the air thickened. When they emerged, it was into an aviary-like interior. A large open column reached up high—no roof, just twinkling stars, and open sky. On all sides, up various split levels, cages jutted out, acting like open rooms. Moss and vines spilled from each cage floor, both dangling and entwining up bars. The foliage provided a semblance of privacy for the fae inside the cages, but not entirely. She glimpsed writhing naked bodies betwixt the greenery. Wow. It really was one of those places. Glass spheres suspended from cages contained glowing balls of light that cast a soft—or shady—ambiance. It was dim, but bright enough to see.

"The cages are filled with natural and live foliage to negate the feeling of being disconnected from the Well. Air fae can also be higher than most others before suffering that disconnection."

"Right."

That made little sense to her, but she had to give him points for trying to educate her.

All manner of fae existed here. It was better than the marketplace. Some were humanlike, some were humanoid. Many were more animal than fae. Orcs. Pixies. Scaly skin. Fae with their wings tucked tight. Skimpy clothing on both males and females. Three haughty looking elves holding a faun by a lead and collar around her neck. They walked to the thriving dance floor that existed around a platform at the center that housed a magnificent archaic cage. It looked more like the bones of a ribcage.

Inside was the band.

Laurel gasped. *They're human.*

No pointed ears. No animal characteristics. Must be.

One violinist. One flutist. One person on the drums. And one woman who sang haunting opera notes. Not one was manacled, or in a state of physical disarray, but she couldn't shake the sense they were prisoners. Each artisan smiled wistfully as they played their instruments, but their eyes screamed in horror. It was surreal, especially compared to the happy, carefree vibe of the patrons dancing around the stage.

Could they be forced? Somehow magically induced to stay there? Was that look in their eyes real?

Laurel scanned the dancing fae to see if anyone noticed, or cared, but they didn't.

"They're human," she whispered to Thorne as he led her toward the curved bar at the back of the establishment. They skirted the dance floor and the surrounding booths.

"Still want to *get lucky*?" he mocked.

"Should we do something?"

He shot her a look as if she was stupid. "Causing trouble here will only have one outcome, being sent to the Ring. And if you want to get out of Cornucopia alive, I highly suggest you don't. Those humans will be spoils of war. I kill their kind."

In other words, they were not worth their time. Anger flashed in her eyes. *She* was their kind. She dropped hold of his arm and strode to the bar. She needed a drink. Things weren't going according to plan. It was supposed to be a fun night where they'd tick one last place off their search list. Just when she thought she was getting used to this place, it surprised her.

She scowled at the barmaid, a cute female fae with wolfish ears, black kohl-rimmed eyes, and with a swishing tail at her rear. She had a similar hairstyle to Laurel, short and dark. Polishing a small glass with a towel, the barmaid noted Laurel's arrival and tipped her chin.

"What will it be?" Husky words.

"Your best elixir." Then she lifted two fingers. Thorne needed to loosen up too.

Two short glasses slammed on the counter, and then the barmaid almost did a double-take at Thorne. Maybe they knew each other?

Huh. Maybe this getting lucky thing wasn't such a good idea after all.

The barmaid was about to pour something blue and glowing into the glasses, but Thorne blocked with his palm. The barmaid raised a brow at Thorne.

He scowled at her. "Not *that* good."

Laurel sent him a questioning look.

"Trust me," he returned. And then darted a glance up at the cages with the writhing, naked bodies. "Unless you were serious about joining them."

When she still looked baffled, he leaned in close and lowered his tone. "It was an aphrodisiac."

Ah. The two-for-one contraceptive offer was starting to make sense. Her brows lifted. "That might not be so bad."

He choked on his drink. "Not in a place like this."

The dim light cast the sharp angles of Thorne's face into soft relief, and she quite enjoyed seeing his face without the stubble. He pretended to be unaffected by the topic of conversation, but his telltale nervous emotions gave him away.

"You've tried it," she accused.

A half shrug was her answer.

She was so right. The thought of Thorne, hot and sweaty, engaged in endless hours of sex made Laurel's heart thump loudly in her chest. She picked up her waiting glass. "You know, for the record, we didn't have places like this

THE SOLACE OF SHARP CLAWS

back home." She took a sip. Minty. Apple fresh. Delicious. It warmed her throat and sent a pleasant sensation of ease into her muscles. She would pay the barmaid a compliment when she ordered the next drink. "Well, I mean, we did have places where people went to have sex, but they weren't advertised so publicly."

Once again, he coughed. "And. Um. Did you, ah, frequent these places?"

A smile touched the corner of her lips. "Wouldn't you like to know?"

For an electrified few seconds, they stared into each other's eyes. There went his simmering lust again, straight down their bond like liquid fire.

"Right," she said and cracked a crick in her neck. She downed the last of the drink and surveyed the room. Her mood darkened when she landed on the band. Before the night was done, she'd have to do something about that. She couldn't leave knowing people were being held captive against their will, whether human or fae. She needed to get closer first. "I'm going to dance. Will you come with me?"

He blinked, perhaps a little panicked, then his familiar mask of discontent slammed down and he sneered at her revealing dress. "If you're going to act like a courtesan, then don't forget to take your pink elixir. Unless, of course, you want to be executed for unsanctioned breeding."

Her jaw dropped. He just called her a whore. Her heart shattered into a million pieces. This jealousy thing wasn't quite working out. But then again, if he was shooting this low with his comments, then she was getting under his skin.

"Suit yourself." She stole his remaining drink, gulped it down, and then wiped her mouth with the back of her hand. She was ready to let loose, dance, and work out some kinks. A giant Thorne-sized kink. Time to feel alive again. Time to feel human. Appreciated.

Just don't look at the musicians in the cage and you'll feel like you're back in a club at home.

CHAPTER SEVENTEEN

*T*his was *not* going according to plan.

Thorne stewed in his dark thoughts on the sidelines of the Birdcage main floor. He regretted every harsh word that sent Laurel to the dance floor. Her hurt had pierced him down their bond, wrapped its barbed wire arms around his chest and squeezed until he hurt too, proving that he had a heart, after all.

Damn. Damn him for saying those nasty things to her, but he was right. She couldn't just let anyone stick their cock in her, fill her with child, and send her to her death. The damned king's stupid law was still in effect and he would not stand by idly and let her fuck her way to her grave.

Shit.

He flinched. He was doing it again. Letting his anger dictate his thoughts. She had done nothing yet. She just wanted to dance. Guilt speared him. Even if she wanted to —he swallowed a lump—do something with another male fae, then shouldn't that be her choice? She was right, he'd been clear to her that he didn't believe their mating was the same as one of the body. But this Well-blessed thing was so new and he was fast surrendering to the idea that it was not only the same as a mating of the body, but more.

Fuck. He scrubbed his face.

He had no other option but to wait with his arms folded and watch over Laurel while she danced. And watch he did. She was hypnotizing. Mesmerizing. The way she closed her eyes, felt the music, swayed, and undulated to the beat was almost like she really had the expert training of a Rosebud courtesan. Seduction pulsed in her veins. It frightened him how she affected him. Every tug of her body, every swerve, roll, dip, twitch of her lip was a direct line to his cock. It sprung to attention the second she went down there. Every now and then, she'd lift her lashes, home in on him, and clash eyes. *Like a hit of divilxir.* A fluttering in his chest. His stomach. The sense of falling. And then the searing hard lust crushing his soul.

Bad. Idea.

Mouth dry, he swallowed. Once again she gave him a beckoning look and then went back to her solo performance. But she wasn't solo for long. He wasn't the only fae watching her. From the dark recess of a booth, a dark shadow had his head riveted in Laurel's direction. Always. Flanking the shadowed figure were two burly orcs who looked more suitable as guards in the Unseelie army. Perhaps they were part of the private security here.

An object on the booth table caught Thorne's eye and a curse slipped from his tongue. It was a djinn bottle. Ceramic, inscribed with runes and uncorked. Meaning it was empty. Used. Was this the fae who'd sent the djinn after the people in Mornington?

He looked closer at one of the orcs and noticed he had saggy skin. Aged. As though he'd used a precious part of his soul to operate the djinn.

Instinctively, Thorne reached for Fury but remembered it was back at the apartment. Twitching, he drew his hand back to his side and made a mental note to pass on this new piece of information to Aeron when he returned to the Order.

Thorne shifted his gaze back to the dance floor and the more pressing concern. Two male pixies, shirts off, wings plastered to their sweaty backs—bumping and grinding around Laurel—potentially looking for a new queen for their harem. *Damned pixies.*

He would kill them. Gut them, pull their entrails out, and stuff them back in their mouths. Maybe he'd use their wings for decoration. Jasper's apartment decor was still a little sparse.

"Another drink," he barked at the bartender. "Ale. Strong."

When the glass slid across the hardwood counter, he caught it and turned his back on the dance floor. Watching Laurel was torture.

Stick to the goal. Interview the patrons. Staff. Anyone.

At least she was enjoying herself. He couldn't fault her for wanting a good time. Crimson knew he'd drowned himself in this place more than once in his younger years. *Just... don't leave with anyone*, he thought. Silently begging.

Thorne pulled out a coin from his pocket and paid.

"Before you go," he said to the barmaid, "Take a look at this."

He cast a spell over his drink and pushed the image of Jasper from his mind into the reflection. A shimmering image of his old mentor appeared in the ale. Not perfect, but good enough. "Have you seen this fae before?"

Thorne waited for the usual clamming up of the tongue —standard response to a Guardian. But the barmaid just stood back with an unimpressed look on her face. And then he recognized her.

"Anise!" he exclaimed.

She raised a vexed brow. "You save my life and you forget my face?"

"No, it's just that I didn't expect to see you here." He frowned. She lived in Crescent Hollow and worked at the Laughing Den. Or had Caraway said he'd not seen her in a while? "Why *are* you here?"

"Not that it's any of your business, but I couldn't live there anymore."

"But isn't Kyra a better alpha than Thaddeus?" He thought the place would be a sanctuary now.

Anise's eyes lost their fire and she picked up a cloth and started polishing a glass. "She is. It's not that."

He nodded solemnly. "It's the memories."

"I can't turn a corner without thinking they're there waiting for me. I can't walk outside the front gate without seeing the cage I was kept in." She shrugged. "It was time to leave. People here don't seem to care about my appearance as much. I should have left long ago."

She said the words, but it didn't look like she believed them. Thorne knew how cruel people could be. They were the same whether in Cornucopia, the Seelie Kingdom, or the dark, chaotic Unseelie. Anise was born to two wolf-shifters, but she couldn't shift. Her tail was permanent. Her nose had a dark tint at the tip. Wait.

"Does Caraway know?"

She scowled at him. "Why would I care? That floater knew the red-coats were in town. He knew Thaddeus and they were up to something, and yet he did nothing. If he'd acted when I told him, maybe a few lives would have been saved. Maybe I wouldn't have nightmares."

"You know Guardians are prohibited to get involved with politics."

"It hasn't stopped you."

He toyed with the rim of the glass. "But I'm an outcast, even with the outcasts."

"No, you're not. You just think you are. And, anyway, I'd rather that than be someone with no backbone." Anise finished polishing her glass and started vigorously cleaning the counter. "Why are you here, anyway?"

He thumbed the dance floor. "I'm with her."

Anise narrowed her eyes at Laurel. "Oh, yeah. She's cute."

"Clarke's friend."

"No shit. Same... like... from before?"

He nodded. Anise scrutinized him for a long time and then pointed at his face. "You know the black shit you put over your Guardian mark is rubbing off."

He scrubbed it. "Stupid idea anyway."

Anise looked back at the image of Jasper in the drink. "So... who's this? He looks familiar"

"An old friend. He's been missing for a long time. He used to frequent this place."

"I've only been here a year. I haven't seen him, but I can ask around."

A little thrill flipped in Thorne's stomach. He cleared his throat and tried not to look excited. "That would be appreciated."

"Stay here a minute." She took the glass and walked over to a security guard, showed him, and moved on. Thorne tracked her as she asked a few more before she came back.

"Apparently he was a regular." Anise blew air from her mouth, raised her eyes to the ceiling, and searched her memory. "I think Fern said the last time they saw Jasper was at least a decade ago."

Bogey's Balls. Thorne knew it was too good to be true.

"Can you tell me more about that last time?"

"Not really. All I know is that he spent a lot of coin. Fucked a lot of Rosebuds. Drank a lot of divilixir."

Same old Jasper-shit. An exasperated sigh slipped out.

Thorne hand-signed his thanks and took a swig of his drink. He swilled the fruity taste around his mouth.

Anise paused and frowned. Her eyes darted over to the dark booth in the corner. "Although," she said. "Mind you. Things have changed a bit since then in here."

Thorne nodded slowly.

"If you need more info, ask Patches."

"He the new boss?"

"As good as. Been around for a couple of years. Right about when the entertainment started coming from captive humans. Honestly, it's the first time I've heard about this kind of captivity outside of King Mithras's Court."

"You don't mind it?" Thorne asked. He didn't think Anise was this kind of person.

"Between you and me, I won't be around for long." She glanced behind Thorne. "That's Patches."

"Right." Thorne followed her gaze to the booth in the corner with the empty djinn bottle. The same booth with the shadowed resident watching Laurel. The one where the resident wasn't sitting in the dark anymore, but standing at the edge of the dance floor, watching Laurel.

The scent of Patches' breed wafted over to Thorne and he tensed. Wolf. Probably Seelie since most wolves were. Fucker wore nothing but leather pants, meaning he was ready to shift at a moment's notice. Yellow eyes. Power-enhancing tattoos slicked over his scarred body. Pumped and threaded muscles. Furred, pointed ears twitching. Patch over one scarred eye.

During Thorne's teenage years, Jasper had taken Thorne

to a place just like this and hired him a Rosebud to "break him in." Some people might think Jasper was a delinquent sexual fiend, but Thorne knew better. It was a cover. Sure, he'd enjoyed the perks of the role, but that first visit hadn't just been about hedonism. It was battle practice. Thorne still remembered walking in behind Jasper and being lectured quietly.

"Scope the joint on entry. Check the exits. Check for threats. Who do you think is the one you need to worry about most?"

"The big one with the tatts."

Jasper whacked Thorne over the head. "No, grasshopper. The biggest threat is the calmest person in the room. Look again."

Tonight, that person was Patches.

A disturbance at the entrance interrupted Thorne's attention. Air shifted and electrified with warning. Sound warped. His ears pricked at the gasps of patrons as they begrudgingly made way for a new arrival. Anise cursed under her breath. The bewitched musicians stumbled, the beat skipped, and then the magic riding their captivity kicked in again and the music flowed as if it hadn't stopped.

Once upon a time, Thorne looked at the latest artisan captives with pity and compassion, but that time had long since past. Being a Guardian had whittled away any part of him that cared for the fate of anyone that failed to fall under the scope of a Guardian's protection. Did it make him jaded? Probably. But no worse than the two Guardians currently walking in a direct line toward Thorne.

Cloud and Shade. Crow and Vampire.

Both resplendently fearsome in their Guardian battle gear, hard eyes, and contempt for those around them. The crowd parted to make way. Cloud's feathered wings draped with menace, and Shade's leathery wings twitched with barely veiled tension. They cared little about the Birdcage's rule to keep their wings tucked tight. Guardians cared little about the opinions of others in general.

Thorne tried to move so they wouldn't see him, but it was no use. They were here *for* him. *Well-damn it.* Probably here on Leaf's orders to drag him back to the Order and face repercussions for leaving when he'd been given a mission. Screw the Order. He was sick of them.

He slammed down the last of the fruity ale just as Cloud strode up to him.

"The fuck you done to your face?" he asked dryly, either meaning Thorne's black smudge over the teardrop tattoo, or the missing beard.

Thorne ignored him and smiled apologetically at Anise. She smirked and went to prepare a drink for the new arrivals.

Shade picked up Thorne's empty glass and inspected it.

"If you're here to haul me back to the Order," Thorne said, "save yourselves some time and turn around now. I'm not coming back. Not until I find Jasper."

"Good," Shade drawled as he put the empty glass back down.

Surprise lifted Thorne's brows. "Then why are you here?"

"Hungry." Shade's predatory gaze scanned the patrons, now over their initial disturbance and back in revelry.

Liar. Shade was hungry, clearly, but they weren't here for the food. A good-looking vampire, as experienced as Shade, had willing donors falling at his feet. To prove Thorne's point, Shade pushed off the counter and crooked his finger at a pretty faun with curved horns flowing out of her curly red hair. She broke away from her group, cloven feet tick-ticking on the marble floor, and the two of them disappeared into the shadows.

That's all it took for Shade. A crook of the finger and females wet themselves. If only Thorne had that much control over the opposite sex, maybe he could get Laurel to follow his instructions more. No. It was Laurel who only needed to crook her finger at him, and his insides turned to lava.

She would be the death of him.

"Why are you here, Cloud?" Thorne ground out. He needed to see if it was the djinn bottle, or something else. "The Prime send you? Leaf?"

Cloud accepted his drink, tossed the ridiculous garnish, and sniffed it. "Nope."

"Then why?" Still didn't trust them.

"Maybe we care about Jasper too. You ever think that?"

Thorne scoffed, "You don't care about anyone."

"Harsh."

"True."

Cloud stared intently at the drink. "Maybe my wings

have been clipped, and that's why I haven't helped in the hunt for Jasper."

Clipped? As in the Prime had something over him? "Fuck the Prime."

"Not today. Not any day."

Thorne slid eyes at Cloud. The fae returned his solid stare. Well-damn. Color him inky. Cloud was serious. Of all the fae to throw in their lot with Thorne, he'd never expected it to be the human-hating, Prime-loving, crow. He was wrong about the Prime-loving part. Which begged the question, who was Cloud loyal to?

"Just so you know," Cloud added. "The young wolf who filled your mission is dead."

Thorne's stomach dropped. "The fuck?"

"Yep. He's monster meat." Cloud leveled his gaze at Thorne. "This is the fallout from neglecting your duty."

Shit. Fuck. Shit. Heaviness closed Thorne's lids. The same weight settled on his shoulders. He braced the counter and breathed deeply. Poor kid. The wolf inside Thorne howled in grief. Another wolf down. Thorne's fault. There was no denying it.

"What happened to your markings?" Cloud asked, eying Thorne's arm.

"Glamored."

A cold, derogatory laugh burst out of Cloud and he slung his gaze at the dance floor. "Trouble in paradise already. Can't say I'm surprised. Didn't expect anything less from a filthy human."

Thorne bared his teeth. "Watch it."

"Then again, she's dancing between an orc and a pixie. Maybe she's about to redeem herself," Cloud added sarcastically.

Thorne tensed. Couldn't look. The wolf in him, already worked up, was now frantic. Part of him wanted to throttle Cloud for his disrespect, the other part wanted to throttle the fae no doubt with their hands all over Laurel. Nothing but fun and elation trickled down their bond. Damn. He needed to figure out a way to block their shared emotions... or accept it. Neither would be easy.

Cloud continued, "And with that dress on—wait. Isn't she your mate?"

The counter creaked under Thorne's punishing grip. "Why?"

"Then why is she—oh, yeah, that's not good. Time for us to get what we came for." Cloud made a shrill whistle, calling Shade back.

Thorne snapped around, heart pounding in his chest. There, in the center of the dance floor, Laurel was stuck between a growing group of male fae and trying to stop a brawl. One of the orc guards, a few pixies, and some elves. Motherfuckers.

This ends now.

Pushing off the counter, he strode into the fray, only vaguely aware of Cloud and Shade heading toward the table where the djinn bottle was. Of course those fuckers would be all about work.

Without thinking, he palmed two males beside Laurel— an orc and a pixie—both staggered back. The pixie's wings flared and vibrated on instinct, knocking a glass from the fae next to them, which in turn spilled on another. The orc bellowed in fury. The sound echoed off the high aviary column and disappeared into the night sky above.

"I had it sorted, Thorne," Laurel snapped.

"The fuck you did. Come on. Let's go." He tried to take Laurel by the arm, but she shrugged out of his hold.

"Don't," she warned.

"Lady said no," the orc grunted and stepped up. He shoved Thorne back.

Despite the big fae's height and brawn, Thorne barely flinched. He looked down at the beefy hand, still pressed to his pec. Red leaked into Thorne's vision and he rubbed the remainder of paint from his eye tattoo. He snarled and shattered the glamor holding his true appearance at bay. The Well-blessed markings on his arm and hand flickered into life, and the fire in his eyes doubled.

The orc's eyes widened. "Guardian?"

"Remove your hand, orc."

"The fucking Seelie-priss started it." The orc snatched his hand back, but recollected his composure and glared at the pixie, still glowering behind Laurel's back.

The pixie's fangs bared and he hissed. "Unseelie trash. You think you can just take what you want. She was with me first."

The orc took a swing. The pixie went down. And then chaos let loose.

The brawl moved over the dance floor like a tumultuous ocean. Lurkers in the shadows made themselves known.

Orc bouncers. Shifters. Other reprobates with sharp bone weapons brandished. Blood would be spilled if this wasn't stopped.

Before Thorne could shift into a wolf, a thunderous crack rent the air. Lightning flashed. Everyone ducked, protecting their head from the elemental fury that was Cloud as he gathered electricity into his body. Next to him, Shade had materialized from whatever nook he'd been supping in, a drop of blood at the corner of his mouth, lethal prowess in his dark eyes. Shade commanded the shadows, and they crept toward him ominously, ready to swallow up anyone who got in his way.

Patrons screamed and shuffled out of the way, hiding wherever they could. A stampede almost crushed Thorne, but he shouldered free and watched the spectacle the Guardians put on.

Casually, as if Cloud had all the time in the world, he strolled over to where Patches stood and collected the djinn bottle from the table.

"This yours, wolf?" Cloud asked him.

"What's it to you, freak?"

Cloud laughed and looked at Shade. "You hear that? He called me a freak."

Shade looked impressed. "Yeah, I did. Must have balls. Because it also means I'm a freak. And, ah—" he looked over to Thorne. "Mean's he called our buddy over there a freak too."

Fuck. *Don't involve me.* Thorne clenched his jaw.

Patches calculated the odds, didn't like them, and then

pointed at the orc who'd tried it on with Laurel. The same one with a slightly aged look to his face. "He's the one who brought the bottle in here. Ask him."

Cloud raised a brow at the orc. "That right?"

The orc paled. Nodded.

"Guess that's us done, then." Cloud secured the bottle to his belt loop and then gestured at Shade.

Shade looked Thorne squarely in the eyes. "You're welcome."

The two of them took one meaty orc arm each, flapped their wings, and then took off vertically, carrying their prisoner kicking and screaming between them until their bodies were nothing but shadows in the dark sky.

Patches hadn't offered the whole truth. That orc may have been the one who brought the bottle in, but somehow Thorne didn't think the orc was the one who'd orchestrated the attack on Mornington. Cloud and Shade weren't stupid. They'd be back for Patches.

"Time to go," Thorne said and looked for Laurel.

But she wasn't there.

Confused, he searched for her. Only then did he notice the music had stopped. The musicians weren't in their cage. The knowledge of what Laurel had done hit him with the force of a hurricane. She'd freed them during the disturbance. The moment he'd noticed, so did Patches. In the space of seconds, more guards appeared from the darkness of the club and dropped from the cages hanging above. This time, it was only one Guardian against many.

Thorne still liked those odds.

Until they dragged Laurel from the bathrooms, kicking and struggling, bleeding from her lip.

"The lady has caused this establishment offense," Patches boomed.

"Take your hands off her," Thorne warned. "Or this won't end pretty."

"Stay out of this, Guardian," Patches replied. "This doesn't concern you."

"Oh yes, it does."

Thorne's fangs and claws elongated, ready to let the wolf out, but Laurel shook her head. He paused. What? Why the fuck not? Forcing himself to calm and assess the situation, he realized there was no fear hurtling down the bond from her, not like it had done with the Sluagh. He arched his brow at her. Her lips quirked. *Trust me.*

Crimson, save him.

"What is the offense?" Thorne asked.

"She released our humans. She can't pay in coin, so she must pay in the Ring."

Shocked, Thorne couldn't stop the snarl that slipped out. But yet again, Laurel didn't flinch. Her smile widened. Which meant only one thing. She'd planned this.

He leveled his stare at Patches. "If you're taking her, then I invoke the rights of a Well-blessed union."

He lifted his marked hand. A chorus of gasps floated around the room.

"But you can't enter the Ring," someone said. "You're a Guardian."

"I'm also her mate. You either take both of us or none."

Patches looked at Laurel, at her still bare arm. "I don't see the same marking on her. And I don't see a wolf's bite on her neck. You don't smell mated, and you don't act it." He slid his narrowed eyes back to Thorne. "I don't want the Order breathing down my neck if we send you in. She goes alone."

CHAPTER EIGHTEEN

"*S*he goes alone."

Patches' words echoed in the room. Laurel tensed, waiting for Thorne to protest. She supposed she could let the glamor on her Well-blessed markings drop. That would solve the argument. But she liked watching Thorne squirm.

That unsanctioned breeding comment Thorne had made cut her deep, but it was a festering wound for him. His pain was worse, and he'd lashed out to keep it hidden. So, when she'd danced, and the orc had danced with her, she couldn't help asking questions about Jasper.

To her surprise, each of the male fae that had danced around her had been more than forthcoming, each eager to please her more with tid-bits of information. Before he'd been taken by Cloud and Shade, the older-looking orc had confessed that he'd been working for Patches for a long time. And he'd been around when another orc had boasted about taking the bastard son of the king to the Ring. Of course, this other orc—Gunther, his name was—was also a prisoner at the Ring and resided under the hill.

From what she'd gathered, "under the hill" was the colloquial term Cornucopians called the place where prisoners were kept before they had to battle in the Ring. Some prisoners never left this jail. They would do battle, and then would be returned under the hill until the next time they were needed. Some battles negotiated were until death, others were first blood, and then if you were lucky, you could walk away.

The only way of gleaning more information from Gunther would be to get herself arrested.

The moment the two visiting Guardians had caused a commotion, Laurel knew that she could help the human prisoners escape and get herself caught in the process.

The guards holding her made to take her away, but Thorne shouted, "*Stop.*"

"You want us to act mated?" he snapped at Patches. "Fine."

Thorne strode to Laurel, fierce intensity in his blue-ice stare. He gripped the back of her neck, pulled her toward him so fast her mind sloshed, and then crushed his lips to hers. Maybe she should have been confused, or surprised, or angry, but all those feelings she'd told to wait, didn't want to wait. They rushed to the surface at the taste of him, and when he gripped her rear with his free hand, she forgot to breathe. She forgot to think.

There was nothing but his tongue, his taste, and his heat.

She was so lost in him, she almost missed his whispered words. "If you don't drop the glamor, they'll drop it for you. All of it."

Panic petrified her.

Her ears. She'd forgotten. With her mind whirling with the potential consequences, she let him gently nibble her bottom lip as her mind caught up. Being a human in front of all these human-hating fae wouldn't mean being sent to the Ring. It could mean immediate execution, or entrapment like the artisans. Thorne was right. She dropped the glamor on her arm and when he eased off, she held her arm up for all to see.

Patches' dark eyebrow lifted over his eye-patch. He looked at Thorne. "Your funeral."

THERE WASN'T a moment of privacy the entire walk from the Birdcage to the Ring, and Laurel had been warned by Thorne not to give away any secrets with so many sharp ears listening. She couldn't tell him about her plan. It would have to wait until they were securely under the hill.

Their guards pushed them up the dirt path toward the colosseum at the top of a hill of rock. There was a fight on tonight, and the bright beam of orange light shot up from the colosseum into the sky. But it was beneath the colosseum that held Laurel's attention. No access points to the hill anywhere she could see, meaning they had to walk up to the top.

Inwardly, she groaned. It looked about four or five floors high. Her heels weren't going to cut it.

Thorne prowled at her side. Not a peep out of him the entire journey through town. She had no idea if he understood why or how she'd done this. He was big and strong enough to take down the four guards flanking them. He didn't.

He knew.

Must.

Or he could be doing what he'd done the entire time they'd been in Cornucopia—letting her lead.

Finally at the top, and with sore feet and heaving breaths, Laurel and her companions came to the large stadium. Fae milled about the many arched entries. Some looked excited about the show, others were nervous or in tears—probably friends or family of some prisoners. Seeing that side of it, Laurel's own nerves hit. Was she stupid to think she could handle this? Even win a battle? Or escape?

Don't lose faith now.

"Here we go," a guard said as they arrived at a small, nondescript hatch in the floor. "Your new home."

That's it? A hatch?

"And we wait down there until when?" Thorne demanded.

"Until you're called upon."

"Which is…?"

The orc smirked. "Whenever we say. You had your chance, Guardian. You gave it up. Now the bargain has been set. You can't leave until you win."

Why did Laurel suddenly have a bad feeling about that? "Who do we have to beat?"

The orc pulled out a strange tool that reminded Laurel of a branding iron, but it wasn't metal. It was made of smooth ceramic.

"What is that?" Thorne growled.

"For your binding." The orc's lips stretched to reveal his fangs. "We can't very well have prisoners portal out of here whenever they want."

"Is that all it's for?"

"Once you're released, it will disappear."

Thorne's brows slammed down. "That's not what I asked. I said, is that all it's for?"

Irritation swam over the orc's features. "It also prohibits your magic leaving the stadium."

Laurel supposed that made sense. Thorne, on the other hand, was infuriated for some reason. Perhaps he'd had another plan up his proverbial sleeve. But neither of them had time for more questions. The orc stamped their cheeks, burning their flesh. Laurel screamed. White hot agony lanced the side of her face. She wanted to touch it but couldn't manage more than a trembling hand hovering over the area.

Thorne took it much better. Not even a wince. When his was done, she was surprised to see no glaring red branding wound, but a blue rune, glowing and glittering with the power of the Well, just like her hand markings and his teardrop tattoo.

"Oh. And it's embedded with a transference spell,

meaning when it's time for you to fight, you can't hide. You'll be transported into the arena."

Then the orc pushed Laurel down the hatch. Briefly, she became airborne in the dark. A scream froze in her throat. *Weightless*. And then… her ass hit slippery dirt and she flew down a slide, hands flailing, desperate to grasp something to slow herself down. Down, down, down she swirled like Alice down the rabbit hole. Until finally, light burst, hurting her eyes. She squinted, became airborne again, and then landed on soft green grass, tumbling until she came to a halt.

When she gathered her bearings, she gasped.

Trees. Grass. Sun? Light came from somewhere. The trickle of water. A sparkling river. Little huts made from sticks and bark. People—fae—of all kinds everywhere. At first glance, at least fifty. Maybe a hundred. She thought perhaps she'd knocked her head. It sure seemed like a Wonderland. But then she looked closer. The fae were rough, brutal, and the type that looked like they would stab you in the back the moment you weren't looking. But there was also fae who looked like they'd lived down here for years. As though they'd been forgotten.

Thorne landed gracefully next to her. He rolled and found his feet swiftly. Immediately, he took up a position of wariness—crouched in a fighting stance, eyes scanning the new Wonderland as though it were about to eat him whole. After he assessed, he relaxed and helped Laurel up.

"You good?" he asked, eyes never leaving those fae residents, now staring at the newcomers with hungry eyes.

She nodded. "Just peachy."

Her ass and thighs stung from the ride down the slippery dirt tunnel. If she looked, she'd bet she'd find scratches under the layer of mud. Her shoes were missing and her beautiful new dress was torn to shreds. If she thought it was revealing before, that was nothing compared to now.

"Shit," she muttered and pawed at the torn shreds.

Thorne reached over his shoulder, grabbed his shirt by the neck, and pulled it off. "Put this on."

With the weight of a thousand eyes on her, she had no trouble doing as she was told. She ripped off any straggling gauze and used a long strip to tie Thorne's shirt around her waist so it looked like a dress. When she was done, she tilted her nose to the shirt. It smelled like him. Now it was on her. She liked that. Their scents mixing.

He gave her a quizzical look. She blushed and quickly looked away.

"So," she said. "What now?"

"You tell me."

Their eyes met. Held. Yeah, he knew.

Laurel glanced around to see if anyone was within hearing range. They were halfway down a soft grass hill that led to a valley below where the people gathered.

"Is it safe to talk?" Even though he seemed to trust her, it was time to explain.

His ears twitched. "Probably not. But also probably the most privacy we'll get in this place."

"While I was dancing, I questioned the orc guard about Jasper. He said another guard many years ago had boasted about sending Jasper to the Ring. That guard is here himself and has been for years. His name is Gunther."

"So you got arrested on purpose. And you didn't think it pertinent to include me in on your plan?"

"Well excuse me for thinking you had no faith in me, especially considering you had just called me a whore."

His eyes widened. "I called you a Rosebud courtesan. There's a big difference."

"What's the difference?"

He didn't answer.

Jesus Christ. With that, Laurel started her trek down the hill.

His footsteps pounded behind her, as heavy as the god of thunder himself.

"Laurel," he said. "I…"

She stopped at the base of the hill. "You're what?"

You're sorry?

He opened his mouth. Shut it. Then scowled at something behind Laurel.

"We're looking for a fae named Gunther," Thorne bellowed.

A line of hard-looking fae stepped up. Each of different breeds, each with a home-fashioned weapon in their hand. Some were made of bone, others of wood. Maces. Clubs. Axes. Swords. Sharp things. Dangerous things.

Next to her, Thorne sucked in his abs and started plucking buttons on his breeches.

"What are you doing?" she hissed.

"I don't want my only pants to be ruined in the shift," he

replied casually, put his thumbs in the loops of his belt and got ready to drop.

She held out her palm in a placating way. "No need to get your panties twisted, Growly. Let's just take a breath before we wolf out." To the line of hardened criminals edging their way, she waved hello. "We just want to talk to Gunther. No one needs to get hurt."

One stepped forward. No teeth, crooked nose, bald, and a stink she whiffed from ten feet away. Pointed ears. Probably elf. For a species that didn't show age, he looked ancient with crow's feet around his eyes and a gnarled and bent figure. But the muscles in his shoulders were corded. He'd be a tough nut to crack. His snarl was full of contempt.

"What do you want with Gunther? What will you give?" He eyed her bare legs salaciously. Perhaps they didn't get too many females down here.

Already in the process of letting his wolf out, Thorne's eyes took on a feral glint, his claws distended, his canines elongated. It was a breathtaking sight.

"Name your price," she said, turning back to the elf. Hopefully he would ask for coin, food, or protection.

But what the fae came back with, she could never have been prepared.

"Your underwear," he said.

He had to be kidding. But he wasn't. A sharp laugh burst out of her. Thorne turned to stone.

Another fae next to the crooked nosed elf stepped forward. "I'll take you there for only half your underwear."

"I'll do it for a quarter," said a third.

"I'll do it for free," piped up a small voice.

"Yes." Laurel pointed to where the sound came from and landed on a scrappy looking boy of about thirteen. "You. You're the winner. Let's go."

Laurel hurried the rest of the way to meet the boy. As she drew near, she found a timid satyr. Wide and low pointed ears twitched and flicked as though a fly landed on them. Curly brown hair. Big doe eyes. But a hardness in them that saddened her. His clothes were hole-ridden and smelled. He looked half starved. She hated to think what had happened to have him thrown in there.

"I'm Laurel." She stuck out her hand. He eyed it as though she had a disease, so she took it back. Right—hand-shaking wasn't a thing. "This is Thorne."

"I'm Sparrow."

"He's my Sparrow. That's what he is." The crooked nosed elf stood between Sparrow and Laurel. "You want him, you pay for him."

Laurel lifted a brow. "And I suppose you want my underwear."

"Mention her underwear again, and it will be the last thing you utter." Thorne loomed over the elf, jaw clenched, part wolf. "I will cut your tongue out, elf. Don't mistake my words."

The elf looked warily at Thorne, caught the teardrop tattoo, lowered his gaze and stepped back. "What's a Guardian doing here? You lot ain't allowed in here."

"They made an exception."

"I own him." The elf pointed at Sparrow.

"Now I do," Thorne returned.

"You ain't paid me."

Thorne leaned forward an inch. "The fact I leave your tongue in is your payment."

The elf nodded emphatically and stepped back. He shooed the rest of them, and the bystanders eased away. Was Thorne truly that frightening? Or had the reputation of a Guardian preceded him? Laurel was yet to see Thorne in battle.

She'd seen the disgust toward Guardians, but not so much the fear. Come to think of it, even Patches had been hesitant.

When Sparrow led them away, Laurel asked him. "Why do they fear Guardians so much?"

It felt like a silly question, considering he was a warrior, but she also felt there was more to it and wanted to learn more about their culture. Thorne slid her an indecipherable glance, considered, and then shrugged. "Perhaps it's because we're stronger, magically and physically. Or that us using metal can stop them using magic altogether."

"What do you mean?"

"If we use metal to pierce, cut, or wound a fae, or mana-warped monster, with our weapons, it can dampen their magic. Leaving metal in a fae's body will completely stop a shift, halt a spell, and…" His focus turned inward, sad. "Push your mana from your body in an excruciating way."

"You sound like you're speaking from experience."

"Rush and Clarke witnessed my aunt, Kyra, have a liquid

metal injected into her veins. They saw her mana pop out of her body. Then that bastard drank it."

Laurel shivered, knowing exactly who Thorne spoke about. "It was the Void. And Bones."

He nodded grimly. "They harvest mana like it's a delicacy."

Once Bones popped into her head, she couldn't get him out. The fury. The hate. The need for revenge. She was lucky to have gotten away with only her fingernails ripped out. They'd grown back. Twisted and warped, admittedly, but still they grew back. If she ever met Bones again, she wouldn't flinch. She would end him and his sick, black heart. The same went for the Void.

"Laurel," Thorne paused. "You good?"

She cleared her throat. Must have let her emotions slip. She nodded. "Let's go."

Sparrow took them through the strange underground world that was its own microcosm of the world above. They left the grassy knoll behind and ventured into a forest of elm trees where water dripped from the sky in a never-ending sprinkle of rain. Insects chirped. The smell of damp earth and wet leaves restored her mood.

Sparrow ducked and weaved through brush, skipped over fallen logs and damp blackberry bushes. After a five-minute walk, they emerged in a clearing where the sun shone brightly and a lone, wooden shanty sat in the middle.

On the porch, rocking in a chair, was a toothless, haggard, and ancient-looking orc. White hair tufted on the sides of his head. Wrinkles sagged his face.

Laurel stopped. Thorne raised a brow at her.

"He's old," she whispered. "How?"

"My guess?" Thorne rubbed his chin, stubble now forming. "He's paid for his possessions with his mana. Could be the only currency down here. And since mana is what keeps us fae immortal, he's almost out."

"But I thought you could replenish it."

"You can. But there's a way of giving your mana that takes a piece of your soul, of your capacity to ever hold it or sense the magic of the Well again. Think of it like filling up the bottom of a well with sand, reducing its ability to hold water. When that well is full of sand, it doesn't take long before you can't sense the magic of the Well at all. You become human. Or in his case, mortal."

"So he's no danger to us."

"I wouldn't go that far. He's kept these possessions down here with no contest. He's got something."

Laurel took a deep breath and let it out slow. She caught Thorne's eyes. "You ready?"

He darted a glance at Gunther, where all his questions might be answered. "Feels like I've been waiting my whole life for this."

CHAPTER NINETEEN

*T*horne strode toward Gunther's hut with single-minded tenacity. He was *this* close to getting answers, and his patience wore thin.

"Stop!" Sparrow chirped.

Thorne halted. His hand whipped out to catch Laurel on the sternum and halted her too.

He turned to the boy. "This better be good."

The boy licked his lips. "You were about to walk into a trap."

Thorne's brows winged up. Yep. That would do it.

He looked down at his feet, didn't see anything suspicious, but when he shifted his gaze to Gunther, the old orc threw his head back and laughed heartily, eyes crinkling, open mouth a black hole.

"What's the trap?" Thorne asked, cringing at the sound of the orc's wheezing laugh.

"It's, um." The boy seemed to shrink away from Thorne. "I, um."

"Spit it out."

"Thorne," Laurel admonished. "Give him a second."

The boy's shy eyes shifted to her in gratitude.

"If it helps," Laurel continued. "You can talk to me, and not Thorne. He scares me too sometimes."

Sparrow picked up a rock and threw it at the orc. A few feet away, the rock hit an invisible force-field and disintegrated in a spark of electricity.

"Wards," Thorne grumbled.

"What does that mean?" Laurel asked.

"It means," Gunther said as he stood up, creaking in his old age, "that you can't get in unless I let you in."

If Thorne had Fury, he could get in. The metal ax would obliterate the magic. He frowned, brooding in his bitterness.

"We don't need to get in. We just need to ask you a few questions," Laurel replied.

"Answer is no," Gunther shouted.

"You don't even know what I was going to ask."

"Come on, Laurel." Thorne touched Laurel on the shoulder. "Let's go. He's probably a waste of time, anyway."

"Now, I didn't say that." Gunther hunched and shuffled closer. "Tell you what, you ask your question, and I'll tell you if I know the answer."

"Well, that doesn't help us," Laurel replied.

"It will if you do something for me as payment for the actual answer."

"What do you want?" Thorne asked.

"Food."

Thorne turned to Sparrow. "What's the deal with meals down here?"

"They drop food down the chute every day, but you have to fight to get it."

"Don't want no chute-food," Gunther said. "Want fish."

"Are there fish here?" Thorne asked Sparrow, who replied with a dubious look.

"Yeah, but... they're ika fish. Too fast to catch by hand. Big, and they have teeth."

"What if we scorch them?" Thorne suggested.

"Won't work. Too fast."

There were a myriad of other spells he could try, but he had no idea if his mana stores would replenish down here in time for the impending battle, and without Fury, he would probably have to borrow from Laurel as it was.

"What about using a fishing line, bait and hook?" Laurel asked. "Make the fish come to us."

"What would we use for line?" Thorne turned his shrewd gaze to Gunther, then to Sparrow. Both gave no indication that they could help. To be sure, he raised his brows at both of them.

"If I could hunt my own ika," Gunther crowed, "do you think I'd ask for help?"

Thorne supposed not. He had no clue as to how to get the fish if they were too quick for magic and too fast for hands to grab. He wouldn't have much better luck if that was the case.

Laurel glanced at his long hair. "You know... we could cut your hair, as weird as that sounds. It's very long. It could be fashioned into a line."

Thorne's hand went to the tail of his hair and ran down the length. Cut it off? But he hadn't found Jasper yet. He shot Laurel a wary glance.

She smiled gently. "It's long and strong. We can split the strands and braid them together to make a long fishing line. Put a hook at one end, and a rod at the other, and we've got our tool."

Thorne's fist clenched over his hair. Seeing his turmoil, Laurel placed a cool palm on his bare chest and pushed him to the side, under a tree canopy, where they had a little more privacy. She kept her palm there and looked up at him.

Moments ticked by until the burn of her touch far outgrew the sensation where his palm met his hair. The blue of her Well-blessed markings seemed to get brighter with their proximity.

The hair was a constant reminder to never give up.

Laurel's palm slid up his chest, curved around the back of his neck, and held.

"Please let it go, Thorne," she said, eyes somber.

"You don't understand."

"I do."

"How?" The word was a whisper, a ghost.

"Because there was a time once when I held onto someone I loved too."

A lover?

Tightness constricted around his chest.

She let go of Thorne, eyes downcast. "I had a twin. His name was Lionel. And he was everything I wasn't. Funny. Smart. But he was always getting sick. Somehow he was the twin that got the weak genes. He died, and I lived. For years I blamed myself for being the one who survived. What made me so special? Why me and not him?" Her eyes teared up when she met his again. "And then my father said 'You can't base your future on the what ifs and dreams of the past. You can only work on the dreams of today.'" She rubbed her eyes. "Anyway. He was always spouting shit like that. I decided to put my energy into something I can control, into having a business where I could help others stay strong, and do you know what? I actually did help people. Lives were changed. The point is. Right here, right now, we put our energy toward something we can control."

Thorne's stark gaze landed on Gunther. "I need information."

"Right. So let's get it."

She made to move, but he let go of his hair and stopped her, bringing her back to face him.

"Is this why you work so hard?" he asked. "Every day you're up and running as though you have a kuturi squawking at your heels."

She gave him a sad smile and trailed her fingers down his braid. "I respect why you did this. In a way, it gives you the same drive that running gives me. And because of this, I feel I can say this: You're not alone anymore. I'm here with you. I'll be your drive. We won't rest until Jasper is safe. Trust me."

Something cracked inside of him. It hurt.

To avoid looking at Laurel, and making the hurt worse, he turned to Sparrow and walked over. "Do you have a knife?"

Sparrow darted a guilty glance to the orc who still stood a few feet within the boundary of his wards. He reached behind him and pulled a small bone carving knife from his waistband.

The orc shouted, "That's mine."

"Well you shouldn't have left your hut a few weeks ago when the wards were down," Sparrow replied and handed it to Thorne.

Thorne swallowed. He took his braid in hand, held the blade to the scalp, but couldn't do it.

Laurel put her hand over the knife. The look in her eye said that she had his back. She would do it.

Trust me.

Gravity failed and he floated, head dizzy, before suddenly crashing to his knees. His skin prickled hotly. Couldn't breathe.

Laurel's cool touch was an oasis. Fingers were on his shoulders, then pressing the sides of his head, fluttering around as she got herself in position. She lifted the tail of the braid. The knife pushed at the scalp.

No no no.

He squeezed his eyes shut.

And then... snip.

A freeing of weight. A sensation of floating. And Laurel.

Laurel behind him, pressing up against his bare back. Laurel's hands on his head as she used the knife to tidy the rest of his hacked hair. Wisps of white hair floated around and tickled his nose. And Laurel's emotions down the bond... compassion, melancholy... love?

His eyes snapped open. He craned his neck to look at her. Up. Up into her eyes where a fondness gazed back at him. No. It was too soon for that. She cupped his jaw and said with a raw voice, "I'll start on the line. Perhaps you can take the knife and find some wood to fashion into a rod."

WHEN THORNE RETURNED to Laurel with two thick, long sticks he'd removed from a tree, he found her tying off a long, thin and braided line made from his hair. He'd only been gone half an hour, yet the woman had not only created the line, but managed to convince Gunther to grind and shape a fishing hook out of stone. He watched from the tree line and marveled at the tenacity of the woman.

Not long ago, she woke from another time, and yet she'd accomplished so much. Faced with a changed world, Laurel had swiftly moved from someone who believed fae were things and feral beasts, to dancing with them in a club, and protecting a wee one in a prison. She'd somehow cajoled the grumpy orc to help secure her end of the bargain and convinced a timid fae boy to guard her back while she worked.

"How did you manage that?" Thorne asked, pointing to the hook.

"Oh, it wasn't hard." She smirked. "I only needed to remind dear old Gunther that the sooner he helps us, the sooner he eats. I know you fae have to do this exchange thing, but it really would be great to have someone doing something nice and not expect anything in return."

Like you? He wanted to say. Because it was true. He hadn't believed it at first, but Laurel was a quick study. If Thorne hadn't bonded to her, she would have learned about her powers all on her own. She didn't need him. This bargain she'd entered to help him find Jasper hadn't been about her needs at all.

Another unsettled feeling snapped between his ribs. This was not a feeling he was used to, and he was hesitant to put words to it, but the undeniable trust blooming in his heart grew with each act of her kindness.

Thorne took the knife and shaved off any lumps and bumps from the wooden length they were to use as a rod. He notched the end, and they tied the long line to it. When it was done, Laurel stood with a proud look on her face. She grinned and gave Sparrow an affectionate pat on the shoulder.

"We did it, buddy."

Sparrow looked up at Laurel as though she were the sun. She didn't know the kid from an inkeel, but she hooked her arm around his shoulders and tugged him to her side.

A rush of primal desire flooded Thorne's system. The wolf in him woke. Its gaze leveled on Laurel. Intensified.

She would make a good mate. She could protect cubs while the hunter was away. She was caring, kind, strong. A perfect mate.

"All right," Laurel said. "All we need now is bait. And I have just the right people to ask."

"Dare I ask?" Thorne replied, wondering if she had removed her underwear after all.

She looked pleased with herself and shrugged evasively. "Let's ask the natives and see."

Five minutes later, they had secured some scraps of food from some other prisoners. Mostly it was worms, bugs, and other insects foraged from under logs and dirt. As it turned out, it wasn't the underwear she used as currency, but the promise to leave the fishing rod to them after they left. Once again, she'd surprised him.

By the time they settled into position by the stream, Thorne was completely and utterly at a loss for words.

CHAPTER TWENTY

*A*fter Lionel's funeral, it had taken six months for Laurel's father to go fishing again. His declaration had come as such a shock. Lionel and her father had always done this together. The exclusive boys fishing trip was an easy task and suited Lionel's poor health, plus it was a cheeky way to get away from the "nagging" women in the family. While they would go, Laurel and her mother would spend the time pampering and doing mani-pedis at home. It had worked for everyone.

But that first day.

When her father had quietly dressed in his gear and packed the tackle box, Laurel and her mother had watched with heavy hearts. Today there would be no Lionel. There never would.

Laurel used to take the fishing trips for granted, and only saw them as a way she got to spend time with her mother, but her father needed her too. It had been too heartbreaking to ignore. She went with him. At first it was to spend as much time as she could with her father, of replacing the hole Lionel had left. Then it became about living for Lionel. It became about being someone worthy of taking his spot in life. She was the first twin. The bigger one who took more sustenance in the womb. It could have easily been the other way. It could have been her who got sick, or both of them. Or even her parents. But from that day forward, Laurel knew that she would never waste her time on earth again.

It was a pity it took the monotony of waiting for an ika fish to bite to remember those quiet moments of solitude fishing with her father. Just being present with each other. Her business had sucked too much of her time, and she'd stopped those important trips with her dad. Shamefully, she'd been so wrapped up that she hadn't even made Christmas the year before the nuclear bombs went off.

Sniffing, she wiped her nose and continued braiding a second line with the last of Thorne's hair. They might have enough for another one. Sparrow was trying to stab a fast swimming fish a few feet down the meandering river while Thorne manned the fishing rod from the shallows.

He needed some work on patience. He cursed and scoffed every time he gathered in his line and found the bait had been eaten, or worse, that the bait was there and not a nibble had been taken. Once or twice, whole pieces of the line went missing and they'd had to make repairs.

Smiling inwardly, Laurel appreciated the simple sight of the large, well-muscled fae doing something so familiar from her time. Gone was his long warrior's tail. A part of her mourned that. She knew what it meant to him, what it had taken for him to make the sacrifice, and what it meant about his faith in her.

In his rolled-up pants, smooth skin and sharp haircut, he was almost a perfect match to the type of men she dated back in her time. A slow bloom of heat unfurled in her lower stomach. In another life, she could almost imagine the two of them spending time together, relaxing by a river, fishing, camping, swimming—playing. Maybe she would splash him. He'd scowl, grouse for a bit, and then when she thought he had moved on from the joke, he would dive under the water and take her down with him. Water would envelope them. Embrace them. Then maybe while they were down there, he'd kiss her. Breathe air into her lungs. Keep her alive.

Her smile came out to dance on her lips and she had to bite down to contain her growing emotions. She glanced at Thorne.

Icy blue rimmed with electric blue already aimed her way. With breathless awareness, she realized he'd intimately felt the journey of her daydream.

Slowly, never breaking eye contact, she got up from her spot on the lawn. When she joined him, she stood at his side and watched the water meander past in the small river. If she forgot about it being a prison, it was peaceful there. The strange light warming their faces, insects chirping, rain pitter-pattering in the forest. Laurel closed her eyes and immersed herself in the moment.

"Why are you so driven?" Thorne's rough voice entered her reverie. "I mean, I know it was about your twin, but I want to understand more."

She opened her eyes and smiled sadly at him. "Lionel was the sick twin. I felt guilty at first because I was the one who grew strong in the womb. But then this turned into staying strong. To avoid getting the same sickness he did. When Lionel died, I needed to prove I was the right choice."

Silence ticked by.

"And how do you know if you are?"

"See... that's the thing. I used to think the more successful I was, and the fitter I was, the better I was, but now I look back at how I lived my life, I realize how many important things I missed while I was striving to be the best. I missed spending time with my family, the single most important people in my life, and I screwed it all up for green smoothies and spin class."

"I don't know what they are, but I can assure you, your family loved you."

"How could you possibly know that?"

The look he shot her, so open, raw and honest, dug deep into her heart. "Because you're not hard to love."

She stared hard at the ground. "And what about you?"

"Naturally, I'm easy to love too. Just ask Cloud."

Laughter burst out of her so hard and fast that she had to cover her mouth.

A smile stretched his lips. A dimple flashed in his cheek. And somewhere, fireworks went off.

Thorne's gaze turned serious. He took her fingers from

her mouth and reveled in her smile. She'd never had someone who looked at her like this. Like she was the source of his joy, the battery that sparked his heart.

"Why are you so driven?" she asked him.

A dark cloud took his smile away and his intense gaze shifted to the river. Laurel wasn't sure he would speak, but he did. And it stole her breath.

"Jasper was the only person I had in my corner."

It stole her heart because that was never the impression she had. "Are you sure?"

His burning gaze slid her way. "What do you mean?"

"It's just that… um… well. And this might be none of my business, but—" She took a deep, steadying breath. "Before I came through the portal with you that first day, Clarke told me a few things. She told me Rush has been trying to be there for you and you're cutting him out."

Thorne huffed. "Of course I'm not receptive. I've been on my own for decades."

"But is that really true?"

"What are you getting at?"

"Rush was cursed. You may not have been able to see him, but he was there for you. Clarke said he used to follow you around as a child. He used to leave you little carved animals. He would—"

"Fuck. How much have you talked about me behind my back?"

"Only a little. She wanted to give me some background since we're married."

A sharp retort was on the tip of his tongue, but he swallowed it down. "I'm not talking about this anymore."

Thorne shifted to get up, but Laurel stopped him.

"Don't, Thorne. Don't stuff this down in a dark place and let it fester."

He bared his teeth. "What do you know about it?"

Her eyes widened. She gasped. "Are you seriously asking me that? Everyone I've ever loved is dead. My whole world is gone, wiped out by some dickhead because I wasn't brave enough to withstand his torture." Her bottom lip trembled because it was the truth she never wanted to admit. If she had been tough enough to withstand Bones, or even strong enough to fight back, maybe none of this would have happened. She'd been helpless. "But if you let all this hurt and pain block your happiness, you will be lonely for the rest of your life. And it won't be circumstance that put you there, but *you*."

The truth echoed in the air, hanging between them. Hostility burned in his eyes. Laurel watched him fumble with the line for a few seconds before helping him.

"You're doing it wrong. Fishing is a study in patience."

She put her hand over his, but he wouldn't give up the rod. His knuckles whitened. The muscles in his torso were threaded and sinewy with agitation. Veins popped. There was a sense of a caged bear about him. One more poke and he'd snap, ripping her to shreds with claws and teeth. Exhaling deeply, she took her hand away and went to leave, but he spoke.

"I don't know how to be any different." The words were raw, deep, and rough.

The courage it took to say those words was evident in every rigid line of his body.

"Start with this."

She kept her hand on his and then ducked under his arms until she was between them. He stiffened. She adjusted their grip so his big hands engulfed hers on the rod. Body heat seared down her back. Breath ghosted her ear. Her pulse quickened.

Biting her lip, she murmured, "First we make sure the line will fly when released. No tangles. Then we pull back" —she lifted the rod—"take a step forward and then let go of the line when the rod is pointed straight ahead. You ready?"

She felt it more than saw it—his readiness. A hitch of breath, a thud of his heart against her spine, his slow and steady exhale tickling her ear.

"Let it go," she rasped.

Together, they cast the line. It zinged from their hands and landed in the deeper part of the river.

"Now put your finger here so you can feel the tension."

"I feel it."

She swallowed.

"Good. Now we wait."

"How long?"

Her eyes fluttered. "However long it takes."

She went to move, but he tensed, locking her in. No words. Just his solid stance, the weight of his stare—on her, not the water—and the prickle of awareness down the hot side of her face that told her he was shifting closer. Closer. Until he did the strangest thing.

He nuzzled into her neck, inhaled deeply, and then rested his teeth gently on the flesh between her neck and shoulder. That's all he did as long seconds ticked past. For a moment, she thought he might bite her, but then he unlocked his jaw and shifted his chin to the top of her head with a heavy sigh.

"We wait," he repeated.

She nodded dumbly.

And wait they did. Minutes passed. Five. Ten. Fifteen. They did nothing but brace against each other and feel the tension in the line as they watched Sparrow play downstream, giggling softly every time he stabbed a fish and came up short.

The weight of Laurel's lids grew heavy, and she hazily realized they'd been thrown down the chute during the night. Light still sparkled on the water.

"Why is it always daytime down here?" she asked with a yawn.

Behind her, Thorne took a breath and answered. "It's the manabeeze."

She craned to look up at him with questioning eyes. "What?"

"Remember I told you how stolen mana can be used for artificial purposes."

"Well, you didn't quite elaborate. You said the orc may have sold his in some bargains and that once gone, you can't replenish it."

"Right. So manabeeze are little balls of sacred energy. Some say our very soul. They release naturally from your body when you die. They buzz about until eventually they rejoin the cosmic Well. If you look closely at the ceiling, it shimmers. My guess is a vast amount have died down here over the past few centuries. The manabeeze are somehow trapped. Enough has amounted that it creates an artificial light."

"Ghosts," Laurel murmured.

"Pardon?"

"Just like the stars in a night sky, only brighter. I don't know if you're aware of this, or if time has erased the knowledge, but stars are suns from solar systems far away in space. But the sad thing is, by the time the light travels millions of light-years to us, the actual star would be dead in real time. So when we're looking at the stars in the night sky, we're looking at ghosts. It's a bit like this." She sighed. "I suppose it could be romantic."

"Why?"

"If two people who loved each other were trapped up there, they'd be together for eternity."

She glanced over at Sparrow. The boy was too young to lose his life down here. For stealing food?

Thorne let go of the rod briefly. His touch came to the side of her face where the binding rune itched. Tracing around it, she felt his frown in every place his body connected with hers. His stomach tensed, drawing tight across her spine. His arms bracketing her locked.

"I hate that they've done this to you, marred your face."

"It's temporary." Right?

She sensed he was about to say more, but then the line under their fingers *pinged*.

Years of honed fishing instincts launched into action. She locked the line around a notch they'd created and yanked.

"Help me," she gasped.

The line vibrated with tension and promise. She yanked, gathered the line. Yanked. Gathered. Each time the fish came closer.

"We caught one!" Thorne exclaimed.

"Not if you stop reeling it in."

"Right." He joined her again, keeping the line from unraveling and drawing the fish in.

With each tug, a shadow popped under the water, coming closer and closer until finally it broke the surface, flip-flopping about. It was heavy. Thorne took over and hauled the three-foot beast onto land where he clubbed it and then held it up with an incorrigible grin.

"Dinner."

CHAPTER TWENTY-ONE

Thorne kept watch while Laurel slept. After they'd reeled the fish in, she was dead on her feet. He'd gutted the fish, cooked it on a campfire, and the three of them ate in companionable conversation while the nasty orc watched from his side of the ward. Gunther would give them information, but not until after Thorne was clear about who was running the show.

Thorne didn't think they would be called into battle immediately. Having their first ever Guardian would be a draw card. They'd want to advertise the battle and find an opponent worthy enough of bringing in a crowd. Someone who would likely have beef with the Order.

That's what he'd do, anyway. It would make for the better show.

He threw around options in his head as he continued to fish while Laurel and Sparrow slept. Standing in the river shallows, waiting for another bite, strangely settled him. It didn't take long before his tension ebbed away and a calming peace washed over him.

Enjoying the moment, he kept fishing. Even when he caught another, he threw in a line for a third.

He felt the unseen eyes of other prisoners all around him, always watching, waiting for him to slip up. It wouldn't happen. Hours later, he'd caught a total of three large fish and kept them in clear view of Gunther by laying them on the lawn between their camp and the wards. It was probably courting danger, knowing many other eyes were wanting, but he couldn't help himself. The orc had the balls to bargain with a Guardian, then he'd suffer the consequences. *A study in patience*, Laurel had said. He was beginning to see the benefits in that. They would get their information, whether now or later didn't matter. And they would get it on their terms.

With the fish caught, and not much else to do, Thorne found himself staring at his reflection in the river water, pondering over Laurel's words earlier about not having someone in his corner. Rush's curse had made him invisible and untouchable. It wasn't the first time he'd heard Rush had been around Thorne as a child, and the more he thought about it, the more he saw old memories in a new light.

The time when he'd been a tribute to the Order, and pushed into the waters of the ceremonial lake, there had been Guardians who'd strangely fallen in the water. Thorne's young mind had reasoned that it was his own kicking and screaming that had somehow pushed those

Guardians in, but now he knew the strength it took to move someone as solid as him. If those Guardians fell because someone had pushed them, someone like Rush, then it was true—he'd been around. And the act of touching those Guardians would have made Rush violently ill from the curse.

That notion sank in. His father had made himself *ill* trying to protect him.

There were other times Thorne had noticed Rush's presence.

Once a group of young wolf shifters had teased Thorne about his lack of parents. They'd been playing by the Whispering Woods near Crescent Hollow, and Thorne distinctly remembered more than one of them accidentally hitting themselves with the sticks they'd been playing with. They'd thought the spirits of the woods had come to tease them.

Thorne rubbed the back of his neck, contemplating. Perhaps he should reach out to Rush and Clarke. Let them know where they were and to check on Laurel's other friend who would wake soon. Laurel would want to know.

A communication spell through water might work. He had a blood link to Rush. The Well would connect them. Thorne used Sparrow's knife to cut his finger and drip blood into the river. Then he allowed a tiny drop of his mana to drive the spell. The water shimmered a bright blue, and then Thorne mentally sought out Rush. Because the Well connected everything in Elphyne, if Rush was also around water, he'd be alerted by a glow.

It took a few goes, a few drops of blood and a few of

mana, but eventually an image formed in the reflection. It was dark and shadowed, but Thorne made out branches and night sky. Then a tense face loomed over. White hair. Golden eyes. Rush.

"Thorne?" Rush said, voice hollow through the connection.

Because it was never just Rush, a shock of red flashed over Rush's shoulder. Clarke poked her head into view. "What is that?" she asked curiously.

"Communication spell," Rush explained. "Works best between blood relatives."

"Cool." But then Clarke narrowed her eyes. "Hi Thorne. What's wrong. Why are you calling?"

"You mean you don't know?" Thorne joked knowing she hated that she couldn't control her visions.

"Har-har," Clarke replied. "Very funny. When did you get a sense of humor?"

Rush pushed her out of the way so his face filled the view. "Is something wrong?"

"Not exactly." Thorne scrubbed his newly shorn hair. "Have you returned to the Order?"

Rush shook his head. "We've only just arrived at the site where Clarke thinks she'll find her friend. But"—Rush's gaze hardened—"you wouldn't be asking that if you were at the Order."

"Willow is fine," he assured Rush. "It's just that I left with Laurel. We've got a lead on Jasper."

"You were supposed to wait for me."

"I didn't."

Silence.

"Okay. So what's the plan?"

"We're under the hill."

Rush's eyebrows lifted. "You mean, under the Ring?"

Thorne nodded. "Laurel's plan. Trust me, if I knew about it, I wouldn't be here."

Thorne could almost feel Rush's exasperation through the connection. "These human females are hard to deny."

"I heard that!" Clarke called from the distance.

"I'm calling because I think you should know where we are. Just in case."

"Do you need help?"

"Not at the moment."

"Understood."

Thorne darted a glance to Laurel's sleeping form, then back to Rush. "Laurel is sleeping, but she would want me to ask about her friend."

"Not much we can tell you at this stage, but now that we know this connection spell works, I'll try to contact you when we know more."

"Until next time." Thorne dipped his chin.

Rush nodded and the connection ended.

Thorne collected the fishing rod and went back to where Laurel and Sparrow slept huddled together. He settled down, with his back to Gunther, and kept his eye on the forest where he sensed their voyeurs. The fish were behind him, and there was nothing between the fish and the wards. But if anyone else tried to steal the fish, Gunther would see. Knowing how long it had taken to catch the fish, Thorne was sure Gunther would sound an alarm.

Thorne stayed like this until hours later, Laurel began moving in her sleep. She twitched, frowned and whimpered. Must be a nightmare.

Leaning over, he trailed his knuckles down her rune-free cheek and sent calming emotions down their bond. Within moments, she settled and then didn't wake until he supposed it was morning. There was no way to tell with the artificial light.

She sat up, rubbing her eyes. "How long was I out?"

He shrugged.

"Right. No way of knowing, I suppose." Stretching, she met his eyes. His were still locked on the way her lithe body moved. His inner wolf paced restlessly. Since he'd almost marked her when they'd been fishing, it had set off a chain reaction of primal instincts. He'd teased the wolf with completion, now it wanted to finish what he'd started.

It wanted to bite the sexy human.

It wanted to mate with her.

It wanted to keep mating with her until she was tired, spent, and satisfied, but still hungry for his cock. Until she looked much like she did now, after sleep. Puffy eyes. Rosy cheeks. Plump lips. Messy hair.

She smiled hesitantly at him. "Your turn. I'll keep watch."

His brow lifted with indignation, to which she returned with a roll of the eyes.

"You need your rest for this coming battle," she insisted. "Even big strong warrior types like you need rest."

"Not going to happen. Let's speak to Gunther first." He pointed to his stash of fish. "We have plenty to pay him with."

"Oh great. Well done, Thorne. I can't believe you caught more!"

He had the sudden urge to go to her, to bask in her praise. He wanted it.

Laurel's mood sank when her eyes hit Sparrow, still fast asleep. "He's so innocent like this."

Thorne shrugged. "Not too innocent to get put in here."

She shot him a glare. "Do you even know what he did?"

"Doesn't really matter. He's in."

She clicked her tongue. "That kind of attitude sucks. What are you fighting for, Thorne, if not for a world where injustice doesn't rule? I think we have a duty to this kid. The system here has failed him."

He opened his mouth to retort. Then shut it. She was right. And Thorne knew better than anyone about collateral damage from a broken system. He'd failed in his duty recently. A young Guardian wolf shifter had died. Cloud had berated him for it.

"We'll work something out for him."

"Really?" Her eyes lit up, and it was everything Thorne wanted to live for.

That hope.

Trust.

Validation.

He cleared his throat and bent over Sparrow to wake him gently.

"Nap time is over," Thorne said.

Groggily, the boy woke up, but he didn't complain. Tough kid. Thorne handed Sparrow's knife back to him and kneeled until they were at eye level. At first, Sparrow blanched, but then Thorne spoke, and Sparrow's eyes widened to big saucers.

"Thank you for the loan of the knife," Thorne said.

"Y-y-you said thank you," Sparrow stuttered. "Y-y-you owe me."

"Well, look at that. So I did," Thorne agreed, a twitch to his lip. "Guess that means you can now make me do anything you want."

"Keep me safe," Sparrow blurted.

"Already doing that. Pick something else."

A small frown between those tiny brows. "Keep me… fed?"

"Try again."

"Help me escape?"

"That'll do. Agreed." Thorne clasped the boy's hand and sent mana into the agreement, marking it as binding between them. "We will get you out. Alive."

He leaned down closer and whispered, "Don't forget to be specific. If we didn't specify the alive part, escaping could also mean in death."

"Oh. Got it."

When Thorne straightened, he found Laurel smiling at him. And for the first time in a long time, he didn't revolt. He smiled back.

Together, they strode toward the barrier line for

Gunther's warding. He held up the catch of three fish by the tails. "I think you've waited enough."

Gunther, who'd seen them coming, had come off his porch chair to meet them with a sour look.

"Tell us what you know," Laurel demanded, chin up.

A rush of affection surged in Thorne. It was enough for Laurel to dart a questioning glance at him. And what do you know, he Well-damned smiled again. When he turned that smile toward the orc, it turned wicked. He let his fangs elongate.

"If we're satisfied with your information," Thorne said. "You can have the fish."

"The king's guard paid me to bring Jasper in."

"Which king? Mithras?"

"Yes."

Thorne narrowed his eyes. "How long ago?"

The orc shrugged.

Laurel, the brazen female that she was, arched her brow and took the fish from Thorne's hands. Or tried to. It was heavy. In the end, she decided to let him keep hold and put her hand beneath the catch. Fire sparked on her fingertips.

"I don't have any problem cooking an early breakfast," she said. "I'm sure we have plenty of others watching in the wings who will want what we're too full to eat."

Gunther raised his palm, crinkled eyes widening. "He's the champion," he blurted. "Or he was the last time I fought."

Shock reverberated through Thorne. Jasper was the champion? Pushing his reaction way down, he continued.

Now they were getting somewhere. "Is Jasper still the champion?"

"I don't know. The champion gets his own quarters, separate from down here. I ain't seen it, but heard it's real luxury."

"And you have no idea if he's still fighting?" Laurel asked.

"No. Now can I have the fish?"

"I don't know." Thorne rubbed the stubble on his chin. "Doesn't sound feasible that they would be able to hide a Guardian in plain sight, fighting in the Ring all these years."

"They put a mask on him," Gunther added. "It's metal. Hides his face."

A snarl ripped out of Thorne. His voice came out animalistic. "Metal? How is it the Order hasn't discovered this?"

"They painted it to look like bone. Maybe done some other things. But…" Gunther hesitated.

Laurel's flames sparked brighter.

"The mask stays on because it's bolted to his flesh. Even a Guardian can't resist the magic halting effects of metal piercing flesh. They force him to start the shift, then put the mask on. When he fights, he's frozen mid-shift."

Cold fury settled in Thorne's stomach. He'd heard of an undefeated beastly warrior of the Ring, but never had he imagined it would be a wolf shifter. Rush and Clarke's enemies had used that tactic on Kyra to halt her shift. They'd put a bullet in her and left it in. Until the bullet was clawed out, Kyra had been stuck mid-shift, a grotesque half-beast, half-fae. A permanent mask would also hide Jasper's distinguishing Guardian tattoo, eliminating any chance of discovery by the public.

The metal being a part of him could have been what was stopping Thorne's scrying attempts at finding him too.

But what about his other tattoos? Jasper had a myriad of them over his body. He'd sullied his skin as much as he could, gotten tattoos, and brawled and reveled regularly as a way to counteract his pretty face. He hated that his appearance took after the ethereal beauty of his father, the king.

Jasper had been here all along.

Sparrow let out a pained shout. When Thorne looked over, the binding rune on Sparrow's cheek glowed. He was being called to the Ring.

No. Not now. Thorne wasn't finished questioning Gunther. But as the rune glowed brighter, burned hotter, he knew they were out of time.

Thorne threw the fish at Gunther's wards. He leaped at Laurel, took her hand, and then grabbed Sparrow just before the transference spell finished activating. And when it did, all three of them teleported.

A whooshing displacement shot his equilibrium, but he dared not release his hold on Laurel or Sparrow. If he did, Laurel and he could end up in pieces. When the transference was over, and the dust settled, they found themselves standing in the middle of a large oval dirt stage. A multi-tiered crowd roared around them. And twenty feet away were two other prisoners, just coming out of their transference, getting ready to fight.

They were in the Ring.

CHAPTER TWENTY-TWO

*T*he roar of a crowd surrounded Laurel.

It took her a moment to gather her bearings. Sparrow had been called, and Thorne had latched onto Sparrow and her, so they all came. They were in the Ring.

About two-hundred feet long, and one-fifty wide, the fighting arena smelled like dirt, blood and urine. Sky and sun above. A twelve-foot-high wall surrounded the fighting floor. Three closed gates led somewhere and were possibly the only way of escape. Laurel shielded her eyes and looked higher. Three levels of bleachers housed patrons cheering from their seats—what looked like fae gentry and the echelon of Elphyne were on the ground level, then the general public were on the next two. It was like a football game. Only, there was no game. No. From the spilled blood in the sand beneath her feet, it was a fight for survival.

For the first time since she'd hatched her plan to find Jasper, she had doubts.

Worse. Could she keep Sparrow safe? The small boy was trembling with fear and as pale as the bone sword in their opponent's hand. Thorne looked ready to decimate as he scanned the arena for threats and presumably exits. Skin pulled taut over the slabs of hard muscle on his body. Fists flexed at his side.

"Stay behind us," Laurel said to Sparrow, eyeing the only other inhabitants of the Ring—two prisoners from under the hill.

Sparrow had been called up here on his own, which meant the people who ran this farce would make him fight those two much older, more capable, fae. Two adults against one boy? It sickened her.

To the side of the arena, behind a barrier of thick glass, she saw a cluster of guards or soldiers manically discussing the run sheet they had in their hands, most likely wondering how two other people had appeared with Sparrow.

So they were the ones to speak with.

Knowing Thorne would keep Sparrow safe, Laurel lifted her chin and strode straight for them. In all her experience rising to the top of her business, she learned the best way to succeed was to go in guns blazing from the start. The last thing she wanted was to be sent back under the hill. She must do this now.

"Laurel," Thorne growled, halting her.

"I'll be back," she replied with a look over her shoulder. "Look after him."

Laurel continued her brisk pace until guards manning

the boundary started to approach. Most of them were the big burly orc type, but a few were her size. She could take them on if necessary. She could burn them all.

But she'd only get one chance, and then they might use a spell to protect themselves much the same way Thorne had during training.

She just needed to talk to the organizers.

She dared a quick glance back over her shoulder. Thorne, Sparrow, and their opponents weren't engaging. Everyone knew something wasn't quite right. Good. The longer they avoided fighting, the better.

"I'd like to talk to the person in charge, please," Laurel said to the orcs blocking her way.

"How about we send you back downstairs instead?" one replied with a smirk at his comrade.

"How about I set *you* on fire?" she returned. Flames sparked at her fingertips.

They scoffed, unperturbed. They wouldn't be so complacent if she sent the full force of her power at them.

"You either get your boss, or I'll get him myself." She eyed the fae who'd turned from the run sheet with sharp interest. His nose had been recently broken. Long brown hair was fashioned into braids at the front of his face. A thorny headdress perched on his head like a crown. No. It wasn't a crown. It was a part of him. Antlers. He must be the boss with his entitled posture.

"Try," said the guard.

Back at the ceremonial lake, Thorne had said emotion was her trigger. So she let the anger already building in her body have free rein. She thought about them bringing Sparrow up here to fight two adult fae. A growl slipped out. Then she thought about the fact the boy had been thrown under the hill in the first place. Then it was the humans she'd released from the cages. Whether they were even alive. She thought about the unfairness of feeling guilty about how her world ended. At feeling partly responsible, just like Clarke had. It wasn't their fault. They were the victims. *It was Bones's fault. The Void's fault.*

Flame grew from her hands, licked up her arms and became an inferno of mana pouring out of her hands. The heat was a pleasant companion to her rage and she let it all shine on her face, oblivious to the sound of the crowd shouting their excitement.

She wasn't doing this for them. Sick, sick bastards.

She was doing this for all the victims of this cruel world, all the women who'd had men pulling their metaphoric nails out. Rage turned her vision red.

"I'm only going to offer this once," she shouted to the organizers, still safely ensconced behind the boundary wall. But they were engaged. "Let the boy go, unharmed, and we will voluntarily fight your champion."

The antlered fae broke away from the pack, a self-satisfied smile on his twisted face.

He sneered at Laurel. "You're in no position to *volunteer*. We can send you back under the hill until we're ready for you."

The audacity in his eyes made her fingers twitch, and she ached to raze the smug dismissal from his face. She leveled her stare on the stag fae and welcomed the power brimming in her soul. She opened the floodgates. Let it out.

The flames from her arms cast a glow of orange and yellow and white, but also emanated from her body, her skin. She felt nuclear, like she was going to explode. As power rose through her body, a gust of wind tousled her hair. At once, all glamor on her body melted away. The rune on her cheek crumbled to dust, and the glamor on her ears dissolved.

A half smile curved her lips. "Clearly, your binding rune isn't as powerful as me."

The breath of the collective crowd held. The organizers gaped. The guards paled.

"What are you?" The stag-fae stuttered.

"Unstoppable. And human."

Shocked silence deafened her.

She hurtled onward. "This will be your first and only chance to have a powered human with her Well-blessed and mated Guardian do battle. You can either accept that, or we leave. What do you say to my offer?"

The stag nodded, but then stopped when his colleague tapped him on the shoulder and whispered something. Returning to her with an indecipherable expression, the boss said, "Be the last ones standing in a fight with the champion, and then you become the champion." He held up three fingers. "We get you for three battles. If you win all, then you are free to go after the third. Consider your sentence over."

Remembering Thorne's warning to Sparrow about being

specific, she added, "Two battles, and you let the boy leave unharmed and unhindered after the first battle."

The organizers conferred, then nodded in agreement.

Laurel snuffed her flames out. She cast a glance over her shoulder and flinched at Thorne's furious face.

Surely he knew this was the only way to get what he wanted. She waited for his approval. He gave a surly nod and she released a breath. Good.

"We have a bargain," she said to the organizers and turned away. With any luck, they wouldn't realize they hadn't shaken on it, or made the binding, or whatev—

"Not so fast," one of them called.

Dang it.

Biting her lip, she turned back slowly. Sure enough, the boss had stepped onto the floor and approached, flanked by two guards. "We need to make it official."

To his credit, he repeated the bargain terms word for word. When it was done, he asked for Sparrow.

From the simmering anger down their bond, it was clear Thorne would have words with Laurel later, but for now, he squeezed Sparrow on the shoulder. "We will win. Don't worry."

Sparrow's eyes watered. "Than—"

"Don't!" Laurel interrupted. "We're not doing this for a favor. Thorne is a Guardian. It's his duty to protect Elphyne, and you're the best part of that." She turned to Thorne. "Where will he go after he's released?"

Thorne crouched low so he was at eye level with Sparrow. "There is a female fox-shifter who is the merchant of the vegetable cart in the south end of the markets. She is looking for someone to help her with her stall. If you permit, I will leave an endorsement on you to take to her."

"What is that?"

Thorne took Sparrow's thin arm and pointed at the inside of his wrist. "It is my mark spelled with a message. She only needs to touch it, and she will see. It may hurt a little."

Bravely, Sparrow nodded. Thorne's claw sprung from his fingertip and he scratched a shape onto the boy's soft skin. But Sparrow didn't cry. He nodded grimly once it was done and left the floor, joining the organizers on the sidelines.

Now it was just Thorne, Laurel, and the two prisoners. The murmurs and occasional shouts from the crowd meant they were getting restless. They'd expected a bloodthirsty fight to have started minutes ago. When Laurel glanced up, Thorne's mask of hate and anger was back. He stared at their opponents, but the irritation simmering down their bond was for her.

"Do you not agree with what I did?" she asked.

Still, he stared forward. "I don't agree with you thinking you speak for all of us."

Thought so. Damn. She felt a little bad about that. It ended okay, but like he said, it wasn't her place to decide. Thorne was more knowledgeable. He may have had an alternative solution that didn't mean they had to fight two battles.

"And you revealed your true identity," he growled. "You

put yourself in jeopardy. Even if we get out of this, even if the champion is Jasper, they could be gathering armies beyond the walls, waiting for it all to be over." Now he glared at her. "Did you even think about the consequences of that? Word will get around about a powered human. Word might get to our enemies. It's bad enough the Void knows about the humans waking from your time, but if Queen Maebh or King Mithras get wind of it, don't you think they would exploit powered humans too? Maybe they'll want payback for all the fae humans have harvested mana from. Maybe they'll come for you!"

He growled again and looked away.

Shit. She really did mess up. "Sorry?" she tried.

But not even the tempt of a debt placated him. All she could do was face the two prisoners, wait for the champion and hope she wouldn't die.

CHAPTER TWENTY-THREE

*T*horne sized up his opponents. Both hardened criminals had horns, were brawny, and scarred. But the most despicable part of this scenario was the bone weapons. One held a sword. The other, an ax. And they had been prepared to use them on Sparrow.

Something about that situation hit too close to home. Instead of Sparrow, Thorne saw himself as a child. He saw his uncle, Thaddeus, hand him over to the Order. Saw the Order pushing him toward the ceremonial lake—the inkeels.

Thorne bared his teeth.

It was time to bring Fury back. The binding rune on his cheek blocked his magic from leaving the arena, but Laurel had broken her rune. And with the bargain she'd made with the organizers, he didn't think there would be repercussions if he did the same to his own rune. Who cared if there was?

He could take them. He would have Fury. The battle would be as good as won.

The crowned stag took the podium at the end of the arena and lifted his arms like a showman. His voice echoed across the bleachers as he riled up the impatient crowd with shallow words and inflammatory taunts. The crowd would get their money's worth.

Thorne used the opportunity to talk quietly to Laurel.

"When you used your power, how much did you spend?"

"What do you mean?"

"Do you have a sense of how empty your personal well is?" He frowned at her confusion, so clarified. "The abundance of magic within you."

"It feels the same. Why?"

Crimson. She'd expended that much and felt the same? Truly she had a bottomless well, but it gave him an opportunity.

"How did you remove the binding rune?" He tapped his cheek.

"I just got angry and let myself fill with power. Like, really angry. I think you were right, and emotion is my trigger."

It could be a confluence reaction. He'd stopped her from getting too mad at the ceremonial lake, but hadn't now, meaning that without boundaries, she excelled. The problem with uncontrolled magic was that combined with unchecked emotion, it could have combustible consequences. Not only could the power pulled from the Well be stronger, but it could be more chaotic. There was no certainty that if Thorne did the same, he would have the same outcome, but he had to try. If for some reason he was cut from his ability to shift, he would need his metal ax. It would kill any magical creature they threw at them.

He had to try.

A stab of guilt pricked him at the thought of taking her mana again without her permission, but she had spared no thought to his opinion when she'd strode over to the organizers and demanded her terms. Nor had she consulted him at the Birdcage.

Slowly, he focused on their bond. Her mana leaped to him as though waiting for his call, such was the connection of a Well-blessed mating. Such was the harmony of their unique soul bond.

As he drew on her mana, he burned his own, sending it into every fiber and cell of his body, letting himself welcome his old friends: wrath, fury and rage and hate. More. More, he drew, until Laurel shivered and didn't know why. Until his cheek started to burn. And yet more he took and tried not to let the disbelief get into his system and taint the confluence. *So much power. And there was still more to take.*

If anyone found out about this, anyone like the human leeches from Crystal City, then Laurel would be in danger of having her mana harvested.

"... And they think *they* can dictate how the game is played in the Ring," the announcer continued. Thorne pushed his voice out of his head, ignored the consequent roar of the crowd, and concentrated.

With a crack like thunder, the binding rune crumbled on

his cheek, littering dust to the floor. Crouching, he distended a claw and scraped a rune into his right palm, the same rune as on Fury's handle back at Jasper's apartment. Now all he had to do was wait. Wait for the spell to find his ax, and wait for it to arrive in his palm. But when Laurel landed on her knees beside him, he wasn't sure they had enough time.

Her pallid skin held a sheen of sweat. Her head looked too heavy for her neck. Short dark hair was plastered to her cheeks. She looked at him with glassy eyes.

"Are you not well?" he asked.

No words. Perhaps no energy. She shook her head.

He took her hand, tested her pulse at her wrist and found it sluggish. Was this his doing? Had he taken too much of her mana, too fast? Well-blessed matings were rare and untested. Apart from Clarke and Rush, the last pairing was centuries ago. He should have searched the archives at the Order academy library before they'd left, and then perhaps he'd be armed with knowledge before attempting a drawing of this magnitude.

She will gain it back.

Simply by having her feet on the earth, she would start to replenish from the cosmic Well and rebuild her stores. Finding a source of power would be better, faster.

Thorne zoned back in on the announcer's speech. Something about making Thorne and Laurel pay for their disobedience. The hairs on the back of his neck raised in warning.

"What do we say to that?" the announcer shouted.

A roar of defiance merged with an undercurrent of

collective boos and disgruntled comments. The spectators wanted blood, and Thorne and Laurel had taken that away from them. They wanted compensation.

The announcer waved down the horde. "Never fear, my friends, I may have bargained for only two battles for their freedom, but I never specified how long those battles would be." A roar of excitement. "Or how many opponents they shall have." Even more excitement. "Or what species they will be fighting!"

Deafening.

The crowd was inconsolable. Thirsty. They wanted blood? Thorne would give them blood.

"Laurel, you may have used too much of your mana at once. Take it easy. Let me handle this." Thorne stood before the crowd and let his claws loose. He met Laurel's curious stare with steadfast certainty. "You may change your opinion of me after this."

Too tired to respond, she simply met his gaze.

The cacophony from the crowd grew to a stadium-trembling roar of white noise and sparks exploded between Thorne and the prisoners. Must be the signal to start.

Begin.

The prisoners rushed toward Thorne, their eyes full of fury and desperation. Unfortunately for them, there was another Fury, the one that arrived via transference spell into Thorne's hand. He clenched tight around the handle and almost sighed at the relief of having his sworn weapon back where it belonged.

A slow, wicked grin stretched his lips.

Upon seeing the ax, the prisoners balked, but only for a stutter-step, and then they kept coming.

Thorne widened his feet. Braced. He rotated the ax in his hand. Once. Twice.

His opponents split, intending to go around him. He snarled, held Fury to the side, and clotheslined a prisoner at the neck with Fury's handle. With the first opponent down, he kept swinging the ax around and embedded Fury's bit into the other fleeing prisoner's back. The prisoner bowed, screamed in pain, and then collapsed to the ground.

Thorne ground his teeth and yanked Fury out, but the prisoner's body lifted with the ax. He used his boot to separate body from blade and then slid a warning glance to the first prisoner on the floor. He wasn't moving. *Probably broke his windpipe.* Possibly neck.

Briefly, Thorne considered chopping those antlers off to use as a makeshift weapon, but the binding runes on both prisoners' cheeks flared blue, and they sank into the ground, heading back under the hill. Surprised, Thorne lifted his brows. He expected the transference spell to react differently. Perhaps there was more they'd neglected to tell Thorne about the binding rune. *Doesn't matter now.* No doubt they would continue to travel through the dirt until they landed somewhere under the hill, and if they died, manabeeze would escape their body and join the rest of the ghosts in the false sky.

He tapped the ground with his foot. Maybe the earth was spelled, and that's why no manabeeze could escape from under the hill. But that was a question for another day.

He lifted his face to the crowd, held his ax high and roared, "That all you got?"

The crowd cheered. He cast his gaze around at the tiered seating and tried to commit to memory the brutes and heathens who believed this sport was righteous. He caught sight of a cluster of black-coats, Unseelie royal guards with their eyes locked in the distance, somewhere on the opposite side of the arena. Thorne followed their gaze and found a group of red-coats, Seelie royal guards staring right back at them.

Thorne sneered. Perhaps he should shift to wolf. Perhaps he would break the boundary of the Ring and meet some of them in the stands. They might be tasty.

"Thorne?" Laurel asked, now holding Sparrow's puny knife as she stared at something over Thorne's shoulder.

He whirled and caught one of the arena gates opening, cranking heavily upward. Something pawed at the gap beneath. Dust clouds bloomed. Muzzles sniffed, jaws snapped in haste to get out. With each increment the gate lifted, more of the beasts became visible. One. Two. Three. Four waradas. Small and hoglike, their insectoid armor made it extremely difficult to pierce and maim. Unless you knew where to hit. But the pincers on the sides of their jaws were sharp. If just one of them got Laurel...

"Holy shit," she gasped.

"If you are cornered, strike beneath the jaw where it is tender," he barked at her.

Waradas may be small, but they were quick. Once again, he considered shifting to wolf, but the ax would have better luck cutting through the wararda armor than his fangs. The little beasts broke free of their containment and charged.

With his left hand, Thorne threw a blast of hard air, and then propelled himself forward in the slipstream. The waradas scattered from his spell, but Thorne caught two of them in the head, splitting their skulls before they knew what had happened. The other two had rolled and recovered, then charged him. One. Two. He chopped. They were down. Dead. He twirled like a dancer, swung his ax, and caught the final warada under the chin as it charged. It flew back, airborne, and then crashed. When the dust settled, nothing moved.

It was all over in a matter of seconds, but he'd got them all. Laurel was unharmed.

He thought.

He turned back to Laurel and his stomach dropped.

She stood at the center of the arena, unharmed, but it was what he saw behind her that worried him. Another gate had fully opened. Bright light shone from the tunnel, and the dark silhouette standing in the hollow was tall, bulky and humanoid. But it wasn't human. Nor animal. It was something between.

Tribal drums started beating. The crowed whipped into a frenzy.

The thing in the tunnel was head to toe black fur. Sharp claws protruded from gnarled fingers. It had a thick neck, broad shoulders, and a bushy tail. Was this a wolf shifter caught between shapes? Jasper? While his face was covered by a bone mask that only showed yellow eyes through two holes, shaggy brown hair and pointed ears aimed skyward. Thorne sniffed, catching the metallic tang on the air. Not bone. *Iron.*

A growl ripped out of him. Gunther had been right.

Fur covered any power-enhancing tattoos. The mask hid the Guardian teardrop tattoo. But it was Jasper. Thorne knew it by the champion's scent.

Gripping Fury until his knuckles hurt, Thorne stalked warily toward his old mentor, one eye looking out for more danger.

The tick-tick-ticking of the gates opening.

The thump-thump-thumping of the drums.

And then a gurgling, hissing sound Thorne would never forget in his life. Well-hounds. Without turning, he knew there would be one, maybe two or three waist high beasts behind him. Canine cousins of wolves, but warped by mana so much that it bled from their eyes in a stream of blue iridescent acid. But he dared not turn, for the most dangerous beast was to his front, on the other side of Laurel.

CHAPTER TWENTY-FOUR

*Y*eah. This wasn't good.

Laurel didn't know which was worse, the strange Doberman like dogs stalking closer behind Thorne, or the thing she knew was behind her, but was too afraid to look at. Thorne's hard eyes locked over her shoulder, and he took slow and wary steps toward her, almost as if he didn't want to startle what was behind her.

She squeezed her eyes shut, imagining the worst. Something from Stephen King's IT maybe, or a fricking T-Rex. Who knew with this world? Who knew what fricking monsters were going to attack next?

Something had happened to her earlier and she felt wretched. Like she needed to sleep for days. Her arms were weighted. The breath dragged into her lungs. And her lids drooped heavily. But after seeing the dogs with dripping eyes, adrenaline hit her system and she started to wake up.

Taking a deep breath, she reached for her magic and

held it ready. Plenty was still there, so it made no sense why she'd felt so woozy. The moment one of those dogs came at her, she was letting loose.

Thorne got to her side. Blue eyes crystalized with alarm.

"What is it?" she asked. "Behind me... no. Don't tell me. I don't want to know."

"It's Jasper," he grunted.

"Oh." Maybe that wasn't so bad.

And then a howl ripped through the arena. She slowly looked over her shoulder. Froze. That was *not* Jasper. That was a fucking werewolf.

"Holy mother of all."

"I'll take care of him," Thorne said. "You fire at the Well-hounds. Once they're burning, try to get the blade into them." He gritted his teeth. "No. Actually, you can't. I'll have to do it."

"Why?"

"Because the little dagger you have will be eaten by their acidic blood. The only reason my ax won't is that the Well-hound is a magical creature. Its blood is only acidic because of magic. My ax will nullify that. I'm not even sure if your fire will work on the Well-hounds. Their coats can deflect magic."

"So, I have to..." She turned fully to face Jasper realizing that her only other option was to fight him. She gulped.

"Just keep him busy. Throw fire at him, but don't... don't hurt him too much. Make a smokescreen. The metal mask will not only stop him from accessing his magic, but impede his sense of smell."

"Got it."

And then it was on.

The hounds leaped and Thorne whirled to fight, ax brandished high, and then cleaved down, taking his first hound. A devil come to life, his muscles bulged with deadly intent, and his eyes were lit by the blue fires of hell.

Laurel turned back to Jasper who ambled, slow but steadily toward her. Big wolf ears pricked forward over his mask. Shaggy brown and black hair, a matted mess behind his head. It was a small mercy his teeth were hidden. But not those claws. She licked her lips. "You can do this, Laurel."

Find your fire. Your only weakness is you.

Goddamn it. Those sayings worked better in picture frames on her gymnasium wall. The crowd roared louder. The drums beat faster. And Jasper threw his head back and howled from beneath his mask. The sound wrapped around her bones and rattled.

Good God. This was Thorne's mentor? He was *enormous*.

Flexing her fists, she waited for him to come. She intended to let him get closer before she released her flames, but in a blink of an eye, he launched, faster than her eye could see. She let the flames go on instinct but had no idea if they burned.

She was hit. Full body. By a big, furry, shaggy human-shaped monster.

She screamed and felt hands around her shoulders, claws digging into her skin. *Don't hurt him.* This was the person Thorne had been searching for. But the pain stabbing into her flesh, it was frightening. She didn't want to die.

She used fear to gather power. It gushed like a geyser and exploded from her in a blast that rattled the arena. Not fire. Just a tornado of air. How she'd managed that, or if Jasper had been disabled from the gust, she had no idea. Without waiting for the dust to settle, she got to her feet. An enormous cloud of arena dirt bloomed, masking everything. She tested her shoulder wound. It was shallow. She was fine.

For now.

The werewolf had caught her in its claws. It could have killed her, but it had gripped her more... out of curiosity?

She looked for Thorne in the screen of dust.

The crowd booed and her pulse sped up. Why were they booing?

Was it because they couldn't see through the dust cloud? Or was it...

A dog whined. Shrieked. Snarled.

"Thorne!" she shouted urgently.

She put her hand to shield her eyes as if that could help with visibility. Another whine cut off mid sound. Another snarl. The kind that sounded like a beast had something in its mouth and rattled from side to side. Twirling, she squinted, trying to see.

"Thorne!"

No answer. She coughed. The dust was thinning.

A shadow. Ahead. Was that the direction Thorne had gone? Or was she disoriented? Was it the werewolf—Jasper?

"Laurel!"

Her heart leaped. It was Thorne. Where? Where? She waved her hands before her face, trying to clear more dust-smoke. Thorne strode out of the bloom, more bloody than before. His ax dripped with a blue substance that hissed upon meeting the ground. Bright eyes scanned wildly, landed on her, and then burned with a light that squeezed her heart. He rushed to her, gripped the back of her neck and forced her to look into his eyes.

"You good?" he asked.

She nodded. "Just a few scratches."

"Jasper?"

"He's... I don't know. I was scared. I blasted. I... I don't know." *I'm sorry.*

Thorne gave a short, grave nod, and then pushed her behind him.

With nose lifted and scenting, he strode forward into dust. At least they could see the blue sky now. His hand moved from her hip, down to her hand, and forced it to a belt loop on his pants.

"Hold on until we get to a clear spot."

She nodded. Took hold. When she'd been body hit, she'd lost the bone knife. It was somewhere on the ground, buried beneath the dust. Thorne stepped forward cautiously, scenting the air, letting his nose guide them. Every so often, he would sneeze, clear his olfactory, and start again.

Suddenly, the boos stopped. The drums stopped.

Eerie silence.

The crowd cheered. Crazed. Dread coated Laurel's bones. What the...?

A thud. Another thud.

Footsteps?

Something drew close.

Out of the dust, a face from a horror movie. Yellow frenzied eyes peering from a full-faced mask. Gnarly claws. Brown fur.

Thorne ran to meet Jasper, but Laurel was still holding onto him. Her arm almost ripped from its socket as she was dragged along. She unhooked from his belt loop just in time. Thorne clashed with Jasper. He used the ax butt to push against Jasper's chest, forcing him backward. They wrestled. Went to the ground. More dust and sand exploded.

"Jasper!" Thorne roared. "It's me."

Laurel felt like a dumbass just standing there, but what could she do?

Nothing Thorne did changed Jasper's single-mindedness. The feral glint in his yellow eyes raged as he attacked.

"Have to get the mask off," Thorne muttered, grunted, and tried to rip it from Jasper's face.

Jasper howled in pain and lashed out.

"Fuck!" Thorne cursed.

Blood ran from Jasper's neck, where the mask was attached.

"What if I melt it off?" Laurel suggested. "Can we insulate his skin at the same time, as you did at the lake?"

Thorne pushed the long ax handle across Jasper's throat, choking and incapacitating him.

"Do it," he bit out. "I'll insulate him. Do it now."

Thank God. Fire was the only spell Laurel knew how to do well. She summoned her magic, let the flames build until sparks ignited at her fingertips.

"Move!" she shouted.

Thorne jumped back. She thrust her hands at Jasper and sent napalm his way, hoping to dear God that Thorne's insulation spell kept the heat, as well as the fire, from Jasper's skin because if it didn't... she didn't want to know.

"More!" Thorne yelled through the inferno. "Hot. Like at the lake."

She did as was told.

More fire. More flames. More heat. Until she felt giddy with it.

"Enough!" he roared.

Laurel snapped her hands closed, shutting the valve to her power. When it cut off, she felt like it rebounded in her body. Waves of dizziness came over her. The same lethargy she'd experienced before hit. But this time, she rolled to the side and vomited as she vaguely heard Thorne's voice.

"Jasper. It's me. Fuck, what have they done to you?"

Laurel gagged again. God, she felt awful.

A male moan. A groan. "Rush?" A gasp. "Rush." A whimper. "You came. You... I don't deserve it. I don't deserve to be rescued. Not when I left you... not when—"

"Hush, Jasper. It's Thorne. Not Rush."

"No. no. No. I shouldn't have let her die. Véda. She was pregnant. Not her fault. I should have said something."

"Jasper!"

"I looked after your son, just like you asked. I kept an eye on him for you." Another moan. A whimper. "Please don't hate me."

The air was clearing. The dust was settling. Laurel heaved in a breath to steady her nausea. The shadowed silhouettes that were Thorne and Jasper became clear. The plan had worked. The mask was now a molten puddle beside the fae with shaggy brown and black hair, pointed ears, and deeply tanned skin. Blue glowing marks circled his neck like a collar. He was naked. Distraught. Tortured. Manic.

Jasper's untamed eyes fixated on Thorne but failed to see him.

The look of anguish in Thorne's expression said it all. Jasper wasn't quite right in the head.

Drip. Hiss.

Drip. Hiss.

Laurel frowned. What was that?

Drip.

Hiss.

She turned her head, glimpsed black animal, blue leaking eyes, and then fangs snapped at her. She lifted her arm to shield herself. Teeth clamped down.

Pain exploded. Her scream curdled. Something snapped. Bone. Oh God, it was her bone. Crushed. The hound dragged her backward by her arm. Kicking and whimpering, she tried to keep up so the arm wouldn't tear from her body. That was her fear.

A roar of fury rattled from somewhere and she couldn't tell where. Tears ran in streams from her face. She managed to look down her body, to where she'd last seen Thorne.

Time stopped.

Pain stopped.

It was as though they'd split the fabric of the world and there was a space between breaths as her eyes met Thorne's across the distance.

His eyes were *torn*. Just like his emotions hurtling down their bond. Desperation. Indecision. He had Jasper in his grasp. Finally...

And Laurel?

What was she to him?

Nothing.

She exhaled. Tears brimmed. And she hurtled all her fury and rage and pain back at the beast still locked around her arm. She had no other weapon but her magic. Drawing on it as best she could, she sent fire at the beast, but it fizzled and sputtered as it hit the hound. Flames died out... doused as though drowned in water.

Helplessness swamped her. Magic didn't work against the beast.

This is it. I'm dying. Maybe this was why I was given a second chance. To help Thorne rescue Jasper. Now it's done.

Her eyes shut. Blackness. Then opened heavily. Tired. Tormented.

An anguished roar created an earthquake. She heard

thudding. And then the beast latching onto her arm was gone. Or maybe her arm was gone. She couldn't tell. It hurt so much. Acidic fire burned in her veins.

"Laurel." Thorne's sweet, rough voice. "Hold on."

Pressure on her arm... or what was left of it.

He kept his hand clamped on her wound, a deep furrow to his brow. "You'll be fine. They have healers here. I can triage a little. Here. Bite down."

He put something between her teeth. Hard. Dirty. Salty. The ax handle. It barely fit between her teeth, but it did the job.

Searing white-hot agony engulfed her arm. She screamed around the wooden bit, eyes streaming with tears. Blinking, she craned her neck and saw a bright light bleeding from Thorne's hands. He was doing something. Healing her somehow... the pain ebbed like cold water had been thrown on it.

She spat out the handle.

"Jasper?" she croaked.

Thorne's brows lifted in the middle. He looked beyond Laurel's body. She followed his glance and found Jasper, safe, and sound. One knee up, elbow resting on it, looking at them with a strange curiosity, as though he should know them.

Those blue glyphs around his collar winked in the sun. Like Thorne, Jasper was well built. But where Thorne was hewn from rough rock, Jasper was smooth marble. Stunning face, perfectly carved, almost pretty in his masculinity. The rest of him was solid, strong and infallible, but for his mind and confused golden gaze.

"He's cursed," Thorne explained quietly. "Doesn't quite remember me. But I don't think it's the curse that's done that to him. I think his mind is protecting itself. He's been tortured. Maybe it's both."

A hush swept over the crowd.

And Laurel's heart stopped. This was the moment of reckoning. Would the organizers send more opponents out? Was this enough to beat Jasper?

As if reading her thoughts, Thorne grit out, "I won't kill him. I'll kill everyone in the crowd if they try to make me."

Turned out, they didn't.

Jasper's blue glyphs flared brightly. He howled in pain, clutching his head.

"No!" Thorne shouted. He darted a panicked glance to Laurel's arm then back to Jasper. "I can't." He choked. "I can't get to you, Jasper. *I'm sorry*."

Then, like the transference spell that had taken the first prisoners, Jasper started to melt into the ground. All around them, the animals did too.

"I'll come for you," Thorne shouted, and then one by one the hounds and Jasper all disappeared until nothing but blood and acid stains were left.

"Ladies and gentlemen," shouted the announcer with a note of disdain. "We have our new champions!"

CHAPTER TWENTY-FIVE

*T*horne glared at Laurel. Bitterness leaked from his eyes like the acid from the hounds, and it was all directed at her.

She was to blame. She was wounded. She couldn't protect herself. She led them here.

Here—where he'd found Jasper and lost him. Thorne's entire life had boiled down to that moment when he couldn't save the male who had saved him.

He'd chosen her instead.

Pain squeezed his heart at the image of Laurel being dragged by one of the hounds he'd failed to dispatch. The sight burned into his retinas. The blood. The caustic acid. Her blood-curdling scream. His hand trying to stem the bleeding. Her pale face and blue lips and blood pooling on the ground beneath them.

He sucked in a deep breath, let air fill his lungs, and then *roared*.

It frightened Laurel. She balked from his touch. His fingers slipped from her blood-wet arm. But it didn't matter, the bleeding had stopped. It wasn't as bad as he'd originally thought, just messy. The healers would take care of the rest.

He roared again.

And the crowd thought it was in victory.

Not again.

He rubbed his aching chest. *Not again.*

"Thorne," Laurel tried. She reached for him, but he shook her off.

Storming to his feet, he picked up Fury, and then scooped Laurel into his arms. She was his now.

CHAPTER TWENTY-SIX

Thorne carried Laurel with confident strides toward the gate leaving the arena. She felt safe cocooned in his arms, protected by his body, despite the turmoil coming from him. So much pain, confusion, and just... feelings. It suffocated Laurel. Full body trembles wracked her body. Her arm stung, itched, and she was afraid to look at it. But it was functional. Her fingers moved. She could bend at the elbow. Thorne had saved it.

He'd saved her.

The enormity of what had happened sank in.

He could have let her die. There was a moment she wasn't sure what he would do. But he'd chosen her. Over Jasper.

The words kept repeating in her head—he chose me—along with disbelief. Everything after that happened in a blur.

They stopped at the exit in the shadow of the tunnel that

led from the arena. The smarmy announcer waited for them.

"You think you've won?" he sneered. "Maybe this time. But you'll be back for another battle, and we'll be ready for you."

Thorne's return stare said he wanted to rip the announcers crown of antlers from his head and then gut him.

"What did you do with the champion?" Thorne pulled Laurel in tighter.

"He's not the champion anymore. You two are. At least for tonight. Enjoy it while it lasts."

The ground rumbled. The walls shook. Thorne leveled his glare at the announcer. "Don't make me repeat myself."

"Relax. He's gone under the hill. He'll be back for a rematch. We can't let the crowd miss out on that opportunity." Sweat over the announcer's brow betrayed his nerves.

"When?"

"Whenever we decide."

With that, Thorne turned and called for a healer like he owned the place.

Laurel patted Thorne's chest. "Sparrow?"

His eyes softened on her and then hardened as he turned to the announcer, still watching from the wings. "Where is the boy?"

"We let him go."

"You're not holding him?"

"We don't need another mouth to feed. He's gone with the crowd."

Laurel breathed a sigh of relief. With any luck, Sparrow would be just about at the market stall with Thorne's acquaintance. Still, she couldn't help but worry.

"Where is the healer?" Thorne barked.

"You'll get one in your room," the announcer replied. He gave them one last scornful look and then shouted some directions to the guards and left. Five guards weren't enough to hold Thorne back. One look at his battle-ax told them that. But they did their job anyway. Because if Thorne got through them, there were probably more somewhere. Thorne was strong, but not invincible. They escorted Thorne and Laurel through a labyrinth of dark tunnels until they came to a stone staircase and went up.

At the top of the stairs, they walked down a corridor to a single bolted door at the end. Waiting was a slim, female elf who pushed through the soldiers to get to them. Voluminous pantaloons gave Laurel pirate vibes. Various bottles and tinctures dangling from her belt tinkled as she moved.

Thorne gently put Laurel on her feet.

"Are you hurt anywhere else?" The healer reached for her arm.

Thorne caught the healer's wrist and growled in warning.

The healer didn't balk. She glared back at Thorne. Laurel liked her already.

"What are your qualifications, healer?" Thorne demanded.

"I studied with the Royal Apothecary in the Autumn Court for fifty years under Rubrum rule."

Thorne let go of her wrist and gave a disgruntled nod.

The healer quickly took Laurel's arm, assessed no immediate threat to her life, and then ushered them inside the room.

The guards left them at the door.

Inside was a vast suite with polished marble floors. Furthest at the back, enormous ceiling-to-floor windows overlooked the arena. Before the window was a giant bed, bigger than king-sized, and with fabric overhangs draping from the roof. Closer was a series of lounges with velvet embroidered cushions. And before the lounges, inset in the ground and surrounded by brightly colored and glittering tiles, was a long Roman-style bath fit for at least ten people. Steam lifted from the vanilla-scented water.

"Sit," the healer ordered and pointed to two facing wooden benches before the bath.

Thorne helped Laurel to one bench, and then sat on the opposite with his fists on his thighs, glaring at them, silently daring the healer to make a wrong move.

The healer took Laurel's arm, tested it, and asked a few questions about pain and mobility. She cleaned it, found Laurel's skin was healed over, and then was in the middle of applying a salve that tingled and burned when a group of beautiful female fae came in. Dressed scantily, each carried different supplies. Food. Clothes. Drink. Perhaps wine. A large bowl of hot water, soap, perfume, and towels.

The healer massaged Laurel's arm, and she felt her entire body relax. Her lazy gaze wandered back to the new arrivals.

Three females. Two elves. One a brunette, the other with long black hair and a plump-lipped smile. The third was a pretty faun with cloven feet, small bumps on her head for horns, and voluptuous curves at her hips and breasts. All were stunning. Each wore similar pants to the healer, but where the healer wore a modest jacket, these wore revealing bustiers that showed ample midriff and cleavage. A rosebud tattoo graced their upper arms.

Rosebud.

After putting down their trays, two walked over and demurely offered each Thorne, and Laurel an elixir.

"For your energy restoration." The black-haired fae curtseyed.

Laurel accepted her elixir with a smile and drank it. She licked her lips. It tasted like ginger.

Laurel's curiosity turned to irritation when all three Rosebuds went to Thorne and began washing him, doing their best to lather him with extra attention. He stiffly watched Laurel, blue eyes blazing, hardly paying attention to the female attendants, even when their small hands slipped and caressed his body, inching lower over his abs, closer to his belt with each pass.

Could he not see what they were doing?

Laurel squirmed with irritation.

"Sit still," ordered the healer. "They'll relieve you next."

Relieve me!

As in... she snapped her gaze back to Thorne, then down to the very big bulge in his pants. He was hard. Was that there before or after the Rosebuds had touched him?

Sensing her unease, the healer clarified. "A warrior's body is flush with excitement post battle. It is customary for the champion to have his needs met. In this case, we have two champions. You'll have to wait until I'm done before your turn."

Oh, hell no.

The Rosebud attendants made cooing sounds and little feminine moans of appreciation as they washed Thorne. As if they were getting off from cleaning Laurel's man. And he *was* her man. She knew that now. He may pretend otherwise, but deep inside, he knew it too.

They'd gone through too much.

The black-haired elf with the killer lips bent to Thorne's ear and whispered something. When he didn't answer, or even flinch, the elf nodded to her companions. The faun began to unplug the buttons on his breeches. He did nothing. The brunette's hand slipped down his stomach, bumped over his abs, and dipped inside his pants, gasping in delight at what she found.

He did nothing.

Enough.

Laurel shot to her feet, yanked out of the healer's grasp, and slapped the Rosebud's hand away.

"Out," she ordered, pointing at the door. *"Out!"*

They blinked in surprise at Laurel, so she screamed it again. And again. Until everyone in that room scurried in fear. Even the healer picked up her things.

Laurel chased them all out, not satisfied until the last pair of bouncing breasts left the room. She slammed the door behind them, only vaguely registering the five guards still outside before they closed and bolted the door. She whirled back to Thorne.

He had just sat there while they fondled him. While they put their hands on places that even she hadn't touched yet.

She stormed back and stood before him, hands on her hips. His gaze still looked ahead, his fists were still clenched on his thighs. Was he... in shock?

No. He had a fricking boner. It strained against his pants. He'd let them touch him. The image of that slut's hand moving down his pants infuriated her. How dare he let her do that. Laurel wanted to shake him. Wanted to shout in his face and slap him.

"What's wrong with you?" she accused and shoved him squarely in the chest.

He barely moved backward.

Slowly, his eyes lifted to hers and her stomach bottomed out. Something dark flickered in the depths of his blue ocean. Dark, dangerous, furious.

"Me?" He tensed. Sinews and tendons became visible. Veins popped. Red-colored his face. "What's wrong with *me?*"

He stood so fast, Laurel stepped back. And then he advanced, crowding her space. Hot, demonic eyes glared at her. Another step back and she fell onto the bench, staring up at him.

"You're the one who got me into this mess," he growled, looking down at her. "From the very beginning, you've been a thorn in my side."

She gasped. A thorn in his side? Flabbergasted, she wanted to rail at him. She thought they were beyond this! After everything they'd been through.

Then it hit her.

Maybe he needed to work through it all verbally. Maybe they needed clarity.

She scowled at him. "You're the one who's so Goddamned angry and mean. You called me a whore!"

"You danced and dressed like one," he shot back.

"You're an ass!"

"You do whatever you want, no thought for the consequences."

"That was the point! You wanted me to. I did that for you!" Because she was so eager for his approval, she realized suddenly. All the fight left her. The next words came out a vehement whimper. A bitter accusation. "All you've wanted to do was to save him. But you saved me."

He blinked. Deadpanned.

"Why did you pick me?" Tears stung her eyes. Her throat clogged up and in that one question, the weight of the world suffocated her.

Why her?

Why did she get to live when others died? Why not her family, her parents, her neighbor? Why not someone who was a saint in her time, a soldier or a philanthropist? Why the woman who worked herself to the bone, and the woman who was afraid she was broken inside. Why. The. Fuck. Her?

Thorne growled, grasped the back of her neck, and

roughly lifted her to her feet. Gasping, her eyes flared. Her heart hammered painfully against her ribcage. He squeezed the column of her neck, tight and almost painful. He studied her, seemingly at a loss for words. All she could feel down their bond was a raging torrent of emotion. Nothing she could decipher.

"Why?" she whispered bravely. "Why choose me?"

Confusion warred with hate on his face. "Because... because..."

"Let it go, Thorne. I can take it."

His gaze hardened. But still, nothing.

"Say something!" She shoved him, caught the sight of her twisted nails, turned her fingers into fists and hit him again.

And again.

Each time she lost energy until she slid her palms up his smooth chest and stilled, over the thudding beat of his heart.

The rough pad of his thumb swiped up the delicate front of her neck and circled against the hollow of her throat, her airway. Was he going to strangle her? Snap her neck? She held him with her stare, the question in her eyes.

"Because I can't breathe when you're around," he rasped. "And I detest it. I can't think. I can't move. I've survived a decade without him, but the thought of a single day without you... I hate it. I hate that I chose you. Hate that I want you so bad I can't sleep at night. Hate that it took me so long to realize you want me too."

He crushed his lips to hers and flattened her to his hard front. Thank God. *This*. This is what she'd been waiting for.

A sign that he wanted her. That he needed her as much as she needed him. A strangled groan escaped him as his tongue demanded entrance to her mouth. She opened to him, and surrendered as he sank into the kiss with wild, hungry strokes of his tongue.

I hate that I chose you.

She shoved him away. "Fuck you, Thorne."

Heaving in ragged breaths, they both stared daggers at the other, but he refused to let her go. His fingers flexed against her shoulders.

No. Fuck him because she wouldn't be that person to him, the reason for his hatred, an excuse for his behavior. It wasn't fair. This wasn't her fault. She never chose to be mated to him. She never asked to be brought back to life. She didn't deserve it. Lip trembling, she broke the hold he had on her and turned her back on him, intending to go anywhere she could.

He grabbed her wrist, yanked her back, and slammed her body against his where he held it.

"No," he growled, eyes on fire... desperate. "You don't walk away from me."

"I do whatever the fuck I want. You hate me."

His eyes widened. Then his brows slammed down again, infuriated. "I hate me, Laurel. Not you. *Me.*"

Oh, God. No.

No, Thorne.

Her anger melted away. She cupped his stubbled jaw and he flinched. She brought his gaze back to hers. What stared back at her wasn't a fearsome Guardian, but a lost little boy.

Someone hurting for so long, the pain had become the poisoned air he breathed.

"I don't hate you," she murmured.

"You should."

"But I don't."

His breath turned ragged, rough, big. He gulped in air, pressed her to his chest. Harder. As though he really were afraid she would leave him. His heart pounded as though it would break through his flesh and leap into hers.

"Laurel." Panic tightened his deep voice. "I don't... I don't..."

"Know how to be different? I know," she said gently. "Let me show you."

More panic down their bond. More ragged breaths.

"Thorne," she whispered, lifted on her toes and drew close to his lips. "Let me show you how to be loved."

She kissed him. At first, he tensed, so she pressed her lips to his jaw. Then to the corner of his mouth. To the other side. To the bottom of his ear where she licked and suckled his lobe lovingly. Slowly, he relaxed.

"Let it go," she muttered. "All that armor you wear over your heart, let it go."

A long guttural moan rattled his body. His legs buckled. He spun them until he landed on the bench and she straddled him, still cupping his face. He buried his face in the crook of her neck, nuzzled into her hair and inhaled deeply. He held her tight. So tight.

"Don't..." he whispered against her neck. "Don't ever walk away from me."

It was more of a plea than a demand. And that's why she shook her head and replied, "I won't."

Another long shuddering breath left him. His teeth grazed over the skin running from her neck to her shoulder, kindling her desire. Beneath her, he hardened again until she felt it between her legs.

"Be mine, Laurel," he murmured against her flesh as he licked and suckled her sensitive spots.

"I already am."

His teeth sank in. She gasped, arching into him. Pain and desire held court in her body. The sting of his teeth versus the pleasure between her legs, at her breasts pushing against him, at his mouth as he suckled her skin, licking and paying homage to it. Part of her wanted him so badly, she rocked wantonly. The other part was aghast. He'd bitten her! Aghast, but delighted at his passion. His need for her was so strong, he played rough. She needed that too. Needed to know how much he wanted her.

She wanted all the fire. Even if it burned.

He came off her, pupils dilated, drugged, fangs elongated and bloody. Her blood.

And he was happy.

Her hand clamped over her neck. "Is it bad?"

The propriety glint in his eye sent shivers down her spine, right to where it pooled with heat in her groin. She squirmed. He steadied her on his lap.

"I marked you," he replied, voice thick and deep. "Now everyone can see that you're mine."

Laurel touched her tender skin, cupping her palm over

the bite mark. Her badge of honor, the markings of love. She grinned.

"Maybe next time, just buy me a ring?"

"I'll do that too. Whatever you want. And this is the one and only time my teeth will sink into your flesh. Mating is for life."

His lazy, heated gaze raked down her body, what he could see of it anyway. Deciding her shirt was a hindrance, he pushed it up her thighs and then growled with barely restrained longing as her underwear came into sight. He thrust his hips and watched where their intimate parts joined through the fabric. He did it again. She moaned as sparks of bliss shot from their connection.

Thorne pinned her with his icy-blue stare. Something wholly inhuman stared back at her. It was the wolf. Hungry. Demanding. Primal. "I'll have my mate now."

Claws distended from his fingers and ripped her shirt clear down the middle. She gasped in delight. Bolstered by her response, he did the same to her underwear, flinging bits of torn fabric until there was nothing left on her body. He drank in her nakedness, loved what he saw, and licked his lips.

"Let's get you cleaned up."

"I don't mind if you don't mind," she said cheekily. Dirty sex. She was down for that. Down for it dirty. Down for it clean. Down for it all.

He shot her a hard stare. "Laurel. I'm going to lick every inch of your body. I mind."

Oh.

Plumping the pillows of her bottom, he gave a self-satisfied grunt and then slapped her. The sting hit her ass and rocked her most sensitive part. She moaned in earnest. Then he carried her to the bath, where he lowered her feet first into the hot water. She slithered down his body and immersed alone, bereft.

The water was thigh high, but she sank until completely under. Heat infused her tired muscles. Laurel held herself underwater for a moment to collect herself. She was about to do this. With Thorne. He'd marked her. She was his.

I'll have my mate now.

A yearning so strong and pure surged through her. He'd finally let go of his hatred and put his passion to good use. And he was invigorating. She surfaced and found him staring at her, eyes at half-mast and full of greedy need. He idly played with the button on his pants, erection straining so hard it looked painful. He caught the direction of her gaze and a slow, indecent smile curved his lips.

There went those dimples, stopping her heart. *Damn, boy.*

Pretending she had control of her hormones, she paddled backward until her back hit the tiles and she rested her arms along the bath length. Her top half emerged from the water, and he clearly enjoyed the sight.

"Strip," she demanded.

With a cocky lift of his brow, he did. Slowly. He hooked thumbs in the belt loops and lowered his pants to the ground. No underwear. A body made from every woman's fantasy. Defined musculature, broad shoulders tapering to a narrow waist of perfection. The light fuzz of dark silver hair. And she knew she'd seen it before, but never like this. His cock was thick, proud, and long. Rock hard and waiting for her. He took it and squeezed.

"I like the way you look at me," he murmured hoarsely.

"Don't make me wait too long," she teased.

He slid into the bath and swam to her where he crowded her with his big body. All that power under the skin. Strong enough to cleave through those vicious arena beasts all on his own.

God, he was hot. Sexy. Heady. Vanilla steam everywhere. Coming right off his skin. His gaze dipped to the mark on her neck and flared with possessive pride. He kissed the wound gently, licked around it, and rumbled appreciatively. It drove Laurel wild. Then he came up until his lips hovered over hers, teasing with his breath. The look on his face showed he struggled to believe this was real too. That it wasn't some dream gone in the morning.

A drop of water trickled down Laurel's cheek and ran to her lip. His pink tongue darted out, licked, lapped, and then ran along her bottom lip until he sucked it completely into his mouth, biting between his teeth. The same teeth that had pierced flesh but were now so gentle.

That was it. The button on her restraint.

She pawed at him, touching everywhere, scratching, needing, dying... until she found his shaft, wrapped her fingers around it, and pumped. His breath came in ragged bursts as he thrust into her. But he didn't forget his promise. He licked and kissed over her entire face, shoulders, ears.

He nibbled, nipped, and drove into her hand. And then he drew back, eyes glassy and full of dark promises.

"You're incredible," he said.

Stupefied.

A breath later and he lifted her onto the edge of the bath. She gasped at the cold tiles beneath. He tasted her lips, her stomach, breasts, nipples. She threw her head back. "Yes, Thorne. Everywhere."

"Everywhere," he grunted and spread her thighs. Upon seeing her intimately, his eyes lit up. They flared blue. She was sure the color changed... became vibrant. Luminescent.

"Fuck." He gave a throaty groan as he stared between her legs. And then he buried his face there, feasting. He kept going. Licking and laving and thrusting with his tongue. He inserted a finger and stroked, plunged, and thrust deep into her core. Like a relentless machine, he worked her until her nerves coiled tight. Until she felt it coming but was helpless against it. Screaming, she broke apart, thighs quivering around his head with her release, fingers clawing into his hair as she struggled to hold on.

When the last of her throes died, he dragged her from the tiles, turned her, and bent her over the bath edge, face first.

"I'm going to have you like this," he growled softly into her ear. "And then I'll take you again with you on top. But for the first... like this."

She nodded and grinned. "For the first."

He slapped her rear. She jolted, felt the echo of her

orgasm between her legs, and then went liquid against the tiles. Couldn't speak. *Do it again.*

"And I'm going to spill my seed on your back."

She nodded. Whatever he wanted. God, that was sexy. Even the way he spoke about it. Men were so crude in her time. This fae was...

"So I don't get you with child."

Her heart clenched. She held her breath and turned slightly to lock eyes and then nodded. *My poor baby.* The damned unsanctioned breeding law had done a number on him. She placed her palms on the hard, wet tiles and lifted her rear in invitation. His big hand landed on her head, almost completely covering it as he pushed gently until her cheek pressed against the tiles where he pinned her.

For a moment, she froze, confused. Fear wanted to rear its ugly head, but... *Trust.* She trusted him. Completely. This was more about his fear.

For the first... like this.

Once the realization hit, and she'd surrendered to that trust, every feminine muscle clenched in anticipation. She was excited. Intoxicated by his masculine smell. The heat of him against her spine. The steady press of his hand against her head. Firm, but not unforgiving. Pleading. He needed her to stay still.

A finger, maybe a claw, traced lightly down her spine, eliciting a gasp from her lips. He traced a circle on each cheek of her bottom. She squirmed and tried to look, but he pushed her head back down. This time, he curled fingers into her hair and gripped tight, perhaps readying himself.

Please ready yourself. The sensation of her hair being strained at the roots did something inside. It was tight, but not painful. Passionate, but gentle. Loving, but rough. A rush of pleasure surged at her swollen apex. She would come again, without even being filled.

The anticipation was killing her.

A desperate moan released from her lungs. "Hurry," she pleaded.

But he didn't. With his free hand, he continued to explore her rear, smacking her playfully, tickling her right where the blood rushed and still pulsated from her recent release. He swiped his fingers through her wet entrance, dipped inside, pressed against her nub. She bit into her palm, whimpering.

I'm so ready.

Blunt pressure at her entrance came in a gentle, almost hesitant manner. She wiggled to let him know she was good, and he slid his length along her wet folds, through the gap between her thighs. A strangled groan later, and he murmured, "I could come just like this. Your ass and thighs are so firm."

Gasping, she pushed back into him. "Don't you dare. I want you inside me."

A hoarse chuckle. "Yes, my queen."

And then he thrust in. All. The. Way. In. She cried out, palms slapping the tiles. Water splashed. Sensation exploded inside her. He filled her completely. Stretched her. But he didn't move. He held her prisoner.

He cursed repetitively, coming to terms himself.

God, she needed to see him. She could imagine his incredible physique straining too. Muscles that were corded and sinewy. Neck tendons and veins distended. His sexy face contorted in determination.

The weight at her head disappeared only to reappear at her waist. He gripped steadily, fingers flexed, and then he pulled out... only to slam back in with a force that sent her sliding along the tiles. He dragged her back into position and held tighter.

"You will take me," he declared. Thrust. "Always."

Her eyes rolled in pleasure.

"Always." He thrust again. "Just me." And again. He kept going, mad, driven, hard, fast. Skin slapped. Pounded. "No fucking dancing pixies."

And again.

"No fucking dancing orcs."

She grinned.

He picked up the pace. Heat gathered at the base of Laurel's spine again. She bit her finger and let herself come apart, whimpering in breathless gasps as he grunted, pulled out, and released on her back, using the gap between her bottom to wring the last of his desire. When he was done, he yanked her back to him in a punishing embrace.

Boneless, they sank into the water and almost submerged until he swam backward to settle on a step. He positioned her between his legs. They floated in a way that felt like heaven, but as her gaze slowly lifted to the ceiling, she knew they weren't.

They were prisoners.

CHAPTER TWENTY-SEVEN

*H*ours later, Thorne had taken Laurel in the bed, on the couches, and against the glass windows facing the empty arena under the moonlight. They couldn't get enough of each other. With her beneath him, she was accommodating, encouraging, and always eager for what he wanted. Patient for what he needed. And she was sure to tell him what she desired too. With her on top, she was a minx with never-ending stamina.

And if he panicked about releasing inside her, she handed him control. Without question.

After their last time, they'd ended on the big bed and were now tangled in silk sheets. She was quite honestly his perfect match, meeting him pound for pound of flesh until they'd both dropped exhausted and slipped into sleep.

Thorne didn't sleep long. He woke near dawn and stared at the overhang of fabric above them, gently stroking her arm as she curled into his side, drifting in and out of sleep.

There were no words to describe how it felt to have her in his arms, knowing that she would be there every night from now on. He couldn't stop thinking about what his future would hold. They would get out of here, there was no doubt in his mind. And there was no going back. He'd marked her. Completely and irrevocably, she was his mate. Forever. Both in soul and in body. The idea both scintillated and worried him. He was uncertain if she understood the gravity of this commitment.

She'd thought the bite mark was cute. She'd grinned when he told her she would never dance with another male fae. But there was more to this than cute or a grin. Every male fae would be able to smell Thorne on her. If they were decent, they would treat her respectfully. He would also react viscerally when seeing other males too close to her. He would get possessive and irrational if they overstepped their bounds. The wolf in him would react differently too, now that he'd sunk his teeth and claws into her. It wouldn't let go, no matter what. Even if she came to hate him for it. Even if she tried to walk away.

You know I'm not the marrying type.

Those had been her words on the day he'd met her. Was marriage the same as mating, or was it different? At that time, he'd not been keen about it either. But now he found he hoped for things he dared not dream before.

The blue Well-blessed markings sparkled on both their arms, shining brighter than before. Perhaps the Well had been right to pair them up. He would give it that. And he would not give her up. Even for Jasper.

A rush of guilt swamped him. His touch tightened on her arm. She stirred and opened her eyes.

"What is it, Growly?" she murmured, running her fingers over his stomach.

She caught sight of her warped nails in the dawn light and snatched her hand back.

"Don't do that," he rumbled.

"What?"

"Don't hide yourself around me, Laurel. We're beyond that now."

"I know." She exhaled and rolled to her back. She said nothing for a long time before speaking again. "It's just... no matter what I do, how boss-lady I feel, it's still there in the back of my head."

"What is?"

"Bones is here. In this time." Her eyes flared with emotion. "And I hate him. I want him gone. I've never said that about anyone before."

He kissed the top of her head. "Then I will make it my life's mission to remove him."

"Just like that?"

He nodded. Whatever she wanted, he would give it to her.

She frowned and looked away again. "I hear you say that, and I believe you—I mean, jeeze, you're a one-man army—but then I wonder if it will be enough. Is it even right? I don't want this need for revenge to define me. Do you know what I mean?"

Sometimes pain occupied a permanent place in your

soul. It was an unwelcome tenant, festering until it came back to haunt you when you least expected. Jasper's iron mask came to mind and Thorne knew that his mentor would have his own tenants to worry about when they found a way to get him out. But looking at Laurel, flushed and spent in his arms, he knew that his pain was smaller. His tenant grew quieter, more obedient.

She touched him again. "You're thinking about him."

"Are you sure your arm is healed?"

"Bit late to ask now," she joked. She gave him a look that said she knew he'd avoided the topic but nodded. "It's been fine since we got back from the Ring. I don't know what you did, but it's like new."

This brought a frown to his face. His spell wasn't supposed to completely heal her. He didn't have the skills. His healing magic was triage at best. But he did heal her. And the only explanation he could come up with was that their union was Well-blessed. Perhaps this knowing of each other's emotions had helped. There was much to learn about their special, intimate union.

"There's something else." She sat up and brushed loose strands of hair from her eyes. "I can feel it. You're the one who said we're beyond hiding things now, so spill."

He didn't want to burden her with this, so he pushed aside the silken sheets and got to his feet. He went to the window. The first rays of dawn peeked over the horizon of the arena. They were on the uppermost level, above the highest tier of bleachers. Around the stadium, he saw their room wasn't the only one above the stands. But he couldn't see into any windows and suspected the glass was manufactured to allow users to see out, but not in. All the better to manage secret prisoners.

Jasper could have stared out at the arena, just like this.

He could have done it for years locked in here, wondering if any of his friends were down there, or if they'd come to view a match and recognize him... to save him. Thorne wondered if Jasper had worn the iron mask permanently, or if it had been removed while he was in this private space. If any attendants came again, he'd ask, but he was afraid he knew the answer. The mask had nails that pierced Jasper's skin at the sides of his face and neck. He'd seen red welts festering around them. The blood when he'd tried to remove it.

A Guardian was resistant to the mana-damaging effects of holding metal, yet they couldn't resist it invading their bodies. The iron had halted Jasper's shift mid-way. What was the point of suffering the inkeels in the ceremonial lake if this advantage over metal didn't extend inward?

Laurel's cool palm on his back startled him. Her hands wrapping around his waist made him soften.

"Please tell me what's on your mind," she whispered against his back.

He turned, slung his arm around her, and brought her to his side where she joined him watching the dawn of a new day.

"I was thinking about how much I never wanted to be a Guardian."

"And now?"

"I don't know," he admitted. He couldn't remember a time he'd wanted it. But he wouldn't give up the advantage it gave him over his opponents. Not when it meant keeping her safe. "Now you make me want things I've never wanted before."

"Such as?"

"Such as this. Us." He swallowed, thought of Rush and Clarke... and little Willow. "Family."

The confession sent his pulse sky rocketing.

She tensed beneath his arm, and for a moment, Thorne thought he'd scared her silent. But then she spoke quietly. "You make me want things too."

His lip quirked. "Such as?"

"I've never been a relationship type of person," she admitted. "I was too busy running my business and being a queen. But here's the thing. Queens are lonely. Spending time with you, fishing of all things, made me remember how much joy there is to be present in a moment. And after everything I loved was taken from me, I realized how little time I spent on what mattered. I don't want to make the same mistakes I made before."

He looked down at her. "Are you saying I matter to you?"

She smirked. "You could say I'm warming to you."

He feigned shock and smacked her gently on the rear. "We're mated. You have no choice."

"So we're mated. And that's that? No wedding ceremony? No party? Do fae not have them?" she pouted.

"We have them. Usually if one wants to mate with another, they must go on a quest the other has set for them."

Her eyes lit up. "What, like, to prove your undying love you must go behind enemy lines and steal their most precious jewel then bring it back. That sort of quest?"

His eyes danced at her interpretation. "Behind enemy lines. That's a high task indeed. Usually it's not so dramatic and something well within each betrothed's means. Like picking special flowers for the garland crowns, or something."

"Oh." She laughed. "Okay. Go on."

"On the day of the mating, each betrothed will present the result of their quest to the other at the ceremony."

"Where the male bites her before everyone?" she exclaimed.

This time, it was his turn to laugh. "Every fae breed has a different ritual. The pixies have a queen and she has a harem. She mates with multiple males. If they all bit her, she'd be covered in scars."

"So what do they do?"

He waggled his brows. "You'll have to ask a pix. Anyway, the celebration goes for seven days. Three before. One on the day of the commitment. And three after."

"Sounds like fun." She tweaked his nose. "I especially like the quest part. I'd be down for that. Sounds like an adventure. We just didn't do that sort of thing back in my time. It was all about the clothes, the looks, the money..."

He stared into her eyes until he got lost in them. "Do you want one, a celebration?"

"I don't know, I just... I guess so. I mean, isn't that what you want?"

"I've never thought about it. Guardians don't mate." Lowering his lips, he touched hers gently. "More things that are changing."

Thorne was mid-blink, trying to decipher her body language when a knock came at the door. Laurel rushed to cover herself with a blanket. He strode to the door in his current state—nude.

He was about three feet from the door when it opened. The black-haired and plump-lipped Rosebud from yesterday came in holding a tray of food. Behind her was the healer. The Rosebud winked at him and then went to place her tray on a table. The healer eyed him warily.

She stepped inside and a guard shut the door behind her, bolting it.

"Are you well?" the healer asked.

He nodded. "Clearly."

"And your mate?"

Laurel arrived at his side, now dressed in similar pantaloons to the healer and with a wrap top. It looked good on her. Laurel didn't seem to have the same appreciation for his state of undress. She shoved a package into his arms.

"Dress," she ordered.

His lips curved at how she glared at the Rosebud, even though the courtesan was busying herself with unloading the tray. He liked Laurel possessive. His wolf liked it too. But there was no need to poke the bear. He slipped on his pants, grimacing at the pantaloon style. Breeches were much better for battle. Less voluminous fabric to get caught in claws or weapons. He left the disgusting vest.

"I would like a word with you, healer."

She ignored him and went to Laurel. "How is your arm?"

Laurel tested her movement. "Perfect."

"Amazing." The healer traced Laurel's Well-blessed markings, perhaps having the same thoughts as he about why Laurel had healed so well. "And your energy?"

Laurel's gaze turned inward. "Excellent, actually. I should be tired, but that restorative elixir worked a treat. I'm as chirpy as a cricket."

"Healer," Thorne repeated. "I would like a word with you."

She met his stare. "Unless it's about your injuries, I am bound not to talk to you. Neither is the Rosebud... unless it is about your pleasure, or your wellbeing, that is."

Laurel stepped closer to Thorne.

"You have a geas on you?" he asked.

The healer nodded.

"Of course you do," he replied bitterly. A magical geas was like a curse, but less harmful to one's soul—for the fae casting it. Where a curse was rigid and difficult to break, a geas was bendable. There was always a workaround or a loophole to a geas. He just needed the right words to say.

"I have an injury, healer," he said.

She narrowed her eyes at him, understanding where he was going with this.

As the fae do not lie, the healer had to take his word for it. She glanced at Laurel, then at the Rosebud, just finishing up. Thorne understood. She was wary of listeners, of someone who would reveal her betrayal to her boss.

"Rosebud," Thorne shouted. She looked over. "That will be all. I will speak more about my injuries with the healer. In private."

The Rosebud nodded, and then made her exit.

"Go on," the healer said. "Tell me about your injury."

"It is one of the heart. Someone dear to me was kept prisoner in this room for decades. It has caused me many years of pain. In order to heal, I need to know more about him."

"Are you saying this act of imprisonment was what caused your injury?"

"Yes."

"What can you tell me about the previous champion?"

The healer lifted her brows and then went to the setting of food where she bit down on some fruit. "This is going to take a while, so I suggest you get comfortable."

For the next hour, the healer told Thorne and Laurel how Jasper was brought in forcibly almost a decade ago. His power-enhancing tattoos were stripped from his body, but they couldn't remove the distinctive teardrop tattoo of a Guardian no matter how hard they tried, so used the iron mask to cover it.

The person who'd ordered Jasper's imprisonment was someone well off. This person had paid for a Dark Mage to paint the curse runes around Jasper's neck. When Thorne questioned the iron mask, she told them of a human companion to the Dark Mage. A man wearing all black, who had the look of a hawk, and held metal weapons for his own defense. Two years ago, this same human returned, this time wearing the colors of Seelie High King Mithras, a red velvet coat with flames embroidered along the hem. The human no longer had round ears but pointed.

But it was the same human. She'd been sure of it.

Upon hearing this last bit, Laurel went quiet.

"Is the old champion under the hill?" Thorne asked. "This still relates to my injury."

"He was last night."

"And now?"

"I don't know."

Thorne scratched his chin. "One last question," he said. "The champion. Was the iron mask always on his face?"

The healer nodded gravely. "But occasionally it was removed to allow him to shift back to fae form."

Banshee's balls. This meant Jasper had been stuck between a wolf and fae form for most of a decade. The iron might have poisoned his brain. There was no telling how dark Jasper's state of mind would be when they rescued him.

And they would rescue him.

Thorne hand-signed his thanks to the healer. "Your time has been invaluable. So I will give you something of value in return. This establishment has committed a grave offense against the Well."

"The iron mask," she said.

He nodded. "There will be a raid. The Guardians will come. You should be very far from here when that happens."

The healer signed her gratitude and then left.

Laurel picked at the last of the bread. Her eyes were unfocused, and anxiety trickled down their bond. She'd been like this since the healer had talked about the human turned fae. It was this Bones person. Must be. The one Thorne was going to hunt down and kill for her.

While it twisted his gut to see her so upset, he knew it would have to wait. First, he would see to the raid.

He collected the bowl the Rosebuds had used the previous night and refilled it will bath water. He went back to the table, pierced his finger, and instigated a communication spell. While he waited for it to connect with Rush, he thought it was regrettable that Jasper's only blood relative had been the king, the very man who had imprisoned him. Jasper was unable to get word out, as those communication spells only worked for blooded kin. It might not have mattered anyway if the iron mask had kept Jasper in a state of flux the entire time. His mind might not have been lucid enough to cast spells.

"Thorne?" Rush's deep voice came from the bowl.

"Rush," Thorne greeted, relieved to see his father's visage in the water. "Have I caught you at a bad time?"

Clouds of air puffed from Rush's mouth. He must be somewhere cold.

"You could say that," Rush replied in a grave voice. "But I'm afraid, there won't be a good time for a while."

"What's happened?"

"It's Ada," Rush replied. "We found her, but she won't wake up."

Laurel's hand covered her mouth. Thorne reached over and squeezed her on the shoulder.

"But she is safe?" he asked.

"Yes. We are about to leave for the Order where the healers can see to her. Her blood is pumping. But she will not wake. You didn't contact me for that, though, did you?"

Thorne's fingers clenched on the bowl, and he couldn't make the next words come out. He must have taken too long, perhaps frowned too much, because Rush noticed.

"I know that look," Rush remarked.

"How?"

"When you were young and Thaddeus asked you to collect water from the lake as punishment, you would wear that face and stand on the shore for hours until you knew someone would come and hasten you. And only when the time you'd been allotted for the task was drawing close, would you complete the task. So, I know that face. You are procrastinating. You need help."

Yes, Thorne had made that face at the lake. The realization swam from his deepest memories. He'd been afraid of the lake because, even though the one where he'd been tasked to collect water wasn't the ceremonial lake, it still reminded his young mind of the place he'd been told had taken his grandfather, the original alpha of Crescent Hollow.

Thorne stared at Rush, at the male he'd accused of never being there for him, somehow only now understanding that Rush had *always* been there. Just not seen. Thorne scrubbed his face. He swallowed.

"Yes. I need help."

"Anything."

A warm feeling flooded Thorne and the next words spilled out of him. He told Rush about what they'd discovered, about the iron mask, the need for a raid, and then Jasper's words to him in the arena.

Before Jasper was Thorne's mentor, he was Rush's friend, possibly his mentor as well. Rush had asked Jasper to look after his son. It should dampen Thorne's feelings about Jasper's involvement in his life, but it didn't. He could see how both had only wanted the best for Thorne.

Someone spoke out of view from Rush. Rush turned, listened, and then met Thorne's eyes again.

"I will arrange the raid and be at the Ring by the time the sun sets, if not before. The rest of the Twelve will be with me."

"What about the Prime? She's not my biggest fan."

Rush's vicious growl of discontent came through the connection, rippling the water. "You leave her to me."

"Good."

"Thorne?"

"Yes?"

"I'm proud of you." And then the connection cut. Rush's visage disappeared and the water turned opaque.

"What do we do now?" Laurel asked.

"Now we wait."

CHAPTER TWENTY-EIGHT

*L*ater that day, Laurel sat on the floor of the champion's room, her head pressed to the glass window, watching the fight happening all the way down at ground level. She hadn't expected Rush to pull together something so quickly, but when a flock of shadows passed across the sun, and a squadron of winged fae dropped to the arena roof, she knew it could only mean one thing. The raid had begun.

"Thorne!" she shouted, hopping to her feet. "It's happening."

He rushed to her side from where he'd been listening at the door with his keen wolf ears, hoping to garner some nugget of information from the guards. She pointed at the opposite roof where two Guardians had taken position. He squinted.

"That's Indigo and Shade," he said, then cast his eyes around, noting more fae he recognized. "Haze. Cloud. Ash, and River." He turned to her, eyes wide. "That's all the winged fae in the Twelve—the crows and the vamps."

"Why are you surprised?"

"I just didn't think they'd all come."

She squeezed his arm and smiled. "You asked for help, and they came."

His nostrils flared, and he nodded. "There's always a ground fleet during a raid. With this many on top, Rush probably has the rest of the Twelve down below. Plus more." He shook his head. "I still can't believe it."

"Get used to it, Thorne," she said. "Your friends support you. And Jasper."

"I don't know how Rush convinced the Prime to let them come." He narrowed his eyes. "Unless she's only approved the bit about the iron-mask, and not taking Jasper."

"We'll find him."

He nodded, collected his ax, and ushered her to the front door. "Let's go. Stay behind me. We might have to fight our way out."

"Wait." She stopped him. "What about the bargain I made with the organizer to have two battles?"

Thorne shot her a wolfish grin. "Fighting these guards outside our door consists of a battle, does it not?"

She returned his smile. "Yes. Yes, it does."

"Perfect." He shooed her back a step. "Don't want to hurt my queen."

"Of course."

When she was a safe distance back, he cleaved his battle-ax at the door, splitting the wood straight down the middle. Shouts ensued on the other side. Guards rushed and called for backup, but within another two strokes, Thorne had burst through the bolted door and kicked it wide open.

Laurel's fierce warrior cast a glance over his shoulder and said, "A blast of your fire will suffice."

Bouncing on her toes with excitement, she let flames consume her fingers and sent an inferno through the door, pulling the power at the last moment when she heard a pitiful scream. When the smoke and flames died down, there was no one in the hall. For a moment, she thought she might have burned them all to a crisp, but then one by one, the guards came back up from the stairwell and charged. Thorne threw a spell of dense air at them, knocking them back like a tidal wave, and then dispatched each guard by clocking them with the flat edge of his ax. When it was done, his ears pricked up alert, checking for more danger. Satisfied there was none, he waved Laurel onward and went down the stairs.

They reached ground level and found the gate to the arena wide open. Sun shone from the bright entrance. Thorne slowed his approach, wary and steady with his ax at the ready. When a shadow blocked the light, he lifted his ax, ready to inflict pain, but then dropped it to his side.

It was Rush.

Standing as tall and broad as Thorne, Rush looked fearsome in his Guardian uniform, great sword gripped in his hand, silver hair tied back and ready for battle. Golden eyes landed on Thorne, then flicked to Laurel.

"Vacation is over," Rush joked and gestured for them to exit the tunnel.

"Har-har," Thorne replied. He took Laurel's hand and walked out with her. When they emerged, they found the arena virtually empty. Only a few Guardians combed the bleachers.

"Jasper?" Thorne asked Rush.

"He wasn't down there."

Thorne let loose a string of curses.

Two Guardians came over. One was the tall gilt-haired elf, Leaf, and the other was the serious brunette elf who at first glance somehow looked more suave than the rest, even though he wore the same badass battle uniform.

Leaf opened his mouth to speak, but Thorne cut him off. "If you're going to reprimand me about skipping out on my mission, don't."

Both Leaf and the other elf narrowed their eyes at Thorne. Rush also cast him a wary look but said nothing.

"I wasn't," Leaf replied. "A new tribute will have to replace him. Your guilt is reprimand enough."

Thorne's face reddened, and true to Leaf's word, guilt surged down their bond to plunge into Laurel's heart. This was the first she'd heard of this. Someone had died because Thorne had left?

Thorne frowned and rubbed between his eyes. He turned away and took a few steps where he stopped and stayed with his back to them.

Two vampires landed in a whirl of leathery wings and dust. One was the sinfully good-looking vampire she'd glimpsed at the Birdcage, the other was one she'd never met. He was tall, athletic, and had light brown wavy hair—longish on top, buzzed on the sides. Somehow, there was a carefree vibe to him, despite his blood-streaked leathers. She could almost see him partying on a yacht in the Caribbean or part of the Brazilian soccer team. Maybe both.

And then she looked closer. He wore spiked metal rings on his knuckles. They were covered in fresh blood.

He caught her looking, gave her a curious once-over, and his lips curved on one side, flashing fang. His pointed tongue darted out to lick the blood off his knuckle-duster.

"Fangs to yourself, Indigo," Thorne growled at the vampire. He rested a proprietary arm over Laurel's shoulder.

Indigo kissed the air in Thorne's direction, then turned to Leaf.

"D'arn Shade. D'arn Indigo," Leaf acknowledged. "Status report?"

"Clearly no one is accepting blame for the iron mask," Shade drawled. "But we found evidence of it in the dirt on the arena floor. What was left of it, anyway. Completely melted."

Laurel gingerly lifted her hand. "That was me."

A stare from six extremely tall and lethal Guardians, all dressed in black battle gear spattered with blood, was the most intimidating thing Laurel had ever experienced.

She lifted her chin. "It was necessary to remove the mask from Jasper's face."

"And you did this with your power?" Leaf confirmed.

She nodded. "Thorne put an insulation spell on him for protection."

It was the brunette elf who responded. "Interesting. I would like to know more about the spell you both used when you get a chance."

She didn't exactly use a spell. It was more like instinct. She nodded. Thorne's grip tightened on her shoulder.

"Right," Shade continued. "As I was saying, no one is owning up to it. But Cloud isn't finished interrogating them."

"And Jasper is missing," Thorne added. "Is there news on where he was taken?"

"Unfortunately," Shade continued, "the most we have is that he went under the hill, but not for long before a portal opened and he was taken away by someone wearing the colors of the Seelie High King."

"How long are we going to let him get away with this?" Thorne growled. "Let's just infiltrate Helianthus City, find Jasper, and take him back."

"Sign me up." Indigo's eyes flashed. "That sounds like fun."

Rush shook his head. "He might not be in the city. Even if he was, there's no evidence. We can't just break in without just cause. Not with the power of the Order behind us."

"What if we do it without?"

Leaf's blue eyes blazed. "I've told you once, and I'll say it again. We have a duty to the Well. We can't spend years chasing Jasper down. There simply aren't enough resources."

"More like you're the Prime's little lackey," Thorne shot back.

"Actually," Rush interjected. "The Prime has given us permission to run an extraction for Jasper. He is one of our own. She regrets the outcome of her bargain with the king. It just needs to be above board."

"You mean the bargain where she gave him Jasper in return for keeping the unsanctioned law active. So she could ensure you were cursed, unseeable to the scrying eyes of the enemy, and in the right place and time to find your mate," Thorne shot back.

The air thickened with tension. Thorne became solid rock next to Laurel.

Rush's brows lowered at Thorne. "You want to do this here? Now?"

Laurel looked up at her mate. *Let it go*, she tried to tell him through their bond. He had to let it go. This poisonous hold on his past was eating him. As if hearing her plea, Thorne looked down. His eyes softened, and he released a breath. He looked at Rush, his father, and hand-signed an apology.

"It's not your fault. I shouldn't have spoken out," Thorne said.

Shade made a choking sound. Indigo coughed and raised a brow at Thorne. "Did you just apologize?"

A few of them chuckled. Rush just gave a short nod, then changed the conversation. "I suggest we gather some intel before we make a decision."

"Yes," Leaf added. "When Cloud is done with his interrogation, we might know more about the link between Patches and the Birdcage, this place, and the Seelie High King."

"He's only going to confirm what I've been saying for the past two years," Rush growled. "The humans are setting up the Unseelie. They're trying to instigate a war. They know that with the Sluagh, they can't kill us, so they're trying to make us kill each other."

Leaf scrubbed his jaw. "It's certainly the kind of crafty we've come to expect from them, but all we have to go on is hearsay and circumstantial evidence. No one has caught the humans in the act."

Thorne opened his mouth to say that they had—when the humans had kidnapped Kyra and Clarke two years prior, but Leaf lifted a finger to silence him.

"No," Leaf added. "That wasn't catching them in the act. Only Rush laid eyes on the humans. Not a single one of us did. And the only evidence we found showed that the humans were feeding Thaddeus metal, not the king. Thaddeus is now dead."

"So we're back to playing the same cat-and-mouse game we've been playing for years," Thorne replied, throwing his hands in the air. "Why can't we tell Queen Maebh or King Mithras that it's all a setup?"

"That might have worked a few years ago," Rush said. "But we've learned today that Mithras is working with a human. How else would he get his hands on enough iron to make a mask?"

"Yes. He is working with a human," Thorne confirmed with a grave look at Laurel. "His name is Bones."

Rush's golden gaze narrowed. "He is the right-hand man of the one Clarke calls the Void. The human leader. And you know this for sure?"

Thorne nodded. "The healer here was under a geas not to talk about anything except our injuries, but I found a loophole. She confessed she had witnessed a person matching Bones' description was here two years ago as a human, then more recently dressed in Mithras colors and with elven ears."

"Once again, this is hearsay," Leaf pointed out.

"Well, we won't have hard evidence unless we go on the offensive," Thorne said.

For some reason, Thorne's words threw the group into silence... almost as if *offensive* was a dirty word. Laurel supposed it might be. From what she'd gathered, their roles were to preserve the integrity of the Well. Up until recently, this duty had revolved around hunting mana-warped monsters, policing metals and plastics, and keeping the current day humans from entering Elphyne. But their duty was becoming convoluted as time wore on. Clarke foretold another war, one where the man who'd originally defiled the world did it again, ending life once and for all this time.

"Has Clarke *seen* anything?" Laurel asked.

Rush winced. "Not about this. And to be fair, her mind is occupied with the health of her friend."

Laurel's heart clenched. Ada was in a coma. How could she have forgotten that?

They continued talking, but Laurel tuned out. All she could think was that she couldn't handle this for another decade. Jasper had already been missing for that long. She didn't know how to help. She was a fish out of water.

"More discussion is required," Leaf declared. "We will return to the Order until we exhaust all avenues and come up with a plan of attack."

As each Guardian took off through a portal, Laurel caught the bitter look on Thorne's face, and if she guessed correctly, she knew why. It seemed the Prime had indoctrinated the Guardians to her way of thinking. They couldn't make decisions without consulting her. They weren't living in a democracy. It was a dictatorship.

CHAPTER TWENTY-NINE

*A*s they crossed the threshold to the house of the Twelve, Thorne watched his mate draw Clarke into a fierce embrace. From that moment, Thorne was not much but an afterthought in Laurel's eyes. Seeing the twinkle in them, and the way she invigorated around her friend, he couldn't help feeling a little envious at the friendship. And then there was the rush of love he sensed from Laurel. They must be close friends, indeed. But when Clarke's expression turned grave, and she gestured for Laurel to follow her, the twinkle in Laurel's eyes disappeared. She cast a concerned glance to Thorne, and he gestured that he would be right behind.

"Is she still asleep?" Laurel asked Clarke as they took the staircase.

Clarke nodded. "Hasn't moved an inch. The healing Mages don't know what is wrong. They're trying to use magic to keep her sustained, but if she doesn't wake soon, I'm afraid she'll slip away."

Laurel's nose turned pink and her eyes watered. "Where is she?"

"We put her in Jasper's old room." Clarke sent a nervous glance to Thorne. "It was the only room free, and we need her close."

He gave a short nod. There wasn't much he could say to that. Jasper wasn't here. And if this newly awoken woman, Ada, was as close to these two as they were to each other, then she must be like family.

Thorne followed the women down the hall and stopped at the open doorway to Jasper's old room. He leaned against the frame with a shoulder. Lying on Jasper's bed was a petite female with long, wavy golden hair spread around her like a mermaid. Her eyes were closed, her body still, her mouth pinched as though she were in pain. She'd been cleaned and dressed in fresh clothing.

Laurel sat next to Ada on the bed.

Thorne watched his mate brush her friend gently down the arm and was reminded of the time she did that to Willow. Laurel would make a good mother one day. It wasn't the first time he'd thought that, but it was the first time he'd done so knowing what it meant to him directly.

He should give them some space. Rubbing his chest, he turned and headed to the kitchen, hungry and ready for food. Or a drink. When he got there, he found Rush scrounging around too. Both still in the attire they'd been in during the raid, and both led by their stomachs. Their eyes met briefly, and then Thorne joined him in the search. It was too early for dinner, but food was required before he cleaned up. Silently, they found a collection of nuts and dried berries, and a jug of ale before heading outside and into the back garden where Willow played while under the watchful eye of Jocinda as she tended to a patch of herbs.

They sat on a wooden bench before a long table used for communal meals. The weather had been unseasonably warm. A few years ago, it snowed at this time of year, but now the sun shone brightly and the flowers bloomed. A long strip of lawn stretched from the back of the house to the tall stone wall that separated the Order campus from the poisonous forest surrounding them. Before the wall was a thick grove of Willow and Cherry trees, blocking much of the wall from sight and catching most errant poisonous leaves from the external forest. They still had to watch Willow in case she found a leaf and ingested it.

"You are comfortable with her outside now?" Thorne asked with a nod in the direction of the house of the Six.

Rush poured ale into two steins and exhaled deeply. "I've accepted she's not going to shift into wolf, it would have happened by now, but she has shifted from human into a fae form, or rather something closer to an elf. I don't think the Sluagh will bother her."

Thorne frowned as he recalled her change in appearance that night she'd wanted to sleep in his bed. "I remember fangs coming out, and her ears elongating."

"Claws too," Rush added, "but that is all."

"Should be enough to mark her as different from the humans."

"Agreed. Plus, her mana-holding capacity is strong for her age. We will still keep her indoors when the sun goes down, though."

Thorne settled back on the wooden bench, the stein in his hand, and joined Rush as he watched the little silver-haired child chase down a butterfly—or a possible sprite—with single-minded tenacity.

"She is fearless," Thorne remarked.

"She is," Rush agreed.

Willow landed, caught something, carefully opened her hands, and then pouted. Not there. She resumed her hunt.

"Leaf has called a meeting with the Council first thing in the morning," Rush said. "We will discuss a plan of action."

Weariness coated Thorne's bones. "I don't know what more we can do being shackled as we are by the rules the Prime has put in place. We have exhausted our options."

"There are always more options," Rush replied. "Ada has been found. Now I am free to go on the hunt with you. If we can't use the Order to get to him, then we do it on our own. We won't stop until we bring Jasper home."

Thorne let those words settle, and something tight around his heart loosened. He was learning Rush was a fae true to his word, a male who didn't mince words or skirt around manipulation and misdirection. He'd promised to go on this hunt when he could, and now he would.

"There is something you should know," Thorne said.

"I'm listening."

"When Jasper was freed from the mask, he confused me with you."

Rush's brows snapped together.

Thorne scrubbed his hand through his newly shorn hair. "He babbled about looking after me like you'd asked, but not deserving to be rescued." Thorne paused. "He apologized."

Rush went still.

Even though Jasper was fae, and his words should have been the truth, Thorne had to ask. "Was your request why he mentored me?"

"Jasper and I were longtime friends and would often partner on missions into the wolf territories. When your mother was executed, and they took me into custody, I threw some regrettable words at him." A dark shadow passed over Rush's expression. "Jasper had refused to help Véda, and I found it unforgivable. It didn't make sense. Now I understand that perhaps the Prime had something to do with it." Rush's gaze fogged as he stared into his stein. "While I'm eternally grateful he looked out for you, I had no idea he took those harsh words to heart."

"He failed to remember me," Thorne muttered into his stein, took a breath with his lips on the rim, and then sipped.

When he lowered the cup, he felt Rush's shrewd gaze on him. "This is most likely because of the curse marks that were on his body. Or his state of mind. Not because of you."

"I never said it was," he groused.

"But you were thinking it."

Thorne kept his mouth shut. Had he been thinking it? Perhaps it was there, simmering beneath his conscious thoughts. Perhaps his face showed his inner turmoil more than he liked to admit.

"I know," Rush added. "Because—"

"You know me," Thorne finished.

Willow leaped over Jocinda's feet as she kneeled and dug into a herb patch. She took two wobbly steps and then launched with her whole body onto something on the grass. She looked over to Rush with excitement—*look at me!*—opened her fingers, squealed in excitement, but then her catch flittered off.

"Dad!" she shouted. "See?"

"Yes, squirt. I saw." Rush turned to Thorne. "I see your mate has been marked. These mana-filled humans are hard to resist, no?"

Thorne barked out a laugh. "That is one way of putting it."

Rush smiled over his stein. "They are also very bossy."

Thorne laughed some more. When his humor died down, he confessed, "I think I needed that."

"Me too."

They shared a small smile, and it was... nice. But Thorne wasn't settled. He wouldn't be for a while. Not with Jasper in the wind, and Laurel worried over her friend. And when Laurel worried, he worried. It was more than their shared bond.

Rush noticed Thorne checking the door to the house and raised his brows in question.

"Laurel is unsettled," Thorne explained. "About this new friend."

"So is Clarke," Rush agreed and scowled into his cup. "I don't know what to do. Usually, Clarke is the one who knows such things."

"And they are strange things, are they not?" Thorne replied. "From their time, I mean."

"Yes. This is true."

They both turned their scowls to their steins. A few minutes of awkward silence, then Thorne offered, "Laurel used to own a business where females would pay coin for her to show them how to make their bodies physically fit."

Rush frowned. "Like the training we do on the fields?"

"I guess so."

"And these females would pay Laurel. Not the other way around?"

Thorne shrugged. "Something like that."

"The training. Did that make her a general of her own army?"

"She said she was a queen. But not like our queens. I don't believe she had subjects. Or a castle."

"Odd."

"Indeed."

"Clarke was a thief," Rush blurted.

Thorne sprayed out his mouthful of ale and laughed.

Rush's lips quirked. "Don't tell her I told you."

The sun warmed Thorne's face and he tried to experience this moment for what it was. Laurel had mentioned this sort of simple awareness was something she'd regretted. He could see the wisdom in that. It was the first time he'd come together with his father on level ground. They had something in common. Both had Well-blessed mates—the first fae in centuries to do so—and both were mated to women of the days past. Humans with power. Another first. They were the only people in this time to share such a bond. And they were kin. Thorne knew that Rush and he would stand together, united, if anyone came for their humans. It was because of this notion of connection that he was prompted to speak his next words.

"I would like to do something for Laurel," he said. He felt a little silly, but continued. "She talks about something called a smoo-thie."

Rush lifted his gaze to Thorne's. "Smoo-thie?"

"Yes. She wishes for one in the morning, usually when she is hungry, yet she talks about it as though she drinks it. I don't know what it is, but I would like to give her one."

Rush's gaze turned foggy, and he looked inward, as though trying to remember. He tapped his lip. "Smoo-thie."

"I believe it is green. Perhaps it involves fruit."

"I suppose if it is a meal, we could enquire with the house brownies. I could also ask Clarke when Laurel is not within hearing distance, if you permit."

Thorne studied Rush for a moment and decided he liked this new thing between them. He sensed Rush did too. "I would like that."

"Consider it done." Rush chugged back the last of his ale, thumped his chest, belching softly.

"Da-*ad*." The sound of a little voice trying to entice

attention drifted over. "Where's Willow?"

Both Thorne and Rush looked to the garden.

Thorne barked a laugh. There, behind a sparse bush was Willow. He could see her clearly, but a single leaf covered her lower face. She clearly thought it was enough to hide her entire form. Earnest eyes twinkled at her father.

Thorne raised his brow at Rush, who chuckled back and then shouted, "Oh dear, I've lost Willow. Wherever can she be?"

Giggles.

And then Rush stood, clapped Thorne on the shoulder and walked past to collect a squealing and giggling Willow before zooming her around and lifting her onto his shoulders. Then he returned and headed for the house.

"I'll be back," Rush said and mimed having a drink.

The smoo-thie?

"You're going to ask now?" Thorne asked.

"No time like the present." Rush shrugged. "I'll no longer put off for tomorrow what I can do today. You never know when time is taken from you."

AFTER DINNER, Thorne took a plate of food up to Jasper's room where Laurel still sat a vigil at Ada's beside by candlelight. Night had long since fallen, and he'd already bathed and dressed. Clarke was asleep next to Ada. She must be weary after keeping vigil herself for so long.

Laurel was still in the clothes she'd taken from the Ring.

Her feet were tucked under her bottom and she rested in the high-back chair by the window-side. Her melancholy reflected down their bond. It reminded him of her first night awake in this time, where she'd sat on a chair just like that in his room, brooding out the window while he'd taken his bath.

She didn't think he'd paid attention, but he did. She'd been homesick, and he'd felt every last minute of it while he'd taken a bath. He'd lifted the blanket to cover her and tucked her hair as she'd drifted to sleep. It was then that he'd first thought maybe she was worth getting to know more thoroughly. He was glad he now had.

He rapped his knuckles gently on the door.

Laurel looked over.

"I have food," he said.

She smiled. "Perfect."

He took the plate to her. She raised her brows, impressed at the selection. A selection of roast vegetables and savory pastries filled with fish and cream. She made short work of eating the selection.

"Will you be retiring soon?" The thought of having his mate in his bed awoke every instinct in his body. Since he'd marked her, it was all he'd thought about, but he wouldn't push the subject. As he'd mentioned to her, a mating ceremony lasted days. But what he hadn't mentioned, was that the last three days were spent in privacy, enjoying each other's bodies while the rest of the family continued the party without them. This may not be practical given their current situation.

He would, however, push the subject of her needing rest.

She glanced at Ada. "Clarke and I are taking shifts watching her. When she wakes, I'll come."

A sound at the door drew their attention, and a little white head poked around from the shadow of the door-frame. Willow came stumbling in, hair wet from a recent bath, and dressed in sleepwear. The scent of fresh powder wafted in. She looked over at them hesitantly, then dragged a small blanket into the room.

"Sleeping Pretty is cold," she mumbled and looked at the bed.

Thorne thought perhaps Willow meant her mother, but she crawled onto the bed and tried to cover Ada. Seeing her difficulty, Thorne helped her spread the blanket. When Willow was done, she curled between her mother and Ada.

Laurel came to stand next to Thorne. "That's weird."

"Not really. The temperature is dropping."

"No, I mean..." Laurel shook her head. "It doesn't matter."

Thorne pulled her into his arms. "It does, else you wouldn't have mentioned it."

"It's just that we used to call Ada 'Pretty Kitty' because she used to rehabilitate big wild cats, and clearly, she's very pretty. Eventually, we shortened it to just Pretty." She bit her lip. "Maybe Clarke said something."

"Most likely." Thorne lifted Laurel's face and kissed her deeply, making sure to let her know what would be waiting when she made it to his bed. *Their* bed.

"Don't be too long," he said, patted her gently on the rear, and went back to his room.

CHAPTER THIRTY

*A*fter Thorne had left, Laurel sat on the bedside chair, occasionally testing the temperature on Ada's forehead with the back of her hand. She was afraid that Ada would suddenly stop breathing if she stopped checking. Laurel didn't want to lose her, not when she'd lost so much already.

Ada had a dry, sarcastic sense of humor that not everyone understood, but Laurel and Clarke did. They were often in fits of laughter over something Ada refused to believe was funny, only the truth. Of course, that made it funnier.

Seeing Clarke and her new family gave Laurel a taste of what a future could be like here and sharing that with Ada would be even better. Laurel dug into the pocket in her pantaloons and pulled out a small vial of pink elixir. After learning Laurel's relationship with Thorne had gone to the next level, Clarke had given it to Laurel the moment they were alone. Take a drop a day and it would stop Laurel from becoming pregnant.

Laurel had taken her first dose hours ago. She would tell Thorne about it as soon as she could. It would relieve his concerns and allay his fears about the unsanctioned breeding law.

She put the vial back and went back to staring at her friend, watching the air draw in and out of her lips as she slept. Since Willow had brought the extra blanket, Ada's cheeks had taken more color. Maybe she had been cold, after all. Perhaps Willow had a little of her mother's psychic powers.

Either way, if Ada had been cold, and now she wasn't, it could only be a good sign.

Hours passed, and Laurel's eyes grew heavy, but she didn't want to wake Clarke. The poor thing had a small child. She'd be exhausted. Laurel looked over at her redheaded friend and noticed a deep frown between her brows. Laurel picked up the candlestick holder at the table and brought the flame closer to Clarke. She was definitely whimpering with shallow breath.

Dreaming?

Laurel put the candle on the bedside table and took hold of her friend's shoulder.

"Clarke," she whispered.

"No." Clarke spoke vehemently through her teeth. "You stay away from her."

Clarke's eyes pinged open and seemed to look beyond Laurel's shoulders. The hairs on the back of Laurel's neck lifted, and she checked, half expecting to see Bones, or perhaps the Sluagh, but there was nothing. Clarke kept talking. No. It was more like pleading with someone not there. Glistening tracks of tears ran down her cheeks.

"Wake up," Laurel said and shook Clarke's shoulders.

With a gasp, Clarke's eyes focused. "Laurel?"

"Yeah, it's me. You were dreaming."

Clarke jackknifed up, and drew Laurel into a hug, whimpering, "Oh, thank God. I thought he had you again."

"Shh." Laurel stroked her friend's sobbing back. "I'm fine. I'm fine. It wasn't a—" Laurel swallowed the lump in her throat. "Vision, was it?"

"I don't know. It felt more like a regular nightmare. Did you see my eyes? Where they white?"

"They looked normal."

Clarke exhaled heavily. "Nightmare then."

Willow stirred on the bed. Clarke wiped her nose and then checked on her daughter. Once satisfied she was asleep, Clarke picked up the candleholder and took Laurel's hand. She dragged Laurel into the adjoining bathing chamber—as far as they could get from little fae ears.

"What's wrong?" Laurel asked.

Flickering candlelight revealed the panic in Clarke's eyes.

"I keep dreaming about *him*."

"The Void?"

Clarke nodded. Her lip curled. "It's worse than before, and it's also not only him but..."

"Bones."

Another nod. Then Clarke burst into tears. "I'm sorry."

"Hey. Hey, don't cry." Laurel squeezed Clarke's arm. "Whatever it is, we'll work it out. We've got badass warriors for husbands."

"Mates."

"Same thing."

"Better. But here's the thing," Clarke continued. "Every version of the future I dream, it's not our fae warriors who beat the Void. Well, it's not them alone."

Laurel stiffened. "You mean it's us?"

"They're trained to avoid fae politics. It's ingrained in them. But the Void uses fae politics to infiltrate Elphyne. Don't you see?"

No. She didn't see. Clarke wasn't making much sense. Laurel frowned at her friend while her brain whirled. The healer at the Ring had mentioned the human who'd been described as looking similar to Bones coming back disguised as a fae in the king's colors. Was that what Clarke meant by politics? The Order might have the power, but they were ill-equipped to battle on the same frequency as someone so manipulative and deceptive as Bones.

This man who had destroyed their world could be sitting by King Mithras's side, right now, plotting the end of another world, but this time, he'd have the power of a fae king behind him. Not just any king, the High Seelie King. Ruler of half the land.

Clarke's eyes met Laurel's. "Before you woke up in this time, I had a vision of you walking ahead with Thorne, Jasper, all of us behind you. You lead us to a table where we enjoyed a meal together. I know it's you, Laurel. You'll somehow lead us to Jasper. Some decision you make is going to make us all very happy. For a time, anyway."

Silently watching through the doorway to the two sleeping on the bed, the profound realization of their situation hit home. This was their life now. They were alive. The world was flourishing. Laurel had *hope*. She had dreams. She wanted her own family some day.

A ghost of pain in her fingertips caused a tremble in her hands. She rubbed her nails on her thighs.

Clarke had a *child*. She had a family now. That was too much to lose.

"We need to kill Bones," Clarke said grimly. Perhaps she'd been thinking the same things.

"I agree. But I need to kill him. You need to stay here."

The words hung in the air.

Laurel? Kill. Had she really said that?

Yes. She was strong, now. More powerful. The Bones she knew didn't have magic. Not like her. He was here, in Elphyne. In their realm, on their terms. Now was the time.

"I want to help more," Clarke whispered. "I hate that you're the one who has to do this when it was my fault we're all in this mess."

Laurel turned to her friend. "Clarke, it was never your fault," she said vehemently. "It was none of our faults. It was theirs. Bishop. Bones. The Void. *Theirs*. You want to help? Tell me what you know. Then Thorne and I can be ready."

Clarke nodded. Her eyes watered.

"Rush would help too, but... there are too many variables in that chain of events."

"What? Have you seen something?"

"I know that Bones is directly linked to the end of the world. I know that the Order want to help, but they need us to finish it. I know that sometimes, they have the right intentions, but they don't get the job done." Clarke glanced to where Ada was sleeping in the other room. "We're the only ones who know what Bones and the Void are really like. We've seen the old world. We know what was lost. I'm afraid... I'm afraid that if they get their hands on Bones, they'll keep him alive to question him."

"He's a cancer. It's better to cut it out and be done with it." Dark bitterness coated Laurel's vision, and she was surprised at how right those words sounded. *Cut it out. Be done with it.*

"Exactly. We don't need to interrogate him. We can find out the Void's plan some other way."

None of them wanted to voice their fears. Could they really do this? Take this ruthless and cold step? Could Laurel become a killer?

Were they acting irrationally *because* of their fears?

Laurel rubbed her aching nails again.

"We need to keep this between you and me," Clarke said, meeting Laurel's eyes. "I'm talking about our end game. If we tell Rush or Thorne, or even the Prime about how serious we are about this, they might try to stop us."

"But Thorne said he would kill Bones for me. He wants the same thing."

"He might not have the choice. He might have to choose between you or Bones, or Jasper and Bones. I just..."

"I know what you're getting at." Laurel inhaled deeply and exhaled. If it came to Laurel's life, or Bones', Thorne would pick her. Without a doubt. But Laurel wouldn't stop until she cut out the cancer. She had to. "We keep the killing part between us then."

"At least until the deed is done."

"Agreed."

"In the meantime, I'll work on the Prime. The Guardians might not be trained for manipulations and politics, but she is. She's a master of it. If I can find a reason to convince her to help us, perhaps we can get you into the Summer Court, and then half the job is done."

Laurel nodded grimly. Already, she was preparing her mind, making herself harder, colder. She could do this.

Just think about how it would feel to finally know Bones wasn't in the world anymore. That he was never coming back.

⚖

LAUREL RETURNED to Thorne's room not long after midnight. After their decision to kill Bones, she and Clarke had gone over as many variations of a plan as they could, but there came a point where they couldn't continue without going around in circles, so Laurel left. Now, she pushed it all out of her mind, telling herself that for the rest of the night, she would pretend things were as normal as they could be.

That she didn't have to turn herself into a cold, ruthless killer just yet.

Closing the door softly, she padded quietly into the room and to where Thorne was fast asleep on the bed, naked and twisted in his sheets. The soft warm glow of her candlelight clashed with the blue of his Well-blessed markings. It was breathtaking. She didn't think she'd ever get used to these magical moments. Of course, ogling his perfect physique could also be another reason she was out of breath. The sharp lines of his body, the slabs of muscle, the smooth skin, and the peaceful expression on his face as he slept. It all made her insides ache with want. She put her candle on the bedside table and then undressed.

She would get in and curl up beside him.

But she wasn't tired anymore. Her mind was buzzed from what she'd discussed with Clarke.

Crawling onto the bed, she straddled him gently and began kissing down his front—starting with the hard column of his neck, and trailing down his torso. When her lips tickled the hair at his groin, he stirred with a low, pleasure-filled moan and she was pleased to see a hard rod take shape beneath the sheets. Big hands landed on her head. Fingers threaded into her hair and massaged meanderingly.

"Laurel," he murmured, voice deep and husky. "What is the meaning of this?"

"Are you complaining?"

She hooked her finger in the sheet that covered his hips, drew it down to reveal he was indeed hard and ready. She lowered her lips and licked the long, responsive length, taking special care as she hit the crown.

Another masculine groan, an instinctive gentle thrust of his hips, and his cock entered her mouth. She hummed appreciatively and sucked deep.

Thorne cursed and bolted upright. She jerked back, grinning and licking her lips. Now completely awake, his eyes landed on her state of undress, settling on his favorite parts of her with smoldering intensity. He reached for her.

She straddled his hips, fitted him beneath her, and sank down on his length, shuddering at the sensation of being filled completely. He steadied her waist and looked softly into her eyes.

"You should be resting," he insisted.

She undulated her hips, reveling in the way stubbornness eased out of his expression. Loving how he soon forgot about his protests and started kissing down her neck, licking around the mark he'd put there, and moving with her.

Hard pants. Ragged breaths.

"My queen," he murmured, half to himself.

Laurel took her pleasure in her warrior fae and enjoyed the night for what it was—possibly the last time he'd look at her without hurt or betrayal again.

Secrets never ended well.

But sometimes, they were necessary.

WHEN MORNING CAME, Laurel woke to find Thorne already gone. But next to the bed on the side table was a pottery cup with condensation running down the side. She shuffled over and looked inside. Frothy green foam. Next to the cup was a small piece of parchment with the words "Drink me" written in a chicken scratch scrawl she could only guess was Thorne's handwriting.

She sniffed it. Fruity, yet... herby.

Her eyes lit up and she braved a sip. Her taste buds rejoiced. Full of dense flavor and exactly what she'd been craving. A smoothie. Not exactly like the wheatgrass one she had every morning, not as smooth, but similar. A taste of home.

Tears sprung to her eyes, and she gulped it all down, trying not to think about how this made her task even more difficult. She had to lie to Thorne.

And that made her feel sick.

She didn't want to do it.

But if anything, sleep had solidified the notion that Bones had to die. And Thorne would always pick her if it came to it. She couldn't just send the Guardians on an assassination mission. Clarke was right not to trust them to complete the deed. They might keep Bones. And then he might escape. He might do something worse.

No. It had to be this way.

Laurel bathed and dressed into something she could jog in. She needed to feel that burn in her lungs today more than any day. She needed to chase her demons away. Once ready, she headed out.

The house was abuzz with activity and large, half-naked male fae. Some she recognized and gave a shy wave to, others she stayed clear of. The dark crow-shifter, for one. The way he looked at her gave her the heebie-jeebies—as though he wanted to knock her out, gift wrap her and deliver her next door to the thing that ate souls.

No. Not *thing*, she reminded herself. That's how she used to think. She was different now. She was a part of this new world. Every creature in this time was owed respect, even if it lived off the souls of others. She was sure there was no other way for it to gain sustenance. Like vampires.

The door to Ada's room was closed, and Laurel suspected Clarke was in there with a sleeping Willow, so avoided going in. Clarke would have told Laurel if Ada's condition had changed.

She went out the front door in search of Thorne and found him and a group of three other fae in hand-to-hand combat on the front lawn. Rush, Aeron, and a big, body-builder type vampire she thought was named Haze. Behind them, about a hundred feet away, and across the grass field, were the Guardian barracks where those who weren't in the special cadres resided. A few Guardians she'd never met sat out the front, watching the informal sparring match while they ate breakfast.

Thorne must have sensed her arrival. He turned, got knocked in the head by a meaty fist, scowled at his attacker —Haze—and then jogged toward Laurel. When he arrived, all sweaty and in leather breeches, he drew her to his frame and gave her an open-mouthed kiss.

"Mm," he said, licking his lips and looking very pleased with himself. "You found my gift."

Laurel didn't know what to say. She was all warm and gooey inside. He'd not only made the most public display of affection, but he'd given her the taste of home, and he was... smiling. Dimples and all.

She wasn't the only one lost for words. All three fae on the lawn stood agape. But Thorne didn't care. He put his lips near her ear. "For the record, any time you want to wake me as you did last night, is fine with me."

Clearly, fae had good hearing, because one of them let out a taunting wolf whistle. Laurel's cheeks heated.

"Don't be shy," Thorne chuckled. "They probably heard last night too."

"What!" she gasped.

He shrugged. "You took me by surprise last night, but I'll spell the room tonight to give us some privacy." Then his gaze turned wicked. "Unless you want me to spell it now. I think we have a few minutes before the council meeting."

Apparently, they didn't. Across the lawn, Leaf strode toward them, his golden hair gilded by the morning sun. He wore a grave expression on his face.

"Something is wrong," Thorne murmured, eyes on Leaf.

When Leaf arrived, he gestured for them all to go indoors.

"What is it?" Thorne asked.

"I'll tell you when everyone is together."

"Just tell us now."

Leaf put his hands on his hips, shot a glance to the other

concerned Guardians, and exhaled. "We received an invitation from High King Mithras last night."

Thorne tensed beside Laurel.

Leaf continued, "It's for a ball in honor of his announcement to recognize his first and only heir."

"Fuck off, he is," Haze spat.

A growl ripped out of both Thorne's and Rush's throats. The rest of them held a glower on their face that could cut stone, but Laurel wasn't quite understanding.

"Why is this not a good thing?" she asked.

"The king assassinated his offspring years ago—both legitimate and illegitimate," Leaf explained. "Unless he's secretly produced an heir none of us know about, his only living heir is Jasper."

"Who is the invitation for?" Thorne asked.

"The Prime, plus one."

"I'll go with her," Thorne decreed.

Leaf raised a brow. "I think not."

Thorne raised his palm. "This has always been *my* hunt."

"At the expense of your duty to the Well," Leaf reminded.

"I understand that. And I will make amends, but this is—"

Leaf shook his head, cutting Thorne off. "It is not up to me to decide. The Prime will bring someone with her."

"Then we find a way to get in ourselves," Rush added.

"This is impossible," Aeron, the brown-haired elf, said. "This ball will be by invitation only. Unless we find due cause to enter the citadel, we won't be able to get in. We can't even disguise ourselves." He pointed at his teardrop tattoo. "Glamor won't cover this."

"Is it a masquerade?" Thorne asked, eyes hopeful.

Leaf shook his head. "It matters not what we discuss now. The Prime has requested we all meet in the council chambers as soon as possible. You lot head there, and Aeron and I will gather the rest."

Leaf strode into the house with Aeron. The remaining Guardians got into a heated discussion about how, and who, would be the best person to go with the Prime. Laurel stood back, letting them talk, because her mind was already whirling.

The opportunity was too fortuitous. An invitation. She just had to make sure her name was on it.

CHAPTER THIRTY-ONE

*T*horne led Laurel up the temple steps and into the room adjoining it where the Council usually met. An open pantheon, the temple overlooked the entire Order grounds. They'd passed acolytes and novitiates seeing to the upkeep of the floral arrangements, and water integrity as it flowed in a stream from the fountains to culverts to staircases, all leading down to ground level.

He'd not been up there often. The sacred pools, with the elemental obelisks sticking out of the center, always grated on him. One of his earliest memories of entering this place was moving from pool to pool after his initiation ceremony, and having his elemental affinity tested before being sent to his rooms at the barracks the first time. When Laurel tensed next to him, he realized she would have her own memories of this place now. She, too, had been tested upon arriving in this place.

The council chamber was crowded with Guardians from the Twelve. Three blue robed Mages, council members, were also there. Barrow was a preceptor at the academy. He'd had an accident with his mana a few decades ago that left him a little aged and with long white hair. Colt, the pixie, was also a preceptor, and Dawn was the head Seer.

The Prime stood at the front of the room, at the edge of the pantheon, and with her back to the view of grounds below. White feathered wings draped like a mantle over brown shoulders and blue gown. White coiled ringlets bounced when she turned her head Thorne's way. Her large owl-shifter eyes tracked him as he made his way into the room with his hand gripped tightly around Laurel's.

This should be fun, he thought bitterly.

As Thorne was the last to arrive, Barrow cast a privacy ward around the room, ensuring not one word of their conversation would be heard beyond their immediate proximity. Thorne took Laurel to where Rush and Clarke stood near a pillar. He faced the front and drew Laurel to his chest, firmly clasping his arms around her front.

"I have asked you to come here today as there is some news pertinent to us all and we must come to a decision together," the Prime said.

Thorne scoffed. Since when did she consult them all?

The Prime cocked her head Thorne's way. "Do you have something to say, D'arn Thorne?"

"Why bother asking us?" he replied. "You'll make up your own mind, anyway."

She stared at him long and hard. So long, that Thorne believed she would either erupt with offense or ignore him. But her face suddenly lost its defense. She sighed.

"This is the way it has been in the past. True. But..." She glanced at Clarke, of all people. "I am learning that change is a good thing, and I must embrace it if we are to overcome this new threat."

New threat. Did she mean the humans from Crystal City or King Mithras? Perhaps it was both?

"It is no secret I am responsible for the loss of D'arn Jasper from our ranks."

"You mean you sold him," Thorne shot out again. "Don't mince your words, Prime."

Her jaw clenched, but to her credit, she didn't back down. "This is one way of naming what I did. Another way is to say I have secured us your mate."

She gestured at Laurel, who tensed in his arms. He tightened his grip. "Clarke is the one who led us to Laurel."

"And who led Rush to Clarke?" the Prime raised a brow.

Dammit. She was right. He knew it. He knew it a long time ago, yet he still couldn't let it go.

The Prime lowered her brows at Thorne. "You cannot believe that the events that led to Clarke's discovery were easy for me to decide. The fae who have died as a result will be a burden I, and I alone, carry. It will weigh me down when I finally rejoin the cosmic Well."

A hollow ache filled Thorne's chest. He'd not yet met these humans they were so fearful of, the ones who'd destroyed the planet the first time around, but he'd seen the evidence of their destruction, not only in the icy wastelands that covered most of the planet today, but in the aftermath of Clarke's kidnapping two years ago. They'd preyed on Thaddeus Nightstalk's vulnerable inky side and used him to carry out their wishes, harvesting mana from the souls of fae to feed the humans and their false immortality. Thorne still remembered the cages lining the Crescent Hollow village boundary walls. He still remembered Anise's weak body as he drew her out of the cage suspended from the ground. And if these humans were the same ones somehow behind Jasper's capture at the Ring... a low growl rumbled in his throat.

"I may not have shown it," he said to the Prime, "but I understand this threat. I am here, Prime, because I stand on the same side as you."

She gave him a slight nod and turned to the rest of the congregation. "High King Mithras has invited me, and a guest of my choosing, to a ball in honor of naming his new heir. It is in a week's time. Considering Jasper's recent sighting, we're all assuming he is the one the king is naming as his heir."

A murmur of discontent and discussion arose, but the Prime raised her hand.

"I'm not finished. As anyone who is over the age of three hundred is aware, when the thaw began, and King Mithras broke away from the Unseelie Kingdom to create the Seelie Kingdom, he subsequently and systematically assassinated every fae he'd sired. The only offspring he was unable to touch was Jasper, and that was because Jasper sought refuge with the Order and his identity was stripped from him, thus removing any claim to the throne."

"He's also a bastard," Barrow said, his white busy eyebrows drawn down. "What makes you so sure he's the one the king is naming as heir?"

Cloud stepped forward, dark smudges under his eyes. "Because Ash, River, and I have spent the night confirming this is true."

Thorne straightened. All three crows in the Twelve had gone on a reconnaissance mission. To Helianthus? "You've seen him?"

A solemn nod. "We flew over the citadel, gathered gossip, and then watched in the palace grounds. Not only did the serving staff talk freely of the new prince, but we saw him being fitted for his party attire."

Rage surged in Thorne.

"How is it Dawn hasn't *Seen* this?" Leaf gestured toward the Seer.

But Thorne knew it was the same way that Rush was able to go *unseen* during his curse. It was the reason he was cursed in the first place.

"Jasper has curse marks around his collar," Thorne said. "Both Mithras and Bones have been linked to this act."

The Prime's wings flared dramatically with an irritated snap. "They're working together, and they've used our own technique against us," she noted. "They're fast learners."

A rumble of dissent rippled across the room. Cloud

muttered general insults at the human race. Thorne glared at him.

"So Mithras is working with them?" Colt asked.

"It seems so," the Prime answered.

Colt frowned. "Then we need to stop the spread of their blasphemy before the rest of Elphyne believe they are more important than the Well. If we don't make a move against these dissenters, they will soon have the upper hand. Clearly it's time to bring the kings and queens in on this threat. We must warn the other rulers."

The Prime looked to Clarke for answers, who cowered a little under the intense gaze. Laurel gave Clarke a slight nod, an act which seemed to bolster Clarke's confidence.

Clarke lifted her chin and leveled her gaze at the Prime. "You know who you must bring with you."

Good. Finally some sense. Thorne let go of his mate and stepped forward. But the Prime's gaze settled on Laurel. The walls closed in, and, in a rush of paranoia, Thorne suddenly felt as though he was the last to come to this conclusion because everyone in the room nodded as though it made perfect sense. Even Laurel. Why her? Because of her fire power?

"No," he barked, pre-empting the Prime's response. "She is not going with you. Take a Guardian. It doesn't have to be me, but you need a warrior beside you."

Laurel's eyes flared in irritation. "I fought with you in the Ring. I'm not that incompetent."

"You would have died if I didn't save you," he shot back.

"I know the humans, I've seen what they look like, I can

point them out. I know how they think. I can help the Prime get the information we need to bring Jasper home."

Maybe that was true, but it still wasn't good enough for Thorne. Blinding panic heated his face. "Are you mad? You're not ready. You've been awake in this time for but a week!"

"You've trained me well enough."

"Don't be daft, Laurel. You can't even sense when I'm siphoning your mana without your permission."

She gasped and the silence in the room became deafening.

Shit. He shouldn't have said that. Not here. Not in front of everyone. He'd planned to explain how it all worked properly when they had the time. He needed to ease her into what he'd done. What he'd already promised himself he wouldn't do again.

"You've been doing what?" Laurel ground out through her teeth.

He looked to the ceiling and tried to calm the rising sense of helplessness. May as well let her know all. Then she'd understand what a fool's errand this was. He was sure everyone would agree. "During the battle, when I broke the binding rune they put on me, I used your mana to do it. It is why you almost collapsed in the midst of the battle."

"You put your mate in danger?" Rush growled. "Without even asking her permission?"

"I needed to use a transference spell to bring Fury to me," he shot back. Could none of them see that had been the only decision to make, whether he'd asked permission or not. "Having Fury was the only reason I defeated the Well-hounds." He rounded on the Prime. "So you see, I can do whatever you need her for. She doesn't need to be in the thick of it. Just nearby in case I need to replenish my mana."

"If I had known that's all I meant to you, Thorne, I wouldn't have..." Laurel choked. Hurt, betrayal, and pain surged into Thorne through their bond. She was taking this all the wrong way. How could she not see that he only wanted to protect her? Couldn't she *feel* that from him? Wasn't that enough?

And then she did something that cleaved his heart in two, more than any stroke of a blade. She straightened her spine, walked over to him, took his hand, and looked him squarely in the eye. "We have located Jasper. You have taught me the ways of this land to my satisfaction. Consider our bargain ended."

"No," he said. "You can't walk away from me. We're bonded."

She shrugged. "That's your rule, not mine."

"It's the Well's rule. You're stuck with me, Laurel, whether you like it or not."

She glared at him. "Being *stuck* with you isn't exactly how I imagined this going. If you can't trust me to be on my own, without you, and with the Prime, then what are we doing? As far as I can see, the Well-blessed mating works well when we're together, but there are no adverse affects when we're apart, except the strength of our shared mana and emotions is weakened. So, technically, I can walk away."

"That's not what I meant. You're getting this all wrong."

His heart thudded. His skin went hot and prickly. She promised she wouldn't.

"Well, let me say it in a way you understand. In the binding words of our original bargain, we must walk away from each other."

A spark of heat zapped between their palms as their agreement ended with a snap.

Laurel turned and walked out of the temple.

She Well-damned *walked away* from him.

"We need her, Thorne," the Prime said gently. "Not only can her Well-blessed markings be hidden by appropriate attire, but I believe your mate has the power within her to keep a cloaking spell active for an extended period. She can get into places in the castle none of us can. We just need to train her."

All he heard was waffle because the blood in his ears was roaring. The wolf in him snarled with fury. Claws sprung from his fingertips. Fangs elongated in his mouth. He glared at her and spoke with a voice no longer human.

"You," he spat. "What more will you take from me?"

The Prime blinked, surprised.

And it infuriated him all the more. But then she filled with her power, letting the electric currents of the Well crackle along her skin, sparking and lighting with raw energy.

"Now you, D'arn Thorne, must walk away before you go somewhere dark you may not return from."

Every pair of eyes in the room watched him warily, readying their own power in case he released his. But they weren't worth it. None of them were. If his own mate couldn't understand him, then why was he trying? Thorne turned to the only one who'd given him comfort over his years... his wolf. He shifted, burst out of his clothes, and trotted out of there.

CHAPTER THIRTY-TWO

*L*aurel stood at the window in Ada's room and looked at the front lawn as the sun came up. A fire crackled on the hearth, keeping the brisk cold air outside, but condensation had gathered on the window, casting much of the view into warped bubble patterns.

It had been three days since Thorne had shifted into wolf and ran out of the Order compound.

Three days and she'd not heard a peep.

The markings on her arm told her next to nothing. Just a distant presence meaning he was alive, somewhere out there in the wild, poisonous forest surrounding the Order campus walls. And that was the icing on her pain-filled cake. Thorne preferred to live in a poisonous forest, possibly as a wolf, rather than coming home and working through their argument.

He'd hurt her immensely.

She would have given her mana freely if he'd asked at the Ring.

If he'd asked.

But this was about keeping the truth from her. The fae couldn't lie, but they could certainly keep the truth to themselves and, in doing so, he'd unwittingly committed the most heinous crime to her person. He'd taken away her ability to protect herself.

He *knew* how Bones had made her feel.

He *knew*, and yet he'd said nothing about what he'd done.

She felt like she didn't know him at all. What kind of man would do that to someone he supposedly loved?

But did he? Did he love her?

She'd felt warm emotions from him, but who was to say that was love? Their mating wasn't one of their choosing. They didn't even have a wedding ceremony. When he'd described one to her, it had made her pine for one. She felt like they'd missed a whole part of a normal relationship. The part she never used to want, until him.

Thinking back on the time they'd spent together, it had always been Laurel making the sacrifices.

It ate her up inside.

But she wouldn't chase him. No. She was done with telling him to let his anger go. Done with being the one to sacrifice. It was his turn. The ball was in his court.

Maybe this was a good thing. A blessing in disguise. Everyone else believed the Prime and Laurel were going to gather intel, and to rescue Jasper, but Laurel knew. Clarke knew. Laurel wouldn't come back without seeing Bones' dead body with her own eyes. After Thorne's behavior, it was clear there was no way he'd let her go through with this secret mission.

Rush had tried to apologize for Thorne. He'd said a male wolf shifter was highly possessive after mating, but this didn't excuse Thorne's behavior prior to their mating. The stealing of her mana. That was inexcusable.

"I wish I could come with you," Clarke said from behind Laurel. "But someone needs to stay with Ada."

Laurel turned to her friend sitting next to Ada on the bed. "Pretty is lucky to have you as a friend, Clarke. I am too."

"I hope that is true."

"After I go to Helianthus City, you'll see it is. I won't let you down."

Laurel turned back to the window and ran her finger down the condensation on the window. Water trickled to land in a pool at the bottom windowsill.

"Thorne will be back," Clarke declared.

Laurel couldn't find it in herself to feel. "Is this something you've *Seen*?"

"No. It's something I know because he's mated to you. I know how he would be feeling right now."

Like his heart is being ripped out? She hoped so. Because hers was.

"I don't think it's the same for us, Clarke. Thorne and I are different from you and Rush."

"The only difference is that Thorne is extra stubborn." Clarke took a breath. "And he was extra hurt. He never had a loving family like you."

"I know that," she snapped.

"I don't think you do. And don't take this the wrong way, but the scars of a broken and lonely childhood stay with you forever."

Laurel wanted to snap her anger at Clarke again, but her friend was right. Losing Lionel hurt. Deeply. But she'd had two loving parents to fill the gap. She'd had *people*. Some had no one. Some were empty for a long time.

Clarke had grown up with a mother who hated and vilified her. Her father had died young. She was alone until a bad man seduced her vulnerable state and manipulated her. If it weren't for Laurel and Ada befriending Clarke, she might still be with that bad man, but the world as they knew it would still be gone.

Including the loving family Laurel left behind.

A surge of defiance ran through Laurel. Clarke was wrong. Laurel deserved to feel anguish over missing her family. What made Thorne's pain more worthy than hers? It was all relative. Everyone had a right to hurt in the way that mattered to them. It didn't mean they could take it out on those they supposedly cared for. What allowed him to get away with his behavior? He'd had Jasper. He'd had his aunt. And now, he had Rush, Clarke, and Laurel. Yet it still wasn't enough for Thorne.

No. She frowned at the window. She was a queen. A boss. She wouldn't be treated this way. By anyone.

"Are you prepared?" Clarke asked.

"The dress is made. I've practiced the cloaking spell until I've gone cross-eyed."

"That's not what I meant."

Laurel turned and met her friend's grave eyes. She glanced at her ruined nails, but this time, she resisted the urge to rub them on her thighs in an attempt to erase that feeling. No. She curled her fingers into a fist and used that sensation to drive her resolve.

"I won't hesitate when I see him, don't worry. I don't care if it's in a crowded room." Dark, bitter anger filled Laurel. "If I see Bones, I'll burn him to ash."

CHAPTER THIRTY-THREE

*I*n his wolf form, and from the shadows of the trees surrounding the Order walls, Thorne watched the procession bound for Helianthus City leave the grounds. It was unusual that the Prime had chosen to travel by horse and carriage. A portal would have been faster, unless she wanted to travel the long way on purpose.

He hated not knowing why.

A curtain in the carriage window twitched, and Thorne caught sight of his mate's sweet face as she stared out the window, perhaps looking for him. He'd never know because she turned her face back into the dark recess of the cabin where a shock of white ringlets bounced before the curtain was dropped.

Bitterness seethed anew.

And then with each passing moment, the carriage drew away, his battered emotions ebbed, draining away with the distance.

The sense of Laurel's presence lessened in his soul until she became naught but a ghost of a feeling down his bond, and he was once again as lonely as he'd always been. An ache in his chest grew.

He let loose a howl that shook the trees. When the last notes died, his ears pricked up at the sound of footsteps. His hackles rose as he concentrated on the sound: crunching fallen leaves and twigs. And then he scented kin. A white wolf padded out of the shelter of trees and turned to him, golden eyes piercing.

Rush.

A shimmering light haloed the wolf's body, and then Rush shifted into fae form. The deep scowl on his face softened inexplicably. He opened his mouth to speak, but Thorne, still in wolf form, growled at him.

He didn't need a lecture. He knew exactly what a floater he'd been, but he didn't know how to handle the feelings that had been choking him in that council room. He'd only meant to come out here until he could breathe better... and somehow he couldn't work up the courage to find his way back. He couldn't face Laurel with his tail between his legs. Shame had never been in his emotional canon.

Until her.

"I don't know how to help you mend this wound between you and your mate," Rush said. "That's not why I'm here."

Thorne stilled. He sat on his hind legs and looked up at Rush.

351

"Laurel will need your help where she is going." Rush scrubbed his beard, anguish on his face.

Alarm prickled Thorne all over. Laurel needed his help? He shifted back to fae form.

"What is it?" His throat felt raw from under-use.

"I overheard them speak." Rush met Thorne's eyes, then looked away with a frown. "Shit. If Clarke finds out I'm here, she'll have my balls in a vice."

"Rush," Thorne growled, now filling with apprehension.

"But just because we're mated, doesn't mean we always agree. I'm the only one who knows how you feel right now, Thorne. I understand these overwhelming feelings you must have. The urge to protect is so strong after mating. It drove me to do something that almost ended in Clarke's death. If you don't travel to Helianthus City, you won't be able to stop Laurel from making the worst mistake of her life. She's going to kill the one who tortured her."

"Good," Thorne spat. "He will deserve to have his life cut short."

Laurel deserved a little reparation.

"Yes, he does. But does Laurel deserve the burden of such an act?"

Thorne's blood slowly drained from his face.

Rush continued, "Perhaps she's not told you enough about her time and where she was from. Before the very end, they lived peacefully. The only death they knew was from disease or old age. Murder was reserved for the lowliest of them, and few and far between suffered the consequences. Not like now."

The gravity of what Rush said settled in Thorne like a falling stone. If Laurel took on this mantle, it would ruin her. Such an act would eat at her soul. He thought back to all the ways she'd used her power. None of the times had ended in the death of the enemy. She'd been strong, powerful, and at times ruthless. But she wasn't a killer.

He was.

It had been Thorne who'd ended their opponents without a second thought in the Ring. If her time had truly been more peaceful, then having to become this person that killed, so soon after waking from her time, it would irrevocably change her.

"There's more," Rush added. "Cloud and Shade went back to interrogate Patches about the djinn bottle. With what they gathered from his guard too, they've pieced together more mercenary acts of terror paid for by Mithras coin."

"Meaning?"

"Someone close to the king has been paying Patches to make it look like Unseelie are attacking the Seelie."

"So it is true. Someone is inciting a civil war between fae-kind."

"Yes."

"You think it's the humans?"

Rush nodded. "Clarke and I suspected it's been happening for some time, but after we were rid of Thaddeus, there wasn't much activity. When I'd visited the human city while I was cursed, I saw nothing of this magnitude. That coupled with the fact Clarke's recent visions were mainly about finding Laurel and Ada, we thought we had time to deal with the Void. Now we know the humans were using this time to get a stronghold within the Summer Court."

A new flood of irritation swam through Thorne. "Knowing all this, then how can you be happy with the Prime's plan to take Laurel with her? There is more we can do on behalf of the Well. The Order has a right to raid the palace."

Rush scoffed. "No, we don't. We need more evidence. But if you'd stuck around long enough, you'd have learned the Guardians pushed for our own extraction plan for Jasper. And the Prime has approved it."

"She has?"

"It is why she left by carriage and not portal. She is creating a distraction, making the journey to the Summer Court in Helianthus a spectacle. And we have time to prepare." Rush's gaze turned inward. "Do you know I almost killed the Prime for what she did to us? I went to her office, drew Starcleaver, and swung it at her head. I caught naught but a tail-feather as she flew out of the window. And now I am glad that I missed." He leveled his stare on Thorne. "Killing anyone because of perceived injustice is no way to honor the Well. It makes us no better than the ones who came before us."

"Perceived injustice?" Thorne growled. "How can you say that? It was real."

"I only meant the Prime has been different since the news about Jasper came out. I believe she is regretful. I now understand the toll it takes to keep Elphyne flourishing. She had to make an untenable decision. Any way she chose, someone was going to get hurt. She picked the fate that ended with Clarke alive. And with Clarke alive, Laurel is alive. More will live because of this choice. Possibly the rest of the world will be born anew. I will never forgive the Prime for what she's done, but I believe she deserves a chance to make amends for her mistake with Jasper."

His words hit Thorne hard.

It *had* been an untenable decision. Less death vs more death. Could Thorne say he'd be able to take that burden on?

No.

Which meant Thorne had been a fool. A giant floating piece of useless, Well-rejected trash. Not only to Laurel, but to the Order. He'd let his anger get in the way, and because of his inability to see past it, they'd have learned about the link with the djinn's owner before he'd even met Laurel. They'd know the humans had infiltrated the Summer Court long before Jasper was removed from the Ring. But it took Laurel to teach him to let go of that anger. So, in a way, Clarke had been right. Laurel had led him to finding Jasper in more ways than one.

All they knew about the Void now was that he wanted Elphyne for himself, and he believed he could use magic without having to follow the rules the Well had given them. He wanted to bring metals and plastics back. He wanted to dominate the new world. The fae knew that this would have catastrophic consequences. For centuries, the world struggled to gain its life back. Survival in the harsh, frozen land-scape was nothing more than that… survival. There were those among the fae—the Prime, namely—who still remem-bered that world. She made sure to remind them of it often. They weren't living back then. They were surviving. It wasn't until Jackson Crimson discovered the link to the Well, and the rules about metals and plastics, that life flour-ished anew.

Life came back to the planet. New species were made in both animal and plant life. Some species thought extinct had thawed and were brought back to the living. And it was only through the grace of the Well that this happened. Letting the Void go back to the old, greedy ways would spell the end, and if they got rid of Bones, the Void would only find another to fill his place.

"We should capture this Bones person. He is the Void's right-hand man. We should capture him and not kill him because it could set off a chain reaction of revenge with the Void. For all we know, they are lovers. They've traveled through time to be here. I might not be anywhere near the truth, but if there's one thing I've learned this year, it's that I don't know everything," Thorne said. "We should capture him, and then give him to Cloud to interrogate."

"Agreed."

Thorne's gaze snapped to his father's, a mirror image of his own except for the color. Thorne inherited that from his mother. It may have taken Thorne some time to come to terms with Rush's presence, but now Thorne could see he was a fae of honor, and he was doing his best to put the painful past behind them—something they couldn't change —and look to the future. Something they *could* change.

There was much Thorne could learn from his father.

"If Laurel is allowed to end this human," Rush continued. "It could cause catastrophic consequences. I don't know why or how Clarke has not *seen* this. I think sometimes we rely on her knowing too much from her visions, we fail to see that she is just as fallible as the rest of us. Her emotions get in the way too. She is afraid. I sense it every day. We all make mistakes. How we deal with them is our true test of character."

"How are you so wise?" Thorne joked.

"I've spent a long time watching the behavior of others."

This made a sadness well inside Thorne. "You were there when I grew up," he acknowledged.

"Yes. Until you got to the Order I shared in your pain. And then... seeing you with Jasper." Rush looked away. "It was then I realized you were moving on without me. It hurt too much to watch, so I moved away. I trusted Jasper to look after you."

It took a long moment before Thorne had the courage to say, "I understand this now. And... I am sorry no one was there to share your pain."

Rush's eyes watered. His jaw clenched. And he nodded.

For it was known that only family apologized so freely to one another. Only family didn't expect a boon in return.

Emotion clogged Thorne. And then, for the first time in his decades-long life, he hugged his father.

CHAPTER THIRTY-FOUR

*T*he journey south from the Order of the Well to the Helianthus City took three days.

It was only three days.

She could wait three days to hear Bones scream as he melted in her fire. To smell his scorched flesh. To feel an echo of the pain he'd inflicted on her. It was all she cared about now, and somehow, she'd equated the end of Bones with the release of the bitterness left from Thorne's betrayal.

How could he?

He'd used her.

Left her vulnerable.

He'd left.

And didn't come back.

She knew he was hurting. She knew she'd walked away from him first. But she was hurting too. She'd had her whole world ripped from her, and she was tired of trying to stay positive about it.

The long journey to Helianthus City meant they had to stop at many villages along the way. At each stop, the Prime would get out and wave regally and bestow blessings on the townspeople. Laurel would stay in the carriage or regale herself to any room or lodgings volunteered by the grace of townspeople loyal to the Well.

Without Clarke, or the distraction of keeping Ada hydrated and alive, Laurel slipped into a dark, resentful state of mind.

No guards traveled with them, only two Mages. One was the Prime's assistant, Maryweather, who was another owl shifter. Maryweather looked very similar to the Prime, minus the curly hair. Maryweather's was straight. She sat up on the driver's box seat with Thistle, the coachman—a male fox-eared fae with red hair. Occasionally, Laurel caught shadows flittering over the carriage, and she looked outside, expecting to see clouds, but only caught a white owl coasting. Occasionally a crow or two.

But after the first day, she'd stopped checking to see who followed them and her thoughts became consumed with how she would find Bones and assassinate him. He might not be in the palace. He might not be in Elphyne. But if he was, she would find him.

She also had to go along with the Prime's plan to rescue Jasper.

Thistle was extremely zealous in his newly self-appointed

role as the tour guide and narrated stories about the towns they passed. Annoyingly, he kept interrupting her dark thoughts with his chirpy rundowns of the towns they stopped in. Like a proper gentleman, he would help Laurel and the Prime down from the carriage when necessary. He confessed to Laurel that they wouldn't be able to do this sort of fanfare in the Unseelie Kingdom. Residents there would shut their doors and stay inside, and it wouldn't be a personal insult, it was just how the Unseelie were. They didn't like outsiders, even those who dedicated their lives to serving the Well.

Maybe that was where Laurel needed to go. She might need to escape the Seelie kingdom after what she planned to do. Surely there would be someone willing to help her relocate. And if not, she had a handy cloaking spell in her canon of skills now. She would find a way. Living in the Unseelie kingdom, undisturbed by outsiders… it was definitely appealing.

As they neared Helianthus City, Laurel decided she wouldn't get another chance to discuss something that had been playing on her mind. The Prime wasn't particularly talkative during the journey, and she was a little frightening. Men trying to mansplain things to Laurel, she could take. But a strong woman, possibly as powerful as Laurel, *that* she found intimidating.

But there was one thing that had been playing on her mind. If she didn't speak up now, she might never have a chance to ask the Prime again.

"Is it really necessary to force tributes to obtain more

Guardians?" she asked. "Can they not be sourced another way?"

The Prime, who had been staring out the window on her side of the carriage, a stack of papers in her hand, turned to Laurel with a knowing smirk. "I see D'arn Thorne has been in your ear about the subject."

"He has," she agreed. "But I would also like to hear your version of the truth."

The Prime looked at Laurel with a mix of suspicion and something Laurel believed was respect, then she turned back to the window.

"Our numbers are dwindling," the Prime admitted. "Elphyne is growing, flourishing, yet there are empty beds in the barracks. Guardians perish too often. Mana-twisted monsters are springing up from the depths of the Well. The threat from humans is also expanding." She sighed heavily. "Once, there was nothing more important than dedicating your life to the service of the Well. The fae knew that if we made sacrifices, the Well would reward us with a treasured world beyond our imaginations. Now we live in our imagination and our dreams have become reality. It is hard to see beyond into a future where we don't dominate. I fear the fae will have to see nightmares again before they realize how good they have it."

Laurel agreed, in a way. "Humans suffered the same affliction. We are too smart for our own good. We built the bombs, we destroyed the land, and we suffered for it. It is a pity I don't have a lesson learned you can use to teach the people of this time. We were always aware of the sinking ship but could never stop it."

The Prime leveled her stare at Laurel. It lasted so long that Laurel squirmed. "Has anyone told you the tale of the first fae who discovered the link between the Well, the magic within us, and that of the planet?"

"Jackson Crimson?" she suggested. She'd heard snippets about their first leader during her training at the academy for the cloaking spell.

"Did they tell you what happened to him?"

Laurel shook her head.

"No," the Prime said. "I suppose no one has told you. It's nowhere near as glamorous as the start of his story."

"What happened to him?"

"He dedicated his life to building the Order. He built everything you see that we have today. And then he went to the ceremonial lake, offered himself, and never came out." A sadness came over the Prime, as though she had been there, as though she'd known him. "The scriptures say he'd reached enlightenment. The Well took him into its depths and he became one with it, all-powerful, all-seeing. But... I know the truth. He was tired. Tired of fighting for Elphyne, when it didn't seem like the fae were learning from the mistakes the first humans made."

"Are you talking about metals and plastics?"

The Prime nodded. "And more. The magic. Dipping into the dark arts, thinking of themselves as gods. Cruelty. Greed. You will understand more when you meet King Mithras. I fear it is as you said. A sinking ship."

With that, the Prime turned back to her papers, effectively dismissing Laurel. But she wasn't done with the Prime.

"The fae don't need nightmares," Laurel said. "People are defensive when they believe no one is on their side. Your trouble with recruits is a classic branding problem." The Prime arched her brow at Laurel, so she continued. "In my time, we had businesses and corporations that had thousands of staff. My own company employed twelve-hundred people. To make my workplace attractive to work at, I offered free fitness clothes, free equipment, and free gym memberships. It not only made them feel of value, but it encouraged them to look after their health, which in turn made them more productive. I marketed Queen Fitness as, not only a place to work, but a way of life. Work healthy, live longer."

The Prime snorted. "We can't make that promise. Living longer isn't necessarily something we can offer. You're more likely to live longer if you *aren't* a Guardian."

"You're taking me too literally. There are plenty of things you can offer."

"Such as?"

"Such as a place to live. A warm home and a roof over their heads. Belonging. Clothes. Food. Education. Power. Glory. The knowledge that you are doing something good for the world."

"Altruism has never been a core value of the fae, despite Crimson's best efforts."

Laurel shrugged. "Perhaps. But it's a start. I saw how

much the fae liked watching the ruthless battles at the Ring. Maybe you could host something like the Guardian Games, where you pit each Guardian against each other and they battle for glory—not to the death, obviously—but maybe something more sporty. Children could collect cards or place bets on their favorites. If you make these games a regular thing, soon others will want to join. It doesn't have to be a sport, but it's a popularity contest. We need to make ourselves look better than the Crown."

The Prime tapped her lip. "I think sometime later, I would like to hear more about your time and how your businesses handled these situations."

"I also would like that," Laurel replied. She hoped that one day the Order could do away with tributes. With a pang in her chest, she realized Thorne would have liked that too.

Thistle shouted down from his position outside the carriage.

"Helianthus City coming up on the right."

Laurel pulled the curtain from the window and peeked outside. Her breath sucked in hard at the beauty and found her mind inexplicably shift to Thorne. She would have liked to share this experience with him.

He'd hurt her, and she'd hurt him back. It was petty, childish, and not the way she'd normally behave.

She'd waited for days in their room for him to come back so they could talk about it, but he didn't. And with each passing day he stayed away, her heart broke a little more, and the scars between the broken parts had hardened. It was easier to turn her attention toward Bones and let him be the focus of her wrath. But now, as the city came into view, all that hatred ebbed away, and all she could think was that she wanted to share it with Thorne.

Those little small moments of joy they'd been collecting were missed.

Pushing aside her sadness, she focused on the magnificent city they approached. Helianthus City was unlike anything she'd seen before. No such cities existed in her time. This one sparkled in the sun as though it were made from diamonds.

While the carriage traveled over the uneven road, Thistle explained the impenetrable citadel walls were made from mana-fortified glass that looked like someone had frozen a wave of water as it reached breaking point. Laurel honestly couldn't tell if there was actual water inside the glass walls, or if it was sparkling manabeeze like the false sky under the hill. Would this wall glow at night, or was it the sun's rays reflecting in it now?

The weather had turned warmer. Seagulls squawked. It still wasn't the summer as she remembered it, but she supposed to these people, who had lived centuries in winter, this would indeed be very warm.

The carriage crossed a long, arched bridge to get to the city walls. As they traveled over it, a sparkling river ran from the city harbor and into a vast turquoise sea. This was the first time Laurel had seen the seaside since arriving in this time, and it was incredibly clear and pristine. Laurel gasped as they drove by a rocky beach with white sand where she could have sworn humanoid creatures basked on a warm slab of stone. Each had a fish tail. And a human head.

She whipped around to the Prime. "Were they mermaids?"

The Prime, who'd not been paying attention due to her flicking through some documents, shrugged. "Possibly. There are such fae named mermaids, but there are also fae emerging from the oceans who've lived there unnoticed for millennia until recently. With the habitable stretch of land increasing every year, we're still discovering new breeds of fae."

Holy mother-of-pearl. Laurel turned back to the window as they arrived at the citadel gates and were stopped by the soldiers guarding the entrance. All were distinguished in coats of shocking red, clean-cut appearances, shiny bone weapons or bows, and arrows. After the guards checked in to see the Prime, they were allowed through the gates. Within moments, they were moving again and driving into the citadel itself.

Laurel didn't think she could be filled with more wonder, but once inside the citadel, she saw there were not only streets, but canals that led from the estuary and wound through the packed houses, like those she'd once seen in Venice. Most townhouses weren't made from glass, like the wall, but they had glass features, enough to make it all twinkle brightly, making Laurel wish for a pair of sunglasses. Fae of all kinds came out of their dwellings to see the Prime's carriage. Some of them opened the hatches of their windows, smiled and waved. Others frowned.

Most frowned.

Definitely a branding issue.

As they took the main road, Laurel noticed fae putting up decorations in the streets. Some were already celebrating roadside with food and drink. She supposed the festivities tonight in the palace would spill out into the streets, making the king's announcement something the entire city could be a part of. Laurel's mood darkened when, as they drew closer to the palace, she noted more food, more drink, and more wastage.

What had happened to having too many mouths to feed that they resorted to killing fae for having children?

An animal roasted on a spit, but the people carousing next to it had completely forgotten. It had burned black, and they didn't care because they'd already had their fill with other food. Empty plates and cups were scattered everywhere. Seagulls scavenged and gorged. Rotten food had flies buzzing around. Had they been celebrating for days?

It certainly didn't look like the people here in the city wanted for necessities so much that they needed an unsanctioned breeding law to ensure enough resources went around. It looked like they had too much.

A tomato, or similar fruit, smashed against the carriage window and she drew back suddenly.

The Prime sighed. "Here we go."

"Why are they throwing fruit?"

"They see the Order of the Well emblem on the carriage."

"You know," Laurel commented dryly, "You should be

LANA PECHERCZYK

taxing the king and this city for your monster-hunting services, not the people you save."

The thud of more fruit hit the carriage, the occasional derogatory shout from a passerby, and the responding curse from Thistle.

Laurel faced the Prime, who watched her with unguarded curiosity. Laurel thought perhaps she'd spoken out of turn, but the Prime nodded.

"You first humans are constantly astounding me. You and Clarke, I mean. The ones who live today, they're descended from your kind, but I believe they're different. Before you and Clarke arrived, I never would have thought working with the humans would be a possibility. But you keep proving me wrong, and for that, I am grateful. Not only because all the sacrifices I've made are founded, but because it gives me hope for our combined futures. Crimson always wanted us all to live in harmony. Until then..." The Prime tapped her lip. "I believe taxing the king just might be a solution we can entertain." She pointed at Laurel. "Remind me when we return to the Order."

Pride swelled in Laurel as she turned back to gazing out of the window. Yes. Perhaps she was going to find her feet in this world, after all. Whether it was with Thorne, the Prime, or otherwise. She wouldn't let Bones take this away from her. Not this time.

CHAPTER THIRTY-FIVE

*S*tanding before a black-glass mirror, Laurel watched her reflection as Maryweather fussed about, tying Laurel's turquoise blue shoulder straps and securing a small beaded headdress. The dress was too much, but the Prime had insisted Laurel look eye catching enough to gain the king's attention.

Eye-catching meant a neckline that dipped to her navel and showed ample cleavage. The same cut existed at the back, showing skin all the way down to the curve of her very awesome rear-end. So low that she couldn't wear underwear. The dress hugged her hips and then flared near the floor, fishtail style, ending in patterns of red, yellow, and orange.

Sky on fire.

That's what her dress reminded her of.

Scattered along the base hem of the dress, sparkling beads glowed sporadically as though powered by electricity.

Her favorite pearlescent crushed powder highlighted her smooth skin. When she walked, she shimmered, as though she truly were on fire.

With strong black eye makeup, pale glossy lips, and long dangling earrings, she felt like she was going to the Met Gala. She'd been once with a Cross-fit champion on her arm. It had all been for publicity, but it was fun. Maybe this could be too. The fae certainly knew how to dress. She was truly extravagant, and she wasn't ashamed to admit it. The only part she didn't like was the way her pinned back hair showed her very round ears.

They'd discussed at length whether Laurel would go in disguise. In the end, they decided that the king was already liaising with humans. Laurel had already declared to Cornucopia she was human, so why not use her humanity to their benefit? This was essentially Laurel's debutante introduction into the fae society as a powered human. It not only signaled that she was here, but that she was accepted by the Order, and that they would stand behind her if anyone tried to hurt her. Still...

"It's too much," she said. "The cloaking spell works better if I'm already inconspicuous."

The Prime barely looked up from the letter she penned with quill and ink at a desk. Her simple white dress draped down her legs to pool at the floor.

"We've been through this," she said, eyes still on her work. "The cloaking spell is a backup. First, we want you to attract attention. The king has been refusing to grant me an audience for the past two years. The only way to speak privately with him is for you to catch his eye. He likes new things. He likes beautiful things. He likes collecting human artisans and holding them captive. Word about the human with fire power who fought in the Ring will have reached him by now. And since you have Well-blessed markings on your body, he will be very curious. He and I have a history. We compete. He won't like that I have you and he doesn't. He will endeavor to steal you for himself. Even seduce you."

"Even knowing I'm mated?"

"Nobody can erase that mating, but he won't want to do that. He'll want to conquer you and use you. Then he will throw you away."

"You make this sound so appealing," she muttered under her breath. And then louder, "Why can't you demand he hand Jasper back to you? You're the Prime of the Order of the Well. I thought you were above Elphyne law."

The Prime lifted her head, smiled, and arched a brow. "Now, if that was the case, we wouldn't be here, would we?" She went back to her letter. "No. The sorry fact is that the courts are starting to shun the Order, and powerful as we are, we are small. On our way in, I noticed emissaries from the Autumn and Spring Courts. This does not bode well."

"Why not?"

"Because the Autumn Court is part of the Unseelie king-dom. If Mithras is attempting to sway them, he's trying to amass power. He wants them to defect and to join him with his attack on Queen Maebh. Our job at this ball is not only to retrieve Jasper as one of our own but to put in a show of force. To say that we know what is happening, and we are as strong as they are."

"Force?" Laurel asked. "But it's just you and me."

The Prime blinked. "Whatever gave you that idea?"

"Oh. I just assumed because you never told me otherwise."

"Why would I tell you my plans? You've yet to pledge loyalty to the Well. You haven't even discussed tenure at the Order. The only reason I trust you this far is that my Seer, Dawn, has foretold that for us to have a beneficial outcome from this ball, you are necessary."

Laurel turned back to the mirror and tried to keep her beating heart to a minimum. What else had the Prime planned? Was any of it going to interfere with Laurel's intentions to assassinate Bones? Should she tell the Prime? Unease swam through Laurel's stomach and she pressed her palm there. Maybe going out half-cocked and just killing some random person in the royal court might not be a good idea, even if he was one of the worst humans in history.

She felt sick with doubt and ached for Thorne's steady presence. A hard lump formed in her throat. She missed him. More than she'd ever imagined. Would he miss her too, if all this went south?

Laurel cast one last glance at herself in the mirror. It was a beautiful dress. Sky on fire. She flared her fingers at her stomach. Maryweather had offered to glamor her nails, but Laurel declined, as she always did. They were her battle scars, a reminder of everything Bones had taken. A reminder for her to stay the course. She rubbed her nails against her thighs.

HUES of the setting sun glimmered into the palace through the crystal clear ceiling. Laurel waited patiently with the Prime in an anteroom beside the ballroom, catching glimpses of the ballroom every time a guest entered through the long red, velvet drapes. From what she could see inside, more curtains lined the walls, covering masonry so that it looked like a room made from velvet and glass, opulent to its core.

From the loud conversation, the string quartet, and the jingling of bells—something the Prime explained probably belonged to a jester—it seemed like festivities were well underway. Laurel had yet to glimpse Jasper, or Bones, or the king. But she saw plenty of glamorously dressed fae, just like her. She didn't feel so out of place.

The Prime stood next to Laurel, and fumed. They'd been waiting for at least thirty minutes to be admitted to the ballroom and announced. Her great white owl wings were packed away—shifted into her body, so she looked virtually human, if it weren't for the aura of otherness to her.

Finally, a fae with large curling ram horns and a waistcoat called them through the drapes. Once inside the ballroom, he made them stop. He pinched his lips. Looked down at them, and then raised his trumpet, taking the attention of the ballroom. He read from a sheet where they'd written their names down.

"May I present Aleksandra, Her Illustrious Prime of the Order of the Well, and, er... Miss Laurel Baker, Fitness Queen of Las Vegas."

Laurel grinned at her title. None of them knew where Vegas was, but like the Prime had said, they needed to use her humanity to an advantage. It would intrigue the king, and it would flush Bones out. If he was here.

She strode into the room with her chin held high, her spine straight, and her eyes wary.

But she couldn't see past the crowds of curious gentry, the lords and ladies of Elphyne. Perhaps even a queen or a king. And she couldn't see past her own disgust. Not only were the fae here grossly overdressed, but the food was extravagant, as was the drink. Hanging from the glass ceiling were large chandeliers with half-naked fae dangling, performing acrobatics and swinging from thick, green vines. As they walked around the perimeter of the room, Laurel heard dallying laughter, and the occasional sound of couples clearly enjoying themselves. There must be hidden alcoves behind the curtains.

At round tables, fae behaved badly, throwing food into each other's mouths, shooting back drinks from the bosoms of ladies, dipping under the tables to play with pet animals on leashes. Some of them weren't even animals. Some were fae. Or perhaps... human.

And then they walked into the center of the room, right before the dais leading up to the king's throne, flanked by

Jasper on one side, and Bones on the other. Laurel's heart threatened to pound out of her chest, but she forced herself to ignore both of them and keep her eyes on the king. As they stopped before the dais, Laurel's eyes lifted and landed on the golden-haired, svelte fae with eyes like honey. His wolfish ears stuck out from the weight of a delicate blown-glass crown. His long golden locks looked more like a lion's mane than that of a wolf.

But it was clear he was a wolf. She could see it in the wild shadows of his eyes. They were the same as Jasper's. But where the king was golden, Jasper was dark. Laurel bet that he would shift into a black wolf with that brown and black-tipped hair. He looked better than he had at the arena —face cleaned, no wounds in sight. His high, frill-neck shirt covered his curse marks, and a velvet orange coat hugged his physique. On his head sat a smaller, blown-glass crown. Clearly, he was the heir, but he wasn't even allowed to sit.

A statue with empty eyes.

Was he drugged?

Sadness bloomed in Laurel, and then she shifted her gaze to the other side of the throne where a face she'd never forget stared back at her. Bones. In a red embroidered coat. He was part of the king's royal guard.

Heat prickled Laurel's face and under her arms. Without helping herself, her fingers rubbed and flexed against her thighs. There he was. And with pointed elf-ears. He watched her with a black, evil gaze. He caught the movement of her fingers and then smiled.

He fed off fear. She wouldn't give it to him. She stopped

rubbing her nails. Cold, hard fury seethed in her blood. That's all he would receive from her now. That was the last time she'd let her panic take over.

The king looked at Laurel, then down to the Prime. His finger tapped on the arm of his throne as he stared at her in contemplation. But then Bones whispered something in the king's ear, and his gaze snapped back to Laurel.

The king stood up.

He stepped down the dais and came toward Laurel, like a lion stalking its prey. Mithras pushed past the Prime and stopped mere inches from Laurel's feet. This slight was exactly what the Prime had hoped, but she acted affronted, all the same.

The crowd cleared around them, giving ample room for the king to inspect Laurel. The Prime made a very loud, obvious huff, and then retreated to another table where she struck a conversation with two bronze-skinned and auburn-haired fae.

"Human," the king drawled, drawing her attention back to him. He gave her the once over, like she was a prized mare on auction. His golden gaze, a brand down her body. "You are simply breathtaking."

Laurel met his gaze and nodded. "I am."

The king blinked, shocked by her admission, and then paused as though recollecting his strategy.

In Laurel's experience, men didn't like it when an empowered female accepted their compliment. They wanted to be the one with the power, lauding their attention as though it were a gift from a god—them. So the easiest way to establish a power balance was to meet him halfway. Laurel knew she was beautiful. She knew she had a trim body that men drooled over. She'd worked damned hard for it. She'd earned her confidence.

She held out her hand. The one with her Well-blessed markings glowing brightly on her skin. The king's gaze flared with some hidden emotion, and then he took her hand and lowered his lips to it, ensuring he smelled her with his keen wolf senses.

Laurel didn't miss his gaze catching on her nails and watched curiously to see what he would do. He rubbed his thumb over her hand and straightened but didn't let go.

"You are a most curious human."

"My name is Laurel."

"Laurel," he tested. "A name as beautiful as the person it belongs to. Tell me, Laurel, do you have any special artistic gifts?" He gestured to the string quartet currently playing in the corner. Like the musicians she'd seen at the Birdcage, these played with bleeding fingers. "I most like the human artisans from Crystal City. They're unlike anything we experience here in Elphyne."

She smiled at him. Name dropping the impenetrable human city was a veiled display of his influence and reach. Perhaps he assumed that Laurel thought because he could take these humans whenever he wanted, he could take her too. They were chattel to him.

Laurel darted a glance to Bones. He'd traded in metal cages and weapons to Thaddeus, and now he was using his own kind to get in the king's good graces.

"I'm not from Crystal City."

His brows winged up. "No?"

He still held her hand, idly rubbing his thumb over her skin, making sure to touch her blue mating marks. He also looked occasionally to the one at her neck and it seemed to titillate him further, as though he planned to take what belonged to someone else. She had the sudden urge to vomit, or to take a long hot bath and wash his taint away. But she settled for letting her power build until it heated her hand. He gasped and let go, looking at her shocked. Her grin stretched.

"No," she repeated. "I'm not from Crystal City. But I suspect you knew that, even before I had it announced at my arrival."

His playfulness disappeared and something wild flashed in the shadows of his eyes. His wolfish ears twitched, dislodging golden hair and nudging his crown. Laurel imagined the wolf he shifted to was dark, ruthless, and a little mad. And then the king's countenance snapped back to one of joviality.

"Come," he said, holding out his hand, proving he wasn't afraid of her fire. "Dance with me."

A murmur of surprise, shock, and awe rippled around the room. The king dancing, let alone with a human, probably didn't happen often. And she also got the sense that one didn't refuse an invitation to do so. She smiled thinly and put her hand back in his while holding the bile down in her throat.

He tugged her to his frame. Beneath the embroidered

suit was a hard body she had no doubt was lethal and strong. She forced a smile on her lips. "I'm afraid I'm not versed in the dances of your world. I may step on your feet."

"Oh"—he smiled darkly—"It's not hard to follow my lead."

One hand clasped hers and lifted to the side, the other grasped her rear. No. Grasp was the wrong word. Groped was better.

A surge of fury gushed down Laurel's bond. It wasn't hers.

Thorne?

Hope flared in her chest. She cast her gaze around the room but couldn't see him. The king must have sensed her distraction. He lowered his nose to her neck, right over the bite scar, and inhaled deeply.

When he came back to face her, she saw his eyes had turned slumberous.

"You smell divine, even with the taint of your mate on there."

She frowned at him. He could smell that? "I haven't seen him for days," she mumbled.

The king gave her a rakish grin. "I wouldn't care if you did."

In other words, he might be the only male in Elphyne who couldn't care less about the rules of mating. She was told that no other male would want to be with her after she'd been sworn to Thorne—a fact he'd neglected to tell her before he'd bitten her.

Her chest constricted. *Better get this over with.*

"Why did you assume I was from Crystal City?" she asked demurely.

The king's grip on her rear tightened so much, it impeded her movement. He shifted and danced them around in a circle. "Where else would you be from?"

"The same place Bones is from."

He didn't stutter. He didn't flinch. "Bones," he said. "Such a barbaric name, don't you think?"

"So you don't deny it. You know him."

"And you lie. There is only one human city."

Two realizations hit Laurel. If the king believed there was only one human city, then Bones hadn't revealed he was from the past. The second thing was that the king clearly knew Bones was human, so the glamor on Bones' ears wasn't for the king's benefit, but for the people of Elphyne. The king knowingly colluded with Bones and didn't want them to know about it. This was all the Prime needed to know to take the matter further.

"Can Bones use mana as I can?" she pressed.

"Why so many questions about my advisor?"

"Your advisor?" she laughed. "I'm just curious if he woke from my time with the same unending power, or if he was shunned by the Well, as I've heard."

Mithras narrowed his eyes. "What do you mean, 'he woke from your time.' And no one has unending power."

"Well, perhaps not unending. But close. It's true. The Order hasn't seen the likes of this much power in one person since they started recording it. Ask the Prime if you don't believe me." She waggled her arm with the blue markings. "And I can share my power with my mate, making him all the stronger too. Did you hear about our little situation at the Ring?" She leaned closer. "My mate drew enough power from me to shatter binding runes, and I'd done the same to myself only moments before."

The king stopped dancing. She could virtually see his thoughts ticking over, wondering about the prize he had in his hands, and why Bones hadn't revealed he had this kind of power, or if Bones had it at all. Whatever he was thinking, Laurel knew she'd cast doubt into his mind.

"I want to make you an offer," she said, as a sudden thought came to her. "Release Jasper, and you can have me for as long as you want."

"Why would I want you over my kin?"

That riled. She glared back. "Because I know you like to collect things. I know you like to look better than Queen Maebh, but the sad fact is you simply aren't as powerful. Correct me if I'm wrong, but she commands the Sluagh, right? Didn't she create them?" She blinked innocently. "Tell me, King Mithras. What have you created? I'm fascinated to know."

Cold, hard menace flickered in his dark eyes.

And there it was. She'd found his core trigger. He'd broken away from the Unseelie Kingdom years ago to create the Seelie Kingdom, but Queen Maebh was one of the original fae. She was far more powerful than him, and he knew it. He feared it.

He swung her roughly around in a pirouette.

She leaned in close to him and lowered her voice seductively. "I can burn your palace of glass down in one sitting and still have power left over. Isn't that worth having in the war you're about to incite?"

"Killing you won't have the same rallying effect, I'm afraid. Even with your power, you're not worth as much as the fae upon that dais."

They were going to kill Jasper? Laurel gasped. Of course. Why else would a selfish king announce an heir when he'd assassinated all other offspring? He was greedy. He wanted to rule Elphyne. But he only had half of it, and he was no match for the Unseelie queen.

But if he made it look like she killed his only heir, then he had a symbol to rally fae armies behind. They would seek revenge, not just for the fake attacks around the realm, but for the murder of his only son.

"This was Bones' idea, wasn't it?" she accused.

The king smirked and then shrugged. "So what if it was?"

"You realize that whatever he's told you about his origins is false. Humans can lie, or have you forgotten that? He is one of the people who destroyed the first world. And the reason they did that was so the new world was smaller, more manageable, easier for them to take over." She studied the king's face. "You seem to be proving them right."

Outrage shattered the king's superior countenance. "If that were so, then why are they stuck behind their Crystal City walls, deep into the barren ice wastelands?"

"But they're not stuck, are they?" she replied. "I can see at least five in this room. The musicians you assume are your prisoners. And Bones. How many more has he smuggled into Elphyne under the guise of captives?"

The king blinked, shocked. Obviously, it had never occurred to him that this could be occurring. Laurel had no idea if it was, but at least the idea cast doubt in his mind.

She pressed on. "If the humans get the fae to kill each other, then they won't be stuck in the wastelands, will they?"

Indignation colored the king's cheeks. He glared at her and stepped away. "Enjoy the rest of the ball, Laurel. And tell that bitch owl that her plan failed to work. Jasper is my kin. I decide what to do with him."

And then the king walked away, back to take the steps of his dais to take a seat on his throne. Laurel noticed with great triumph that he gripped the glass arms until his knuckles were white. And his crown was crooked. Through it all, Jasper didn't even flinch. But on the other side, Bones stared at her with glimmering eyes full of dark thoughts, hatred, and a promise of pain.

Had he heard her interaction with the king? Were those glamored ears also spelled to hear better? She hoped so, because if they were, then he'd know she wasn't the demure, frightened woman she was the last time he met her. *Bring it on, ass-wipe.*

A hit of emotion hurtled into Laurel from her mating bond. Hurt, anger, and eye-watering, skin-prickling fury wracked Laurel's body. She almost choked on it and had to push her way through the crowd toward the sides. She needed a breathing space. Somewhere quiet. The volume of noise started to suffocate her. The chandelier lights were blinding. Too many things sparkled.

That king was infernally stupid, greedy, and cruel. He deserved to be burned to ash, too. Her fingertips heated as she got to the curtained wall. Combustible red velvet drapes hung from the ceiling on all sides. This would be a good place to start the fire.

She glared at the king until the crowd started to swirl around her, partially blocking her view as they returned to dance and shenanigans. It was time to move to Plan B.

Her breathing calmed. She was ready. She would burn both those suckers right there on the dais. So strong was her focus, that she failed to register the sense of Thorne's emotions getting stronger, and when she took a step toward the dais, but was stopped by an arm, she almost screamed. A hand covered her mouth, and then she was dragged through the billowing drapes, between a gap, and right into a dark, hidden alcove only big enough for her... and Thorne.

CHAPTER THIRTY-SIX

*T*horne pushed Laurel up against the dark alcove wall and pinned her with his hips. He held her shoulders and glared at her, despite every cell in his body rejoicing to hold her again.

"I know what you're planning to do," he growled.

He could still smell traces of Mithras on her skin. His wolf howled with indignation, with outrage. It also wanted to make Laurel submit, to pay for flirting with someone *not* him. That's what she'd done, flirted and allowed the king to paw at her in places only Thorne had the right to touch.

She struggled beneath his hold. "It's none of your business, Thorne."

"Yes, it is," he said, digging his claws into her. He wanted to let his fury out, to stoke the fire, but he didn't want to go back to being that person he was before he met her. That person was angry all the time. That person was bitter. That person missed out because of his pride. Thorne exhaled and let her go. "I made a mistake, Laurel. I should have told you about the sharing of our mana."

She blinked. Her lips parted.

He continued. "But I'm not sorry I took what I needed to in order to save your life. I will never be sorry for keeping you alive. I am, however, very sorry that I let you walk away from me without fighting for you."

Her hands lifted to rest on his stomach, and damn, he wished he wasn't wearing his Guardian uniform. He wanted to feel that touch on his bare skin. Like he had once before.

"Laurel," he pleaded. "Don't do it. Please."

"Do what?"

"You know what I'm talking about. Don't kill Bones."

Darkness entered her eyes again.

"He's the man who tortured me. You should understand that. He's the one feeding lies to the king. And guess what? He's the one who's convinced the king to name Jasper as his heir... so they can murder him."

Thorne's breath froze in his lungs. "Murder Jasper?"

"The plan is to set Jasper up as the treasured heir to the Summer Court, then to kill him and make it look like Queen Maebh ordered it. This is the spark that will set all of Elphyne ablaze. Bones has to be stopped. The king didn't even know Bones was from my time."

"This is what you were discussing with the king?"

She nodded, eyes still alight with emotion. "He thinks he's invincible. Unaccountable. He didn't care that I knew he colluded with a human. I tried to offer myself in exchange for Jasper. I figured it would get me closer to

Bones *and* set Jasper free, but he saw through it. He doesn't even care that I have the kind of power I do, or that I'm human. There must be something else they're offering the king to make him betray his own kind like this."

Thorne's mind whirled.

The air in the small confined space grew thick.

She'd offered herself as an exchange.

She would take Jasper's place.

Sacrifice herself for one of them.

Fuck. He'd made a big mistake in letting her go. Big mistake.

"Let me out, Thorne," she demanded. "He's right there. Right through that curtain. All I need to do is get within a few feet and hurl fire at him until I'm drained. He won't survive."

"No," he ground out. "I'm not letting you go."

"What?" she gasped. "You can't stop me."

Sharp claws sprung from his fingers and he bared his teeth. "I won't let you make the same mistakes as me, Laurel. Only a week ago I destroyed something in anger, where if I'd approached it with a level head, we would have known about the king's plans earlier. Don't you see? You taught me to let that anger go. Now I need to do the same for you."

She scowled. "I'll burn you if you don't release me."

"Then we both burn."

"*Thorne*," she pleaded. "I have to do this."

He shook his head. "The Guardians are about to raid. They have this in hand. Let them capture Bones and take him back for questioning. Let us figure out what he's offering Mithras that's more powerful, or more enticing than you. It must be something dangerous to give him an edge over a war with Queen Maebh. Or at least he *thinks* it is. You know this is the best course of action."

"He'll get away."

"No. He's human. And I don't believe Well-blessed like you. He steals his mana. You were gifted with it. If you think any other way, that's your fear talking. Rush believes it was Clarke's fear talking too. You need to let it go."

Laurel's fury surged through their bond. Panic engulfed him. She was going to leave. What he'd said hadn't been enough to sway her.

"Laurel." He took her face gently between his palms. "I'm sorry. What more do you need from me? An oath to the Well? Because I will gladly make that oath, just tell me what to say."

"What is that?"

"It's a mana-infused bargain you make with the Well, not another fae. It's an all-encompassing vow. But be careful. If you want me to say I won't take your mana without permission, the oath will be enforced forever. It's unbreakable. Even if you're dying and you need me to take your mana in order to protect you, I won't be able to do it. Even if I need it to save my own life, or the life of our future children, I won't be able to. But if that is what you need for me to prove that I love you and that I never wanted to hurt you, then I'll do it."

She tensed beneath his touch. Her fury dissipated. Something else flickered down their bond, like a tiny candle coming alight, something he dared not hope for in his wildest dreams.

"You love me?" she asked, eyes glimmering.

His face screwed up with the flood of emotion engulfing his heart. He loved her so much it hurt. So much he couldn't speak. So he nodded. "I would die for you. I would die with you."

Her lips parted. Air puffed out as though she'd been holding it tight. Her face crumpled too, and he knew from their shared emotions that she was trying not to cry.

"You love me?" she asked again, hand moving to his heart.

"Yes," he managed. "I've been so caught up with worrying about being left behind, that I failed to realize I should be holding onto you. And Laurel"—his voice deepened—"I'll hold on to you until we become ghosts in the sky."

She slid her hands around his neck, locked them fiercely, and then pulled his lips to hers, whispering, "I love you too."

He claimed her mouth in a searing kiss. There was no restraint holding him back, no care for the ball guests beyond the curtain, no want or responsibility. Just her lips. Her heart.

She was his.

He felt it.

Knew it.

He'd been stupid to doubt it. Stupid to not fight for it.

He kissed her with all his passion until his balance slipped. His palms slapped on the wall beside her head, and he deepened the kiss, making sure to press against her with his body. She plucked at the studs holding his battle jacket closed. He let her. *Crimson*, he wanted to touch her as she was touching him. To put his fingers where the king's had been, to claim his rights back. Undeniable primal instinct urged him onward.

But he pushed apart and heaved in a ragged breath. "Laurel," he whispered.

Her hands had finished with his jacket, and were now at his belt, already working at the bindings, trying to get to his achingly hard erection. He threw his head back, hissed at the sharp pleasure of her touch as she found her mark.

"We can't," he growled at the ceiling. "There's work to do."

Her touch left him.

When he looked back down, he found her lust-filled eyes suddenly focused. She wiped her mouth. "You're right. Bones. I have to kill him. I promised."

Panic flared in his heart again, and he dipped to take her mouth in another hot and demanding kiss. She groaned as his tongue pushed in. He knew she loved it. He felt it. She dueled back.

Maybe this was what he needed to do. Keep her distracted. It just had to be long enough to let the Guardians' plan kick into action and stop her from making a mistake.

Yesterday, Cloud had finished interrogating Patches. As it turned out, Patches was ready to make an oath to the

Well, one that confessed the king was the one who paid him to use the djinn bottle. The king directly. They had him.

The Guardians were poised to raid the ball. Ready to blackmail the king into releasing Jasper. Ready to take Bones into custody. And then they would get their answers about the Void's plans, and then Thorne would end Bones once and for all. But they had to do this the right way. All Thorne needed to do was keep Laurel busy.

He grinned into her mouth. "I'm going to take you, Laurel, hard against this wall. Shall I put up a privacy ward, or can you stay quiet, little queen, so as not to rouse attention?"

"I can stay quiet," she breathed and dipped her hands deep into his pants. She took hold of his length and squeezed. "Can you?"

Pleasure sparked at his groin. Thorne's vision lost focus.

"Fuck," he grunted and thrust involuntarily into her hand. He buried his face into her neck, kissed her skin, licked his mark, bit down gently. But...

He pulled back so their eyes could meet. He wouldn't start this relationship the second time around with deception. It might be their ruin, the nail in their coffin. He had to be truthful.

"I'm distracting you," he confessed, studying her face.

"I think you got it the wrong way around." She smiled and pumped his length.

His eyes rolled at the bliss.

"I don't think you understand," he ground out.

"Mm." She licked along his bottom lip, nipped him, and then every primal instinct in his body surged.

"Laurel," he warned. "I'm distracting you so you don't make the biggest mistake of your life. Because I don't want you to regret the dark stain on your heart from taking a life. I'm doing this because I love you. Do you understand?"

She paused. Silent. Eyes glistening under the blue glow of their mating marks. His words were finally sinking in. Hitting home.

"You're keeping me from Bones," she accused.

"You have to trust me," he said. "There is a plan to take him into custody. It's a good one. He will receive his justice. This is the best way to honor the people of your time, and the family you lost. We will get the Void's plans from Bones. We will *use* him before we *eliminate* him. Do you understand?"

"Distract me," she demanded. "So I'm not thinking about it. So I don't go out there and..." She swallowed.

His lips curved.

Then he gathered her dress and hiked it up her smooth legs. The raucous cheers and shouts from the party-goers blended with the music. Anytime now, the Guardians would have the place surrounded.

Thorne slid his fingers between Laurel's thighs, found her naked and wet. It should have turned him on, but he saw red. All he could think was that the king had his hands on her, so close to this... this that was his. *Mine*, his wolf growled. All he could see behind his eyelids was the imprint of it happening. He imagined the king's scent still on her.

Every possessive instinct flared to life. The wolf snarled. He would kill the king.

"He touched you," he growled. "No one will touch you like that again. No one but me."

"If they try, they'll lose their hand," she agreed with a smirk. "I'll burn it off."

"I'm serious, Laurel." He plunged a finger into her tight, moist sheath.

Her lips parted with a gasp. "Again."

"Laurel," he ground his teeth. "Do you understand? You and me for life. However long it is. The wolf in me won't have it any other way."

"Tell your wolf not to run away next time."

He smiled. "I think that can be arranged."

"Yes," she breathed. "Let's get married."

He took her mouth, plunged his tongue, and worked her harder with his fingers. Then just as she started to make little sounds signaling she was close to her release, he changed their position. He hooked her legs around his waist, leaned her against the wall, took hold of his shaft and entered her, watching as she moaned with the feel of him stretching her. Every time, this part held him captive. His eyes fluttered with the sensation of her surrounding him.

She'd been wrong.

She couldn't keep quiet.

CHAPTER THIRTY-SEVEN

*L*aurel was still coming down from her high, hugging Thorne, so grateful that they were now past their troubles when a loud crashing sound came from the ballroom and she jolted.

"What was that?" she asked.

Screams.

Shouts.

Men barking orders.

"Sounds like they're here," Thorne grumbled against her neck. "Is it so terrible that I don't want to leave this spot?"

He drew back, and they straightened each other up. Somehow, Laurel's beaded headdress was gone. Thorne's ax-baldric had ridden up his neck. His hair was adorably skewiff. And he had a look about him that seemed very pleased. She gave his jaw a fond caress.

This moment right here was one that she would

remember with joy, despite the chaos brewing in the ballroom.

Another loud crash—this one like breaking glass. All straightened, Thorne's expression grew hard. He held Laurel back and peeled open the curtain so they could peek outside.

It was pandemonium.

Red-coated royal guards were running about. Fancy dressed fae panicked and screamed as they ran from the room. A draft came from somewhere. As the people cleared, the throne dais came into view.

King Mithras sat with a furious scowl on his face, watching as Guardians dropped from the broken glass ceiling. The king's guards had taken up formation between the king and the ballroom floor where more Guardians approached, including Rush, Leaf and the ground fleet.

Mithras's eyes located and locked on the Prime, who was still sitting at a table, calmly sipping from a teacup.

Rush snarled at the king and released his sword, Starcleaver. Not even a king would get in the way of a Guardian's metal weapon. Laurel's heart gave a little flip as Rush climbed up the dais and took hold of Jasper's hand.

After Jasper had confused Thorne with Rush at the arena, Laurel would have thought he'd recognize his old partner, but all Jasper did was stumble vacantly as Rush pulled him down the dais to where the Prime sat.

Movement on the other side of the dais caught Laurel's attention.

"Look," she said and tapped Thorne. "Bones is getting away."

While the king was refusing to budge, Bones slinked off to the side and disappeared down a back exit.

"There are too many red-coats between us and there," Thorne said. "We'll not make it through without joining the fight."

"Bones will escape then."

Panic welled inside Laurel. She couldn't let that happen. Not after coming so close. For a minute, regret surged through her, as did guilt over ignoring her original mission. Thorne caught her change and cupped her face. "Don't," he started. "Don't go there. We will find him. And we will work together."

"I can cloak us."

"Good idea. I can track his scent."

Within seconds, Laurel had completed the cloaking spell, exactly like she remembered from training. It involved using light and shadows against each other. She nodded to Thorne, and he opened the curtain, taking them into the fray.

Both invisible, they kept their hands locked and kept to the outskirts of the room, hurrying as fast as they could between the gaps of frightened fae and scattering staff. The guards were amassing to protect the king.

Laurel glimpsed the severe gazes of Guardians as they formed a circle around the Prime and Jasper. Things were about to get heavy.

"Should we help them?" Laurel asked.

She wanted to find Bones, but not at a cost to their allies.

Thorne glanced over his shoulder as they hurried. "No," he replied. "Rush is there. They'll have it under control."

Laurel and Thorne jumped up on the dais and then darted out the door Bones had run through. It was a service corridor.

"Keep the cloaking spell up," Thorne said and pulled her behind him as he tracked Bones by scent.

Laurel gave herself over to Thorne, trusting his instincts. She concentrated on keeping the spell up. This was what their partnership should be—working together.

A shout ahead and then a clash of utensils had Thorne increasing their speed. The smell of food grew stronger. They reached the kitchens, and Thorne caught her eyes, put his finger to his lips, and released Fury.

They entered the large kitchen together. It was at least fifty feet long. Aisles of counters lined the kitchen. Stoves were against the walls. Cooks and servants everywhere tried to straighten the mess someone had just made by running through. Herbs and food had scattered over benches. And down the center aisle, at the other end of the kitchen where the only other exit was, a furious chef bared his fangs and blocked Bones from leaving.

They'd found him.

Laurel's heart leaped into her throat.

Thorne let go of her hand, releasing himself from the cloaking spell. He quietly motioned for Laurel to go around the counter and head down to the back of the kitchen until she was behind the cook. He would block this exit to stop Bones from retracing his steps.

Sheathed in her cloaking spell, she skipped and darted through the staff in the other aisle as they cursed and shouted at the intruder to get out. Coming around to the chef's rear, Laurel searched for a weapon she could use before dropping her cloaking spell, just something else in case the fire wasn't practical.

She picked up a ceramic knife, brandished it, and then dropped her cloaking spell. Standing behind the enormous cook, she couldn't even see Bones, but she was ready. She tapped the cook on the shoulder.

He glanced over his shoulder, confused.

She smiled sweetly. "I got it, big guy."

But the cook didn't believe she had what it took to stop Bones. He frowned and turned back, but not before Bones pilfered a knife from the bench and drove it into the cook's belly.

Well, that's what he intended to do. Thorne grabbed Bones by the throat and wrenched him backward. Bones was smaller than Thorne, but an experienced mercenary. He flipped the knife in his hands, aimed backward, and stabbed in the gap under his arm. The blade sank into Thorne's stomach.

Thorne grunted. But didn't stall. Bones must have missed. His face contorted into blind rage and he threw Bones across the counter as though he weighed less than a sack of flour. Bones slid across the surface, crashing into bowls of salad, knocking cucumbers and potatoes, skittering glass to the floor with a tremendous crash.

"Let me past!" Laurel shouted at the cook and tried to shove him.

"No, little lady. You stay back. Stay safe."

Rage filled her. She let her hands burn. The cook's eyes widened at the flames and he quickly moved to the side.

Laurel squeezed past him, intending to go to Thorne, but he'd moved around the counter to drag Bones to his feet. Thorne's huge fist crunched the wiry wrist, slamming it onto the counter. In Thorne's other hand, Fury rose behind his head. Laurel's comprehension lagged behind her mate's actions. It wasn't until Bones' skinny fingers were convulsing on the floor, reaching for the wrist still in Thorne's grip, that she understood.

"Cauterize it," he said.

She nodded and sent fire to Bones' arm. His screaming intensified, but she didn't burn him for long. When it was done, Bones cradled his arm. Sweat poured down his face. His eyes rolled, but he locked them onto Laurel with pure, obsidian hatred.

"You'll pay for that."

Thorne took Bones by the neck and squeezed painfully. "Shut up. Or I take your other hand, and she won't cauterize it."

Bones spat into Thorne's face. Thorne dodged, and that infuriated Bones even more. "Doesn't matter what you do to me. You won't make me talk."

"But I will," drawled Cloud as he prowled into the room,

eyes full of something wicked and frightening as he locked onto Bones. "I'll make you sing like a little bird."

Bones' eyes widened in what looked like recognition. "*You.*"

What was going on here?

Laurel's gaze darted between Bones and Cloud. Did they know each other? How was that possible?

Cloud and his fellow crow shifter, River, collected Bones from Thorne and dragged his sorry ass out of there. Just before they got to the exit, Laurel shouted, "Wait!"

Cloud tensed and looked over his shoulder. With Bones dangling between him and River, they turned to face Laurel. She clenched her jaw and strode over. She leaned down so she was eye to eye with Bones. "Pity your Seer didn't see this coming."

She punched him in the face.

Both Thorne and River looked at Laurel with amusement. Cloud held something else in his electric blue gaze. Respect? Understanding?

And then the crows took him away. His feet dragged on the floor and his obsidian gaze was still locked on Laurel.

She shivered. She knew it was more important to keep him alive, yet she couldn't shake the feeling they should kill him while they had the chance. Fear.

That's what it was, nothing more.

Thorne came up to her and held out Bones' dismembered hand.

"I know it's not his nails, but hopefully this is retribution enough," he said. "For now."

She stared at the disgusting hand, then back at Thorne's eager face. And then she burst out laughing.

Tears watered her eyes. This was so surreal. She felt as though she were in a dream. She didn't think she'd ever shake the feeling. Wiping her eyes, she looked at her mate with warmth and touched his cheek tenderly.

"Thank you, my love," she said. "But I don't know what to do with that."

Thorne frowned and turned the hand over. He fiddled with the king's signet ring on the little finger. "Interesting. Perhaps we should rejoin the main party and take this with us."

Laurel linked arms with Thorne. "Okay. But you're carrying it."

⚖

IN THE BALLROOM, tensions flared.

The first thing Laurel noticed was the king no longer sat calmly on his throne. He stood on the ballroom floor surrounded by his guard, shouting at the Prime about her audacity to accuse him of treason to the Well.

The rest of the ballroom had been cleared of guests, and all that remained were a few Guardians manning the exits. Haze and Shade were at the front entrance, and to the back of the stage, Aeron stood next to a new auburn-haired elf she'd not met. Deeply tanned and with brown eyes, he looked as though he spent a lot of time outdoors. He might be Forrest.

Up high on the glass ceiling, to the backdrop of a starry night sky, was Indigo dangling his feet. The vampire had seen Laurel enter and winked when she looked up. A hand shot from the darkness to thwack him on the chest. Laurel vaguely saw the shadowed outline of another fae with wings. She did a quick calculation in her head of all the winged Guardians and realized it must be the third crow-shifter she'd also not met, Ash.

Eyes back to the floor, Leaf and Rush stood guard next to a docile Jasper. The Prime was in the middle of laying out the offenses the king was charged with. Letters she'd appropriated from her handbag were being unfolded on the table. So that's what she'd been working on during the journey, an official record of the treason.

Rush noted their arrival and caught Thorne's eyes. Thorne nodded and held up the severed hand. Rush nodded back. Laurel almost smiled. They were getting along so nicely. Clarke would be proud.

Oh, no. *Clarke*.

She would be furious that Laurel couldn't go through with it. She bit her lip, worried. No, it would be okay. Cloud looked like he would take care of Bones. He'd get the information they needed.

This was the right thing to do. She would help Clarke understand that.

Thorne strode right up to the base of the king's dais and dropped Bones' hand.

Mithras looked down, sneered, and then scolded Thorne. "You dare?"

"Does the ring look familiar?" Thorne asked.

"I don't answer to you," he clipped.

"Well, you should," Thorne replied. "How else are you going to explain why one of your advisors is wearing a metal ring with your signet on it. It matches the wax seal on the letters instructing a certain shifter from Cornucopia to commit acts of terror against the Seelie, your own people." Thorne gave a smug smile. "I hope you weren't planning on activating that transference rune beneath it. You know, the one the metal ring hid from our scans. Possibly the one that would return Bones to you if he was ever taken captive."

The king glared at Thorne like he wanted to chew his heart out. "All that proves is that a man wearing that ring wrote those letters. Not me. I accept no responsibility for the acts you're accusing me of."

The Prime stepped forward. "We don't need you to accept responsibility. We have a witness who will swear an oath to the Well. We have your human. We can try you for treason right now."

"What you have is circumstantial evidence at best."

"You put curse marks on Jasper," Rush accused.

"They were there when we rescued him from the Ring. And for the record, he belongs to me. You can't take him."

"Oh, we'll take him," the Prime said. "And you'll let us because if you don't, we'll go straight to Queen Maebh with proof of your machinations to incite a war. Whether you admit it or not, she will invade your territory and find out for herself. Or perhaps she'll send the Wild Hunt to collect you and bring you back to her."

"You don't get involved in fae politics," he spat back.

"For this, I will make an allowance."

King Mithras stared down at the Prime. "You've turned into a cold-hearted bitch, Aleksandra."

"And you, a spineless coward."

"Fine. Take him." Mithras gestured at Jasper. "He is broken, anyway."

Assuming he was free to go, the king turned to leave, but the Prime had one last demand.

"You will end the unsanctioned breeding law," she said. "As you promised the first time."

"A promise is not a bargain," the king said over his shoulder.

"No. It's worth more. It's between friends," the Prime shot back. "Clearly, I was wrong to trust you. You promised that if I handed Jasper over to you, you would treat him as your treasured son. I was stupid to think you would treasure your children a different way. I won't make the mistake again. Fail to follow through with your word, and not only will I try you for treason, but I will visit Queen Maebh."

King Mithras's eyes glowed molten gold. He ground his teeth and then eventually said, "By the morrow I will send out a decree that the unsanctioned breeding law be abolished in Seelie territory, and then I trust this insane idea of my treason will be forgotten and you will focus your attention on where it needs to be—toward the humans invading our land."

He glared at Laurel. Thorne growled low in his throat. The king looked back to the Prime.

She nodded brusquely. "If you do not make this decree, and stick to your word, I will personally portal into the Obsidian Palace and go directly to Queen Maebh. You have until noon tomorrow, and then I expect to see fae all over Seelie territory fornicating in celebration."

Mithras gestured to the guards. "See them out. I want no Order representatives left by the time the moon is high."

Thorne's lip curled at the king's retreating back. "We were leaving, anyway."

CHAPTER THIRTY-EIGHT

JASPER – THE HOUSE OF THE TWELVE, IN
THE LIVING ROOM.

*T*here were things he remembered—things he didn't.

He knew he shifted into a wolf. He knew he'd lived here before. The smells were the same. He knew he should recognize these people who'd taken him from the king's palace and into their home filled with leather-clad warriors, fussing brownies, and citrus and cedar cleaning solution.

He should know how to play the game of cards the three vampires engaged in at the table in the adjoining room. He should know why they sat him in the worn, comfortable chair by the empty fireplace, or why they handed him a rolled-up stick of mana-weed to smoke. But it sat dwindling on a tray, unused.

Fae would come before him, speak to him, and welcome him home.

But he didn't know them.

He didn't know anything.

Days passed.

Eventually, they stopped trying to get him to talk. They left him alone, watching from his chair, frowning at the empty fireplace. He wasn't sure how long he stared.

Something touched his arm. He looked down. A small, pale and chubby hand rested on his forearm. His gaze followed the arm and found a cherub face with silver-white hair. She bared little sharp fangs and growled viciously. Did he know her?

He bared his teeth back.

She relaxed, cocked her head, and inspected him. Then she pouted and tugged on his hand. "Sleeping Pretty needs you."

He looked over to where the people who'd brought him talked at a table. They looked happy. Comfortable. Friendly. He didn't belong there.

Quietly, unnoticed, he stood and followed the little girl up the staircase and down the hall to a wooden door. He'd been here before. Many times. Long, long ago. The little one pushed open the door and told him to hush. Then she creeped inside and pointed at the bed in the dim room.

Lying on it was a golden-haired female. Asleep.

The little girl tugged him closer. He stumbled until his knees hit the bed.

"Sleeping Pretty needs a kiss to wake."

He looked down at the child and frowned. He looked back at the sleeping female. His frown deepened.

An undeniable urge to go to her swam through him. It was as though something pushed him.

He didn't know how, he didn't know anything, but he knew her.

So he went to her. Her mana called to his like a siren at sea, and like a wave rising to meet the shore, his mana called back. He touched her arm. A spark of heat zipped up his arm. Blue flames engulfed them both, and then he heard a scream.

Behind him.

A redheaded woman.

"Leave her alone!"

Footsteps thudded up the stairs. Down the hall. The people he should know came barging into the room, scowling at him as though he'd done wrong. They frowned at his golden-haired female on the bed. The one inexplicably linked to him. They wanted to take her away from him.

She was his. *Mine.*

Something wild and feral within him growled. His fangs elongated, and a snarl ripped out of his lungs. He picked up Sleeping Pretty, carried her in his arms, and he wished himself gone.

CHAPTER THIRTY-NINE

"Any news?" Laurel asked as she fitted a floral wreath to her head.

Clarke turned to her friend with a placating smile. "Laurel, you've asked me that every day for the past three weeks and the answer is always the same." Clarke shrugged. "I can't *see* anything about Jasper. Since he took Ada, his curse marks block him from my visions. They must still be together because I can't see her either."

"Yeah, but that's a good thing, right?" Laurel asked.

"I think so." Clarke gave Laurel's floral headdress one last tweak. Her eyes glittered with worry. "I was so afraid when I first saw him with her, but she'll be fine. Jasper is her mate. I saw the blue markings with my own eyes before he took her away. They have to be fine."

Laurel took her friend's hands and squeezed. "They will be. I just wondered if there was news. It would be nice to share this day with her, that's all."

"I know," Clarke said with a sigh. "I also know that I was wrong to ask you to kill Bones. You can't know how sorry I am."

"I wanted to. Don't think it was only you."

"I'm glad our big, overbearing mates stopped us."

"Me too."

Clarke checked her appearance in the mirror. She straightened her bridesmaid floral garland on her head. "Maybe we'll keep them."

Laurel chuckled. She gathered herself and stood back for one last look. Yeah. She looked like a boss. Like a queen. She'd even painted her nails and displayed them proudly.

Clarke came up behind her and hugged her. "Your parents would be proud. I'm proud."

Laurel's eyes teared up. "You'll make me cry and ruin my makeup."

"Then let me focus on how amazing you look." Clarke quickly gave a low whistle of appreciation. "Thorne is going to carry you off and have his way with you before you even finish walking down the aisle."

Laurel's cheeks hurt as she smiled. She dashed away her burgeoning tears and picked up her bouquet of jasmine. "But that's what the last three days of the celebration are for, right?"

They laughed and left the bedroom together. It was sad that Ada wasn't there, but none of them could dispute the coincidence that Jasper had triggered a Well-blessed mating with Ada. They had to have faith that the Well had chosen their union for a reason. It's what their partners kept insisting, and none of them were worried. They couldn't keep putting their lives on hold while they waited for them both to turn up.

Clarke led Laurel down the staircase to the kitchen where they walked through to the back door. Outside in the sun, set up on the back lawn, was a seating arrangement reminiscent of a classic wedding ceremony. All the Guardians, some Mages, and even a friend or two were present. Rush sat to one side with Willow on his lap, both of them grinning at the fun "first human tradition" they shared in. Thorne stood at the end of a floral carpeted aisle, waiting nervously. The Prime stood behind him, ready to officiate.

Thorne had promised Laurel a mating celebration, and she'd realized she wanted a wedding. Old school. Something to remember her time. So he wore a suit, and she wore a white dress.

Laurel stood at the start of the aisle, not a tremble in her fingers, not a doubt in her mind.

This war with the Void may only be beginning, and King Mithras was up to something. She also hadn't forgotten that she owed the Prime a debt for thanking her, as was the fae custom, but she was starting to trust her too. She might collect one day, she might not. Things were changing in Elphyne, and Laurel was proud to be a part of it.

For now, she would enjoy this small moment for what it was—perfection.

When the flute started playing, Clarke turned to Laurel and smiled. "You ready?"

She nodded. When they arrived together at the front, Laurel handed her bouquet to Clarke. Thorne took her hands, and without waiting for the Prime's instructions, he slipped a glass ring on her finger.

"Is this right?" he murmured, voice hoarse.

"You're supposed to wait for the celebrant to tell you when."

He made an awkward face. "I couldn't wait to show you."

Laurel looked down at the ring he'd put on her finger and gasped. It was as beautiful as the day she'd first admired it at the Cornucopia markets. A clear glass ring that sparkled with trapped light. He'd gone back for it.

"I may have not told the whole truth when I said I wouldn't take your mana again without permission," he confessed. "I took a single drop and infused it in the ring. I also added one from mine. Now a part of us will always be together. For eternity."

"Like ghosts of the past. The stars in the sky."

He nodded. "You're never alone, Laurel."

Tears burned her eyes as she blubbered, "Neither are you, my love."

She looked around at all the people who had gathered to share in this momentous occasion. And from the sheer joy radiating down their bond, she believed him.

She only wished this moment would last forever.

The End.

That's not the last of the Fae Guardians... Keep reading for some exclusive awesomeness.

Subscribers get a FREE EXCLUSIVE copy of the Novella
***Of Kisses and Wishes*, featuring a side story with Caraway and Anise.**
GET IT HERE
https://dl.bookfunnel.com/wl7wsatsu1

WHAT'S NEXT?

CAN'T WAIT THAT LONG FOR YOUR FAE GUARDIANS FIX?

Join Lana's Angels Facebook Group for fun chats, give-aways, and exclusive content. https://www.facebook.com/groups/lanasangels

ACKNOWLEDGEMENTS

Writing a book is hard, y'all. Even harder for an indie author who has to be their own publishing team. Indies have to not only write the damn book, but edit, market, and promote. So, with that in mind, I'd like to thank the following people:

Thank you first and foremost to my husband, Matthew, and our two kids for putting up with my crazy writing process (hint, hint, it all happens at the END of the deadline, not spaced out in an entirely logical way).

Thank you to my editor Ann Harth. She's the legend who puts up with my "hot mess" of a manuscript, and whips it into shape.

Thank you to my ARC team, who put up with my last minute ARCS, who scour and do their best to find typos, and who are always encouraging and fill me with much love and the wherewithal to continue writing when some days I feel like crawling under a rock.

Emma James, Helen Walton, Sahar Husseini, Trish, Tracey, Carmin Misner, Fizza Younis, Traci Burch, Angela Dee, Veronica Albertson, Chloe Knoll, Crystal Goh, Sue Tilson, Angelica Luevano, Claire Bloom, Scarolet Ellis, Patti Hays, Sheila Gabler, Dawn Dohey, Stella Mascia, Linda Lehesaho, Rachel Joi Maples, Dawn Mulligan, Dani Hopping, Jennifer Johnson, Mary-Anne, LaTasha Watson, Lorna Coon, Sandra Kirnbauer, Karen Ayoub, Teresa Bruno Woodard, and more. If I've missed your name, it's an oversight. Please let me know and I'll update. I'm grateful to everyone!

Thank you to my author buddies, Louisa West, Kimberley Jaye, Anna Hackett, Michelle Diener, Claire Boston, Daniel DeLorne, Shona Husk who are always happy to chat story ideas and more.

Thank you to the fabulous readers in the Facebook reader group, Lana's Angels. You all know who you are. I love you.

Lastly, thanks to me for putting up with myself and designing awesome covers. I love you too, Lana. Go take a break.

ABOUT THE AUTHOR

OMG! How do you say my name?

Lana (straight forward enough - Lah-nah) **Pecherczyk** (this is where it gets tricky - Pe-her-chick).

I've been called Lana Price-Check, Lana Pera-Chick-ywack, Lana Pressed-Chicken, Lana Pech...*that girl!* You name it, they said it. So if it's so hard to spell, why on earth would I use this name instead of an easy pen name?

To put it simply, it belonged to my mother. And she was my dream champion.

For most of my life, I've been good at one thing – art. The world around me saw my work, and said I should do more of it, so I did.

But when at the age of eight, I said I wanted to write stories, and even though we were poor, my mother came home with a blank notebook and a pencil saying I should follow my dreams, no matter where they take me for they will make me happy. I wasn't very good at it, but it didn't matter because I had her support and I liked it.

She died when I was thirteen, and left her four daughters orphaned. Suddenly, I had lost my dream champion, I was split from my youngest two sisters and had no one to talk to about the challenge of life.

So, I wrote in secret. I poured my heart out daily to a diary and sometimes imagined that she would listen. At the end of the day, even if she couldn't hear, writing kept that dream alive.

Eventually, after having my own children (two fire-crackers in the guise of little boys) and ignoring my inner voice for too long, I decided to lead by example. How could I teach my children to follow their dreams if I wasn't? I became my own dream champion and the rest is history, here I am.

When I'm not writing the next great action-packed romantic novel, or wrangling the rug rats, or rescuing GI Joe from the jaws of my Kelpie, I fight evil by moonlight, win love by daylight and never run from a real fight.

I live in Australia, but I'm up for a chat anytime online. Come and find me.

Subscribe & Follow
subscribe.lanapecherczyk.com

lp@lanapecherczyk.com

facebook.com/lanapecherczykauthor
twitter.com/lana_p_author
instagram.com/lana_p_author
amazon.com/-/e/B00V2TP0HG
bookbub.com/profile/lana-pecherczyk

Game of Gods

(Romantic Urban Fantasy)

Soul Thing

The Devil Inside

Playing God

Game Over

Game of Gods Box Set

Printed in Great Britain
by Amazon